DUDLEY PUBLIC LIBRARIES

The loan of this book may be renewed if not required by other readers, by contacting the library from which it was borrowed.

With Love From

COLLECTION

With Love From Florence

SCARLET WILSON

HEIDI RICE

CHRISTINA HOLLIS

MILLS & BOON

First Published in Great Britain 2020
By Mills & Boon, an imprint of HarperCollins*Publishers*
1 London Bridge Street, London, SE1 9GF

WITH LOVE FROM FLORENCE © 2020 Harlequin Books S.A.

His Lost-and-Found Bride © 2015 Harlequin Books S.A.
Unfinished Business with the Duke © 2010 Heidi Rice
The Italian's Blushing Gardener © 2010 Christina Hollis

Special thanks and acknowledgement are given to Scarlet Wilson for her contribution to *The Vineyards of Calanetti* series.

ISBN: 978-0-263-28124-8

0420

MIX
Paper from
responsible sources
FSC™ C007454

FSC
www.fsc.org

This book is produced from independently certified FSC™ paper to ensure responsible forest management.

For more information visit: www.harpercollins.co.uk/green

Printed and bound in Spain
by CPI, Barcelona

HIS LOST-AND-FOUND BRIDE

SCARLET WILSON

This book is dedicated to my fellow authors Susan Meier, Jennifer Faye, Michelle Douglas, Cara Colter, Teresa Carpenter, Rebecca Winters and Barbara Wallace.

It has been so much fun creating this series with you!

PROLOGUE

'SIGNOR! SIGNOR, VENGA ORA!'

Logan Cascini was on his feet in an instant. As an architect who specialised in restoring old Italian buildings, to get the call to help transform the Palazzo di Comparino's chapel for a royal wedding was a dream come true.

The property at the vineyard was sprawling and over the years areas had fallen into disrepair. His work was painstaking, but he only employed the most specialised of builders, those who could truly re-create the past beauty of the historic chapel in the grounds and the main *palazzo*. Most of the buildings he worked on were listed and only traditional building methods could be used to restore them to their former glory.

Timescales were tight in order to try and get the chapel restored for the royal wedding of Prince Antonio of Halencia and his bride-to-be, Christina Rose. No expense was being spared—which was just as well considering he had twenty different master builders on-site.

'Signor! Signor, venga ora!'

He left his desk in the main *palazzo* and rushed outside to the site of the chapel. His stomach was twisting. *Please don't let them have found anything that would hold up the build.* The last thing he needed was some unexpected hundred-year-old bones or a hoard of Roman crockery or coins.

This was Italy. It wouldn't be the first time something unexpected had turned up on a restoration project.

He reached the entrance to the ancient chapel and the first thing that struck him was the fact there was no noise. For the last few weeks the sound of hammers on stone and the chatter of Italian voices had been constant. Now every builder stood silently, all looking towards one of the walls.

The interior of the chapel had been redecorated over the years. Much of the original details and façade had been hidden. The walls had been covered first in dark, inlaid wood and then—strangely—painted over with a variety of paints. Every time Logan came across such 'improvements' he cringed. Some were just trends of the time—others were individual owners' ideas of what made the building better. In restoration terms that usually meant that original wood and stone had been ripped away and replaced with poorer, less durable materials. Sometimes the damage done was irreparable.

His eyes widened as he strode forward into the chapel. Light was streaming through the side windows and main door behind him. The small stained-glass windows behind the altar were muted and in shadow. But that didn't stop the explosion of riotous colour on the far wall.

A few of the builders had been tasked with pulling down the painted wooden panelling to expose the original walls underneath.

There had been no indication at all that this was what would be found.

Now he understood the shouts. Now he understood the silence.

Beneath the roughly pulled-back wood emerged a beautiful fresco. So vibrant, the colours so fresh it looked as if it had just been painted.

Logan's heart rate quickened as he reached the fresco. He started shaking his head as a smile became fixed on his face.

This was amazing. It was one of the most traditional of frescoes, depicting the Madonna and Child. Through his historical work Logan had seen hundreds of frescoes, even attending a private viewing of the most famous of all at the Sistine Chapel.

But the detail in this fresco was stunning and being able to see it so close was a gift. He could see every line, every brushstroke. The single hairs on Mary's head, baby Jesus's eyelashes, the downy hair on his skin, the tiny lines around Mary's eyes.

Both heads in the fresco were turned upwards to the heavens, where the clouds were parted, a beam of light illuminating their faces.

Part of the fresco was still obscured. Logan grabbed the nearest tool and pulled back the final pieces of broken wood, being careful not to touch the wall. Finally the whole fresco was revealed to the viewers in the chapel.

It was the colour that was most spectacular. It seemed that the years behind the wood had been kind to the fresco. Most that he'd seen before had been dulled with age, eroded by touch and a variety of other elements. There had even been scientific studies about the effects of carbon dioxide on frescoes. 'Breathing out' could cause harm.

But this fresco hadn't had any of that kind of exposure. It looked as fresh as the day it had been painted.

His hand reached out to touch the wall and he immediately pulled it back. It was almost magnetic—the pull of the fresco, the desire to touch it. He'd never seen one so vibrant, from the colour of Mary's dark blue robe to the white and yellow of the brilliant beam of light. The greens of the surrounding countryside, the pink tones of Jesus's skin, the ochre of the small stool on which Mary sat and the bright orange and red flowers depicted around them. It took his breath away.

He'd hoped to restore this chapel to its former glory—but he'd never expected to find something that would surpass all his expectations.

'*Signor? Signor?* What will we do?' Vito, one of the builders, appeared at his elbow. His eyes were wide, his face smeared with dirt.

'Take the rest of the day off,' Logan said quickly. 'All of you.' He turned to face the rest of the staff. 'Let me decide how to proceed. Come back tomorrow.'

There were a few nods. Most eyes were still transfixed on the wall.

There was a flurry at the entranceway and Louisa, the new owner of the *palazzo*, appeared. 'Logan? What's going on? I heard shouts. Is something…?' Her voice tailed off and her legs automatically propelled her forward.

Louisa Harrison was the American who'd inherited Palazzo di Comparino and hired him to renovate both it and the chapel back to their former beauty. She was hard to gauge. Tall and slim, her long blond hair was tied up in a ponytail and she was wearing yoga pants and a loose-fitting top. Her brow was furrowed as she looked at the fresco and shook her head. 'This was here?' She looked around at the debris on the floor. 'Behind the panelling?'

He nodded while his brain tried to process his thoughts. Louisa would have no idea what the implications of this could be.

She turned back to face him, her face beaming. 'This is wonderful. It's amazing. The colours are so fresh it's as if the painter just put down his paintbrush today. I've never seen anything like this. Have you?'

He took a deep breath and chose his words carefully. 'I've seen a few.' He gave a nod to the wall. 'But none as spectacular as this.'

She was still smiling. It was the most animated he'd seen her since he'd got here. Louisa rarely talked to the tradesmen or contractors and when she did it was all business. No personal stuff. He'd learned quickly that she was a woman with secrets and he still had no idea how she'd managed to inherit such a wonderful part of Italian history.

But her intentions seemed honourable. She'd hired him after going along with the request for a wedding venue from Prince Antonio. And with his growing reputation, thriving architecture business and natural curiosity there had been no way he'd turn down the opportunity to do these renovations.

'It will be the perfect backdrop for the wedding,' Louisa said quietly, her eyes still fixed on the fresco. 'Won't it?'

He swallowed. Exactly how could he put this?

'It could be. I'll need to make some calls.'

'To whom?'

'Any new piece of art has to be reported and examined.'

She wrinkled her nose. 'And a fresco falls under that category?'

He nodded. 'A fresco, any uncovered relics, a mosaic, a tiled floor...' He waved his hand and gave a little smile. 'We Italians like to keep our heritage safe. So much of it has already been lost.'

'And you know who to call? You can sort this all out?' He could almost hear her brain ticking over.

He gave a quick nod.

'Then I'll leave it to you. Let me know if there are any problems.' She spun away and walked to the door.

Logan turned back to the wall and stood very still as he heard the quiet, retreating footsteps. The enormity of the discovery was beginning to unfurl within his brain.

He could almost see the millions of euros' worth of plans for the prince to marry here floating off down the nearby Chiana River.

In his wildest dreams the prince might get to marry his bride with this in the background. But Italian bureaucracy could be difficult. And when it came to listed buildings and historic discoveries, things were usually painstakingly slow.

He sucked in a deep breath. The air in the chapel was still but every little hair stood up on his arms as if a cool breeze had just fluttered over his skin. He knew exactly what this fresco would mean.

He knew exactly who he would have to contact. Who would have the expertise and credentials to say what should happen next. Italy's Arts Heritage Board had a fresco expert who would be able to deal with this.

Lucia Moretti. His ex.

CHAPTER ONE

LUCIA STARED OUT of the window, sipped her coffee and licked the chocolate from her fingers.

If her desk hadn't been on some priceless antiques list somewhere she would lift her aching legs and put them on it. She'd just completed a major piece of work for Italy's Art Heritage Board. Months of negotiations with frazzled artefact owners, restorers and suppliers. Her patience had been stretched to breaking point, but the final agreement over who was going to fund the project had taken longest. Finally, with grants secured and papers signed, she could take a deep breath and relax.

She pushed her window open a little wider. Venice was hot, even for a woman who'd stayed there for the last twelve years, and the small-paned leaded-glass window obstructed her view out over the Grand Canal. A cruise ship was floating past her window right now—in a few months these larger ships wouldn't be allowed along here any more. The huge currents they unleashed threatened the delicate foundations of the world-famous city. So much of Venice had been lost already—it was up to the present generation to protect the beauty that remained.

Her boss, Alessio Orsini, put his head around the

door. His eyes were gleaming and she straightened immediately in her chair. Alessio had seen just about every wonder of the world. There wasn't much left that could make his eyes twinkle like that.

'I've just had the most interesting call.' She waved her hand to gesture him into her room, but even though he was in his late seventies he would rarely sit down.

'What is it?'

He gave a little nod. 'There's been a discovery. A new fresco—or rather an old one. Just been discovered in Tuscany during a chapel restoration. I've given him your number.' He glanced at her desk. 'Seems like perfect timing for you.'

She smiled. Alessio expected everyone around him to have the boundless energy he had. But her interest was piqued already. An undiscovered fresco could be a huge coup for the heritage board—particularly if they could identify the artist. So many frescoes had been lost already.

It seemed as though the whole of Italy was rich with frescoes. From the famous Sistine Chapel to the ancient Roman frescoes in Pompeii.

The phone on her desk rang and she picked it up straight away. This could be the most exciting thing she'd worked on in a while.

'*Ciao*, Lucia.'

It was the voice. Instantly recognisable. Italian words with a Scottish burr. Unmistakable.

Her legs gave a wobble and she thumped down into her chair.

'Logan.' It was all she could say. She could barely get a breath. His was the last voice in the world she'd expected to hear.

Logan Cascini. The one true love of her life. Meeting him in Florence had been like a dream come true. Normally conservative, studying art history at Florence University had brought Lucia out of her shell. Meeting Logan Cascini had made it seem as though she'd never had a shell in the first place.

He'd shared her passion—hers for art, his for architecture. From the moment they'd met when he'd spilled an espresso all down her pale pink dress and she'd heard his soft burr of Scottish Italian she'd been hooked.

She'd never had a serious relationship. Three days after meeting they'd moved in together. Life had been perfect. *He* had been perfect.

They'd complemented each other beautifully. He'd made her blossom and she'd taught him some reserve. He'd been brought up in a bohemian Italian/Scots family and had often spoken first and thought later.

She'd had dreams about them growing old together until it had all come to a tragic end. Getting the job in Venice had been her lifeline—her way out. And although she'd always expected to come across him at some point in her professional life she hadn't realised the effect it would have.

Twelve years. Twelve years since she'd walked away from Logan Cascini. Why did she suddenly feel twenty years old again?

Why on earth was he calling her after all this time?

He spoke slowly. 'I hope you are well. Alessio Orsini suggested you were the most appropriate person to deal with. I'm working in Tuscany at the Palazzo di Comparino in Monte Calanetti. I'm renovating the chapel for the upcoming wedding of Prince Antonio of Halencia and Christina Rose, and yesterday we made the most amazing discovery. A fresco of the Madonna and Child. It's exquisite, Lucia. It must have been covered up for years because the colours of the paint are so fresh.'

His voice washed over her like treacle as her heart sank to the bottom of her stomach. How stupid. Of course. Alessio had just told her he'd given someone her number. He just hadn't told her *who*.

Logan Cascini was calling for purely professional reasons—nothing else. So why was she so disappointed?

It wasn't as if she'd spent the last twelve years pining for him. There was a connection between them that would last for ever. But she'd chosen to leave before they'd just disintegrated around each other. Some relationships weren't built to withstand tragedy.

She tried to concentrate on his words. Once she'd got over the initial shock of who was calling, her professionalism slipped back into place.

This was work. This was only about work. Nothing else.

Being involved in the discovery and identification of a new fresco would be amazing. She couldn't believe the timing. If she'd still been caught up in negotiations, Alessio could have directed this call to someone else on the team. Even though frescoes were her speciality, the Italian Heritage Board expected all their staff to be able to cover a whole range of specialities.

She drew in a deep breath. Her brain was still spinning, still processing. This was the man she'd lived with, breathed with. What had he been doing these last few years?

Her heart twisted in her chest. Was he married? Did he have children?

'Lucia?'

His voice had been brisk before, but now it was soft. The way it had been when he'd tried to cajole or placate her. Just the tone sent a little tremor down her spine.

She cleared her throat, getting her mind back on the job. She had to take Logan out of this equation. This discovery could be career-changing. It was time to put her business head on her shoulders.

'What can you tell me about the fresco?'

He hesitated. 'I almost don't know where to start.' His voice was echoing. He must be standing in the chapel now. She squeezed her eyes shut. She didn't need to imagine Logan—his broad shoulders, thick dark hair and oh-so-sexy green eyes. He was already there. Permanently imprinted from the last time she'd seen him.

After all the emotion, all the pent-up frustration and anger, all the tears, she'd been left with his face on her mind. A picture of resolve. One that knew there was no point continuing. One that knew walking away was the only way they would both heal.

She'd known he wouldn't come after her. They had been past that point. He might not have agreed but he'd realised how much they'd both been damaging each other.

The vision of him standing in the stairwell of their apartment, running his hand through his just-too-long hair, his impeccable suit rumpled beyond all repair and his eyelids heavy with regret had burned a hole in her mind.

'Just tell me what you see.' She spoke quickly, giving her head a shake and trying to push him from her mind.

He sighed. 'I can't, Lucia. I just can't. It's just too... too...magnificent. You have to see it for yourself. You have to see it in the flesh.'

Flesh. Every tiny hair on her arms stood on end. Seeing it in the flesh would mean seeing *him* in the flesh. Could she really go there again?

'Wait,' he said. She could hear him fumbling and for a second it made her smile. Logan wasn't prone to fumbling. 'What's your email address?'

'What?'

'Your email. Give me your email address. I've just taken a photo.'

She recited off her email address. It was odd. She didn't even want to give that little part of herself away to him again. She wanted to keep herself, and everything about her, sealed away. Almost in an invisible bubble.

That would keep her safe.

Being around Logan again—just hearing his voice—made her feel vulnerable. Emotionally vulnerable. No one else had ever evoked the same passion in her that Logan had. Maybe it was what they'd gone through together, what they'd shared that made the connection run so deep. But whatever it was she didn't ever want to re-create it. She'd come out the other side once before. She didn't think she'd ever have the strength to do it again.

Ping. The email landed in her inbox and she clicked to open it.

As soon as the photo opened she jerked back in her seat. Wow.

'Have you got it?'

'Oh, I've got it,' she breathed. She'd spent her life studying frescoes. Most of the ones she'd encountered were remnants of their former selves. Time, age, environment had all caused damage. Few were in the condition of the one she was looking at now. It was an explosion of radiant colour. So vivid, so detailed that her breath caught in her throat. She expanded the photo. It was so clear she could almost see the brushstrokes. What she could definitely see was every hair on the baby Jesus's head and every tiny line around Mary's eyes.

'Now you get it,' said the voice, so soft it almost stroked her skin.

'Now I get it,' she repeated without hesitation.

There was silence for a few seconds as her eyes swept from one part of the fresco to another. There was so much to see. So much to relish. The palm of her hand itched to actually reach out and touch it.

'So, what now?'

The million-dollar question. What now indeed? 'Who owns the property?' she asked quickly.

'Louisa Harrison—she's an American and inherited the property from a distant Italian relative. She hired me to renovate the *palazzo* and chapel for the upcoming royal wedding.'

Lucia frowned. 'What royal wedding?'

Logan let out a laugh. 'Oh, Lucia, I forget that you don't keep up with the news. Prince Antonio of Halencia and Christina Rose. It's only a few short weeks away.'

'And you're still renovating?' She couldn't keep the surprise from her voice. All the Italian renovation projects that Logan had been involved with before had taken months to complete. Months of negotiation for the correct materials sourced from original suppliers and then the inevitable wait for available master craftsmen.

This time he didn't laugh. This time there was an edge to his voice. 'Yes. I have around forty men working for me right now. This fresco—it was more than a little surprise. There was wood panelling covering all the walls. Every other wall we've uncovered has been bare. We expected this one to be the same.' He sighed. 'I expected just to use original plaster on the walls. It should only have taken a few days.'

Now she understood. This discovery was amazing—but it could also cause huge hold-ups in Logan's work. She'd known him long enough to know that would be worrying him sick.

Logan never missed a deadline. Never reneged on a deal. And although she hadn't heard about this wedding she was sure it must be all over the media. If Logan couldn't finish the renovations of the church in time the whole wedding would be up in the air and his reputation would be ruined.

Not to mention his bank balance. She'd no idea who the owner was, but there was every chance she'd put a clause in the contract about delayed completion—particularly when it was so vital.

'I'll come.' The words were out before she really thought about it. She grabbed a notebook and pen. 'Give me the address and I'll make travel arrangements today.' As her pen was poised above the paper her brain was screaming at her. *No. What are you doing?*

She waited. And waited.

'You'll come here?' He sounded stunned—almost disbelieving.

Her stomach recoiled. Logan obviously had the same reservations about seeing her as she had about him. But why—after twelve years—did that hurt?

But he recovered quickly, reciting the address, the nearest airport and recommending an airline. 'If you let me know your flight details I'll have someone pick you up.'

His voice was still as smooth as silk but she didn't miss the implication—Logan hadn't offered to pick her up himself.

It didn't matter that she was alone in her office, she could almost feel her mask slipping into place. The one that she'd used on several occasions over the years when people had started to get too close and ask personal questions. When past boyfriends had started to make little noises about moving to the next stage of their relationship.

Self-preservation. That was the only way to get through this.

'I'll email you,' she said briskly, and replaced the receiver. She ignored the fact her hands were trembling slightly and quickly made arrangements on her computer. Alessio would be delighted at the prospect of a new fresco. As long as it wasn't a complete fake and a wasted journey.

But it didn't sound like a fake—hidden for years behind wood panelling in a now-abandoned private chapel. It sounded like a hidden treasure. And even though she didn't want to admit it, Logan was so experienced in Italian architecture and art he would have enough background knowledge to spot an obvious fake.

She sent a few final emails and went through to give the secretary she shared with five other members of staff her itinerary for the next few days. It was five o'clock and her flight was early next morning. She needed to pick up a few things and get packed.

She turned and closed her window. Venice. She'd felt secure here these last few years. She'd built a life here on her own. She had a good job and her own fashionable apartment. There was security in looking out her window every day and watching the traffic and tourists on the Grand Canal. The thought of heading to Tuscany to see Logan again was unsettling her. She felt like a teenager.

She picked up her jacket and briefcase, opening her filing cabinets to grab a few books. She had detailed illustrations of just about every fresco ever found. There were a few artists who'd lived in Tuscany who could have painted the fresco. It made sense to take examples of their work for comparison.

She switched on her answering-machine and headed for the door. She needed to be confident. She needed to be professional. Logan would find this situation every bit as awkward as she would.

She was an expert in her field—that's why she'd been called. And if she could just hold on to the *career-defining* thought and keep it close, it could get her through the next few days.

Because if that didn't, she wasn't sure what would.

CHAPTER TWO

LUCIA STEPPED DOWN from the chartered flight with her compact red suitcase in her hand. She'd spent most of the flight going over notes, trying to determine who the likely artist of the fresco would be.

The style was vaguely familiar. But there were a huge number of fresco artists spanning hundreds of years. Often the date of the building helped with the determination of the artist, but it seemed that Palazzo di Comparino had existed, in some state, for hundreds of years. The chapel even longer. There were a number of possibilities.

The airport in Tuscany was private—owned by some local multi-millionaire—so she was practically able to walk down the steps into the waiting car.

She gave a nod to the driver. '*Grazie*, I will be staying at Hotel di Stelle.'

He lifted her case in the trunk of the black car. 'No, *signorina*. A room has been prepared for you at Palazzo di Comparino.'

Her stomach clenched. She'd been definite about booking her own accommodation. Working with Logan was one thing, living under the same roof—even for a few days—was too much.

'No, I insist. I must stay at the hotel. Can you drop my bag there, please?'

He gave a little smile and climbed into the driver's seat. The Tuscan countryside flew past. The roads in the area were winding, climbing lush green hills, passing hectares of olive groves and vineyards, filling the air with the aroma of Mediterranean vegetation. Tuscany was known for its rolling hills, vineyards and fine wines and olive oil.

It was also unique in its representation of class. Every kind of person stayed in these hills. They passed a huge array of houses and tiny cottages dotted over the countryside. Medieval villages, castles—some ruins, some renovated—and old farmhouses crowning hilltops.

After thirty minutes the car passed an old crumbling wall and turned onto a narrow road lined with cypress trees, then rolled into the picturesque village of Monte Calanetti. Lucia put down her window for a better view. The village had two bell towers that were ringing out the hour as they arrived. There was also a piazza surrounded by small shops and businesses, cobblestoned walkways going up and down the narrow streets and a fountain where a few children were walking around the small wall surrounding it and splashing water at each other.

There was an old well on one side next to red-brick houses with gorgeous flower boxes and laundry strung overhead.

A few blue and red scooters whizzed past, ridden by young men with their trousers rolled up at their ankles and their hair flapping in the wind. Helmets didn't seem to be a priority.

She smiled. It was gorgeous. It was quaint. It could

be a setting for a film. Every character that was needed was there—the small wizened woman hanging her washing from a window, the young mother hurrying past with her child, a shopkeeper standing in a doorway and a couple of young girls whispering and watching the guys zipping past on their scooters.

The car turned onto another winding road, again lined with cypress trees. It only took a few moments for the *palazzo* to come into sight.

It was a sprawling, grand building with lots of little scattered buildings around. Lucia twisted in her seat, but it wasn't until the car pulled up outside the sweeping entrance of the *palazzo* that she finally saw the building she was after on the other side of the courtyard.

An old traditional chapel. Dark stonework, arched windows and door. It had two stained-glass windows, which had obviously been added at a later date than the original build.

But before she had a chance to focus on the beauty of the building something else took her breath away.

Logan, emerging from the entrance of the chapel. It had been twelve years since she'd seen him and she hadn't quite expected the jolt that was running through her body.

He ran his fingers through his dark hair, which was still a little too long. Logan had always been stylish, had always dressed as if the clothes had been made personally for him. Today he had on cream suit trousers and a pale blue shirt, open at the throat with the sleeves pushed up. Only Italian men could get away with cream suits. She imagined his cream jacket would have been discarded somewhere inside the chapel.

It wasn't just that he'd aged well. He'd aged *movie*

star well. He was still lean, but there was a little more muscle to his frame. His shoulders a bit wider, his shape more sculpted. He lifted his head and his footsteps faltered. He'd noticed her at the same time she'd noticed him, but she could bet his body wasn't doing the same things that hers was.

The car halted and the driver opened her door. There was no retreat. There was nowhere to hide.

She stared down at her Italian pumps for the briefest of seconds, sucking in a breath and trying to still the erratic pitter-patter of her heart. Thank goodness she'd taken off the stilettos. She'd never have survived the cobbled streets of Monte Calanetti.

She accepted the extended hand of the driver and stepped out of the car, pulling down her dress a little and adjusting her suit jacket. The cool interior of the car had kept the heat of Tuscany out well. It was like stepping into a piping-hot bath. This situation was hot enough without the sun's intense rays to contend with.

Logan walked over. His faltering footsteps had recovered quickly. He reached out his hand towards her. 'Lucia, welcome.'

For the briefest of seconds she hesitated. This was business. *This was business.* She tried to appear calm and composed, even though the first little rivulet of sweat was snaking down her back.

She grasped his hand confidently. 'Logan, I hope you've been well. I take it that is the chapel?' She gestured to the building from which he'd emerged.

Straight to the point. It was the only way to be. She had to ignore the way his warm hand enveloped hers. She definitely had to ignore the tiny sparks in her palm and the tingling shooting up her arm. She pulled her hand back sharply.

If he was surprised at her direct response he didn't show it. His voice was as smooth as silk. 'Why don't we go into the main house? I'll show you to your room and introduce you to Louisa, the owner.'

He waved his hand, gesturing her towards the *palazzo*, and she could instantly feel the hackles rise at the back of her neck.

'That won't be necessary. I'm not staying. I've booked a hotel nearby.'

Logan exchanged a glance with the driver, who was already disappearing into the *palazzo* with her red case. 'Why don't you have some refreshments in the meantime? I'd still like to introduce you to Louisa and I'm sure you'd like to see around the *palazzo*—we've already renovated some parts of it, including the room Louisa has set aside for you.'

He was so confident, so assured. It grated because she wished she felt that way too. She was trying her best to mimic the effect, but it was all just a charade. Her stomach was churning so wildly she could have thrown up on the spot. It wasn't just the intense heat that was causing little rivulets of sweat to run down her back, it was Logan. Being in his presence again after all these years and the two of them standing here, exchanging pleasantries, as if what had happened between them hadn't changed their lives for ever, just couldn't compute in her brain.

Business. She kept repeating the word in her head. She was probably going to have to keep doing this for the next few days. Whatever it took to get through them. She had to be professional. She had to be polite. The

Italian Heritage Board would expect her to discuss her findings and proposals with the owner directly—not through a third party. Maybe this way she could take Logan out the equation?

She gave a nod and walked over the courtyard towards the *palazzo*. The first thing she noticed as she walked into the wide entrance hall was the instantly cool air. The *palazzo* may be hundreds of years old but it seemed as though the amenities had been updated. She gently pulled her jacket from her back to let some air circulate.

Logan showed her through to a wide open-plan sitting area. Glass doors gave a wide, spectacular view over the vineyards. She was instantly drawn to the greenery outside.

'Wow. I've never really seen a working vineyard before. This is amazing.'

A beautiful slim blonde emerged from another doorway, her hair tied in a high ponytail, wearing capri pants and a white top. She smiled broadly and held out her hand. 'Welcome. You must be Lucia. Logan told me to expect you. I'm Louisa.' She nodded to the view outside. 'And I knew nothing about vineyards either before I arrived here.'

Lucia shook her hand easily. Should she be cautious? What exactly had Logan told her?

Her eyes flitted from one to the other. Was there a relationship between Logan and Louisa? She watched for a few seconds. Logan had his hands in his pockets and was waiting in the background. He wouldn't do that if he were in a relationship with Louisa and this was their home.

Louisa nodded towards the doorway that must lead

towards the kitchen. 'Can I get you coffee, tea, water or…' she gave a smile '…some wine?'

Of course. She was in a vineyard. Would it be rude to say no? She was Italian, she loved wine. But she was here for business, not pleasure. 'Just some water would be lovely, thank you.'

There was a few seconds of uncomfortable silence as she was left alone with Logan again. He moved over next to her, keeping his hands firmly in his pockets.

'How is your job at the heritage board? Do you like it?'

She gave a brief nod but kept her eyes firmly on the vineyard outside. 'It was always the kind of job that I wanted to do.' She left everything else unsaid. If things had turned out differently there was a good chance that she would never have taken the job in Venice. It would have been too far away from the life they had planned together in Florence.

Something inside her cringed. It was almost as if she'd wanted things to turn out this way and that just wasn't what she'd meant at all.

But Logan didn't seem to notice. He just seemed more concerned with filling the silent space between them. 'And how do you like living in Venice, compared to Florence?' It was his first acknowledgement of anything between them. They'd lived together in Florence for just over a year.

Louisa came back out of the kitchen holding a glass of water. 'You've lived in Florence and now Venice? How wonderful. What's it like?'

Lucia took the water gratefully. Her throat was achingly dry. For the first time since she'd got here she felt on comfortable ground—questions about Venice were always easy to answer. 'Venice is amazing. It's such a welcoming city and it absolutely feels like home to me now. It is, of course, permanently full of tourists, but I don't really mind that. My apartment is on the Grand Canal so at night I can just open my doors and enjoy the world passing by on the water. Some nights it's calming and peaceful—other nights it's complete chaos. But I wouldn't have it any other way.'

Louisa gave a visible shudder. 'Too many people for me. Too much of everything.' She looked out over the vineyards. 'I can't imagine what this place will be like when the royal wedding takes place. There will be people everywhere.' She gave a shake of her head. 'All the farmhouses and outbuildings are being renovated too. Logan's the only person staying in one right now while we still have some quiet about the place.'

Lucia didn't smile. Didn't react. But her body was practically trembling with relief to know she wouldn't be under the same roof as Logan.

Now she might consider staying in the *palazzo* for the next couple of days.

Louisa gave her a smile. 'I intend to stay out of the way as much possible. Now, about the fresco. What happens next? You do understand that we are under an obligation to get the rest of the restoration work finished as soon as possible?'

Lucia could hear the edge in her voice. The same strong hint that had come from Logan. She chose her words carefully. 'It all depends on the fresco itself. Or, more importantly, the artist who created it.'

'Will you know as soon as you look at it?'

She held out her hands. 'It would be wonderful if we could just look at something and say, "Oh, that's by this artist…" But the heritage board requires authentication of any piece of work. Sometimes it's by detailed comparison of brushstrokes, which can be as good an identifier as a signature—we have a specialised computer program for that. Sometimes it's age-related by carbon dating. Sometimes we have to rely on the actual date of the construction of the building to allow us to agree a starting point for the fresco.'

Louisa smiled and glanced over at Logan, who looked lost in his own thoughts. 'Well, that's easy, then. Logan has already been able to date the construction of the *palazzo* and chapel from the stone used and the building methods used. Isn't that right, Logan?'

He turned his head at the sound of his name, obviously only catching the tail end of the conversation. He took a few steps towards Lucia. 'The buildings were constructed around 1500, towards the end of the Italian Renaissance period. The fresco could have appeared at any point from then onwards.'

It didn't matter how tired she was, how uncomfortable she felt around Logan—it was all she could do not to throw off her shoes and dash across the entrance courtyard right now to get in and start examining it.

She gave a polite, cautious nod. 'I'm keen to start work with you as soon as possible, Louisa.'

Louisa's eyes widened and she let out a laugh. 'Oh, you won't be working with me.' She gestured towards Logan. 'You'll be working with Logan. I have absolutely no expertise on any of these things. I've started to call him Mr Restoration. Anything to do with the work has to be agreed with him.'

Lucia eyes fell to the empty glass on the table. Where

was more water when she needed it? This was the last thing she wanted to hear.

She smiled politely once again. 'But, as the owner, I need to agree access with you and have you sign any paperwork the heritage board may require. I also need to be able to come to and from the *palazzo* at my leisure. I will be staying at a nearby hotel.'

'What? Oh, no. You're staying here. Come, and I'll show you to your room.' She was on her feet in an instant. 'We have renovated some parts of the *palazzo*, you know.' She waved her hand. 'And it will all be finished before the wedding.' As she reached the door she turned, waiting for Lucia to follow her.

The corners of Logan's lips were turning upwards.

'Ms Harrison, I really don't want to put you to any trouble. I'm more than happy to stay in a hotel and just travel to and from the *palazzo*. It will only be for a few days. I don't expect my research to take any longer than that.'

Louisa shook her head. 'Nonsense. You'll stay here. I insist. As for the paperwork, Logan will need to read that first and explain it to me. My Italian is still very rusty.'

Louisa had already started up a flight of stairs, obviously expecting Lucia to follow her. 'You're going to have a beautiful view over the vineyard. And you're welcome to use the kitchen if you want.' She paused. 'But there's a really nice restaurant in Monte Calanetti you should try.'

She wanted to object. She wanted to get away from here. But it was important that she have some sort of relationship with the owner. And because of that the words were sticking in the back of her throat. Louisa hadn't stopped talking. She was already halfway up the stairs. It obviously didn't occur to her that Lucia might continue with her objections. 'I'm sure you'll love the room.'

Lucia sucked in a breath. She wasn't even going to look in Logan's direction. If she saw him smile smugly she might just take off one of her shoes and throw it at him in frustration. At least she had the assurance that he wouldn't actually be under the same roof as her.

Just achingly close.

'I'll be back in five minutes. I want to see the fresco,' she shot at him as she left the room.

She walked up the stairs after Louisa and along a corridor. This *palazzo* had three floors—it was unusual, and had obviously survived throughout the ages. The person who'd built this had obviously had plenty of money to build such a large home in the Tuscan hills. Even transporting the stones here must have been difficult. What with the land, and the vineyard, along with all the outbuildings she'd spotted and the chapel, at one time this must have been a thriving little community.

Louisa took her into a medium-sized room with a double bed and wooden-framed glass windows overlooking the vineyard. Everything about the room was fresh and clean. There was white linen on the bed and a small table and chair next to the window, with a classic baroque chair in the corner. A wooden wardrobe, bedside table and mirror on the wall completed the furnishings.

A gentle breeze made the white drapes at the window flap, bringing the scents of the rich greenery, grapes and lavender inside. Her red case was presumptuously sitting next to the doorway.

'I'll bring you up a jug of water, a glass and some wine for later,' said Louisa as she headed out the door. 'Oh, and we don't quite have an en suite, but the bathroom is right next door. You'll be the only person that's using it.'

She disappeared quickly down the hall, leaving Lucia looking around the room. She sank down onto the bed. It felt instantly comfortable. Instantly inviting. The temperature of the room was cool, even though the breeze drifting in was warm, and she could hear the sounds of the workers in the vineyard.

She closed her eyes for a few seconds. She could do this. Two days tops then she could be out of here again.

Logan. Seeing him again was hard. So hard. The familiar sight of Logan, the scent of Logan was tough. She couldn't let him invade her senses. She couldn't let him into her brain, because if she did a whole host of other memories would come flooding back—ones that she couldn't face again.

This is business. She repeated her mantra once more.

The smell of the Tuscan hills was wrapping itself around her. Welcoming her to the area. Her stomach grumbled. She was hungry, but food would have to wait. She wanted to see the fresco.

She walked over and grabbed her case, putting it on the bed and throwing it open.

It was time to get to work.

Logan had finished pacing and was waiting for Lucia to appear. He'd walked back out to the courtyard and was leaning against the side of the doorway to the chapel with his arms folded across his chest.

It was much warmer out here, but he thrived in the Italian sun.

Seeing Lucia had been a shock to the system. His first glance had been at her left hand but there had been no wedding ring, no glittering diamond of promise. He was surprised. He'd always imagined that after twelve years Lucia would have been married with children. The fact she wasn't bothered him—in more ways than one.

She'd been hurt, she'd been wounded when they'd split. Even though it had been by mutual agreement. But he'd always hoped she'd healed and moved on. When he'd heard she was working for the Italian Heritage Board he'd assumed she'd pulled things together and was focusing on her career. Now he was suspicious she'd *only* focused on her career.

Lucia had aged beautifully. She was still petite and elegant. Her pale pink suit jacket and matching dress hugged her curves, leaving a view of her shapely calves.

And she'd kept her long hair. It was maybe only a few inches shorter than it had been the last time he'd seen her. He liked it that way. Had liked it when her hair had brushed against his face—liked it even more when her long eyelashes had tickled his cheek as she'd moved closer.

It was odd. Even though there were lots of parts of his body that could have responded to the first sight of her, it had been his lips that had reacted first. One sight of her had been enough to remember the feel of her soft lips against his, remember the *taste* of her. And as she'd stepped closer he'd been swamped by her smell. Distinctive. Delicious. In any other set of circumstances…hot.

But not in these circumstances. Not when delays on this project could result in a late completion penalty that could bankrupt his company. Louisa was serious about this place being ready for the royal wedding. She was depending on it.

He straightened as Lucia appeared, walking briskly across the courtyard. She'd changed and was now wearing flat shoes, slim-fitting navy trousers, a pale cream top with lace inserts on the shoulders and a dark silk scarf knotted at her neck. She had a digital camera in her hand.

He was disappointed that her legs were no longer on display.

She stopped in front of him, meeting his gaze straight on. She'd changed a little over the years. There were a few tiny lines around her eyes, but the rest of her skin was smooth. She, like him, had naturally olive Italian skin. Her dark brown gaze was uncompromising. 'Show me your fresco, Logan.'

It was the most direct he'd ever heard her. He tried not to smile. Twelve years had instilled a new-found courage in her. He liked it.

But something else swamped him for a few seconds. There had been a time in his life that Lucia had encompassed everything for him. She'd been the centre of his universe. He shifted self-consciously on his feet. He'd never felt that way again—he'd never *allowed* himself to feel that way again.

It was too much. Too much to have so much invested in one person when your life could change in an instant and everything come tumbling down around you both.

It didn't matter that seeing Lucia again after all these years was swamping him with a host of memories. It was time to put all those feelings back in a box. A place where they were best left.

He gestured towards the entranceway. 'It's all yours. Let's go.'

She walked ahead of him, her tight bottom right in his line of vision. He lifted his eyes to look straight in front of him and smiled as her footsteps faltered as she saw the fresco.

'Oh…whoa.'

He smiled as he stepped alongside her. 'Pretty much what I said too.'

She lifted her camera then put it back down and walked right up to the wall. She lifted her hand but didn't actually touch it. 'It's been covered for…how long?'

Logan shook his head, his hands on his hips. 'I couldn't say for sure.' He pointed to the corner of the room where debris was stacked. 'The wood panelling could be between three and four hundred years old.'

She glanced at the wood and turned back to the fresco. This time she did lift her camera and started snapping, first capturing the full work then systematically snapping detailed sections. Images that she could take time to pore over later.

When she finished she placed the camera on the floor then picked up some tiny fragments of clay that were on the floor—obvious remnants from the uncovering of the fresco. She gathered them in little plastic bags, labelled them, then put them in her bag. Once she'd finished she moved so close to the fresco that her nose was only inches away.

She lifted her fingers. It was obvious she was itching to touch it, but, she was resisting the temptation. 'I can see the movement,' she said quietly. 'I can see the brushstrokes. What kind of brush do you use to paint individual hairs? This is amazing.'

Logan waited, watching her relish her first viewing of the fresco. It was strangely exhilarating. He could see the wonder on her face, see the excitement in her eyes. Just watching her sent a little buzz through his body. Memories were sparking. This was part of the Lucia he'd loved. The wonderful, passionate girl who'd embraced life to the full. When they'd first met she'd been quiet, reserved as a result of her upbringing. But studying in Florence had made her blossom into the beautiful woman he'd quickly grown to love. The buzz, culture and bright lights had been a nurturing environment for the young artistic woman. And the two of them meeting had seemed to spark her even further. All his first memories of Lucia had been about their drive, their passion and their instant connection.

He could feel it even now—twelve years on. The palms of his hands were actually itching to reach out and touch her—just the way hers were obviously itching to touch the fresco. Parts of Lucia had been so easy to read.

Other parts she'd kept tightly locked up and tucked away. Those had been the parts that had sealed the end of their relationship. Every person grieved differently. But Logan just couldn't understand why she'd been unable to talk to *him*, why she'd been unable to share with *him*. After all, he'd been going through exactly the same thing.

He took a deep breath. 'What do you think?'

'The fresco was prepared in sections. *Giornate*— done on a daily basis with small sections of plaster laid at a time to be painted—much in the same way that Michelangelo carried out the work at the Sistine Chapel.'

Logan was incredulous. 'You think this was done by Michelangelo?'

She laughed. 'Oh, no. Of course not. The artist of the time just used the same techniques. Michelangelo used different skin tones from those used here.' She leaned back critically. 'Different draping of the clothes. This definitely isn't his work.'

She finished snapping a few more shots with the camera and turned to face him again. 'I have a program on my computer that I can upload these pictures to. It finds similarities between frescoes and gives the most likely artists.'

He shook his head. 'Why do I feel as if you don't really need it? What's your gut instinct?'

She shook her head. 'I'm not sure. It could be one of a few possibilities.'

He pressed her again. 'But you think...' He let his answer tail off.

She brushed her hair off her shoulder. 'I think there's a chance it's a lesser-known Renaissance painter. His name was Burano.' She gave a wry smile. 'The same as one of the islands in the Venetian lagoon.'

Logan's brow creased. 'He was from Venice, then?'

She nodded.

'So what was he doing in Tuscany?'

She turned back to face the fresco. 'That's my question too. That's why I'm hesitant. I could be wrong. Journeying between Venice and Tuscany in Renaissance times wasn't easy, but we both know the European Renaissance started in Tuscany and centred in Florence and Siena.' She raised her eyebrows. 'Venice was the late starter.'

She walked back to the entranceway. 'Give me some time to run the program and see what it comes up with.'

Logan held out his hand as she made to leave. 'And in the meantime?' He spun around. 'Time is marching on, we've still got work to do in the chapel—even if we aren't anywhere near the fresco.'

She looked around and gave a little nod. 'Let me give you some recommendations on the best way to protect it in the meantime from dust, plaster and paint.' Her gaze connected with his. 'This could be a really amazing discovery, Logan.'

It was the way she'd said his name. Her accent, her lilt. He'd heard it on so many occasions. Last thing at night, first thing in the morning. In the heat of passion and in the depths of despair.

He just hadn't admitted how much he actually missed it.

His feet were rooted to the spot. But Lucia's weren't. She was headed out the door. She was leaving. Who knew how long she would actually stay here. He could get up tomorrow morning and discover her gone.

'Have dinner with me?'

'What?' She stopped. She looked shocked.

'Have dinner with me,' he repeated, stepping closer to her. The words had come out of nowhere. He couldn't take them back. He didn't *want* to take them back.

'We have things we need to discuss.' He saw a wave of panic flit across her eyes. '*Business* we need to discuss.'

'Oh, of course.' She glanced down at her digital camera. 'My program will take a few hours to run.' She was stalling. Of course she was. The last thing she'd want to do was have dinner with him.

'Then you'll have a few hours to kill,' he said quickly. This was embarrassing. Logan Cascini wasn't used to women saying no to him. But Lucia wasn't just any woman. Lucia was the woman he'd once loved. Sure, it felt awkward. Sure, this wasn't an ideal situation.

But this was the first time he'd seen her in twelve years. If this fresco turned out to be important, it could have significant repercussions for his business. He had to keep on top of this.

He almost laughed out loud. His mind was giving him all the rational, professional reasons for having dinner with Lucia. But his heart was giving him a whole host of completely irrational, emotional reasons for having dinner with Lucia.

None of them professional. All of them personal.

His mouth kept talking. 'We can discuss any paperwork that will need to be completed. I'll need to translate everything for Louisa, and if there's going to be any extra expenses we'll need to discuss those too. There's a nice restaurant in Monte Calanetti. It will give you a chance to see the village.'

She was hesitating, looking for a reason to say no, and he wasn't prepared to accept that.

He walked around her in long strides. 'Leave the arrangements to me.'

'Well, I... I...' She was still murmuring while he left.

CHAPTER THREE

FOUR DIFFERENT OUTFITS. That's how many she'd tried on. She hadn't brought that many clothes as she'd only expected to be here a few days and hadn't expected to be socialising at all, let alone socialising with the man she used to live with. Two suits, one pair of trousers, one extra skirt and a variety of tops were all that her trusty red case held.

A white shirt, a pale pink shirt and a bright blue one were currently lying on her bed. She was wearing a flared white skirt and red shirt. And against all her better judgement a bright red pair of stilettos.

The shoes gave some height to her diminutive stature. Right now she was praying that the restaurant wasn't in the middle of the cobbled streets of Monte Calanetti.

Logan was waiting outside for her in an idling car. She'd expected him to drive something black and sleek but instead he was in a four-wheel drive.

He gave her a nod as she opened the door and climbed in. Catching sight of her shoes, a glimmer of a smile appeared on his face. 'We're going to the local restaurant—Mancini's. I hope you like traditional food.' His eyes were gleaming.

She was nervous. And she couldn't quite work out why. Logan had changed into a white open-necked shirt and dark fitted trousers. His dark hair still had that rumpled look that she'd always loved. It was like a magnet—all she wanted to do was lift her hand and run her fingers through it.

She shifted her legs nervously in the car, crossing them one way then the other. If he noticed he didn't say anything. She eyed her shoes warily. 'Where is the restaurant?'

Logan was completely cool. He didn't seem at all unsettled at being around her. 'It's a converted farmhouse on the edge of the village. The chef's family have owned the restaurant for years, his wife-to-be is the maître d'—she's from the US.' He gave a little smile. 'It's an explosive combination.'

With Logan this was all about business. She would clearly have to adopt the same attitude.

He pulled up outside the restaurant, switched off the engine, and before she even had a chance to think he had come around the car and was opening her door and holding out his hand towards her.

She stared at his tanned hand and fingers. *Touch him.* She'd done it once. Her palm had burned for around an hour afterwards. Did she really want to touch Logan Cascini again?

How on earth could she say no?

She placed her hand in his. The sparks didn't fly this time. Probably because she was a little more prepared. This time it was a warm buzz, a little hum running up her arm and straight across to her heart.

Twelve years on, and he could still do it to her.

It was unnerving. She could hardly keep her thoughts straight.

The first glimpse of Logan had sent tingles around her body. But that had been quickly followed by a rush of emotions associated with bad memories. Memories that were locked away deep inside her.

There was a reason she wasn't happily married with a family. There was a reason she always backed off when a few dates started to turn into something else.

Professionally, her life was good. She had a gorgeous apartment, a motivating and challenging job, along with a whole host of good friends and colleagues.

That would be enough for most people. That *should* be enough. And right up until she'd glimpsed Logan again it had been.

Now she felt…unbalanced.

She walked into the farmhouse converted into a restaurant. Thankfully there were no cobbles outside and the added height from her stilettos seemed to buffer her confidence a little.

It was cute. There were shutters on the windows and exposed brickwork on the walls. Wooden tables filled the dining room, but they weren't all uniform, like in most restaurants. They were all different shapes and sizes, perfect for all numbers of guests, and it gave an old-world charm to the place.

They were shown to their table and the waiter lit the candle, then handed over the wine list. He nodded at Logan and pointed to the back wall. 'As you can see, we have a wide variety of wines from all the local vineyards. If you need a recommendation just let me know.'

Lucia ran her eyes down the list and sighed. Italians

were passionate about their wine and the wine list was thicker than the actual menu.

'What's your preference?'

Couldn't he remember? Had he forgotten everything about their time together?

Before she had a chance to speak he waved to the waiter. 'Can we have some bread, olives and some oil while we decide?'

The waiter gave a nod and disappeared. It seemed he hadn't quite forgotten everything after all. Lucia had always enjoyed taking her time to peruse a menu, and Logan had always been starving.

She swallowed, her fingers drifting back to the file she'd brought with her. This made it seem more real. This was work. The reason she'd agreed to dinner to-night.

She licked her lips. Nerves were doing strange things to her. 'I think I'd like to keep things simple. I'd like to have some white wine, I think, something light. A *frascati.*'

She knew he'd be surprised. During their time to-gether they'd both favoured red wines, Merlots and Chi-antis.

'And I like the look of the set menu. Sometimes it's nice to have someone else pick for you.'

She'd only glanced at the set menu and nothing had jumped out at her. Most restaurants offered a set menu of some of their best dishes. She only hoped Mancini's was the same.

In years gone by she'd been picky about her food, sometimes refusing to go to some restaurants if they didn't serve a particular dish that she liked. But she wanted to start this meeting by letting Logan realise that he didn't really know her any more. Just because he was working on this project it didn't mean that he'd get any special treatment. And she wasn't swayed by a royal wedding either.

She took her job seriously. If the fresco had been by Michelangelo everything would have ground to a complete halt. She was fairly certain it was by a lesser-known artist—one who was still recognised and his work would be protected. But the chapel was fairly well maintained. There was no damp, no immediate threat to the fresco—just the new work that was going on to make it ready for the wedding.

Once the identification part was done, things should be fairly straightforward.

Logan set his menu on the table. 'Both are fine with me.' He had a hint of a smile on his face. As if he knew she was trying to be different but it was all really just a pretence. 'How have you been, Lucia?' he asked huskily. That voice. That accent. Little waves were rolling down her spine. It was the memories. It was anticipation of what had used to come next when Logan had spoken to her like that.

Those days were long gone. Vanished for ever. It didn't matter that the words were bland and perfectly normal. It was the *way* he said them that counted.

'Twelve years is a long time, Logan.' Her voice was sharp.

He waited a few seconds before answering. His voice was low. 'You're right. It's been a very long time. Almost a lifetime ago.'

What did that mean? That for him it was gone, forgotten about? How could anyone forget losing a child? She could feel herself bristle.

'How have you been?' She bounced the question back to him. Her insides were curling up in case he told her—even though he didn't wear a ring—that he was indeed married with a houseful of children.

He nodded slowly. 'I've been busy. Building your own business takes time.' He shrugged. 'Nearly all of my time. I like to be on-site for the restoration projects. I like to make sure that everything is going to plan.'

She felt her shoulders relax a little. 'You don't like to sit in your office and drink coffee?' It was something they used to joke about years ago. Creative people ending up in jobs behind desks, drinking endless cups of coffee.

He gave a smile and shook his head as the waiter approached again, taking their order and returning a few moments later to pour the wine and leave the bread, olives and oil on the table.

Lucia took a sip. The first taste was always sharp. The second much more pleasing as her taste buds adjusted.

'Where are your offices?'

He tasted his wine too and nodded in approval. 'Florence. But I don't spend much time there.'

She tried not to raise her eyebrows. Office space in Florence was expensive. His business had obviously done well. 'Do you still live in Florence?'

He hesitated a second. And she wondered if she'd just stepped over some invisible barrier. They'd lived in Florence together. But she didn't expect him still to be in the small one-bedroomed flat a few minutes from the university.

He nodded and dipped a piece of bread in the oil. 'I have an apartment overlooking Piazza Santa Croce.'

'Wow.' She couldn't help it. It was one of the main areas of Florence. Apartments there weren't cheap and although the existing buildings were old, they'd usually been refurbished to a high standard, hence the expensive price tags.

She gave a little nod of her head. 'I can see you staying there. Did you get to renovate the place yourself?'

He shook his head. 'If only. The apartment was renovated before I got there. But all the original architecture is still there. That's what's important.'

'Do you like staying there?' She was dancing around the subject that was really in her mind. *Did anyone stay there with him?* It shouldn't matter to her. Of course it shouldn't. But she couldn't help but feel a natural curiosity. And there was no way she would come right out and ask the question.

'It's fine. It's Florence.' He looked at her carefully. 'I've always loved living in Florence. I just don't get to stay there as much as I would like.'

'Really? Why not?' *Because your wife and child stay somewhere else?*

He shrugged. 'I've spent the last ten years building up my business. I go wherever the work is. It takes time, energy and commitment. When I'm doing a restoration—like now—I like to be on-site. I've stayed in my apartment probably only three months of the last year.'

'I see,' she said quietly, as the waiter appeared and placed their starters in front of them—wild mushroom ravioli with butter and Parmesan sauce. She was glad of the distraction. Glad to stop being watched by those too-intense green eyes.

It made sense. Logan had always been passionate about everything he'd been involved in. From his work, to his family, to his relationships. But it sounded very much like he didn't have anyone back in Florence to worry about.

'How are your family in Scotland?' she asked.

He smiled. 'They're good. They have three restaurants in Glasgow now. The one in George Square is still the main one and my *nonna* refuses to get out from behind the bar. She still sits there every day and criticises what everyone else does.'

Lucia laughed. She'd met his *nonna* on a few occasions. She was fiery little woman who was both fiercely protective and critical of her family.

'They still ask after you,' he said quietly.

Her laughter died and she swallowed quickly. There was a little tug at her heartstrings. Although both families had roots in Italy, Logan's family were much more welcoming and outgoing than her own. She'd felt more at home in their house in Glasgow than in her own mother and father's house in the small town of Osimo.

She didn't reply. She couldn't reply. Too many memories were starting to flood back. This was the problem with seeing Logan after all this time. All the things she'd literally pushed to the back corners of her mind were starting to poke their way through again.

But it wasn't just unhappy memories that were crowding her thoughts. Logan had other little places in her mind. Just sitting here with him now made a little warm glow spread throughout her body. His eyes, his accent, the way he ran his fingers through his hair when he was searching for the right words. Beautiful, sunny days in Florence, long afternoons drinking endless cups of coffee and dusky evenings with wine leading to long nights together.

Passionate. Intense. The two words that sprang to mind to describe their relationship. The third word was tragic. But she didn't even want to go there.

She was still toying with her food, wondering if either one of them would bring up the elephant in the room.

But Logan wasn't ready to go there yet. 'What do you think of Louisa?'

She put down her knife and fork. It was a curious question. The Logan she used to know would size someone up in a matter of minutes. The fact he was asking about Louisa meant he obviously wasn't quite sure.

She frowned. 'I'm not sure. I haven't really had a chance to talk to her yet. She's American, isn't she? How did she manage to own a vineyard in Tuscany?'

'From what I know, she inherited it. She's the last living relative of Signor Bartolini. It seems she might have inherited some time ago but has never visited before. As far as I can make out, Nico—who owns the neighbouring vineyard and who was a friend of Signor Bartolini—has kept it semi-functioning for the last few months. But I'm not entirely sure that Nico and Louisa have hit it off.'

She nodded thoughtfully. She hadn't met Nico yet but had heard him yelling instructions to some of the vineyard workers. He was obviously intent on keeping the vineyard working.

Logan took a sip of his wine. 'How do you find Venice?'

'It took a little getting used to. Florence was always busy, but Venice is off the scale. Cruise liners come in every day and the Piazza San Marco is so busy you can barely move.'

He gave a little nod. 'Where are you staying?'

'I was lucky. I managed to get an older apartment—much like you—on the Grand Canal. My building and street are off the main thoroughfare, but any time of the day or night I can open my doors and look out over the canal. There's never a quiet moment out there.'

'Do you live alone?' She sucked in a breath but couldn't help the amused smile that appeared on her face. It seemed that Logan didn't mind being direct. She'd skirted around the issue but he had no intention of doing that.

A tiny little part of her wanted to lie. Wanted to tell him she had a billionaire husband and three perfect children at home. But she had never been a person to tell lies. Her secret hopes and desires for her own life were just that—secret.

'Yes. It's just me. I lived with someone for a while but things didn't work out. I was consumed with work and didn't really have time for a relationship. It turned out he really didn't want a career woman for a wife anyway.'

She said the words flippantly, not giving away how much it had hurt at the time. But time, in some cases, gave a chance for reflection. That relationship would have always come to an end.

Logan's eyebrows had risen as she'd been speaking. Wasn't she supposed to move on?

But it seemed he'd opened the door now and given her a right to ask whatever she wanted. 'Why haven't you got married and settled down?' she asked.

The waiter appeared, clearing one set of plates and setting down their main course—Tuscan veal chops with Parmesan *tuilles*. The smell drifted up around her.

She picked up her fork and sighed. 'This is the kind of thing I wish I had the time and talent to make.'

'Your cooking talents haven't improved with age?' He laughed. Lucia's cooking attempts had been a constant source of amusement for them. She'd once declared she could burn water—and she probably could.

The initial preparation and cooking attempts hadn't been a problem. Distraction had been the problem. Something else had always managed to crop up while she was supposed to be watching a timer or stirring a pot.

'How have you survived without someone to feed you?'

She gave a resigned nod of her head as she tasted some of the succulent veal. 'I eat out. A lot. The kitchen and I will never be friends.'

He laughed. 'I should get Nonna to package up some food for you.'

She waved her fork at him. 'Nonna should package up food for the world. She could make a fortune if she released a recipe book, or sold them to a food manufacturer.'

Logan's eyes connected with hers. 'You really expect Nonna to reveal her secret family recipes to an unsuspecting world?' He was teasing. She could tell. This was the way it used to be with them. Constant joking back and forth.

She shrugged. 'I'm just saying you have an untapped family fortune out there. That could be your nest egg, you know.'

He shook his head. 'I don't think I'd live to tell the tale.'

'Probably not.' She took a sip of her wine. This wasn't

quite as bad as she'd feared. Logan wasn't being difficult, he was his usual charming self. She'd just forgotten how hypnotic those green eyes could be. Every time
his gaze connected with hers she had to blink to remind
herself to breathe.

Logan had always been charming. His family had
joked he could charm the birds from the trees and the
gods out of Olympus. And she'd loved it. She'd loved
the way he could make her feel like the most important woman on the planet. Because even though Logan
had been a charmer, he'd also been a one-woman man.
He'd never shown a glimmer of interest in anyone else
when he'd been with her. She'd felt assured in his love.

It had been a long time since she'd felt so cherished.

A little warm wave rushed over her skin as she
smiled at him and took another sip of her wine. She
was relaxing more as the night went on, remembering
the good times instead of the bad.

Logan didn't deserve the negative associations that
she'd built up in her brain. He deserved much more
than that.

But if that was how she remembered him, how did
he remember her?

This was more like the Lucia he'd once known. It was
the first time he'd seen a genuine smile since she'd got
here. When she'd walked outside to meet him earlier
his heart rate had rocketed. With her perfect hourglass
figure, the white flared skirt, fitted red shirt and silk
scarf knotted around her neck she'd looked like a nine-
teen-fifties movie star. As for those killer red stilettos…

With her tumbling locks and red lips her picture
could have adorned a thousand walls. His fingers

couldn't decide whether they wanted to unknot the scarf around her neck and pull it free, or run down the smooth skin on her tanned legs towards those heels.

Lucia. It was odd. She tried to act so independent, so aloof, but there was an inherent vulnerability about her that made him lose focus on everything else. He felt strangely protective and proud of her. The last time he'd seen her she'd been a shell of her former self. Losing their child had devastated them both.

Although the pregnancy hadn't been planned they'd both been delighted when they'd found out a baby was on the way. They'd spent hours talking about their future together and making preparations for their baby. At one point it had seemed that the whole apartment had been full of brochures for cribs, cabinets, prams and high chairs.

The twenty-week scan had revealed a perfect daughter waiting to be introduced to the world.

No one could explain the unexpected premature labour.

No one could explain why Ariella Rose hadn't managed to take those first few vital breaths.

Of course, the doctor had tried to say that her lungs hadn't been developed enough and there had been no time to give Lucia steroids to help Ariella's lungs mature.

It had been that terrible time when doctors tried to decide if a baby's life was viable or not.

Some babies did breathe at twenty-three weeks.

Ariella Rose hadn't.

The beautiful, vivacious woman he'd known had disintegrated before his eyes, their relationship crumbling around him. He'd spent months desperate to get her to talk to him. But Lucia had put up walls so thick nothing had penetrated.

Every time he'd tried to draw her out of her shell she'd become more and more silent and withdrawn. He'd pulled back too, focusing on his work, because right then that had been all he'd had. But Lucia had slipped through his fingers like grains of sand from the beach.

He'd been grieving too, watching the days tick by on the calendar, waiting for the day they would have welcomed their daughter into the world.

That had been the day Lucia had packed her cases and left.

No amount of pleading had dissuaded her. Florence had had too many bad memories for her—too many painful associations. She'd accepted a job in Venice. She'd wanted to leave, and she hadn't wanted him to follow.

Now his insides twisted. He'd always regretted that he hadn't fought harder. Hadn't found the words to persuade her to stay.

It was almost a relief to see her now. There was a stillness about her—something reserved that hadn't been there before they'd lost their daughter. He could still see a remnant of sadness in her eyes.

But this Lucia was different. She had a different kind of confidence around her. She was a little more self-assured. She'd been through the worst and come out the other side. There was a real resilience there that bubbled underneath the surface.

Her clothes and demeanour were back to the woman he remembered. She'd always worn her stilettos with pride, as if to take someone to task for her diminutive height. And her hair was every bit as tempting as it had always been. It had always felt like silk and smelled of roses. Even now, there was a faint floral aroma drifting across the table towards him, curling its way around him and kicking his senses into gear.

The waiter appeared to clear their plates. 'Dessert?'

'No, thank you.' They both answered in unison and Lucia threw her head back and laughed.

Now his fingers were definitely itching to reach across and tug that scarf from her neck and reveal the paler sensitive skin around her décolletage.

It was her tender spot. The area that when kissed sent her into a spin. It had always been guaranteed to make her go weak at the knees.

He shifted uncomfortably in his chair. Parts of his body were awakening that shouldn't—not in a public restaurant. 'Do you want to have coffee?'

She shook her head. 'I'm tired. I still need to do some work online.'

Work. Of course. The reason they were here. He'd barely even discussed the project with her. He was normally so pedantic about every detail of his build. It seemed that even being around Lucia for a few hours was making him lose focus.

He should be worrying about delays. He should be panicking that his business could be affected by the non-completion clause in his contract.

If things weren't ready on time for the royal wedding he might have to face the wrath of the wedding planner, Lindsay Reeves. She was already phoning him twice a day for updates and photos of the chapel.

He took a deep breath and tried to collect his thoughts. 'Can we continue our work in the chapel?'

This was useless. Now he was looking at those deep brown eyes. Lucia's eyes had always been able to draw him in completely. In twelve years they hadn't lost their magic.

People said that eyes were the window to the soul. Lucia's brown eyes were very dark, very deep and flecked with gold. He could get lost in them completely. Always had.

She blinked. 'In truth, probably not. Give me another day. I have a few ideas. If I needed to go elsewhere to verify who painted it, would you have someone who could ensure the safety of the fresco?'

He straightened in his chair. 'Why would that be needed? It's been safe for the last five hundred years beneath the panels in the chapel?'

She gave an apologetic smile. 'But now it's been discovered. Now it's open to the elements. And now we have a whole host of tradesmen who know that it exists.' She shrugged. 'What if people have thoughts like you first did? What if they think that there is a tiny possibility this could be a Michelangelo work? What if someone tells the press?'

She held out her hands. 'In the space of a few hours this whole village could be swamped by a whole host of people—not all of them with good intentions.' She spoke with complete sincerity. He'd always respected Lucia's ambition, but he was now seeing a true glimpse of her professional expertise.

He nodded slowly. 'Of course. Louisa has already expressed some concerns about publicity. She's worried enough about the royal wedding without having to deal with something else.' It was easy to know who to discuss this with. 'Connor Benson is the head of security for the royal party. He'll know exactly how to keep things safe and protect the fresco in the meantime.'

She gave him an amused smile. 'Isn't he more at home looking after real-life people than artefacts?'

Logan lifted his hands. 'He has the skill and expertise we need. What's more important is that I trust him. If he says he can keep the fresco safe, then I believe him.'

He signalled to the waiter for the bill. Lucia had told him she still had work to do. It didn't matter that he wasn't in a hurry for this evening to end. He had to respect the job she was here to do.

It only took a few minutes to pay the bill and head back out to the car. The sun was setting behind the deep green Tuscan hills, sending shards of orange and red across the sky.

Lucia took a deep breath as they stepped outside. 'How beautiful.' She spun around in her heels, her skirt swishing around her, a relaxed smile on her face.

He caught her arm as she spun, feeling her smooth skin against his palm. 'You've never experienced a Tuscan sunset. It really is something, isn't it?'

The evening was still warm and pleasant. 'Why don't we go for a walk before we head back to the *palazzo*?' The words were out before he thought about it and he could sense her immediate reluctance.

But what struck him straight away was the way his stomach curled. He hated seeing Lucia like this, prickly and difficult around him. Towards the end of their relationship she'd been so flat. Almost emotionless, as if everything had just been drained from her. It had just been another stage of grieving—he appreciated that now.

But at the beginning she'd been bright, bubbly and vivacious. He didn't know this prickly and difficult version. More importantly, he didn't know how to *act* around her.

He waved his hand. 'Of course, if you want to head straight back, that's fine. I just thought you might want to have a chance to see around Monte Calanetti a little.'

It was official.

She was caught between a rock and a hard place.

Strange as it seemed, getting a sense of the village might actually help her identify who the artist of the fresco might be. Often, if someone had stayed in an area there might be historical stories or some folklore about them. Sometimes getting a sense of a place, seeing other work done in the area could actually help. And, in some respects, Logan's brain worked exactly the same way that hers did.

She sucked in a breath, holding it for a few seconds, her eyes fixing on her red stilettos. They'd seemed like a good idea at the time. But she'd seen the streets of Monte Calanetti. Cobbles. Everywhere. She'd probably land on her back.

She bit her lip. Logan's gaze was fixed on the sunset, his face basking in the orange glow. Her reserve softened. With his dark hair, tanned skin and dark suit jacket he was definite movie-star material. Age suited him. The little lines around his eyes gave him even more charisma, and Logan had oozed it already.

'Okay, then.' *Where had that come from?*

She was almost as amazed at her words as Logan was, judging by the expression on his face. He recovered quickly. 'Great, let's go.'

He drove the car into the town centre and parked outside a bar. He walked swiftly around and opened the door, holding his hand out to her as he had before.

She didn't hesitate. Didn't think about the contact. She was making too much of this. It was probably just all in her head anyway.

Wrong move. She could almost see the spike of electricity.

One of her heels automatically slipped in a gap in the cobbles and he caught her elbow, sliding one arm behind her waist. She pretended it was nothing. Nothing—to feel his body right next to hers.

Her throat was so dry she couldn't even swallow. This wasn't supposed to happen. She was in self-protect mode.

She could smell him. Smell his woodsy aftershave, his masculine scent winding its way around her body. So familiar. So scintillating.

He slammed the car door, keeping one hand around her waist. 'Don't want you to stumble,' he said throatily.

It was an excuse. She knew it was an excuse to keep her close. But she didn't feel in a position to protest. The likelihood of her landing on her backside had just increased tenfold. The cobbles weren't the only thing affecting her balance around here.

He steered her towards the centre of the square, near a fountain and old brick well.

Now Lucia really had a chance to see the beauty of the square, the most quirky thing being that it wasn't exactly a square. The fountain was similar to lots found in small Italian villages. Built with travertine stone, it was circular with a sleeping nymph at its centre. The old well was solid with mismatched stones. Like most of Italy's traditional village wells some modernisation had taken place and water from the well could be accessed via a pipe at the side. Logan pressed the button and reached over for her hand. She didn't have time to pull it back before cool, clear water poured over their fingers.

He lifted his hand, letting the drops fall into his mouth. Her legs quivered. She put her fingers to her lips and tasted the cold water. It was surprisingly fresh. She smiled as a drop trickled down her chin.

Logan moved instantly and caught the drop with his finger. She froze. Before it had just been touching hands, arms. Even holding her close, she was still completely clothed.

But touching her face was different. Touching her face was a complete and utter blast from the past. Logan had always touched her face—just before he kissed her.

It had been their *thing*. She'd used to close her eyes and he'd trace his finger over her skin like butterfly kisses. It had always driven her crazy.

And even though she willed it not to happen, as soon as he touched her chin her body reacted. She closed her eyes.

This was something she wasn't prepared for. This was something she'd *never* be prepared for. She sucked in a sharp breath and forced her eyes back open.

Their gazes meshed. So focused, so intense it made her want to cry.

Logan's deep green eyes were so clear, so solid. He was everything she'd ever wanted. Everything she'd ever needed. The person she'd love for ever. The person she'd never forget.

Something flashed across his vision. Panic. Something she'd never seen before in Logan's eyes. He was the calmest, most controlled man she'd ever known.

He pulled his finger back and stared at it for a second, as if he were being hit with the same overload of memories she was.

She wobbled, adjusting her weight in her stilettos. Logan blinked and lifted his hands onto her shoulders, walking her back a few steps to the edge of the fountain. She sagged down, breathing heavily, trying to ignore the pitter-patter in her chest.

She adjusted her position at the edge of the fountain and her eyes fixed on the nymph in the centre of the cascading water. It was exquisite. Serene and beautiful, holding a large clamshell above her head.

Logan stepped in front of her. She was so conscious of him, of his strong muscular thighs barely hidden inside the dark suit trousers. He didn't speak. He didn't try to touch her again.

Her brain tried to clear a little. This was ridiculous. She wasn't the young woman she'd been the last time she'd been around Logan. She'd lived and aged twelve years. Sometimes inside it felt like she'd aged another forty.

She tried to focus her attention on something else. Something safe. The sculpture of the nymph.

Most nymphs were naked. This nymph wasn't. It was clothed. In a cloak. A cloak with characteristic folds.

She straightened up.

'What is it?' Logan crouched down next to her.

She pointed to the nymph. 'Do you know anything about this?'

He touched the wall of the fountain where she was sitting. 'About the fountain?'

She shook her head. 'No. About the nymph. Do you know who sculpted it? Is there any village history that would tell us?'

His eyes were fixed on hers. 'I know the legend attached to the fountain.'

Her heart started to beat faster. 'What's the legend?' She was watching the fine billowing mist that seemed to glow in the lowering sun. Of course. Every village fountain in Italy would have a legend.

He gave her a wistful kind of smile. 'They say that if you toss a coin and it lands in the clamshell you get your wish.'

Her stomach clenched. It wasn't exactly what she'd wanted to hear. But it reached into her and grabbed a tiny part of her soul. Oh, she had a whole host of things she could wish for. But most of them were in the past. And nothing would change that now.

Wishful thinking. That's all that could happen around this fountain. And a fanciful legend didn't help her identify the sculptor. 'Do you know anything else? Anything more realistic?'

He looked as if he'd been stung. He frowned. 'I have no idea. Is it important?'

She stood up and spun around to face it. 'It could be. See the folds of the cloak?'

He leaned forward. 'Yes...' His voice was hesitant.

She touched his arm. 'Does it look familiar to you?'

His face broke into a smile, there was a mischievous twinkle in his eyes and he held up his hands. 'Is yes the right answer?' It was clear he had no idea.

But something had sparked a fire within her. 'I think it might. Most Renaissance artists didn't just paint— they also sculpted. It could be the nymph was sculpted

by the same person who painted the fresco. The folds of
the cloak are quite characteristic. If I can compare the
fresco and the nymph to the works of art that are held
in Venice, it could help identify the artist.'

He started to nod his head in recognition. 'You still
think its Alberto Burano?'

She smiled. 'It could be.'

This was work. Work she could do. Talking about
work made her feel confident again. Made her feel
safe.

'So what happens now? How long will it take you
to find out?'

She paused. Of course. 'These things can take
weeks—sometimes months. The Italian Heritage Board
is cautious. We have to be careful before we make any
kind of declaration about the potential artist of any
fresco. It can always be challenged by others.'

Logan shook his head. 'But what happens in the
meantime? Can the wedding still go ahead in the chapel? Louisa is absolutely adamant that things must go
to plan. I suspect she's counting on the money from the
royal wedding to help her complete the renovations on
the *palazzo*. If we can't progress…' His voice tailed off.

There were deep furrows in his brow. He put his
hands on his hips and stared out across the village. It
was obvious that something else was bothering him.

'If we can't progress—what?'

He let out a deep breath and turned to face her. 'We
have a non-completion clause in the contract. It's standard practice in the renovation business.'

'What happens if you don't complete on time?' Now
she understood why he looked so worried.

He couldn't meet her gaze. Her brain whirred. She

knew exactly what would happen. Logan's company would have to bear the brunt of any costs.

Something twisted inside her. It had been a long time but Logan had been the father of her child. She knew exactly how much something like this would matter. If he failed to complete this job his reputation would be ruined—he could kiss his company and all his hard work goodbye.

'Is there anything I can do to help prevent the delays?' There was an edge to his voice. Determination.

From the second she'd got here all she'd wanted to do was get away. Being around Logan was claustrophobic, too cluttered—stifling, too many memories.

But she couldn't let his business fall apart because of things he had no control over. This wasn't his fault.

She hesitated. 'There will be a whole lot of paperwork that will need to be completed in Venice. That's always the thing that causes the most delays. If Louisa will allow you to be a signatory for her it could make things much easier. As you know, Italian paperwork can be complicated.'

'You want me to come to Venice?' He sounded a little stunned.

But so was she. Had she really just suggested that?

'Well...it might move things along more quickly. I will be working on the comparisons with other frescoes. If you could find any history of the village that might link Alberto Burano to being here it could also be a huge benefit.'

He nodded slowly. She could almost see him thinking everything over, weighing up the best way forward.

He stepped forward. A little closer than she expected and as she breathed in all she could smell was his woodsy aftershave.

'What day do you want me in Venice?' His voice was determined.

'Friday,' she said quickly, trying not to think about it too much.

Friday was only a few days away. She would have done some of the groundwork before he got there.

He seemed to wait a few seconds before he replied. His voice was low and husky, sending shivers down her spine. 'Friday it is.'

What had she just done?

CHAPTER FOUR

THE HEAT IN Venice was stifling. It seemed the whole
world had descended on it to hear one of the world's biggest rock bands play in a concert. Piazza San Marco was
positively heaving, the streets crowded beyond measure
and tourists juggling to pay the inflated prices in the
surrounding cafés and bars.

Venice was always hot in the summer and Lucia was
used to it. Living in the middle of permanent tourist at-
tractions meant it was rarely quiet but today was the
busiest she'd ever seen it. The queue of people to get
inside St Mark's Basilica snaked around the centre of
the piazza twice.

Lucia glanced at her clock again. She'd expected
Logan to call her over an hour ago. When they'd made
the arrangement for him to come and help complete the
paperwork she'd had no idea about the rock concert.
It hadn't even been on her radar. She didn't want to
think about what Venice Marco Polo Airport was like
right now. She knew that the wait for the water buses
was over an hour and that everything was going much
slower than expected.

But the heat in her office was becoming claustrophobic. Even with her windows opened wide over the

Grand Canal there was no breeze. She glanced at the clock again and pulled her fitted blouse away from her back. The air conditioning rarely worked at the Italian Heritage Board. Today was no exception.

She gathered up the papers she might need, closed her windows and headed for the door. Her mobile sounded just as she walked down the stairs. Logan. She answered quickly, but could barely make out his voice for the background noise. 'Logan, where are you?'

She walked out into the bustling crowds, her feet turning automatically in the direction of San Marco, the waterbus drop-off on the Grand Canal. His voice was lost as she struggled to hear, so she continued through the thronging crowds towards the drop-off point. There, in the distance, she could see Logan and a smile flickered to her face.

His bag was clutched in one hand, alongside a pale beige jacket and his mobile phone. His white shirt was wrinkled, his hair rumpled and his face red. It was the first time in her life she'd ever seen Logan looking hot and bothered. It was kind of nice to know that could actually happen to him too.

He ran his fingers through his hair and looked around him, scanning the crowds. The rock concert had obviously caught him equally unawares.

She lifted her hand and waved at him, snaking her way through the people. A flash of relief was all over his face and gave her an unexpected glow. He moved towards her. 'Lucia, thank goodness.' He held up his hands. 'This place is even madder than usual. It wasn't until I hit the airport that I heard about the concert. I guess I should have got an earlier flight. The queue for the water taxis and buses was a mile long.'

She gave a nod and glanced at his bag. 'You look hot. How about we find somewhere to sit down and get something cool to drink?'

Logan let out a long breath, his brow furrowed. 'Do you think you'll be able to find anywhere?'

Lucia gave a little nod of her head. 'You forget, Logan. I've been here more than ten years. I know all Venice's best kept secrets.' She nodded her head for him to follow and weaved through the crowds. She was glad she'd opted out of wearing her normal business attire today. In these conditions she would have sweltered in her fitted suit dress. Instead, the lighter short-sleeved white blouse and knee-length navy skirt helped to keep her cooler. She pulled her sunglasses down from her head and snaked her way through the cobbled side streets of Venice. These were instantly cooler out of the sun's blistering rays and after a few minutes' walk they were away from the madding crowds.

She pointed towards a café with tables and parasols set on the street. Logan gave a sigh of relief and sank down into a chair. 'Perfect,' he said.

The waitress appeared instantly and they both ordered two drinks, one cool and one coffee for later.

She was still amused by how flustered he looked. 'I'm sorry about being so late, Lucia. I hope I haven't ruined your schedule for the day.'

She shook her head. 'No problem. I'd just decided to leave a little earlier because it was so hot. I'm happy to meet you outside rather than in the office.' She pulled out her files. 'I brought the paperwork with me. We can do it now, if you like.'

The waiter appeared and put their drinks on the table. Logan finished his cool drink within a few seconds, then sat back in his chair and sighed. He gave her a quirky smile and held up his hands. 'I don't remember Venice ever being this hot. What on earth is happening?'

She shrugged her shoulders. 'A cross between a heat wave and an extra twenty thousand people descending on the city at once?' She pushed the papers over towards him. 'These are the ones I need you to complete. Then we can file the fresco as a "new find" with the Heritage Board. They are the ones that can authorise any restoration that might need to take place.'

Logan was scouring the papers. He lifted his eyes towards her. 'And who would do that?'

She paused for a second, wondering if it was an answer he really wanted to hear. 'It would probably be me. I've done most of the work on all of the last frescoes that needed to be restored. It used to be my boss, Alessio Orsini, who handled fresco restoration, but once he'd trained me and overseen my work a few times he was happy to hand over the reins. I think he's looking to retire soon.'

Logan nodded slowly. He sat down his pen. 'How would you feel about working in Tuscany? There is a good chance that I'll still be there for the next few months.'

Logan was being cautious, but for some reason she felt as if a little man with icy feet was marching down her spine. It was almost as if he didn't want her there. She felt insulted.

She looked at him steadily. 'I'll go wherever I'm needed. My job is very important to me. The other personalities involved aren't important.' She picked up her cappuccino and took a sip, breaking the little caramelised biscuit at the side into pieces.

'That's not what I meant.' He reached over and grabbed her hand.

It was unexpected. A little part of the biscuit dropped from her hand onto the cobbled street.

Her eyes fixed on it lying amongst the cobbles, rather than looking at his hands or his face. She didn't pull her hand back. 'I get it, Logan. You'd rather not have to work with me. But I won't compromise on my job. We're just going to have to both be professional about it.' She lifted her gaze to meet his.

His eyes widened. 'No, Lucia. You're reading this all wrong.' He squeezed her hand. 'I know we had a difficult past. And seeing you after all these years…it's been…' He seemed to struggle to find the right word. 'It's been hard.'

She felt her heart squeeze.

He moved the position of his hand. This time his thumb was inside her palm, moving in tiny circular motions, while the rest of his hand rested over hers.

He lowered his voice. 'But it's been good to see you, Lucia. Really good. It's left me wondering why we didn't do this earlier.'

She didn't hesitate. 'Because it would have been too hard.' Her gaze was steady on his. 'And you're right, it is still hard.'

'But it doesn't have to be?' There was an edge of optimism in his voice. A little glimmer of hopefulness.

Tears prickled in her eyes. A lump rose instantly in her throat. This was dangerous territory. Business was business, but this was something else entirely. She swallowed. 'I think it always will be. There's too many memories. Too many associations.'

He didn't move. Didn't flinch. Logan had always

been like this. His thumb kept moving in little circles, the way it always had when he was trying to soothe her. And for the most part it worked. Logan had always been cool, almost like the eye of a storm. Few things made him ever raise his voice. Few things made him rattled.

She looked at him again. He was still her Logan. Still so handsome. Still so protective. Grief had made his love feel suffocating. But the truth was Logan had never been suffocating. He'd encouraged her to blossom and grow while they'd been in Florence together. He'd be the very person to tell her never to hide her light under a bushel.

Why on earth hadn't he met someone over the last twelve years? Why wasn't he married with children? It had always been what he wanted. And he'd seemed to cope so much better with the death of Ariella Rose than she had.

He'd been grief-stricken for sure. The plans they'd made for baby furniture and paraphernalia had silently disappeared. He'd spoken to the doctors regarding a proper burial. Things were difficult when a baby was so young. But Logan's calm and assuring manner had persuaded them to go along with his wishes and they'd got to lay Ariella Rose to rest in a cemetery just outside the city walls.

The short ceremony by the priest had been beautiful, the flowers and funeral arrangements all carried out by Logan—she'd been too numb to help with any of it.

It was only now, in hindsight, that she could appreciate just how hard that must have been for him. She hadn't been the only one to cry over the death of their daughter. And after he'd spent days trying to get her talk and she hadn't responded he'd finally stopped and mirrored her behaviour. Closing in on himself and shutting out the world around him.

He finally replied. 'Let's just see how things are. I'm glad we've met again, Lucia. I'm glad that you're settled in an amazing city and doing a job that you love.'

There it was. The unspoken words.

I'm glad you've finally moved on.

But had she?

All he wanted to do was reach across the table and hold her. Lucia was at her most fragile right now. He could see the hidden pain in her eyes and he hated it that he was the person who had done that to her. Hated that her association with him was her most painful memory.

He had painful memories too. But he was still able to remember the good times in Florence—running through one of the fountains during a rainstorm, watching her face when he'd come home with every flower that the street vendor had been selling, sneaking out in the morning to buy her favourite pastry and watching her nose twitch as she'd woken up to the smell. For a long time Lucia had been his joy—and the feeling had been mutual. He only wished he was still hers.

She'd haunted his dreams on and off for years. Dreams about them meeting again in some random place, having dinner together, or catching each other's eye across a crowded room.

He'd always dreaded hearing the news that she was happily married or settled with a family of her own, but somehow seeing her like this was equally hard. More than anything he wanted Lucia to be happy.

Seeing her again was sparking a whole host of emotions that he'd long forgotten. He'd never imagined that the spark between them would still feel so electric. He'd never imagined that once he'd stared into those brown eyes again he'd feel rooted to the spot and never want to break away.

Lucia brushed her chocolate hair from her shoulder. It was a little shorter than he remembered and it suited her. She pulled her hand back steadily, keeping her gaze on his. He could almost see her retreating back into herself and putting a carefully drawn line between them.

She picked up her coffee cup. 'How soon do you think you'll get the paperwork completed?'

Business. That was all she wanted to discuss with him. Even after all this time.

He nodded, picking up the biscuit from the side of his cappuccino and placing it on her saucer. He didn't miss the little hint of a smile from her.

'How soon can you tell me I can finish my renovations?'

She blinked. 'Well...' She paused. 'Actually, I'm not sure. We have to file your paperwork, then I need to do some investigating. I've made a private appointment tomorrow to view another fresco by the artist we think is involved.'

He sat back in his chair. 'Well, that's fine. I'll come with you.'

She looked surprised. 'Why would you want to come with me?'

He shrugged. 'There's not much point in me going back if I can't give Louisa good news. She needs to know that the renovations and wedding plans can continue. At the moment most of the work in the chapel has ground to a halt. There's still work ongoing in the *palazzo* but it doesn't require my supervision every day.

The chapel will be the difference between this wedding going ahead or not.'

Lucia looked thoughtful. Her fingers started twiddling with a strand of her hair and she crossed her legs, giving him a flash of her tanned skin. 'What do you know about the royal couple?'

He shook his head. 'Virtually nothing. I've mostly dealt with Lindsay, the wedding planner.' He laughed. 'Now, there's a woman I don't want to call to say there's an issue with the chapel.'

Lucia smiled. 'Will she chew you up and spit you out?' There was a little spark of amusement in her eyes. It suited her. It made her more like the Lucia he remembered. The Lucia he *wanted* to remember.

'In a heartbeat,' he said quickly. 'There's no point in going back until I know I'm safe.'

Lucia frowned. 'Where have you made arrangements to stay?'

This time he frowned too. Oh, no. 'Well, I haven't. Not yet anyway.' His brain started spinning. 'There's a small boutique hotel I stay in if I ever come to Venice. I can give them a call.' He pulled his mobile from his pocket and started dialling.

Lucia shook her head and held out her hands. 'Have you seen this place? I've never seen Venice this busy. I think everywhere will be packed out.'

So do I. He was cringing inside. He'd known as soon as he'd arrived that he would never make his flight back. It was leaving right around now. And he hadn't even made any attempt to book another. With this number of tourists he imagined that every flight and train journey, in and out of Venice, was booked for the next few days.

He pressed the phone to his ear. 'Hi, there, it's Logan Cascini. I wondered if there was any chance of reserving a room for the night.'

He listened to the reply and tried to stop the sinking feeling settling over him. 'No problem. Can you recommend anywhere else?'

The crease across Lucia's brow was deepening.

He listened to the receptionist telling him what he already knew. Venice was packed. Every hotel was fully booked for the next two days. He cut the call and gave his best attempt at a shrug. 'I'll try somewhere else.'

Lucia sucked in a breath. 'Why do you want to stay, Logan? There isn't anything that you can actually do. Did you book a flight back to Tuscany?'

Her tone was almost accusatory. He pressed a button on his phone and spun it around, showing her his online boarding card for the flight that was due to take off any minute.

Her eyes widened. 'Oh.'

She bit her lip again. 'Why do you even *want* to stay?'

The same question again. This time with a different emphasis on the words. It was obviously preying on her mind, just like it was preying on his. When he'd booked his flight he'd planned to be in Venice for four hours and leave again later today and go straight back to Tuscany. It had all seemed straightforward. Except in his mind, where a little voice kept niggling at him.

This was the contact he'd always imagined making. The renovations were a perfect excuse to be around Lucia. He hadn't planned it. It had surprised him just as much as it had surprised her. But sometimes fate had a mysterious hand in things.

After the first few awkward moments curiosity had been killing him about Lucia. He wanted to know everything about the last twelve years. He wanted to know her plans for the future. If she was happy. If she was settled.

And absolutely none of it was his business. But that didn't stop the little craving that had always been there growing into something a whole lot bigger.

There would always be something between them. Right now, it still felt as if there was a big black cloud hanging over them. But for him, he could see little remnants of sunlight struggling to get through. And he wanted them to get through. So badly.

But still something was holding him back. Holding him back from saying their daughter's name and asking Lucia if she was ready to talk about her.

So he took the easy way out. The safest way out, if he wanted to still have contact with Lucia.

'I want to stay because I want to help move this project along. I would love to see Burano's fresco. I would love to see how it compares to the Madonna and Child and to the nymph sculpture. You know I love this stuff just as much as you do.'

Part of him felt guilty. These were careful words, designed to push the little buttons inside her and help things spark along.

There was a glimmer in her eyes. He was talking her language. A language she related to and understood.

He pulled something from his bag. 'Look at this. You told me to try and find any evidence that Burano had been around the village. I've photocopied something from the local museum. One of the guest houses had an ancient register. People used to stay for months at a time.' He pointed to a blurred entry from 1530. 'I thought that might be Alberto Burano.'

She screwed up her nose and squinted at the blurred entry. It was difficult to judge but he could see the glimmer of excitement behind her eyes.

'I'm sure we'll have a sample of his writing somewhere at the heritage board.' She met his gaze. 'This could be really important, Logan. You did well to find this.'

It was the first note of approval he'd had from her and it made his heart swell in his chest. He wasn't going to tell how he'd had to bribe the local museum curator to let him riffle through all the old paperwork. He wasn't going to let her know he'd spent all of last night checking through mountains of ancient chests in order to find anything that might help.

'Can I take this?' she asked, holding up the photocopy.

He nodded as he zipped up his bag again.

'This can definitely help.' She looked around them. The number of people in the quiet street was starting to pick up. 'But where will you stay?'

The million-dollar question. He shrugged as he desperately tried to think of someone, *anyone* he still knew in Venice.

His fingers flicked through the numbers on his phone. He had a multitude of contacts in Florence, Rome and Pisa. Venice? Not so much.

'You can stay with me.'

The words came out of the blue. It was absolutely the last thing he was expecting to hear.

'What? No, I couldn't possibly put you to any trouble.' His stomach clenched.

He couldn't miss the expression on her face. She was saying the words, but it was reluctantly—this wasn't a warm invitation.

And he hated that. He hated that she felt obliged to offer him somewhere to stay—when it was obvious she didn't really want to.

That hurt.

But the reality was that he really didn't have anywhere else to go. Chances were he could spend the next two hours phoning every hotel and just get the same answer—fully booked. There was a strong likelihood he wouldn't find a bed for the night.

Part of him wanted to refuse graciously and just walk away.

But something else was burning inside…a persistence.

Lucia used to be his. She used to fill his whole world. And he knew that the feelings had been mutual.

They were both adults. They were twelve years away from their shared past. Determination was overcoming him.

He didn't want to walk away from Lucia—no matter how awkward she felt.

In another world she would love him just as much as she always had, and would be delighted to offer him somewhere to stay and he would be delighted to accept.

But in another world they wouldn't have lost Ariella Rose.

His fingers itched to reach over and touch her soft hand.

Her own hands were knotted together, turning over and over in her lap.

The rational part of his brain kicked in. He needed

to get this job back on track. He needed to finish the renovations at the *palazzo* and the chapel.

And the history-loving part of him would love to see the other fresco. This wasn't such an unreasonable offer to accept. Another night in Venice might give him a little time to get to know Lucia again.

And it seemed as though the rest of Venice might be attending a concert somewhere, leaving the beauties of Venice still to be explored...

He lifted his gaze to meet hers. 'Thank you, Lucia. You're right. I probably won't be able to find anywhere else to stay. As long as you're sure it's not too much trouble, I'd be delighted to stay.'

CHAPTER FIVE

WHAT HAD SHE just done?

Was her apartment even reasonably tidy? She didn't have any food. Well, not the kind of food to entertain with and make dinner for a guest. Chilli-flavoured crisps and orange-flavoured chocolate might be her favourite dinner but she couldn't offer it to a guest. What on earth had she been thinking?

She was desperately hoping that she appeared outwardly calm. But her heartbeat was thudding against her chest at a rate of knots. Logan gestured to the waiter and settled their bill, picking up his bag and giving her a casual smile. 'Shall we finish this paperwork back at your place?'

It was a reasonable, rational question. He couldn't possibly imagine the way the blood was racing around her system and the breath was sticking in her lungs.

'Of course,' she said as coolly as possible, with a nod of her head as she stood up.

'How far away do you live?' he asked.

She tried to smile. 'Well, that depends entirely on traffic and the time of day.'

She weaved her way through the cobbled streets towards the water-taxi stop. 'I'm only two stops along. It only takes a few minutes.'

They were lucky. The water taxis on this side of the canal weren't quite so busy. They jumped on and back off within five minutes.

Her skin was prickling. Every little hair on her arms was standing on end even though the sun was splitting the sky. Now that Logan had had a chance to cool down he was back to his normal, unruffled self. She kind of wished he was still as flustered as he had been for a few moments earlier. It made him seem less infallible. A little more vulnerable—just like she felt.

But Logan had never been vulnerable. He'd always been rock solid. Even in grief.

He jumped out of the taxi before her and held out his hand for her as she stepped from the bobbing boat. She lifted her head and tried to walk with confidence. Although her apartment overlooked the Grand Canal the entrance of the traditional building was around the back. It had been hundreds of years since people had entered directly from the canal, and the original entrance had long since been plastered over.

She couldn't hide her smile. The architect in Logan could never be hidden. His eyes were roaming over the traditional building, his smile growing wider by the second. 'You stay in an old Venetian palace?'

The admiration and wonder in his voice was obvious. She'd always known Logan would approve of her choice. The fifteenth-century building facing the Grand Canal was one of the most photographed in the district. It had distinctive Venetian floral Gothic-style architecture. The façade was pink plaster facing with intricate white detailing around all the windows and balconies that overlooked the canal. The arches on the balconies were topped with delicate quatrefoil windows, resembling flowers with four petals.

She gave him a smile as she opened the entranceway. 'Just wait until you see the inside. We have our own high ceilings, beams, alcoves and frescoes. The whole place is full of original features.'

Logan was nodding, his eyes wide as they stepped inside. She'd always loved this about him. The way a glimpse of architectural details of a building could capture his attention instantly. He would become instantly enthralled, desperate to know more about the building and its history. Architecture had always been Logan's dream. But renovating ancient buildings? That was his calling. Always had been.

A bit like hers had been painting.

The memory swept through her like a gust of stormy weather.

Another part of life put into a box. When she'd first got together with Logan, their apartment had been littered with brushes, easels and oils. She had painted all the time, usually wearing nothing more than one of his shirts. She'd loved the feel of having him right next to her as she'd created, and if he hadn't been there, the scent of him—his aroma and aftershave—would usually linger on one of his shirts waiting to be washed. Thoughts of Logan had always fired her creative juices.

A warm feeling crept across her stomach. Logan had always loved finding her like that, his shirt loose around her body and her hair twisted on top of her head with an errant paintbrush holding it in place. He'd usually pulled it free, followed by the shirt, and the following hours had been lost in a rush of love.

But that light had flickered out and died along with the death of their daughter. For a long time she couldn't even bear to look at a paintbrush, let alone hold one.

Working for the heritage board had helped her heal. She didn't paint her own creations any more. But she did paint. Restoration work was painstaking. In every fresco she restored she tried to re-create the passion and drama that the original artist had felt when he'd envisaged the work.

There was still a little part of her that longed to feel like that again too.

There was a lift inside her building but Logan was captivated by the grandiose staircase inside the entranceway. As it curved upwards there were archways hollowed out in the plaster in the walls. A long time ago each had been painted individually and had held sculptures. In between each hollowed archway was a large circular fresco embedded into the plaster on the walls.

Logan moved quickly up the stairs, stopping to admire each individual one. 'These are amazing,' he said, his hand hovering about them. Logan's professional expertise knew far better than to actually touch.

She followed him upwards. A warmth was spreading through her. She was proud of her home—and secretly pleased that the man she'd shared part of her life with loved it just as much as she did.

As they walked upwards she leaned a little closer and whispered, 'I might have restored some of these.'

His head shot around towards her. 'You did?'

She nodded as his eyes fixed on the walls again. His fingers were still hovering just above a fresco of Moses. 'You've made an amazing job of these.'

'Thank you,' she said simply, as they reached her

floor and she pulled out her key and opened the apartment door.

He walked inside and looked around. Her living area
was spacious and held a dining table and chairs and two
wooden-footed red sofas. As with most Italian traditional apartments the floor was marble. A dark wooden
bookcase adorned one wall, jam-packed with books.

But the most spectacular aspect of the apartment was
the view. Lucia strode across the room and pulled open
the black-and-gilt-edged glass doors. The warm air and
noise from the Grand Canal below flooded in. It was like
flicking a button and bringing the place to life. Next to
the doors was a small wooden table, a chaise longue
and an armchair. It was like having a real-live television. You could sit here all day and night and watch the
world go by.

She knew his head must be spinning. This apartment
was sumptuous. Well out of her price range. She stood
shoulder to shoulder with him, watching the *vaporetti*
and private boats motor past. On the other side of the
canal stood another magnificent long-abandoned palace. Renaissance in style again, with Gothic-styled windows and ornate frescoes on the outside of the building.

He turned towards her and smiled. 'It's almost like
your perfect view, isn't it?' There was an edge of curiosity in his voice. But he wasn't going to ask the question out loud. Logan was far too polite for that.

'Coffee?' she asked, as she walked towards the
kitchen. It was right next door to the open living area
and again had windows looking out on the canal. He
nodded and walked in next to her, sitting down on one
of the high stools looking over the canal. She switched
on her coffee-machine and put in her favourite blend.

She leaned back against the countertop. 'I haven't always stayed here,' she said quietly. 'After I'd been in Venice for two years one of my colleagues retired from the heritage board. They subsidise our living arrangements because—as you know—Venice can be very expensive.' She held out her hands. 'I sort of inherited this place. I pay roughly the same as we did for our apartment in Florence.' She watched his eyebrows rise and couldn't stop the smile. 'It was like all my Saturdays at once.' She laughed as she watched the coffee brew and pointed across the waterway. 'Do you know, they actually asked me how I'd feel about staying here? It was all I could do not to snatch the key and just run.'

The warm feeling was spreading further. She rarely brought friends back to her apartment. This place was her sanctuary. From the moment she'd stepped inside it had always felt like that.

She'd thought having Logan here would be unbearable. She'd been so busy focusing on all the negatives she hadn't even considered the positives.

He was fascinated by the building's history and traditional architecture. He respected the heritage just as much as she did.

She poured the coffee into two mugs and set them on the table, watching the steam rising while she frothed some milk and added it to the mugs.

She gestured with her hand. 'Come and I'll show you where your room is.'

She hadn't even had time to prepare anything and she had to hope that nothing was out of place in her barely used guest suite. She led him down the corridor off the kitchen. It was the only place in her apartment that didn't have natural light.

He grabbed her elbow as they walked down the corridor. 'Are you sure this is okay?'

She turned to face him. He was much closer than she'd expected, his warm breath hitting her cheek. For a second she was frozen. This was as up close and personal as she'd been to Logan in years. The closeness took her breath away.

Even in the dim light of the corridor his green eyes made her struggle to think clearly. He was worried. He was worried about her. And glances like that brought back painful memories.

A tiny little part of her wished that Logan was looking at her in a different way. The way he used to, with passion and laughter in his eyes. She wanted to reach up and touch him. Touch the skin on his cheek, the shadowed outline of his jaw, and run her fingers through his dark hair. She wanted him to step forward just a few inches to see if their bodies still fitted together after all this time.

Her heart was racing and Logan blinked. He was staring at a spot on her neck where she was sure he could see the rapid beating of her pulse.

She took a deep breath and turned away, trying to blink back threatening tears. This was why everything about this was a bad idea.

She swung open a dark wooden door, flooding the corridor with light and stepping into a white and blue room. It was still traditional. A double bedroom with a window overlooking the canal, pale blue walls and fresh white bed linen. It wasn't quite as sumptuous as the other rooms in the house as it was rarely used.

She nodded her head. 'The bathroom is next door. Don't worry, we won't have to share. The box room

was converted to an en suite. Would you like some
time to settle in?'

He shook his head. 'Your coffee smells too good to
let it go to waste. Let's finish the paperwork then we
can decide where I'm taking you to dinner.' There was
a glimmer in his eye. 'I don't expect you to cook for
me—not if I want to live to tell the tale.'

He'd caught her unawares and she threw back her
head and laughed. 'I offer you a room for the night and
this is the thanks I get?'

He gave her a steady smile. 'Let's just wait until dinner.' She could almost hear his brain ticking over and
her stomach gave a little leap.

What on earth did he have planned?

Logan washed up and changed his wrinkled shirt.
Thank goodness he always had a spare in his bag.

He looked around the room. It was comfortable but
sparse—it was clear this room didn't get much use.
Didn't Lucia have friends to stay? She'd had a few girlfriends at university but he had no idea if they'd kept
in touch.

He sighed and looked out of the window. It was ridiculous but he was having a hard time with this.

Lucia had a job she loved and a fabulous apartment
in one of the most cosmopolitan cities in the world. He
should be overjoyed for her. In his head, all he'd ever
wanted was for her to be happy. In a twisted kind of
way this was his ideal situation.

She was happy. She was settled. But there was no
husband and kids on the scene to let the tiny leaves of
jealousy unfurl. To let him know that she'd taken the
final steps.

He couldn't quite work out why he was feeling so unsettled. All he knew was that there was something in her eyes. A guarded part. A hidden part. A little piece of her that didn't look quite...alive.

That was what bothered him. Lucia had a fabulous life. But was she really living?

He glanced around. While this room was sparsely furnished, the rest of the apartment was sumptuous. The reds and golds complemented the grandeur of the ancient palace. There were lots of similar buildings scattered across Venice. It seemed everyone who'd ever been slightly royal had built a palace in Venice. It was no wonder the heritage board wanted to keep someone in here.

He walked through to the main room. Lucia was sitting in a chair next to the open doors, the sights and sounds of the Grand Canal drifting up towards them. She'd changed into a purple jersey wrap-around dress, her dark chocolate-brown hair falling over her shoulders in waves. Her legs were curled up underneath her and she was reading a book.

Sitting on the table next to her was a glass of red wine. He smiled. 'Merlot or Chianti?'

Her head lifted in surprise. 'What do you think?'

He glanced out at the busy traffic on the Grand Canal. 'A warm summer evening? An aperitif before dinner?' He put his finger on his chin. 'I'm trying to think what you've planned for dinner—will it be meat or pasta?'

She used to be so fussy. He could imagine there were only certain local restaurants that she'd visit.

She held up her glass towards him. 'Maybe it will be both?'

She was teasing. He shook his head and pointed to the glass. 'It must be Merlot. It's too warm an evening for steak. You're planning for pasta.'

Something flickered across her face. She didn't like it that after twelve years he could still read her. She gestured towards the dining table where the bottle of wine and another glass sat. 'Find out for yourself.'

Logan walked over and filled his glass, resisting the temptation to smile. 'Where do you think we're eating tonight?'

She raised her eyebrows. 'What makes you think we'll be eating anywhere? Haven't you heard—it's the busiest night of the year in Venice?'

He sat down on the chaise longue next to her chair. 'But I might know an out-of-the-way place that the tourist hordes don't know about—like Erona's in Florence.'

There was a flash of something behind her eyes and she stood up quickly. He'd upset her.

She didn't want direct reminders of their time in Florence. 'You're not from here. How would you know where to eat?'

'Let's just say that your boss, Alessio, gave me a few hints.'

She slid her feet into a pair of red-soled black patent stilettos with impossibly high heels.

'Wherever we're going, I hope they have flat surfaces,' he muttered. Alessio had told him to get to the restaurant—just not what the streets around it were like.

'Let's go, Logan. Our viewing is early tomorrow morning. I want to get an early night.'

The words sent a flurry of sparks across his brain. An early night. With Lucia Moretti. It was enough to send his whole body into overdrive.

His eyes focused on her behind as she crossed the room ahead of him in her impossibly high heels. Her dress clung to every curve.

He swallowed. This was going to be a long, uncomfortable night.

Venice was virtually silent at this time in the morning. The private motor boat glided through the water towards the Venetian island of Giudecca.

Logan was curious. 'I thought all the artefacts of historical value would have been commandeered by the Italian Heritage Board?'

Lucia gave a sigh. 'In theory, they can. But part of this island is private—has been since before Renaissance times. It's owned by the Brunelli family. They built the church here and commissioned the artist, Burano, to paint the fresco. Technically, we're just their guests. We're allowed access to the fresco on request. You'll understand why when you see it—it's a little unusual.'

The boat came to a halt at the dock and they disembarked onto the wooden structure. A white stone path led them directly to the church, where a dark-suited man was waiting for them. Logan recognised him immediately—Dario Brunelli was frequently nicknamed Italian's most eligible bachelor. *He knew Lucia?*

'Lucia,' he said swiftly, bending to kiss her on both cheeks, 'it's good to see you again. How have you been?'

His familiarity with Lucia grated instantly. Her reaction was even worse—she seemed relaxed in his company. 'I'm good, thank you.' She turned towards Logan. 'Dario, this is Logan Cascini, a specialist restoration architect from Florence. He's working with me on the project in Tuscany.'

It was completely true. But it made it sound as if they'd only just met. As if there was no shared history between them at all.

For a second he held his breath, wondering if Dario was having the same thoughts that he'd had this morning when he'd first seen Lucia. Her cream fitted business suit and pale pink shirt hugged her curves. The knee-length skirt exposed her slim legs. And her dark hair and eyes complemented the package perfectly. Lucia looked good enough to eat.

Dario nodded towards Logan but it was clear his focus was on Lucia. 'So, do you think you've found another of Burano's frescoes?'

Lucia's smile was broad. 'I think there is a distinct possibility. With your permission, I'm going to take some high-resolution digital shots to compare the brushstrokes.'

Dario was nodding enthusiastically. 'In Tuscany? I wonder how in the world Burano ended up working there? Wouldn't it be wonderful if it was another of his works?'

A Renaissance art lover. The passion and enthusiasm in his eyes was for the art, not for Lucia. Not for his woman.

Where had that come from?

Cold air prickled his skin and he shifted on his feet. Lucia hadn't been his woman for twelve years—she hadn't wanted to be.

And he'd had to live with that. He'd had to support the fact she wasn't able to continue their relationship and allow her the space she'd needed to heal. No matter how much it had ripped his heart in two.

No one else had ever come close to the love he'd

felt for Lucia. How could they? She'd been the mother of his child. And even though that was something she wanted to forget, her place in his heart had been well and truly cemented there.

But even he hadn't realised how much.

'Forgive me.' Dario nodded. 'I have to go. I have business to attend to. Please, take all the time you need.'

Lucia gave a gracious nod of her head as Dario walked swiftly down the path towards the waiting motorboat.

She turned and pressed her hand against the heavy wooden door of the church and smiled at Logan. There was a gleam of something in her eye. He only hoped it was for the contents of the church and not for the retreating back of Dario. The spike of jealousy had been unexpected—a feeling he hadn't dealt with in years.

'Ready?' she asked.

He nodded and she pushed the door and it groaned and creaked loudly on its hinges as it swung back. The church wasn't lit.

The only light that streamed in came through six muted stained-glass windows above the altar.

It took a few seconds for his eyes to adjust to the dim light. He caught his breath.

The fresco on the wall was magnificent and stretched from one end of the church to the other. His feet moved automatically towards it.

Over his years in Italy he'd seen many frescoes—but none quite like this. It was completely and utterly unique, almost like a timeline through the first book of the bible.

She rested her hand on his arm. 'I've never seen anything like it before, and I'm quite sure I'll never see anything like it again.' He could hear the amusement in her voice at his reaction. 'It's a little different from the Madonna and Child, isn't it?'

He shook his head as he took in more and more of the fresco. He recognised the characters—at least, he thought he did. Adam and Eve, Noah, Moses, Jacob and his sons. But the thing that made these characters unique was the fact they were all completely naked.

He spun to face her. 'What on earth…?'

She laughed. 'I know. It's why the Italian Heritage Board hasn't bothered to make demands on the family. The Catholic Church would be outraged by these scenes.'

Logan moved forward. He just couldn't stop smiling. He was trying to think rationally. 'Adam and Eve—you might expect them to be naked. But the rest…' He kept looking at the scenes. 'It's amazing. I mean, apart from their nakedness the depictions are accurate. Eve with the apple, Moses leading the Israelites through the Red Sea, Noah on the ark, and Jacob with his twelve sons.' He let out a laugh. 'Joseph is even holding his multi-coloured coat instead of wearing it.'

She shrugged her shoulders. 'Naked bodies were pretty much the fashion during Renaissance times.' Her brow creased slightly. 'But usually they had something—anything—draped around about them. These ones are totally original.'

Logan stepped back a little. 'But there's something else, isn't there? I can't quite put my finger on it.' He paused, staring hard at the scenes, looking between one and another.

She nodded, with an amused expression on her face. 'Give it time, Logan. You'll get it.'

She was teasing him. It was almost like throwing down a challenge. So he took a few minutes, concentrating hard until, finally, the penny dropped.

He turned to her in amazement. 'It's the faces, isn't it?' He stepped right up to the fresco, staring first at the face of Adam then at the face of Moses, then Noah. 'It's the same face.' His eyes scanned one way, then the other. 'It's the same man and woman in every scene.'

Lucia was laughing. 'You're right. The family don't have any official records about who commissioned the fresco. The name of Burano has just been passed down through the family. That's why we'll have to do a comparison. And we're not quite sure why it's the same faces in all the scenes. I've spoken to the family about it at length. We think there's something a little narcissistic in it. We think that when the original Brunellis commissioned the artist they asked for the faces to be made in their image.'

Logan let out a burst of laughter. 'You mean, even all those years ago we had fame-hungry people?' He shook his head. 'Wow, just wow.'

He took another few seconds and stopped in front of the young Joseph holding the coat. 'I still can't believe they wouldn't let Joseph wear his multi-coloured coat.'

She bent down in the front of the fresco. In the dim light he could see her dark eyes were still gleaming. 'Yes, but look at the folds in the cloak. What do you see?'

He looked closer. 'Of course. They look exactly like the folds in the Madonna's dress in the fresco in Tuscany. That's what you noticed.'

There wasn't a sound in the dark church. They were entirely alone, crouching on the floor. The lack of artificial light was almost like a safety blanket around them.

His face was only inches from hers. Their gazes meshed. It was a moment. An instant. For just that second she had the same passion and wonder in her eyes that she'd had twelve years ago. Twelve years ago when they'd thought they could conquer the world.

He'd been trying so hard to hold his tongue, trying to keep a handle on how he felt about everything, but the memories of Lucia were just overtaking him. The spark of jealousy, the protectiveness, the connection between them. He was like a pressure cooker just waiting to go off.

Her pupils were dilating in front of him, the blackness overtaking the chocolate brown of her eyes. He was pretty certain his were doing exactly the same.

All of a sudden he couldn't stop himself. He leaned forward, just a few inches, and caught the back of her head in his hand, tangling his fingers through her hair as he pulled her towards him.

And then he stopped thinking entirely...

She was instantly transported back twelve years. The familiarity was astounding.

No one had kissed her like this in twelve years.

No kiss had felt so right.

No kiss had felt so perfect.

Her body moved on automatic pilot, ignoring all the little neurons that were firing in her brain. Ignoring every single rational thought that might be there.

She could only act on instinct. Her hands slid through his thick, dark hair, her fingers tugging and pulling at his head. She could taste him. She could smell him.

Everything about him was familiar. His scent was winding its way around her like a coiling snake. Her hands moved, sliding across his muscled shoulders and arms and down the planes of his chest.

His lips never left hers. Their teeth clashed, his tongue tangling with hers. Crouching on a floor wasn't comfortable for kissing. Logan sensed that and pulled her up against him, his strong legs lifting them both upwards, keeping their bodies in contact the whole time.

She could feel his heart thudding against her chest. Feel her breath catching in her throat.

It was so easy to be swept away. It was so easy to forget about everything else. His fingertips brushed across the front of her breasts as she sucked in a sharp breath, then rounded her hips and stopped firmly on her behind, pulling her even closer to him.

There was no mistaking his reaction to her. There was no mistaking he was every bit as caught up in this as she was.

So when he stopped kissing her she was shocked.

He pulled his lips back from hers and rested his forehead against hers, breathing heavily. His body was still interlocked with hers. It seemed he had no intention of moving.

Her hands, resting against his chest, clenched.

Embarrassment swamped her. She wanted to step back but couldn't.

What on earth was he thinking?

Then, to her surprise, he let out a deep laugh. It wasn't a mocking laugh. It wasn't derogatory. It was more one of astonishment.

In the dark church his voice was husky. 'So that's what I've been missing.' He took a deep breath. 'I sometimes wondered if my mind was playing tricks on me. If I'd imagined how good it was.'

He was echoing her thoughts. She'd felt exactly the same way. Any time she'd allowed memories of Logan to sneak into her brain, she'd always thought it couldn't possibly have been as good as she remembered it. Everything before Ariella Rose, that was.

The portcullis that was always stiffly in place was shaken a little. The thick gate had risen just a tiny bit, leaving the thinnest gap underneath. The black cloud of self-protection that usually cloaked her was thinning in patches.

Their foreheads were still touching. She could feel his warm breath on her cheeks. 'It wasn't all that bad, was it?' she whispered.

His fingers stroked through her soft hair. 'Some parts were really good,' he breathed quietly.

She stayed where she was—for a few more seconds.

This was only a moment of madness. A tiny little step back in time.

It wasn't real. None of this was real.

Real life meant that now she lived and worked in Venice and Logan lived and worked in Florence.

The meeting at Tuscany was merely a blip. The next few weeks of working together would only be a continuation of that blip. She could almost feel the protective coating going around her heart. She had to be careful. She had to be sensible.

She lifted her head back from his, trying to ignore the warm feeling of his beating heart beneath her palm.

It was time to put all the safeguards back in place.

She gave him a rueful smile and stepped back, freeing herself from his grasp.

The movement jolted Logan. He straightened his

back, watching her carefully. It was almost as if he knew what was coming next.

'We don't really have time to reminisce, Logan. I have work to do. You have work to do. The sooner we can verify the artist of the fresco, the sooner we can both move towards our goals.'

What were her goals? She'd always been clear about them in the past, but right now they were looking pretty muddy.

Silence hung in the air between them. It almost shimmered in the slowly brightening daylight.

She could almost hear him processing what she'd said.

He chose his words carefully as he stepped forward and gently touched her cheek. 'You're right, Lucia. It's best we leave things as they are.' He nodded his head. 'We both need to focus on work.'

Something squeezed in her chest. For a few seconds she felt as if she couldn't breathe.

Part of her wished he'd said no. Part of her wished he'd pull her back into his arms and kiss her all over again. Acknowledge this thing that shimmered in the air between them and refuse to walk away from it.

But that was all a fairy tale. This was real life. She could tell from the slight waver in his voice that he was saying what he thought he should. This was just as hard for him as it was for her.

If this was anyone else she might think they were toying with her. But Logan just wasn't capable of that kind of thing. Not after what they'd shared.

This was for the best. It didn't matter that little parts of her brain were screaming at her. Every female hormone she'd ever possessed was currently marching in a charge towards all parts of her body.

She blinked back the tears that were hovering behind her eyes. His fingers felt like butterfly wings on her skin. It was all she could do not to tilt her head towards his hand.

She bent down and picked up her papers, which were strewn on the floor, trying not to acknowledge her trembling hands.

His feet took a step backwards. She could sense him bending over her, probably reaching towards her, then he took a few further steps back. It was almost as if he forcing himself into a position of retreat.

She straightened up and fixed a false smile on her face. 'Let's get to work, Logan. Can you see if we can find some light?' She pulled her camera from her bag. 'The sooner we get these pictures, the sooner we can move forward.'

She tried not to wince at her choice of words.

But Logan's expression was resolute. Guarded. She had no idea what was going on behind those green eyes.

He gave a brief nod. 'Of course.' And walked back towards the door to let in some light.

She turned back to the fresco.

Work. The only thing that was currently keeping her sane.

CHAPTER SIX

WORK WAS THE easy part. It didn't take any time at all for Lucia to take the photos and to take the boat trip back to her office. The rest of Venice had woken up now, with the city becoming loud and colourful as their boat glided back through the water.

The Italian Heritage Board building was every bit as exuberant as Logan had expected it to be. The architecture was a welcome distraction, with some of the really exclusive Renaissance pieces of art housed in the building.

Lucia had uploaded the pictures to her computer and was running a comparison computer program that would take a few hours.

All they could do was wait.

And waiting was something Logan Cascini had never been good at.

After that kiss he was finding it difficult to keep his cool, collected manner in place. One touch of Lucia's lips had been enough to ignite all the sparks in his brain and frustration had been building ever since.

He'd had enough. Not of Lucia. He'd had enough of them being in the same room together and not talking about the big elephant between them. Ariella Rose.

It was twelve years on. It was time. Even if Lucia still felt that it wasn't.

There was no way he was getting on that plane back to Tuscany without tackling the subject. No way at all.

But how?

She had barriers erected so tightly around her she might as well have been wearing a spacesuit. The kiss had been one thing. She'd probably already written it off as a blip.

But Logan couldn't do that. He wanted more. Much more.

No wonder every other relationship he'd had had fizzled out. No wonder he'd never wanted to commit to someone else.

This was nothing to do with losing his daughter. This wasn't about the fear of another pregnancy or another child.

It was much more primal than that. It was about the fear of never finding someone he had the same chemistry with, the same connection with, as he had with Lucia.

Life was hard. Life was tough. But twelve years of drifting had given him new determination.

Seeing Lucia for the first time again had been like a lightning bolt. Kissing her again…well, that had been so much more.

It was time to face things head-on.

He turned from the view of Venice to face her. She was sitting behind her desk, twiddling her long dark hair around one finger.

He reached forward and grabbed her other hand, pulling her to her feet. 'Let's go.'

She looked shocked. 'Let's go where?'

He held out his other hand. 'Out there. Let's see Venice.' He pointed to the screen. 'You already said the computer program would take a few hours. Let's spend them wisely.' He grinned at her. 'Today I am a tourist. Today I want you to show me Venice.'

A hint of a smile appeared on her face. She waved towards the window. 'But it will be crazy out there. There's another concert tonight. We'll have all of last night's gig-goers and all of tonight's too.'

He raised his eyebrows. 'What, we can't handle a few tourists?'

She shook her head and let out a little laugh. 'Now I know you're definitely crazy.' She picked up her handbag and swung it over her shoulder. 'You're right, the program will take another few hours, and as long as we start with ice cream I'm in.'

He held out his hand towards her.

She hesitated. She wavered. He could see it in every inch of her body. She finally let out the breath she'd been holding and put her hand in his.

'Let's go.'

It was hotter than hot. Her jacket was hanging over the top of her shoulder bag to try and deter any pickpockets and her shirt was in danger of sticking to her back.

The queue for ice cream was snaking its way out the door of her favourite gelateria. She tugged Logan towards the end of the queue. His hand was still in hers. It felt odd, but she hadn't quite managed to pull her hand free of his.

The walk through the twisting cobbled streets had been like a step back in time. She'd noticed the women's admiring glances. Logan was every woman's Italian dream—dark-haired, broad shouldered, well dressed and devilishly handsome. His unexpected bright green eyes added a little twist.

And he was free with his natural charm. He nodded and smiled at the numerous pairs of acknowledging eyes. A tiny swell of pride surged in her chest. Memories flickered in her brain. People thought they were a couple. People thought that Logan was hers.

He turned to face her as the queue slowly moved forward. 'What kind of ice cream do you want? I take it you've sampled them all?'

She gave a little smile. 'All in the name of research. Dark chocolate and *limon* are my two favourites from here.'

He nodded at her choices. 'In that case we'll get one of each. Why not try everything you like?' He was smiling as he said the words, and the woman in front turned around with a gleam in her eyes.

Lucia shifted on her feet. She didn't want to allow the tiny seeds in her brain to flower and grow.

Logan reached the front of the queue, ordering their ice creams and only releasing her hand when he reached to pay for them. They walked out into the building heat and he held both hands out towards her. 'What'll it be? The dark, tantalising chocolate or the sweet, zesty lemon?'

He was teasing her. But the surprising thing was, she kind of liked it.

She held her hand out for the chocolate. 'I'll start with dark and delicious.' Her fingers brushed against his. 'But don't count on getting to finish the lemon yourself,' she said smartly as she walked past.

Within seconds he was walking shoulder to shoulder

with her. 'Where do you want to play tourist, then?' she asked. 'I can't imagine that you want to visit Piazza San Marco, St Mark's Basilica or the Clock Tower.'

He shook his head. 'Too busy, and anyway I much prefer Piazza San Marco at night. Much more romantic,' he added.

She ignored the comment.

He pointed over in the distance. 'What I'd really like to do is catch a *vaporetto* to San Giorgio Maggiore and go up the campanile. It's still early. There will hardly be any crowds.'

She gave him a sideways glance as she veered towards the nearest *vaporetto* stop. 'Hmm, so you're still a tourist at heart, then?'

He shrugged. 'It's been a few years since I've been in Venice. But I'm an Italian, I still know where to go to get the best view of the city.' He held out his ice cream towards her. 'Swap?'

She nodded. The dark chocolate was starting to taste a little bitter. She took a nibble of the lemon and sweet, tangy zest nearly made her taste buds explode. But her brain didn't have time to focus on that because Logan had slung his arm around her shoulders and was walking easily next to her as if they did it every day.

And it *did* feel like they did it every day. She fitted under his arm. Always had—always would.

He chatted as they made their way along to the *vaparetto* stop, joining the small number of waiting people and climbing on board as soon as it arrived. Most of the rest of the passengers were heading to Murano—the island famous for its glassware. He glanced at her as the boat stopped. 'Did you want to get off here?'

She shook her head. 'I love Murano glass—I have the

most gorgeous red and gold vase in my apartment—but I don't like the hordes of tourists, or what they make for them. If I see one more orange fish in a clear square cube I'll scream.'

She was standing near the front of the boat and he laughed and pulled her down next to him as the next load of passengers climbed on board. 'You old Venice snob.'

'Oh, come on, you were exactly the same way in Florence. You hated the millions of ornaments of the cathedral and baptistery.'

He lifted his ice cream towards her. 'Guilty as charged.' Then he glanced at the activity on the Grand Canal. 'But sometimes it's nice to play tourist.'

They sat in silence for a few minutes as the boat glided along the canal. It was busy this morning, making the ride a little bumpy, and she inched closer and closer to him. His arm stayed loosely on her shoulders as they reached the stop for San Giorgio. Ice creams finished, they wiped their hands on the napkins provided and climbed out of the boat.

It was getting hotter but most of the tourists hadn't reached the island yet and the queue for the lift to the top of the campanile meant they only had a ten-minute wait.

Logan shook his head as they approached. 'This is one of the architectural glories of Venice. Palladio is one of my favourite architects. Look at it, the gleaming white Istrian marble façade and lithe brick and bell tower—why, it almost seems to float in the middle of the Bacino San Marco, supported on its own tiny island. It's only a few hundred yards off St Mark's Square but most people just take a photo on the way past. They have no idea it's decorated with works by Tintoretto,

Carpaccio and Jacopo Bassano. This is the one place in Venice I just wouldn't want to miss.'

Lucia smiled at him. The passion and enthusiasm in his voice was so good to hear. She could see heads turning at his voice, obviously relieved they'd chosen this venue to visit.

The lift opened to take them up the sixty-metre-high bell tower and a few minutes later they stepped out on to the observation deck. Logan held out his arms and spun around. 'And this is why I love this place. Hardly a queue to get in, only a couple of euros and no crowding up here. The view is perfect.' He pointed across the water towards the campanile San Marco. 'While our brother over there has long lines, a higher price tag, is crowded and doesn't have the same panoramic views.'

Lucia grinned. 'But you can get a full-on postcard shot of the Piazza San Marco just across the water.' She pulled out her phone and held it in front of her, snapping a quick photo.

'Hold it.' Logan pulled out his own phone, but put his hands on her shoulders and turned her, so instead of having a background shot of Piazza San Marco he had a full shot of the Grand Canal. 'Smile,' he said as he held up his phone. 'You know, on a clear day you can see right across the Adriatic Sea and all the way to the Alps.'

The smile was still on her face and she didn't have much time to think about the fact that Logan would now have a picture of her on his phone. As soon as he'd snapped the shot he walked over and leaned his elbows on the balcony, looking out at the panoramic view. 'This is what Venice should be about,' he said quietly.

She spun around and put her elbows next to his. There were a few other people wandering around on the observation deck, but it was nowhere near as busy here as it was on the other side of the water. St Mark's Square was already packed. It seemed most of the people who'd attended the concert hadn't had much sleep.

She could hardly blame them. Anyone who was lucky enough to visit Venice—even for a few hours— usually tried to squeeze in as many of the sights as they possibly could.

Something flickered through her brain. With one concert last night and another tonight there would be a whole host of new people in and out of the city today. 'You won't be able to get a flight home today either, will you?'

A gentle breeze blew across her skin. She wasn't quite sure how she felt about this. Having Logan stay over one night had seemed like an unavoidable hiccup. Having him stay for two nights was something else entirely.

He didn't answer for a few seconds, fixing his eyes instead on the hustle and bustle of the masses of people on the other side of the canal. 'I'm sorry, Lucia.' He ran his fingers through his hair. 'I had no idea about any of this. I didn't mean to put you in a difficult position.'

He looked a little uncomfortable but not entirely unhappy. She'd hardly slept a wink last night. How could she, knowing that the person she used to love with her whole heart had been lying naked next door?

Logan had always slept naked, hating anything on his skin once he was in bed. The only thing he'd ever wanted next to his skin had been her.

She was trying so hard to seem cool, to seem professional. The atmosphere between them today had been lighter, less pressured.

Exactly the opposite from what it should have been after that kiss.

But that kiss had ignited the good memories in her brain. Before that, everything about Logan had been a build-up of frustration and a reminder of grief.

It was almost as if that kiss had brought alive the side of her brain she'd shut off. She just didn't know what to do with it.

'It's fine, Logan,' she said quickly, as she held out her hand towards the busy St Mark's Square. 'The hotels will be every bit as busy again today. Don't worry.'

His head turned towards her and he lifted his hand, running one finger down her arm towards her hand. 'But I do worry, Lucia. I'll always worry about you.' His voice was low, husky and it sent a little tremble up her spine.

She couldn't turn to face him, just kept looking out at the people of Venice as her skin tingled and his hand slid over hers, slowly interlocking their fingers.

Her breath caught in her chest. Just when she'd thought she was safe around Logan. Just when she'd thought she could relax, he did something like this.

Something that made her catch her breath and nibble her bottom lip.

It was the closeness that made her feel vulnerable. Made her feel as if she was on the verge of opening herself up to a whole host of hurt. She'd spent so long protecting herself, hiding herself away.

Logan was a whole part of her life that she'd chosen to close the door on. But having him standing next to her, his breath warming her cheek and his hand interlocked with hers, was like dangling her over a precipice she wasn't ready for.

And it was as if he could sense it. He didn't go any further. Didn't make any other move. Didn't bring up the biggest subject in the world.

Logan was carefully skirting around the edges of her life. But he wouldn't stay there for ever.

'How do you enjoy living and working in Venice?'

She swallowed, trying to push all other thoughts away. 'I love Venice. But it's not the city that captures my soul. I still miss Florence.'

The words took her by surprise. She'd always felt like that. She'd just never said it out loud.

He was facing her again and she could feel his eyes watching her carefully. She wondered if he'd pick her up on what she'd just said. But he didn't. He let it go, keeping things in safe territory. 'How do the restorations work?'

She lifted her other hand and pulled her hair off her neck. It was getting even hotter. 'I've done at least one every year I've worked for the heritage board. Always on frescoes. If they decide the fresco in Tuscany is genuine and is to be restored, then that will be my job.'

She knew why he was asking. He would be in Tuscany for the next few months and he was trying to think ahead. If a few days were difficult, how would they manage to work in the same environment for a few months?

At least, she thought that's what would be on his mind.

It couldn't be the kiss. It *wouldn't* be the kiss. Not when there was so much more to think about.

'How do you feel about coming down to Tuscany?'

It was work. Of course it was work. She didn't know whether to feel disappointment or relief. The touching and handholding was nothing. It was just Logan back to his usual charming self, trying to make everyone around him feel good.

She stared at the packed street across from her and smiled. 'While I love Venice, and I love my apartment, the summer months are extremely busy. Tuscany seems a lot more peaceful than here. It might be nice to have some clean fresh air and some quiet to be able to concentrate on the restoration work.' She turned her body towards him, finally relaxed enough to give him a smile. 'I think I'll like it.'

But Logan wasn't staring at her the way she'd thought. He'd moved his thumb underneath their interlocked fingers and was gently making circles on the underside of her palm, This was what he'd used to do when he was deep in thought…when he was contemplating something carefully. His eyes were lowered and his voice quiet. 'How would you feel…?'

She inched a little closer to hear him.

He tried again. 'How would you feel if I asked you to stay with me when you came back to Tuscany, instead of in the main *palazzo* with Louise?'

Now he did look up. But he didn't have the quiet assuredness that usually always possessed him. Now he looked wary.

The words were very unexpected. She'd just gone back into that 'safe' zone, the one where no one could touch her and no one could threaten her. His words catapulted her straight back out.

The voices in the background blended together into one constant murmur as the rapid beating of her heart thudded in her eardrums. His thumb hadn't stopped moving in those little circles. It was almost as if he'd been trying to prepare her, to soothe her, before he'd asked the question.

Her brain felt jumbled. She didn't quite know what to say. 'I don't think… I don't think that would work,' was all she could fumble out.

His fingers tensed around hers. 'Why? Why wouldn't it work? You're my oldest friend. Twelve years have passed, Lucia, and you and I are still trapped there. Why aren't you married to someone else with a houseful of kids? Why aren't I?'

Now it was too much. That little question had turned into a whole lot more. She was standing overlooking this beautiful city, people all around her, and yet she felt hideously exposed. If she could transport herself, right now, back into her bed and under her covers, that's exactly what she'd do.

'I don't want to be married,' she blurted out, causing a few heads to turn in their direction. Instantly, she understood what she'd done. People were casting their eyes down in sympathy, as if Logan had just proposed and it had gone horribly wrong.

She shook her head. 'I'm happy with my work. I'm happy with my life.'

He put his hand behind her waist and pulled her towards him. His voice was quiet but there was an edge of frustration that only she could hear. Only she could understand.

'Look at me, Lucia. Look at me and tell me that you've tried to have other relationships. Tell me that you've met some suitably nice, handsome men—just like I've met some beautiful and good women—but something just hasn't been right. It hasn't felt the way it used to feel—the way it *should* feel. You could never go on and take the next step because you knew, deep down, that you'd ultimately hurt this good and loving person. You'd never quite love them the way that they loved you.'

It was almost as if he'd stepped inside her brain and was reading her mind and all her past memories. All her hidden regrets. She could see them all reflected on his face. He knew this, because he'd been living this life too.

That kiss had catapulted him into another space. Given him a painful reminder of what he wanted to capture again. Just like it had her.

She put her hand up to her chest, which was hurting, tight.

She was still shaking her head, aware of the anxious glances around them. 'I don't know, Logan. I just don't know.' She looked up and met his gaze. He looked hurt. He looked confused and something twisted inside her. It had been a long time since she and Logan had been like this.

Last time around she'd felt numb. She'd been unable to cope with her own grief so she certainly hadn't coped with his. But now he looked just as exposed as she felt.

His hair was mussed from where he'd run his fingers through it. The wind was rippling his shirt around his shoulders and chest. She almost hated the fact he could relate to how her life had turned out. To how every relationship she'd had since him had turned out.

But she hated even more that he'd mirrored her life with his own. She'd told herself that she'd always hoped Logan would move on, meet a girl, fall in love and have a family of his own.

Seeing him in Tuscany a few days ago and feeling

that flicker of excitement when he'd told her he was unattached had revealed a side to her she didn't like.

He was fixed on her with those green eyes. They were burning a hole into her. To the rest of the world they would be the picture-perfect couple with the backdrop of Venice behind them. No one else would know the way their insides had been ripped out and left for the vultures.

Her heart squeezed. She was bad. She was selfish. Part of her did wish Logan had a happy life but then again part of her always wanted him to belong to her. But at what price?

He hadn't moved. One hand was still wrapped around her waist, pressing her body against his, the other interlocking their fingers. She could break free if she wanted to. But after all these years she just didn't know how.

He blinked. 'I won't pressure you any more. I won't bring it up again. Just promise me you'll give it some thought. You can tell me before I return to Tuscany tomorrow.'

She gave the briefest nod and it coincided with a swell of relief from her chest as he stepped back, breaking their contact. In their exposed position on the observation deck a gust of wind swept between them. It startled her, sweeping away the feeling of warmth from Logan's body next to hers.

The expression in Logan's eyes changed. Gone was the tiny smudge of vulnerability that she'd seen before. It had been replaced by the determined, focused look she knew so well.

'Are we done with photos?' he asked, just a little brusquely.

She nodded as she pushed her phone back in her bag. He took her hand again, firmly this time, no gentle touch, as if he was determined not to let her escape. They walked back to the lift. 'Tonight I'm going to pick the venue for dinner.'

It was clear there was no point arguing. She gave a brief nod as the doors slid closed in front of them.

The stiff atmosphere remained for the next thirty minutes. His hand grasped hers rigidly as they boarded the *vaporetto* and made the short journey back to Piazza San Marco.

It was even more crowded but Logan seemed to have got his bearings in the city and led her through some of the backstreets. Her phone rang just as they were about to cross one of Venice's bridges.

She pulled it from her bag. 'It's work,' she said. 'I need to take it.'

'No problem. I'll have a look in some of the shops around here.'

As her boss spoke rapidly in her ear she lost sight of Logan's broad shoulders in the crowds. It was twenty minutes before the conversation was over and Logan appeared at her side holding a large loop-handled bag with a designer logo on the side. He held it out towards her.

'What is it?'

'Yours. For tonight.'

She was more than a little surprised. She opened the bag and saw a flash of red but he shook his head.

'Leave it. You can try it on when we get back to the apartment.'

In some ways she should feel flattered. Logan had always had exquisite taste. He'd bought her clothes in the past and she'd loved every single item. But they weren't a couple any more—they weren't lovers and she wasn't sure this felt entirely appropriate.

'Why on earth would you buy me something?'

He shrugged his shoulders. 'It's a thank-you gift,' he said casually. 'A thank you for letting me stay at your apartment when I obviously should have planned better.' He made it sound so matter-of-fact, so easy and rational. But the contents of the bag didn't seem impartial.

Red was her favourite colour. And although she hadn't had a chance to examine the dress she was sure it would fit perfectly and be a flattering style. It was all part of Logan's gift.

'What was your call?' He wasn't giving her time to think about this too much. Probably in case she started to object.

She gave a little smile. 'The electronic comparison of brushstrokes indicates the fresco is indeed by Burano. The paint sampling won't be completed until early next week.'

'When?'

'Probably Monday. Technology is a wonderful thing these days. They will be able to give me an exact match of the product and colours that Burano used in his fresco for the restoration work.'

They started to walk across the bridge now, stopping in the middle just as a gondola with some tourists on board passed underneath. 'And how long do you think the restoration work will take?'

She put her elbows on the bridge next to him. The sun was beating down now, rising high in the sky above them. She gave a nervous laugh. 'That's the one thing that doesn't happen quickly. Probably around a few months.'

'And it will be definitely you who does the work?'

Was it possible he didn't want her to be working next to him, no matter what he'd been saying? Maybe Logan was only looking for a quiet life. Maybe he was only trying to keep her onside to make sure his project didn't miss his deadline?

But he didn't look unhappy. He still had that determined gleam in his eye. He pointed to a baker's shop on the other side of the bridge. 'Why don't we grab some food and head back to the apartment? It's going to be too hot for sightseeing this afternoon and we both have work we can probably do before dinner tonight.'

She gave a nod of her head. It made sense— even if the thought of sharing her apartment space with Logan all afternoon made it feel as if the walls would close in around her.

'Where are we going later?' she asked, as they walked over the other side of the bridge.

He tapped the side of his nose. 'Leave that to me.'

CHAPTER SEVEN

IT WAS RIDICULOUS and he knew it. Why did he feel as if so much rested on one night?

He'd planned everything to perfection, pulling strings wherever he could. What he wanted most was for Lucia to be relaxed around him, maybe just enough to let her guard down and let him in.

It sounded cold, it sounded calculating. It was anything but.

He needed her to open up to him, to talk to him. It's what they both needed in order to move on with their lives.

It didn't matter that he had hopes for the direction in which they moved. He had to push those aside right now. He wanted her to talk. He couldn't see any further forward than that.

'Are you ready?'

He'd been pacing in the main room for the last half hour, watching the sun beginning to lower in the sky, bathing Venice in a beautiful orange glow.

'I'm ready.' Her voice sounded a little shaky and he spun around.

She looked a picture. The red dress was exactly as he'd envisaged it, hugging her curves in all the right places. He'd known as soon as he'd seen it that it was perfect for her. A red jersey underlay with red crochet lace on top, it reached her knees and only gave the tiniest hint of skin underneath. Lucia had never liked anything too revealing.

She was wearing her black patent impossibly high heels with red soles and clutching a sequin bag in her hand. But something wasn't quite right.

She flicked her long hair on her shoulders and meshed her fingers together. Lucia was wound tighter than a spring.

He walked over and handed her a glass of red wine. 'Let's sit down for five minutes. We have time.'

He gestured towards the chaise longue.

She waited a few seconds. Her nerves seemed to emanate from her, and even the hand holding the glass had an almost imperceptible shake. After a few moments she sucked in a deep breath and walked across the room.

'Thank you for the dress. It's perfect,' she said simply, as she sat down and crossed her legs.

'I knew it would suit you,' he said calmly. 'You look stunning.' It was true and he was quite sure that every man in Venice who saw her would agree during the course of the evening.

She took a sip of her wine. 'Are you going to tell me where we are going for dinner?'

He smiled. 'We're in Venice. We're going to Rubins overlooking Piazza San Marco. Where else would we go?'

A hint of a smile appeared on her face as she relaxed back and took another sip of wine. 'How on earth did you manage that? You couldn't find a hotel room, but you managed to get into the most exclusive restaurant in Venice?'

He wrinkled his nose. 'Let's just say I might have helped them at some point with an architectural matter. Unfortunately, they don't have beds for the night—so dinner it is.'

He actually couldn't believe his luck. The restaurant overlooking Piazza San Marco and based in the Procuratie Nuove had had issues a few years ago when some of the stonework around the elaborate archways had started to crumble. Logan had been able to help them find the same stone, from the original source, to allow complete restoration. It hadn't been an easy task. And right now he would take any advantage he could get.

They sat for a few minutes longer, watching the world go by on the Grand Canal, as she finished her wine.

He stood up and held out his hand towards her. 'Are we ready?'

She nodded and slid her hand into his. The momentum of pulling her up made them almost bump noses and she laughed and put her hands on his chest. 'Where did this dark suit come from? You surely didn't have this in your bag?'

He shook his head. 'I picked it up an hour ago when you were getting ready. I think you've seen enough of the cream jacket and trousers.'

Her eyes ran up and down his body. It was amazing how that tiny act could make his hairs stand on end and make him feel distinctly hot under the collar.

She gave an approving nod. 'I like it,' she said as she stepped away. 'I like it even more that you didn't bother with a tie.' She spun towards him in her heels. 'I never did like a man in a tie.'

His heart leapt in his chest. Her mood was lifting. She was definitely beginning to relax. He caught her elbow and spun her back towards him, resting his other hand on her hip.

He wanted this to be the start of something new. He wanted a chance to make things work with the only woman he'd ever really loved.

He knew they both had to move on. He knew they might not be able to move on together. And he knew at some point they had to talk about Ariella Rose.

But his heart was squeezing in his chest.

Tonight could be perfect. Tonight could just be about them. And somehow he knew that if he gave her the guarantee of no pressure, it could change everything.

'What do you say that for tonight I promise you that I won't mention Ariella Rose. We won't talk about what happened. And we'll only concentrate on the here and now. We'll only concentrate on the good things.'

He slid his hand through her silky soft hair.

She'd outlined her eyes in black and put on some lipstick that matched her dress. Right now Lucia was every bit the Italian siren.

Tonight wasn't about upsetting her. Tonight wasn't about grieving.

Tonight was about reminding her how good things had been between them. Reminding her what it felt like to truly connect with a person—and hoping she might realise that some things were worth fighting for.

She blinked quickly, trying to lose the obvious sheen on her eyes. Her voice was shaky. 'You promise?'

'I promise.' He didn't hesitate. This was the only way. The only way to try and take the steps to move forward. He wouldn't leave Venice without having that

conversation with her but for tonight—just for tonight—
he wanted to capture just a little of the old Lucia and
Logan again.

She locked up the apartment and they headed downstairs. He gestured her towards the other entrance of the
building, the one that looked out over the Grand Canal
and had a private mooring dock.

She shook her head. 'We never use that any more.'

He smiled as he pulled at the older doors. 'Well, tonight we're going to.'

Her stomach had been doing little flip-flops since early
afternoon and didn't seem to want to stop any time
soon.

The dress he'd bought her was beautiful, elegant
without being revealing and still managing to fit like
a second skin. It might as well have been made especially for her.

When she'd put it on she'd felt a surge of confidence
she hadn't felt in years. And seeing Logan in his dark
suit had almost toppled her off the edge where she was
dangling. It was like recapturing a moment from twelve
years ago, when they'd used to dress up regularly and
go out eating and dancing together. Back when neither
had had a care in the world and she'd had no idea what
could lie ahead.

Logan's green eyes were twinkling as he opened the
door to the Grand Canal. Bobbing on the water was a
sleek black gondola edged in red and gilt with its own
private canopy.

Lucia sucked in a breath. 'What on earth have you
done?' She knew exactly how much these cost to hire.
Every night the Grand Canal was full of wide-eyed

tourists bobbing around in these private hired gondolas. Most of the local Venetians laughed at them being taken advantage of. She'd never guessed Logan would fall into the trap.

'I've decided to start this evening the way it should continue.' He was smiling and his voice was steady. She could swear the orange-bathed canal was almost shimmering behind him. It made the whole evening just seem a little magical.

She glanced down at her towering stilettos as the gondolier held out his hand towards her. Her footsteps were slightly tottery as she stepped over the dark water of the Grand Canal. While it could seem terribly romantic, she didn't want to land in it and re-emerge like a creature of the black lagoon.

Logan jumped over easily, catching hold of her waist and steering her towards the red velvet love seat on the gondola. She laughed as they plonked down onto the seat under a black canopy and the gondola started gliding along the canal.

It was the first time in her life she'd felt like a tourist in Venice. Logan's arm slid easily behind her back. The love seat was unsurprisingly small, making sure they sat snugly together, his leg touching the length of hers.

It had been years and years since she'd done anything like this.

There was something magical about Venice in the early evening. Voices were hushed, music floated through the air, and quiet had fallen over the city.

'This is lovely,' Lucia murmured. Logan gave her shoulder a little squeeze.

As she watched the world go by she started to relax into his hold. He'd promised her there would be no pressure, no tension tonight. A tiny part of her coiled-up stomach didn't exactly believe him. It was hard to be around Logan and not think about Ariella Rose at all—and she was sure he must feel the same way.

But for tonight it might be nice not to focus on the hurts of the past. It hadn't been Logan who had hurt her. She'd never felt let down by him, or felt animosity towards him.

He was just the biggest reminder of Ariella Rose, and until her head could get around that...

The gondolier moved smoothly through the traffic. She had no idea where they were going but it was obvious he was going the picturesque route, winding their way through lesser canals and under bridges. She could see tourists pointing and taking pictures. Thank goodness for the canopy as it gave some ounce of privacy without spoiling their view.

There was something nice about the sound of the water lapping gently at the side of the gondola. Logan took his arm from her shoulder and bent forward, bringing out a bottle of chilled Prosecco and two glasses. He popped the cork and filled them up, handing hers over and holding his towards her. 'Here's to a fabulous night in Venice.'

She clinked her glass against his and sipped, letting the bubbles explode across her tongue and tickle her nose. 'Here's to an unusual night in Venice,' she said.

He raised his eyebrows. 'You mean you don't travel by gondola every night?'

She shook her head. 'I mean I haven't travelled in a gondola *ever* since I got here.'

'Really?' He seemed surprised.

She shrugged her shoulders. 'Think of it this way.

If you lived in Pisa, how many times would you actually climb the tower?'

He wrinkled his brow. 'I get where you're coming from but this is me—remember?' He turned a little more to face her. She could see the faint shadow on his jawline. He'd probably only shaved a few hours ago but that didn't quell the rapid growth of his potential beard. Her fingers itched to reach out and touch.

Logan wasn't finished. 'Remember when we stayed in Florence? How many times did we keep visiting the baptistery at the Duomo or stand underneath the Renaissance dome?'

She shook her head. 'That's because you're an architect junkie and those things were right on our doorstep.' She raised her eyebrows at him. 'I do remember you found a way to charm guards at every attraction and skip the queues.'

He gave a wave of his hand and glanced at her mischievously. 'There's a reason Italian men were born with charm. Anyway, we were natives. The guards knew that.'

'Only because you slipped some money in their hands.'

He gave a deep laugh. 'I don't know what you're taking about.' There were crinkles around his green eyes and her heart gave a little lurch.

Logan Cascini was really every woman's dream guy. She'd forgotten just how much fun they used to have together. It was unusual to meet a guy who shared her passion for the arts as much as he did.

From what most of her girlfriends told her, it was unusual to feel so connected, so in tune with a guy as she had with Logan. Most of her friends went for tem-

pestuous and volatile relationships with plates smash-
ing and clothes being tossed out of windows.

Life with Logan had been passionate but fulfilling.
Something she'd never found again.

The gondola slid up next to the service point for dis-
embarkation. It rocked precariously as she tried to stand
up and she wobbled as the gondolier leapt ashore and
held his hand out towards her.

As her feet landed on steady ground she turned towards Logan again. They were right at the edge of
Piazza San Marco—the busiest place in Venice. The
crowds might be a little quieter because of the planned
concert but it was buzzing with excitement.

'Ready?'

He nodded towards the gondolier, tipped him and
slid an arm around her waist, steering her towards the
Procuraties. The sun was even lower in the sky now.
The Procuraties were lit at night with tiny white lights.
It was like a thousand glittering candles flickering in
the night. There was no denying the beauty of the setting.

Music drifted down towards them. Some of these
restaurants were known as the finest in the world, with
Michelin-starred chefs and award-winning menus.

He pointed to a set of stairs heading up towards Rubins. 'After you.'

She felt her stomach flip over. He was being so formal around her. So controlled. The tiny bit of laughter
on the boat had been the one true time she'd glimpsed
the real Logan. That was who she wanted to spend the
evening with.

The restaurant was beautiful. White linen table-
cloths, more flickering candles and a harpist playing in

the corner. It was full of couples dining in the dimmed lights, capturing a moment in one of the most beautiful cities in the world.

Logan held out her chair as she sat at the table then ordered them some wine. The waiter gave them thick, leather-covered menus. Lucia gave a smile as the wine appeared and was poured. 'It looks like we could have finished the wine by the time we get through this menu.'

Logan smiled at the waiter and closed his menu. 'What do you recommend?'

In the end they ordered a mixture of duck stuffed ravioli, white truffle pasta, fish carpaccio and some veal escalopes with Dobbiaco cheese.

The food was delicious and the wine kept flowing, almost as much as the easy chatter.

'What do you have to work on after the Tuscany project?'

Logan smiled at her. 'I could tell you, but I might have to kill you.' He tapped the side of his nose.

She leaned forward. 'Oh, don't go all James Bond on me. Is it something good?'

He leaned forward too, his voice low. 'It's something great. I'm just waiting for the final word. Let's just say I'll be working on something in Rome. Something I would absolutely love to work on and which could really put my restoration business under the spotlight.'

'Doesn't the chapel and *palazzo* restoration in Tuscany already do that? I'd have thought the royal wedding would mean everyone involved would benefit from the publicity.'

He gave a sigh. 'It does. But this is different, this is real Renaissance architecture. Something special that's needed to be restored for a number of years.'

She shook her head as she kept eating the delicious food. 'You make it sound like my dream job of being asked to restore the Michelangelo frescoes.'

'It's close.'

She almost dropped her fork. 'Really?'

He nodded. 'They are considering a number of different companies. The work definitely needs to be done, it just depends who wins the contract.'

She frowned. She knew just how passionate Logan was about his work, just how particular. 'There can't be many firms that have as good a reputation as you have.'

He met her gaze. 'Thanks for the compliment. Any chance you could be on the selection committee?'

She threw back her head and laughed. The wine was starting to kick in. The venue was exquisite and the food delicious. As for the company...

Logan put down his knife and fork. 'Honestly, what would you do if you got asked to do some restoration work on one of Michelangelo's frescoes?'

His face was completely serious. What on earth had he been asked to do?

'Honestly? I would probably die of shock. And I would be too scared to even contemplate doing something like that.'

He tilted his head. 'But you work for the Italian Heritage Board. Isn't that exactly the place that should be asked to do these things?'

She shook her head. 'We're just one organisation. I would be terrified. The pressure would be overwhelming and the criticism—before I even started—would be even more so.' She sat back in her chair. 'When it comes to things like that, I prefer just to admire along with the rest of the general public.'

'And Burano?'

She shook her head. 'His work isn't as well known. Isn't as criticised. The Madonna and Child hasn't been seen in generations. It isn't even on official records. Restoring it to its former beauty will be an act of joy.'

She could see him suck in a breath at her words. He paused, then looked up between heavy lids, 'And do you think everything can be restored—even people?'

Her skin chilled and her throat closed over. It was almost as if someone had stood behind her and poured icy water over her head.

He'd promised. He'd promised he wouldn't mention this tonight. She stood up swiftly, her chair toppling over behind her.

Logan was on his feet in an instant. It was almost as if he'd realised what had slipped out of his mouth. He walked swiftly over to the waiter, thrusting a bundle of notes at him.

Lucia didn't wait, she turned on her impossibly high heels and took off down the stairs.

But Piazza San Marco wasn't ready to give up on her yet.

As they'd had dinner, a small string quintet had been setting up downstairs outside one of the neighbouring restaurants. With the whole square bathed in flickering lights, the silhouette of the Basilica and Clock Tower at one end and the outlined string players in the middle her feet came to an abrupt halt.

Even she knew that running through the middle of a quintet in the piazza wasn't her best idea.

As she sucked in some air to try and still her thudding heart, she felt a presence behind her. Logan's hand slid across the thin red fabric of the dress covering her belly. She felt his warm breath on her shoulder and he moved in gently, letting her feel the rise and fall of his chest against her shoulder blades.

She was upset. But she wasn't angry at his touch. Instead, it felt like a comfort blanket.

Two of the violinists lifted their instruments and the quintet started to play. It wasn't what she expected. Classical music—usually opera—was often heard in the piazza. But this was different. It was a modern song by a UK male singer, transformed and made beautiful by the strings. She could almost hear his words echoing about love and loss in her ears.

It was almost as if they knew exactly what to play.

She spun around, placing her hands flat on Logan's chest. He didn't say a word, just lifted one hand and let his finger trail down her cheek until it reached her shoulder, where he flicked her curls back.

He was watching her with those steady green eyes and she could see the hurt shimmering from him. He was trying so hard, but was finding this every bit as difficult as she was.

His other hand slid around her hips, halting at her lower spine.

They were locked together. Just the way they should be.

Her palms slid up the planes of his chest and rested on his shoulders. This was her Logan. No one else's. No one else could ever come close to the connection she felt with him.

His body started to sway, tiny movements from side to side. One hand stayed at the base of her spine and the other tangled through her hair.

Dancing. She hadn't danced since…

Since before she'd had Ariella Rose.

She and Logan had once danced all the time. Sometimes in the clubs of Florence, often at family events and sometimes in the privacy of their own home.

Most of all she'd just loved the feeling of being in his arms and the warm touch of his body next to hers.

As the melody moved past the introduction he reached up and captured her hand in his, leading her away from the stairs and onto the patterned floor of Piazza San Marco. Little lights glowed under their feet.

People were still walking past, stopping to listen to the music, with one other couple dancing nearby.

He turned her to face her, putting his hands on her hips. 'Ready to recapture the past, Lucia?' he whispered.

She reached up and put her hand on his chest again. She could feel his warm skin and beating heart underneath the fine Italian shirt.

All she could focus on was the way he was looking at her. It made her feel like the only girl on the planet.

She slid her hands around his neck and rested her head against his chest. 'Always,' she replied.

Their footsteps moved in perfect unison. The warmth of his body next to hers felt overwhelming.

They fitted so well together it almost felt like they'd never been apart. And Logan didn't just know how to sway to the music. He knew how to dance—how to really dance.

It was as if they could read each other's minds and knew exactly what the next steps should be. She moved her hand from his chest, sliding it along the length of his arm and letting their hands clasp.

She felt him stiffen against her and she lifted her head.

There was no doubt on his face. He released her from his grasp against him and spun her outwards. When she danced with Logan she always felt like she could fly.

He could lift and spin her as if she were as light as air. Her dress spun out, the ripples of red fabric twisting high from her thighs, the stiletto heels forgotten as she continued to follow his lead.

She could hear the murmurs around them as people stopped to stare. But all she could focus on was the beat of the music and the feel of Logan's hard muscles as they connected briefly through the parts of the music.

Logan knew how to lead. He knew how to steer her and how to whip her around, like a matador with a cape.

And she kept spinning. The lit arches of the Procuraties flashing past her line of vision. The evening was still warm and her body temperature was rising quickly.

She couldn't even begin to think straight. The only thing that counted was how right everything felt—how *connected* everything felt.

She dipped her head and spun under his arm three times as the crowd gasped. The momentum of the music was building. He caught her around the waist and dipped her backwards. It was one of their all-time favourite moves. The sensuality of the deep arch of her back, followed by her ever-so-slow stretch back up, ending up nose to nose with Logan.

He was breathing just as quickly as she was. A laugh escaped from her lips. Her hair fell over her face, some of her curls connecting with his skin. But he didn't brush them back, he just dipped his head further forward, allowing them both to be hidden beneath the veil of her hair.

'How are we doing?' he murmured. He ran one finger up her spine, sending shock waves everywhere, a thousand beautiful butterflies beating their wings against her skin.

It couldn't be more perfect than this.

Then he moved. The music was slowing, reaching a building crescendo. He spun her once more, letting her skirt billow around her and her hair stream outwards.

He caught her hips suddenly, stopping her in mid-pivot and pressing his head against hers. She didn't even have time to catch her breath before his lips were on hers.

There was no time to think about where they were or what they had been doing. There was no time to think about the audience or the scenery.

His hands skirted around her behind, her hips and up the sides of her waist, stopping as they tangled in her hair, and he anchored her head firmly in one hand.

She couldn't ever remember being kissed like this— even by Logan.

She couldn't get enough of him. His taste, his smell, the feel of his body beneath the palms of her hand. He was hers. He was all hers. And she didn't want this to stop.

He pulled his lips back from hers, staying close enough to let her feel his breath on her skin. 'It's you, Lucia. It's always been you.'

The music died around them, but she hardly noticed. Her heartbeat was roaring in her ears. The world around them was still spinning—just like her brain. It hadn't stopped. Not for a second.

Logan held her tightly to him. She could feel his knotted muscles, the tension as he held her. She had no doubt about the effects she had on his body.

Of the effects he had on hers.

It had been so long. She'd forgotten what passion like this felt like. Something had been ignited inside her. A tiny flame that had been dimmed for so long. Now the fire was burning so brightly she couldn't imagine putting it out again.

Logan's eyes fixed on hers. They were steady but had never seemed so determined—so heated.

He clasped one hand in his. 'Let's go.' He didn't wait for a response. He walked away briskly, pulling her behind him as he parted the crowd around them.

His long strides covered the expanse of Piazza San Marco easily, and she was running in her stilettos to keep up.

She was surprised to see the sleek, black gondola still waiting. He didn't wait for the chatting gondolier to pay attention, just turned and lifted her straight onto the swaying gondola, shouting an instruction to the gondolier.

With one tug the canopy was closed, leaving them in a pool of darkness, with only a few of Venice's lights flickering behind them.

A seed of doubt flashed through her brain. All the rational thoughts that she'd completely ignored for the last few hours started to take seed and let their roots unfurl. She couldn't stop the rapid thud-thud of her heart. Every inch of her skin was on fire, the tiny hairs on her arms standing on end.

Her eyes started to adjust to the dim light. Logan hadn't moved. It could only have been a few seconds, but it felt like so much longer. It felt as if his brain must be crowding with the same doubts that she was feeling. Her stomach clenched. Everything suddenly felt like a huge mistake.

Logan shifted his body towards hers, reaching up his hand towards her face. He ran one finger across her forehead. Her eyes automatically closed and the finger traced down over her eyelids, cheeks, across her lips then under her chin and to the tender skin of her décolletage.

He leaned closer, the heat from his body spreading towards hers.

And then he murmured those words again.

'It's you Lucia, it's always been you.'

Before, she'd been shocked. They'd been in the middle of Piazza San Marco with a crowd of onlookers. Here, it was entirely private. All she could hear was the movement of the gondola slipping through the waters of Venice.

She squeezed her eyes closed again for a few seconds. Her hand reached up towards him. She couldn't help it. She couldn't be this close to Logan and not touch him. It was all she could think about.

She felt him suck in a breath as she ran the palm of her hand along his now-stubbled jaw.

If she could suspend the past—suspend the memories—then everything about Logan was perfect.

Now, as he said the words it was just the two of them. Her heart wanted to melt. Her lips wanted to respond. She wanted to say it had only ever been him. She wanted to tell him that she'd never felt the same about anyone else—she *couldn't* feel the same about anyone else.

Without Logan she wasn't living. She was only existing.

She didn't want to just exist any more.

This time when he bent to kiss her she matched him move for move. She ran her hands through his dark hair and pulled him closer to her, pressing her breasts against his chest.

Logan knew how to kiss. He really knew how to kiss. There was a zing as their lips met. Teeth grazed her lips. Then his lips were firmly on hers. Tasting her, caressing her. Full sweet lips on hers, filling her with so much promise, so much expectation.

The zings didn't stop at her lips but carried on right around her body, like an army on rapid attack. She couldn't help her responses. She couldn't help but push harder against his body, her hands exploring his back and shoulders.

The kiss intensified with every passing second, sparking a whole host of memories throughout her body. It didn't matter that their eyes were closed. With this kiss Logan could see every part of her, burrow his way to the centre of her closed-over soul.

She'd always felt threatened by their closeness after the death of their daughter. Fear had pushed her into a position of retreat, because even though she'd told Logan she couldn't talk about things, once he'd kissed her she always felt at her most vulnerable. Her most open.

His earthy scent swam around her. His fingers stroked the back of her neck, giving her a promise of what was to come.

His kisses moved lower, along her cheek and down the delicate skin of her neck. For a moment she almost objected. She didn't want his lips to leave hers.

But Logan knew all her secret places. Knew the tiny spot at the back of her ear that made her gasp with pleasure and lose all rational thought. Before she'd even thought about it her head was arching backwards, opening up the more sensitive skin at the bottom of her throat.

And Logan didn't hesitate. He was on it in a flash. She wanted to move. Her dress was inching upwards, his hand brushing against her thighs. But space was cramped under the canopy, with nowhere really to go, and they both jumped apart as the gondola jerked suddenly as it scraped against wood.

She sat back in the love seat, trying to still her ragged breaths. There was another couple of bumps.

It had been deliberate. Of course it had. They'd reached their destination and their gondolier had enough experience to allow his guests a moment of warning.

Was this it? Was this where this evening ended?

Logan pulled back the canopy and stood up, straightening his rumpled jacket and shirt and then turning towards her. He didn't speak, just held out his hand towards her.

What happened next was up to her.

It was her apartment. Her space. She'd offered him somewhere to stay for the weekend, without even considering this as a possibility.

The sun had set now. The warm orange glow from earlier had disappeared.

But now Venice was alive with a million different lights brightening up the almost black sky. Logan was outlined like a film star on his final movie shot.

The backdrop was stunning with the beautiful architecture along the Grand Canal and silhouetted gondolas around them.

But all she could focus on was Logan.

Because she knew exactly how this night would end.

It was already written in the stars twinkling in the sky above their head.

She slid her hand into his and he pulled her towards him as the boat rocked on the water.

This was fate. It had to be.

And who was she to fight fate?

CHAPTER EIGHT

THE ROOM WAS bathed in the pale light of morning.

It wasn't what he expected—not at all. Last night he hadn't paid attention to anything around them. They'd barely managed to close the apartment door behind them before they'd stumbled through to her bedroom.

Lucia's room wasn't the stark white of the guest bedroom along the corridor. It was sumptuous and opulent, furnished in the colours she'd used to favour when painting. Purples and golds with a tiny flash of red. It suited the general feel of the apartment—the whole place still had the hint of a palace about it. And the beautiful décor and furnishings in the room were more personal—more Lucia—than the room he'd stayed in.

Lucia was still tangled in his arms, her head resting on his chest and her dark locks fanned out on the purple bedding. Her breathing was slow and steady. The early morning light and noise from the Grand Canal hadn't woken her yet.

He didn't want to move. Didn't want to breathe in case it disturbed her.

This was perfection. This was exactly the way things should be between them but he knew he would have to destroy it all.

It would be so easy. So easy to say nothing at all and ignore the huge elephant that sat in the corner of the room every time they were together. But Logan didn't want only part of Lucia. He wanted all of her. He'd waited this long. And if he couldn't have all of her...

His hand reached up and stroked her head. They would have to spend the next few months working together in Tuscany. They could flirt, laugh, love and sleep together and make a poor attempt at having a relationship.

But the truth was that any attempt would be futile until they'd spoken about Ariella Rose. They had to start from scratch. They could only build this relationship once they'd grieved together for their daughter. And he still didn't know if Lucia was capable of that.

His phone beeped on the table next to the bed. The noise stirred Lucia from her peaceful sleep and she woke gradually.

Her arm drifted across his chest. She was smiling as she woke, as if she were in the middle of some alluring dream.

Her eyelids flickered open, revealing her dark brown eyes surrounded by thick black lashes. All traces of last night's make-up had vanished. Lucia didn't need any. Her flawless skin and naturally red lips were enticing enough.

His stomach clenched as he waited for anything— any trace of regret about last night. 'Good morning, beautiful,' he said softly.

She smiled and closed her eyes again, pushing her naked body closer to his. Her fingers started tracing circles on his chest. 'Good morning, handsome,' she said sleepily.

Some of his tension dissipated. He could leave this. Say nothing. Stroke his fingers across her skin and pull her beneath the covers. It was the biggest temptation in the world right now.

And while it might offer some temporary sanctuary and pleasure it wouldn't take him to the place he ultimately wanted to be.

Somehow he knew it didn't matter how he phrased the question—he already knew how she would react.

It was horrible—knowing that the path they would have to tread would be a painful one. But he was ready for it. He'd been ready for it for the past twelve years.

'How are you feeling?'

She pushed her head up onto one hand as she lay facing him. Her face still had that relaxed, sleepy, dreamy quality about it. It was the most chilled he'd ever seen her.

'I'm fine.' She smiled. 'How are you?' There was a teasing tone to her voice—as if she wanted to take this to a whole other place.

His fingers wanted to reach out and touch her soft skin. It took all his will power not to move and instead to clench the purple sheet in his fist.

'We need to talk, Lucia. You know we need to talk.'

The muscles around her neck tensed. She turned her head away from him. 'No, we don't.'

It was an immediate, instinctual reaction. He knew that. He pushed himself further up the bed. The sheet moved with him, pulling from Lucia's skin. She made a grab for it. It was amazing how a few words could make you feel naked all over again.

He sighed. 'We have to work together, Lucia. We're going to be in Tuscany together. I don't want things to be awkward between us.'

Her head shot around. 'And this is how you stop it?' It was an accusatory tone. And he got that. He did. Lucia would much rather they never spoke about this at all.

He moved to the edge of the bed and picked up his discarded shirt from the floor, pulling it over his head. He shook his head. 'No, Lucia. This is how I start things. This is how we should start things. By talking.' He stood up. 'Now get dressed. We're going to go for breakfast together.'

He moved across the floor, finding his underwear, crumpled trousers and shoes. If he were a young man, concerned about his appearance, he might be cringing right now at the thought of going out in Venice in last night's clothes.

But he was a grown-up. An adult. And he had so much more to worry about.

Lucia was scowling at him. The beautiful red dress he'd bought her was bunched up in a little ball. He doubted it would ever look the same. 'I'm not coming.'

'Yes, you are.' He opened the door of her wardrobe, his eyes running rapidly over the colours, and pulled out a flowered dress, throwing it on the bed. 'Would you like me to select your underwear too?' He didn't mean to be cruel. But he wasn't prepared to take no for an answer. Not after all this time.

She pulled the sheet up under her chin. 'Stop it, Logan. You can't bully me into doing what you want. I'm not a child.'

He bent down next to her. 'I have never bullied you, Lucia. I never will. And you're right, you're not a child. You're a mother—just like I'm a father. Just because our child isn't here any more it doesn't change that.'

Her eyes widened. She was shocked. It was the last

thing she'd obviously expected to hear. And he wasn't quite sure where it had come from.

After a few seconds her fingers released on the sheet a little. He sensed the moment and opened the drawer next to her bed, pulling out matching white underwear. 'I'll give you a few minutes to get dressed,' he said, walking to the door and standing in the corridor.

Every part of him was on edge. He had no idea right now if he'd handled this right. He'd spent so long tip-toeing around Lucia that now it felt as if he'd just leapt in wearing a pair of clown-size shoes.

He held his breath, listening for any sign of movement. Any tiny noise.

After a few seconds he heard something. The gentle movement of a sheet. He leaned back against the wall. It didn't matter that she hated him right now. All that mattered was that they talk. That they *really* talked.

He walked through to the guest bedroom and quickly washed his face and hands, running his fingers through his hair and brushing his teeth. He had another shirt in his bag but it would probably be equally as rumpled. He hadn't planned on staying in Venice so clothes were definitely scarce.

It was too warm for a jacket so he walked through to the main room and waited for Lucia to appear.

It only took a few moments. She hadn't bothered with make-up and her hair was pulled back in a clasp. The yellow and pink flowered dress made her look much younger.

His heartbeat turned up a little notch. It was almost like turning back time. She had a white canvas bag in her hand and some flat sandals on her feet. But she'd never looked so beautiful.

He walked over to the main door and held it open. 'Let's go.'

There was a sinking feeling in his stomach. Almost as if he knew how this could turn out.

Lucia didn't even glance at him as she walked past. She had that determined edge to her chin.

But he could be equally determined. It was time to show her how much.

Talk about an awkward morning after. She couldn't believe she'd allowed herself to get into this position.

She knew so much better than this.

She was an adult and knew exactly what going for dinner and wine with Logan could lead to. The sexual chemistry between them had always been off the chart, but add into that the dress-buying and dancing and, well…what chance had she really had?

She held her head up proudly as she walked down the street towards her favourite café. This wasn't like doing a walk of shame the next day after a night-time encounter.

Logan had been the man she'd lived with. He'd been the man who'd cherished and treasured her. He'd been the man she'd loved with her whole heart.

She still did.

Her feet stumbled on the uneven street. Logan caught her elbow and she tugged it away. Where had that thought come from?

She squeezed her eyes closed for a second. This was because of last night. Memories of what had been and how good they had been together. She was being sentimental, nothing more. So why was her stomach permanently in knots?

She stopped at the tables on the street at her favourite café. Logan pulled out a chair for her. The waiter gave her a wave. 'Usual?'

She nodded. Logan caught his eye 'Make it two.'

Little parts of her were starting to unravel, even at those innocuous words. Logan knew that her usual would be coffee with steamed milk and a heated croissant with raspberry jam. He knew her that well and was happy to eat the same as her.

It was almost as if he were chipping away at the barriers she'd erected around herself all those years ago. The ones that had protected her. Stopped her from getting too close to anyone else and kept her safe from being hurt.

Logan folded his arms across his chest. He was sitting directly opposite her, his eyes watching her carefully.

He waited until the coffee appeared on the table and the waft of buttery croissants filled the air around them.

'It's been too long, Lucia,' he said quietly. 'I never wanted you to leave, but I understood you needed time and space.' He picked up his spoon and stirred his coffee. 'But it was never my intention to leave things this long.'

He had no idea what those few words could do to her.

The rest of Venice seemed completely at ease. People were laughing and strolling in the early Sunday morning light. Shopkeepers were just starting to roll up their shutters and open their doors. A street vendor wandered past, clutching buckets filled with beautiful flowers. The assorted scents started to mix with that of the breakfast croissants. It could be a beautiful day. So why did it feel like the worst?

Logan hadn't finished talking. 'I always hoped things would be different. I thought you would be married. I thought you would be a mother.'

He paused. 'I always hoped you would be.'

She felt tears spring to her eyes. It was almost as if he were twisting the knife that was currently piercing her heart. She knew that wasn't his intention. She knew he was trying his best to move things forward.

But Lucia had never moved forward. She could remember everything about Ariella Rose as if it had just happened yesterday. She could remember the sudden unexpected pain, the cramps, the awkward delivery. She could remember the tiny fragile bundle. Ariella had been so small she could fit in one hand, wrapped in a pink blanket made by Nonna.

The almost transparent skin. The tiny little blue veins underneath. She could remember how she'd had to gently ease up a tiny eyelid in order to see her baby's eyes. Eyes that would never see the world.

Lungs that would never fill with air.

She could remember all her hopes and dreams for the future evaporate with the silence in the air. The heavy, ominous silence of nothing.

Her horror had been so complete she'd only been able to shed a few tears. Tears of shock. It had been as if every emotion in her body had switched off. Gone into complete self-protection mode.

Now Logan was trying to open her all up to this again.

'Maybe I decided that wasn't what I wanted.' The words came out tight, almost angry, and Logan eyebrows arched slowly.

'You were made to be a mother, Lucia.' He held her

gaze as she tried to swallow. 'You would be the finest mother in the world.'

She was frozen. Couldn't breathe. Her mouth had never felt so dry, but the aroma of coffee was acrid to her now. The croissant mocked her.

Some modern career women would find his words insulting. But she didn't. Logan knew her better than anyone. He knew how much she'd relished being pregnant. He knew how much she'd planned for their daughter—they both had.

Although she was passionate about her career, she'd longed to raise their daughter.

She lifted her coffee cup with trembling hands. 'Things change.'

He shook his head and reached across the table towards her.

But she didn't want him to touch her. She couldn't take the feel of his skin on hers right now.

He leaned his elbows on the table and just kept talking. 'I've dreamt of being a father too. But it's never happened. It wasn't meant to happen—not with anyone but you.'

He said the words so easily. As if he'd contemplated them for a long time and had come to accept that this was his lot in life.

'I've met some wonderful women, but none that I wanted to marry, none that I wanted to raise children with. I only ever wanted to do that with you.'

She could feel the anger build in her chest. 'But we never planned Ariella Rose. You make it sound as if we had our future all written out.' She spat the words at him.

She couldn't understand how he could talk about any

of this so calmly. It felt as if he'd reached a fist into her chest and was squeezing all the blood from her pumping heart.

'My future was written the second I saw you, Lucia.' He hadn't raised his voice once. His words were calm and steady. He was so resolute.

She leaned across the table towards him. 'I can't talk about this,' she hissed.

It was the first time she saw a little spark in him. He gritted his teeth. 'Well, you have to. It's about time. You owe it to our daughter.'

She pulled back as if he'd wounded her. But Logan wasn't finished. 'You owe it to our daughter to talk about her and give her the love and respect she deserves.'

Her head was swimming. 'How dare you! You know I loved Ariella.'

'But you don't honour her memory.'

'What does that mean?'

Logan rubbed the palms of his hand on his trousers. It was obvious this was upsetting him just as much as it was upsetting her.

He took a deep breath. 'It means you walked away, Lucia. You walked away from the memory of our daughter and the memory of what we used to have. I think about her every single day. It doesn't matter that you're in Venice and she's in Tuscany. I visit her grave every month. You could too. But as far as I know you haven't been there since the day we buried her.'

Fury erupted inside her. Tears were brimming in her eyes but they just couldn't come any further— she hadn't been able to cry since the day they'd buried their daughter. From that point on everything had been locked inside.

'I can't go there. I can't visit.'

'Why?' He wouldn't stop. He wasn't going to let this go. It would have been better if they'd never seen each other again. The last thing she needed was stirring up the memories of Ariella Rose and any association with Logan did just that.

She wasn't able to separate the parts of him from their daughter. She couldn't just remember his kiss, his touch without remembering where it had led them. Couldn't block out all the pain it had caused.

'I just can't.'

'Then maybe that's what we should do.'

She felt herself bristle. 'Don't tell me what to do, Logan. We haven't known each other in a long time—you have no right.'

He stood up sharply, his chair screeching backwards, and she held her breath, wondering what would come next. The waiter stuck his head out of the door of the restaurant, watching carefully.

But Logan just shook his head, stretched out his back, then took a few steps towards her and knelt beside her chair.

She was still holding her breath as he slid his hand up and took hers. She hadn't realised it but her hands were cold and the warmth from him completely enveloped her.

His voice was quiet again, this time almost pleading. 'I have every right. We lost our daughter together. Who do you think I get to talk about Ariella Rose with? Who do I get to share the memories of our daughter with? I want to remember what we lost, Lucia. I loved her with every part of my heart—just as you did.' He sighed and looked up, meeting her gaze.

'This isn't just about you any more, Lucia. It was twelve years ago. I would have done anything to help you grieve, to comfort you after the loss of our daughter. But I've realised this is about me too. It wasn't enough just to make the arrangements. It wasn't enough to say a prayer. It wasn't about giving you the space you needed. I watched you fall apart right under my nose, I watched you shut yourself off from the world and bury yourself away. I thought I had no right to force you to talk. I thought I had to let you do this your own way. But twelve years on? I was wrong, Lucia. I was very wrong. For you, and for me.'

She squeezed her eyes closed again. She couldn't take his intense and sincere glance. This was exactly what she'd always tried to avoid.

It had been too much. Too much to think about. She couldn't bear it.

And now here was Logan—her strong, able Logan— telling her how much he'd been hurt too. He'd never worn his heart so much on his sleeve as he was doing now and it was tearing her apart.

She'd never even contemplated his hurt. His grief. She'd been too selfishly trying to cope with her own. Logan had appeared so composed, so strong. Now his face looked as if it had worn a river of grief across it. She could see her own pain reflected in his eyes, the tight grip of her hand telling her more than she wanted to know.

'You have to face this, Lucia. You're never going to get past this, *I'm* never going to get past this, if we can't talk together.'

Logan. Her handsome, strong Logan. She'd always hoped he would have married and had kids. He deserved to be a father. He deserved to spend his summer evenings playing in a garden, with his arms wrapped around the woman that he loved.

Twelve years ago she'd hoped that might be her.

He still wanted to save her. Even after all these years he wanted to patch her up and put her together again. But he couldn't do it then. And he couldn't do it now.

But things were different now. He'd realised how much *he* still hurt.

It didn't matter if Lucia wrapped her arms around his neck right now and told him she wanted to try and make things work again. It didn't matter that she might want a future with them together.

Now he'd realised exactly what he needed. For him. And for her.

He lifted his hand then ran his fingers through her hair at the side of her head. 'I loved Ariella Rose. I loved it that her eyes were so dark blue, though they probably would have turned brown—just like yours. I loved the fine downy hair we could see on her head. I loved that her fingers and toes were perfect. I dream about the person she could have become. And I wonder about the type of personality she would have had.'

He moved his fingers down her cheek. 'I wonder if she would have been like me, or if she would have been like you.'

He brought his hand down next to his other, clasping both of her hands in his. 'I love it that we made a little person. But I watch the calendar every year. Every year when it's her birthday I think about another year that we've lost. I think about the little girl who would have grown up and laughed and played and gone to school. I think she would be at an age right now where she would hate her overprotective dad. She would hate the fact I didn't want her to speak to boys or to wear clothes that made her look like a teenager. I would want to keep her all buttoned up in pink dresses and sandals.'

Lucia was shaking. And not just her hands. Every part of her body was shaking. It was as if his words were starting to penetrate her fortress-like exterior.

He could see the waiter casting anxious glances in their direction. But he didn't want to do anything that might distract her.

'Tell me how much you miss her, Lucia. Tell me what your hopes and dreams were for our daughter.'

He couldn't do anything to stop the shaking. He knew it was just her body's natural response. He just kept her ice-cold hands in his, hoping and praying she would finally start to open up.

Her voice was tight. Her fingers started to grip his hand more tightly. Almost as if she were clinging on for her life.

'I miss her every day.' The words came out in a rush. Then there was silence. Silence he was determined not to fill. It was the first time she'd ever said anything about their daughter.

Lucia finally started to talk again. 'I get so angry because I don't know whether she would have had dark hair, or blond hair like your sisters. I don't know whether she would have had curls or straight hair. I don't know whether she would have been a tomboy or a ballet dancer. Whether she would have wanted red shoes or pink or white.' She shook her head. 'There's so many things about my daughter that I don't know.

Will never know. And I feel cheated, completely and utterly cheated.'

His chest was tight. But tiny little parts of the tightness were giving away to relief. She was finally, finally starting to talk. Starting to talk about the life they had lost.

'Then I think about things that would never, ever have mattered. Not in the scale of things.' She looked upwards to the sky.

'What do you mean?' he prompted gently.

'I mean, would she have liked cats or dogs? Would she have been artistic? Would she have liked staying in Florence? How would she have got on at school? All the things that—if our daughter was actually here—we probably would have argued about and fussed over. But in the end, it doesn't mean anything.' Her eyes lowered and fixed on the canal next to the café. A few boats were puttering past. People going about their daily business.

No one else could know or imagine what was at stake at this table.

Logan took a deep breath. He had so much more to say. Even though he'd been much more able to talk about his grief than Lucia, there was something about it just being the two of them here that made it different.

No one else could really understand how they both felt—not unless they'd lost a child too.

He straightened up and sat back down in the chair opposite her again. But this time he pulled it closer, away from the table and round to the side so their legs were touching.

'I miss things,' he said softly. 'I miss us. I miss what

we used to have together. I didn't just lose a daughter, Lucia. I lost the love of my life too.'

He could see her swallow painfully. It wasn't just him that felt this way. But somehow Lucia didn't want to go there. It was as if, now she'd finally managed to say something about Ariella, she didn't know how to stop.

'Sometimes I think we were lucky. Sometimes I think that I'm selfish.'

His head shot up in surprise. 'What?'

She scrunched up her face. Her voice was sad. 'I look at other people who've lost children. You see them on the news all the time. They had a little person, a real little person with life and spark and personality, and it's just…' she shook her head '…ripped from their grasp. One day they have a little boy or girl in their room at home, talking, laughing, playing, then the next day because of disease or accidents or war their precious little person is stolen from them. Gone, in the blink of an eye.'

Her eyes fixed on the uneven ground beneath their feet. 'That's when I think that most of the time I don't know what I missed. I can pretend. I can build up all these thoughts of what Ariella Rose could have been like in my head.' She met his gaze. 'But the truth is, you and I will never know. Is it easier to lose a baby that you loved and hoped for than it is to lose an actual child you've spent years bringing up?' She shook her head again.

'I try to rationalise why I feel so empty. I try to make excuses about why I don't want to be around pregnant colleagues or friends.' She gave him a sad kind of smile. 'I have twelve years' worth of excuses, Logan, with reasons for not visiting new babies or friends playing happy families. It would surprise you how often I'm away with work.'

He could feel the tiny hairs standing up at the back of his neck. It just didn't feel quite right. He could feel her stepping back, detaching herself from the thoughts and feelings she'd been having a few moments ago. It was the slight change in the tone of her voice. The cool way she could look at him now.

For a few seconds her heart had been virtually on display. Her fears and hidden emotions had been coming to the surface. But even though she hadn't moved, was still sitting on the chair next to him, still letting their legs touch, she was pulling back again.

The only reason he could pick up on the tiny clues was because he knew her so well.

She straightened her spine in the chair. He could sense her sorting out her thoughts, finding a way to steal herself back from what she'd almost revealed.

He reached out to take her hand again. 'How would you feel about taking a visit to Florence again? How would you feel about us going together to Ariella Rose's grave?'

She pulled her hand back sharply from his, almost as if she'd been stung. It was too much. It was a step too far.

She wasn't ready to take it. She might never be ready to take it.

And with that realisation he felt the woman he'd always loved slip away from him once again.

Her face had turned into a mask. 'I don't want to do that, Logan. I don't think it's necessary.'

Her phone beeped in her bag and she bent forward, obviously glad of the distraction.

Their coffees and breakfast were virtually untouched, discarded.

A bit like how he felt right now.

She gave a false smile. 'It's work. With the computer program verifying Burano as the artist of the fresco, we can start to plan for the restoration now.'

She stood up quickly. It was almost as if their conversation had been forgotten.

For a few seconds he didn't move. He'd almost got there. *They'd* almost got there.

For him it was all or nothing. He knew that Lucia was the woman that he wanted, but he wasn't just prepared to accept a small part of her. And just when she'd started, just when she'd finally managed to talk about their daughter, it was almost as if he'd been able to see the shutters come down over her eyes, closing off the part of her that was most exposed, most vulnerable and cocooning it back in herself.

He had so many hidden hopes and plans for them. Last night had been wrong. Last night had made him think that there might just be hope for them. That this relationship could actually bloom and grow after all these years.

She didn't get it. She didn't get it that in his head they would grow old together. When they'd both lost their beauty, their youth and their health, they would still have each other. And that would be enough. That would always be enough.

Only it wasn't now. Not when he knew that the woman he loved with all his heart would never love him the same way. She couldn't. Part of her heart was permanently locked away. Had been for the last twelve years and it looked like it would stay that way for ever.

He stood up and put some notes on the table to cover breakfast. Lucia's whole face had changed. It was as if it had been replaced by a mask.

His stomach turned over. He could have played things so differently this morning. He could have ignored the past and just continued with the present, no matter how little of her he actually got.

But it would never have been enough. And even though his heart felt as though she'd ripped it in two, he knew this was right. For him at least.

He kept his voice as detached as he could. He would never make a scene. Never do anything to deliberately cause her embarrassment or upset.

'Shall we make travel plans back to Tuscany?'

Her shoulders dropped a little as he spoke. Was that relief that he saw? Relief that he'd finally let things go?

Her words came out rapidly and her footsteps matched his on the cobbles next to the narrow canal. 'I can arrange the return flights. We should be able to go back first thing tomorrow morning. The samples that I took earlier will be sent for automatic colour and pigment matching. I can only restore the fresco using products as close to the originals as possible. Thank goodness for modern technology.' She gave a wave of her hand and kept chattering as they crossed the bridge.

Logan felt numb. This was it. This was it for him and her.

He'd have to spend the next few months in Tuscany, working next to Lucia but keeping her at arm's length. Every glimpse whipped up a whole host of memories of the night before. He couldn't possibly be in her company and not think about what the two of them had lost and never recovered from.

There couldn't be a Logan and Lucia. Not if she still couldn't mourn their daughter.

It would be best for them both.

CHAPTER NINE

SHE FELT NUMB. It was the only way she could survive.

Last night had been a blur. They'd got up this morning just as the sun had been rising and made their way in a water taxi to the airport. Logan had spoken barely a word to her.

And that was what hurt most.

He'd been polite, of course, courteous even. But it had all been strained. Any time she'd caught a glimpse of his once gleaming green eyes all she'd been able to see was the blankness that had been pulled over them.

They stood patiently in the queue, checking in and filing through to Departures. As soon as they made their way through she made a feeble excuse that she needed to pick up some things.

Logan gave a nod of his head and said he was going for coffee and would meet her at the departure gate. He seemed almost as relieved as she was to get some space.

Lucia ducked into the nearest shop. She didn't even care which one it was—and started walking blankly through the aisles.

Lingerie. Just what she needed. She cringed as she passed a couple winking and nudging each other near the sexiest black and pink lingerie in the shop. She couldn't even remember the last time she'd spent money on matching lingerie. And she certainly wasn't going to need some any time soon. Not at these prices anyway. Who actually spent this kind of money on underwear?

Something inside her sparked a wave of fury. Her steps became quicker, more determined. She marched along the aisles until she saw something that caught her eye, something she might actually wear.

It was a pale pink satin nightdress trimmed with exquisite lace. It was not as short as she might usually wear, reaching down to at least her knees. She reached out and touched it. The heavy satin was silky to touch, pure of quality and luxury. She picked out her size and walked to the cashier's desk without a second thought.

The cashier folded and wrapped the nightdress in tissue paper and Lucia didn't even blink when she handed over her credit card.

Why shouldn't she buy herself something beautiful? As she pushed the package into her bag her mind flashed back to her bedroom and the beautiful red dress that Logan had bought her lying crumpled on the floor.

She hadn't even picked it up. She didn't need any reminder of the night they'd spent together. It was already ingrained in her brain.

She didn't need anything to remember the feel of his fingers on her skin, the feel of his lips on her neck and throat. The smell of his scent winding its way around her. The squeeze in her heart the next day when he'd told her they needed to talk.

And the look in his eyes when she'd finally stood up and walked away, pushing everything else back into a space she didn't have to deal with.

She'd been walking on eggshells ever since.

And not just around Logan. Around herself too.

For a few tiny seconds she allowed herself to think about Ariella Rose. She'd allowed herself to say a few words, to contemplate what might have been and what she'd lost.

But it had been too much. The wave of emotions that had swept over her had had to be quickly quelled. On that warm summer's day she'd never felt so cold. The tremors that had come over her body had been overwhelming.

It would have been so easy to bury her head in Logan's shoulder and just hold on for grim life. But she was too scared. Scared that if she went there she might never come back.

The truth was that no adult should outlive their child. And only someone who'd been there could understand that. Her friends and family had no idea of the type of thoughts that had crept through her brain in the few days after her daughter's death. She'd never acknowledged them to anyone.

Instead, she'd kept things locked away—even from Logan. How did you tell the man you loved with your whole heart that you would rather be with your daughter than him?

It had been too cruel. Even for her.

Her eyes scanned the coffee shop. Logan was sitting staring out of one of the windows, his hand stirring his cappuccino endlessly.

She dumped her bags in the chair next to him. It wouldn't be long until their flight was called. She walked over to the counter. 'Full-fat caramel latte with whipped cream and a strawberry frosted doughnut.'

A whole day's worth of calories about to be consumed in ten minutes. But she just felt like it. Sometimes days were just like that.

And from the look on Logan's face his day was entirely like that too.

It seemed the longest flight in history.

It was amazing the things you could think up to do rather than talk to the person sitting directly at your elbow.

Lucia was wearing a bright orange dress, and matching stilettos. She had a large brown leather bag—which looked as if it could carry the entire contents of her kitchen—slung over her shoulder.

Her wheeled suitcase looked bigger than his car. It was clear she was here to stay.

For a second he'd wondered if she was having second thoughts. She'd disappeared at the airport for a bit, then reappeared, eating a whole host of things that would never normally cross her lips.

Logan was far too wise to comment. Lucia hadn't been known for hormonal binges. But it had been twelve long years. Lots of things could have changed that he knew nothing about.

And, frankly, it wasn't his business any more.

As they landed at the private Tuscan airport and waited for their car, one of the signs at the newsstand caught his eye.

He gave her a nudge. *'When was the last time Prince Antonio saw his Cinderella bride?'*

For the first time since they'd left Venice the glazed expression left Lucia's face and her eyes widened. 'What on earth have we missed? We've only been gone a few days.'

He shook his head as the car pulled up in front of them. 'I have no idea. We'll need to talk to Louisa as soon as we reach the *palazzo*. I wonder if this will have implications for the wedding?'

He opened the door for Lucia and they climbed inside. After a few seconds she pulled out her laptop and started working. Logan sighed and leaned back, watching the green Tuscan hills roll by.

The journey from the airport took them back through the village and he took a few moments to study the surrounding architecture again. It was important that he keep the *palazzo* as in keeping with its surroundings as possible. Any kind of modern renovation would be disastrous. So, while modern fixtures and fittings could be included, they had to be sympathetic to the history of the house.

They pulled up outside the *palazzo*. It was a hive of activity. Monday mornings in the Italian building trade could notoriously start slowly. Not today.

Connor was in talks with someone outside the chapel building. It was obvious he was keeping on top of the security of the fresco.

A delivery of the special pink-coloured stone used in the *palazzo* was being unloaded. Some of the outer restoration work still needed to be completed. He could see his special stonemason signing for the delivery.

Louisa came walking out of the main entrance as Lucia grabbed her case. Louisa looked distracted, as if her mind were on a hundred other things. She hadn't even noticed their return.

'Louisa?' he said, trying to be heard above the building work around them. She was frowning and it marred her pretty face. Her hair was pulled back in a rumpled knot and her long tunic looked like yesterday's.

Her head flicked up. 'Logan.' Her eyes darted over to Lucia. 'Lucia. You're both back.' She walked over quickly. 'Do you have news?'

Lucia gave her a cautious smile. 'We do. The fresco *is* by Burano, he lived and worked in the Renaissance period and we have other examples of his work. He was both a painter and a sculptor. We're making arrangements to look at the sculpture on the fountain in the village. It could be another piece of his work.'

Louisa gave a smile and a quick nod. 'That's great. Really great. What happens next?'

Lucia glanced towards Logan. It was obvious that she was picking up the same vibes that he was. Louisa's body language was all over the place. She was saying the right words but her hands were continually knotting in front of her abdomen.

'Things will be fine. I'll begin the restoration work on the fresco. It could take a few months. All the costs will be covered by the Italian Heritage Board.'

'A few months?' Louisa looked shocked. 'But what about—?'

Logan stepped forward and took her arm, cutting her off. 'Are you okay? Don't worry about Lucia's work. It won't interfere with any of the plans here.' He nodded towards Lucia. 'We'll make sure of that.' He lowered his voice. 'Is this about the headlines? We saw them when we landed at the airport. Is the wedding still going ahead? Is there anything you need to tell us?'

Louisa's face tightened and she pressed her lips together. 'Of course the wedding is still going ahead. There's nothing to tell. Nothing to tell at all.'

It was clear by the tone of her voice that she wasn't willing to discuss anything.

She waved her hand towards the *palazzo*. 'Lucia, you're welcome to stay here, but...' she glanced at Lucia's stuffed suitcase '...you might need to make other arrangements while the wedding is taking place.'

Logan turned and stared at Lucia just as she turned and stared at him. Both of them had wide eyes. It was like a cartoon scene. It was something that hadn't occurred to either of them.

Of course Lucia would need somewhere to stay for the next few months. He'd invited her to stay with him in the farmhouse, but that had been when they'd been at the top of the campanile. It seemed like a million years ago. She'd promised to consider it and they hadn't discussed it again since.

He knew that he should say something here.

Logan's arrangement was different from everyone else's. He was staying in one of the old converted farmhouses on the estate. It was comfortable. It was private. And it was big enough for two people.

There were two reasonable-sized bedrooms. He had hardly set foot in the other one—even though he could have used it as his office. His computer and paperwork were currently spread over the dining-room table. Dining for one didn't really require the full use of the table.

He caught a glimpse of the expression on Louisa's face. She was caught in the middle, probably unable to fathom out what their relationship was. She waved her hand. 'I'll leave that to you two.' She walked away into the vineyards.

Lucia was watching her retreating back. 'Do you think she's okay?'

He shrugged. 'She certainly didn't want to be drawn into any gossip. She could be worried about how this could affect the prospects for the vineyard and the *palazzo*. I can only assume that the wedding costs are covering all the renovations around here. If they back out now...' He let his voice drift off. They both knew exactly what that could mean for Louisa.

Lucia gave a little nod and tugged at her case. 'In that case, I have things I need to do. I'm going back to chart some of the fresco and make an approximate estimate of how long the restoration work will take. I'll share the timetable with you when it's finished.'

Logan looked around. There was a mountain of work here for him too. A little gust of wind swept past and carried Lucia's rose-scented perfume towards him.

He cringed as it automatically evoked memories in his brain. Nights. Days. Passion. Love. And loss.

Avoiding Lucia in Palazzo di Comparino could be harder than he'd thought.

It could be nigh on impossible.

'See you later,' he said briskly as her eyes met his.

For the tiniest second he held his breath. There it was again, that connection. It sparked every time he looked into those deep brown eyes and reflected the pain and passion that had affected them both.

He dug his hands in his pockets and turned away.

It was best to break the connection.

Best for them both.

Lucia couldn't sleep. The windows in her bedroom were open wide and she could practically hear the music of the Tuscan hills calling to her. Every rustle of the vineyard leaves, every noise from the watering system, the tiny cranking noises of some of the mechanical systems were all being carried in the warm night air.

The bed was comfortable, but even wearing just her new satin nightdress and only having one sheet was proving too much. She couldn't settle. Every time she closed her eyes for a few seconds her brain started to replay the last few days with Logan.

And it was infuriating. Because it wasn't one tiny part—it was everything…almost told in parts like a TV series. Her nerves at speaking to him for the first time. That *whoosh* that had swept over her body when she'd set eyes on him again. The way her skin had prickled just from being near him. Feeling the heat from his body when he was in close proximity to her. The touch of his lips on hers, awakening all the old sensations. Being held in his arms as they'd danced at Piazza San Marco. And the feel of his skin against hers when they'd finally gone to bed together.

Being around Logan seemed to have set all of her five senses on fire. And now they'd been reawakened it seemed they didn't want to go back to sleep.

She sat up in bed for the twentieth time and slid her feet onto the floor. The tiles of the floor were cool and it took a few seconds to find her flat sandals.

She stood at the window for a moment, wondering if she should go outside. There was not a single person in sight. That wasn't unusual—it was the middle of the night. She glanced around her room.

There was somewhere she wanted to be. Was it worth getting changed? The chapel was only across the court-yard from the *palazzo*. Could she just sneak across the way she was?

She grimaced at the stuffed-full suitcase. Packing

when your mind was on other things wasn't exactly ideal. She hadn't brought a dressing gown. Or her running gear. Or a hairdryer.

She opened her door. It creaked loudly and she held her breath for a few seconds to see if anyone had noticed the noise.

The air in the corridor was still. Her sandals made barely a sound as she crept along and down the stairs. The front door of the *palazzo* wasn't even locked.

She slipped outside and her footsteps quickened as she crossed the courtyard, the warm air making her nightdress flutter around her. It didn't matter, there was nobody to see her. She couldn't explain it. Couldn't even think about it too much. But she was being drawn to the chapel like a magnet.

Except it wasn't really the chapel she wanted to see— it was the fresco.

The thick wooden door was heavy and she had to put her shoulder to it to finally push it open.

The slightly colder, stiller air of the chapel swept around her as soon as she stepped inside. Her footsteps stopped as the tiny hairs on her arms stood upright.

It was like walking into a scene from a scary movie. She was being ridiculous. Of course the chapel was slightly colder. The walls were thicker than the *palazzo*'s and the cooler air had probably helped with the preservation of the fresco.

It was pitch-black. Only a few strands of moonlight were sneaking through the stained-glass windows. Nothing was really visible. She hadn't thought to bring a candle with her.

She took a few small steps forward, hoping her eyes would adjust to the darkness around her. Her hand reached out to touch the cold wall. It was odd. This chapel must have hundreds of years' worth of history, hundreds of years' worth of stories to tell. Weddings, birth, funerals all held in here.

In a way it was nice the royal wedding was being held here. A piece of history was being brought back to life, back to its former glory. If they hadn't proposed to use this site, Burano's fresco might never have been discovered.

'Yaow!' She stubbed her foot on something—some kind of carpenter's toolbox—and bent to rub her bare toe. Her hand touched something on the floor. She fumbled for a second. A flashlight. Perfect. She flicked the switch and a thin beam of light cut through the darkness.

Now she could move more easily. She spun the torch around towards the fresco wall, the light hitting squarely on the Madonna's face. Lucia sucked in a breath. Her feet moved forward automatically. An invisible hand had reached into her chest and was squeezing at her heart.

This was it. This was what she'd needed to see. She moved the light a little downwards onto the face of baby Jesus, then back towards Mary. She drew up directly to the fresco, her hand shaking a little as Mary's face was illuminated in all its glory.

Every hint of colour, every hair on her head, every tiny line of her face—it was the expression that had been captured so beautifully. The expression that made her knees tremble.

She'd never seen it captured quite so perfectly. Even though it was paint that was centuries old she felt as if she could reach out and touch Mary. Stroke her cheek, feel the warmth of her skin, see the wonder in her eyes.

This was what she'd remembered. It was the thing that she'd pushed to the back of her head when she'd first seen the fresco. Now it was drawing her back.

Now she couldn't deny it. She couldn't ignore it.

This had all been in Burano's imagination. It felt as if he'd stepped back in time and caught that moment when a mother first looked at her child and was overcome by that huge wave of emotions and undeniable love. Baby Jesus was looking back at his mother with childlike wonder and awe. The look of love that only a child could give his mother—making the bond complete. The light behind the depiction of the Madonna and Child was almost ethereal. The glow around them was all-encompassing. All-consuming.

Her legs trembled. Her whole body was shaking.

And something, something from deep inside, was pushing its way out.

This was what she had missed. This was what she'd missed out on. This was what would never be hers. Never be shared between her and her daughter.

Her legs gave way, collapsing beneath her onto the dusty chapel floor as the sobs started to come out.

And twelve years' worth of suppressed grief started to flow.

Logan was pacing. He hadn't even made an attempt to go to bed. He'd heard rustling in the vineyard and had taken a restless walk to investigate. It had been fruitless. He'd found nothing. It had probably only been a fox.

But as he had been crossing back towards his farmhouse, something had caught his eye. At first he'd thought he had finally gone crazy and was imagining it. Then he'd looked again.

Lucia. Dressed in very little with bare legs, bare arms and a pale pink lace-trimmed nightdress fluttering around her in the warm breeze and clinging to every curve of her skin. Was she sleepwalking?

She seemed so focused, so light on her feet, that she almost floated across the courtyard, straight to the chapel entrance. He'd started to move in her direction but his footsteps had faltered as she'd paused at the chapel door, pushing it with her shoulder to lever it open.

Then she disappeared into the darkness.

Logan stopped. His heart was thudding in his chest. Should he follow, or should he leave?

Every part of his rational brain told him to step away. No matter how much he wanted to, he couldn't pursue a relationship with Lucia. Not like this. Not when they were both in different places.

But the protective element in him couldn't walk away. Couldn't leave her like this.

He walked quietly towards the chapel. A little beam of light appeared inside the chapel, cutting across the stained-glass windows. What was she doing?

He held his breath as he reached the doorway. Stepping inside the dark chapel was intimidating—and he was fully dressed. The thin beam of torchlight was focused on the fresco on the faraway wall.

He'd never seen it lit up like this before. He'd only ever really studied it in daylight. It looked entirely different under the concentrated light of a torch beam. The architect-minded part of him wondered how it must have looked hundreds of years ago in flickering candlelight.

Lucia had the beam directly on the Madonna's face. Under the artificial light her face was brightly illuminated. In a reach-out-and-touch kind of way.

The beam wobbled and he stepped forward. Part of his stomach was curled up in a ball. Lucia had come out to the chapel in the middle of the night. In the light reflected back off the fresco he could see her trembling, shuddering skin. Every muscle, every bone was shaking.

His response was automatic. He stepped forward just as she crumpled to the floor, her sobs cutting through the night air. The torch fell to the floor with a crash, the light sputtering out.

He was stunned. In twelve years he hadn't heard her cry. There had been a few tears just after the birth of their daughter—but none after that.

He wrapped his arms around her. Her skin was cold, chilled in the coolness of the chapel, so he pulled her against his chest and stroked her hair. He didn't care about the dust. He didn't care about the broken torch on the ground.

He just held her.

And she sobbed. Like no one he'd ever heard before. These weren't quiet, tiny sobs. These were loud and spluttering, echoing around the thick chapel walls. Her body was racked with them and he could feel her pain, feel her anguish. It was as if twelve years' worth of grief and sorrow had just erupted from her soul.

It was horrible to see the woman he loved like this. But he knew exactly how she felt. Only he could understand. So he waited and he held her, gently stroking her hair and whispering in her ear.

He had no idea how long they stayed that way. Eventually her sobs quietened, turning into little shudders instead of big outbursts. He changed position, pulling her up onto his knees, taking her bare legs away from the cold floor of the chapel.

His hands sneaked around her satin-covered waist and he pulled her against his chest. Her hands snaked up around his neck and her head tucked under his chin. He could feel her ragged breaths against his skin.

'I know, Lucia,' he said softly. 'I know how you feel. I loved her just as much as you did.'

She gave a little whimper and her fingers tightened around his neck. He waited a few seconds then gently lifted her head up. There was only a tiny bit of moonlight streaming through the stained-glass windows but he could see her tear-streaked face and he lifted both hands to caress it.

'Talk to me,' he whispered.

She shuddered, then nodded slowly.

It was odd. The strangest feeling in the world, but it was almost as if his body gave a little cry of relief.

'I miss her,' she said in shaky breaths. 'I miss her every day.'

His heart squeezed in his chest. He wanted to wrap his arms around her again and kiss her. But he needed to let her speak.

'I don't want to talk about her,' she said, her voice tinged with regret. 'If I don't talk about her, then none of it was real. None of it really happened.'

She shook her head as her voice rose in pain. 'Why, Logan? Why our baby? Why did we have to lose her? Do you know where we could be right now? Do you know what kind of life we could be leading?'

He nodded his head. 'Of course I do,' he whispered.

'But you were so calm, so controlled,' she said angrily. 'I couldn't be like that, I just couldn't. You did everything. You organised the flowers, the funeral, the casket. You spoke to the family.' She shook her head, her voice rising. 'How could you even do that? How could you even function? Our daughter was dead!'

'You think I didn't know that? You think I didn't hurt every bit as much as you? I hated that, Lucia. I hated every second of that. I hated the fact you wouldn't eat, you wouldn't sleep and you wouldn't talk to me. Organising was the only thing I *could* do. I wanted the world to know that Ariella Rose had existed. I wanted her to matter. I wanted to bury our daughter with the respect she deserved.' He hadn't realised this had been buried inside him. He hadn't realised he'd wanted to say all this to her.

'And I didn't?' She was crying again. 'You were so... capable. And I felt useless. I couldn't be the person I'd been. I couldn't be your other half. I couldn't look at you without thinking about her and what had been stolen from me!'

He clasped her head between his hands and leaned his forehead against hers. 'Stolen from *us*, Lucia,' he said quietly.

'I needed you. I needed you every second of the day. But I couldn't get to you. You locked yourself away from me and after a few weeks I realised that you needed to grieve differently from me. I didn't want to let you go. I never wanted to let you go. No matter how sorry I was, no matter how much I hurt, I still wanted you, Lucia. Every second of every day. You're the only person in this world for me. The only person I want to grow old with.' He traced a finger down her damp cheek. 'I just needed to see you cry. I just needed to know that you could acknowledge our daughter.'

She was still shuddering. He ran one hand down her

arm and could feel the tiny hairs on her arms standing on end.

'Why now? What's changed?'

She met his gaze with tear-filled eyes. 'You. I've avoided you for so long. Seeing you again, being together, remembering everything we've shared together, I couldn't hide away from it any more. It's just been bubbling underneath the surface the whole time. I couldn't keep it locked away any more. Not if I want to live.'

He gave his head a shake. 'But you wouldn't talk to me in Venice. You said you couldn't do it.'

She squeezed her eyes closed for a moment. 'I know.' Now she reached up and touched his face, his jaw. 'I think something just lined up for us, Logan.' She pointed towards the fresco. 'If you hadn't got this job, if this fresco hadn't been found, we probably wouldn't have met again.' She placed her hand over her heart. 'I *needed* this. I needed all this to happen.' She looked up towards the fresco. 'Hundreds of years ago Burano must have met someone, must have known a new mother, to capture the love and adoration in his painting. Because he's captured it so beautifully. When I first saw his fresco I wouldn't let the painting touch me. I wouldn't let it inside. I was jealous. I couldn't acknowledge the painting because *I* wanted to be that person. *I* wanted to be that mother who looks at her baby with such joy and pleasure, wondering what the world will hold for them.' The tears were falling freely down her face again.

All he wanted to do was comfort her. All he wanted to do was love her.

He sucked in a deep breath. 'Lucia, you can be that person. I want you to know that I love you. I want you— just the way you are. But if you want to try and have a family again then I'll be with you, every step of the way.' He stroked his thumb across her cheek. 'Likewise, if you just want to grow old and grey together and wander through the streets of Venice, or Florence, or even the Tuscan hills, I'll do that with you too. As long as I'm with you, I know I'll be happy.'

Her hands kept trembling as she wound them around his neck again, pressing her body against his and whispering in his ear. 'Can I be enough for you, Logan? Enough for you on my own? What if we weren't meant to have babies? What if that's never going to happen for us?'

He stood up, pulling her to her feet alongside him but keeping their bodies locked close together. He slid his hands along the satin slip covering her back and anchored her to him. He kissed one cheek and then the other. 'Then that's the way things are supposed to be. As long as I'm with you I can take whatever hand life deals us.'

He bent to meet her lips.

It was like the first kiss all over again.

This was the woman he'd fallen in love with all those years ago.

This was the woman he'd had to allow to walk away even though it had broken his heart.

This was the mother of his child.

This was his Lucia.

Her body was pressed against his and she responded to every touch, her fingers threading through his hair. Her rose scent wound around him, pulling him in in every way.

Her cold skin heated quickly, her lips matching every kiss.

For Logan, it was like coming home.

When Lucia finally pulled back he was shocked. She lifted a finger and placed it against his lips, keeping her body tight against his.

She took a deep breath. 'Logan, if this is going to work, there's something I need to do.'

His breath was caught somewhere in his throat. After twelve years there was finally a chance of a relationship again with Lucia. There wasn't anything he wouldn't agree to.

'What is it? What do you need to do? Because I don't want to lose you again. I don't want this chance to slip away from us.'

Her voice was trembling and her hand slid down his arm, interlocking their fingers. 'I was kind of hoping you would agree to do it with me.'

Her dark eyes met his gaze and he squeezed her hand tightly. 'Anything, Lucia,' he whispered. 'Anything for you.'

CHAPTER TEN

IT WAS A gorgeous summer's day with the sun high in the sky above them.

Logan was standing in front of her in his trademark cream suit and pale blue shirt. 'Ready?' he asked.

Her stomach was churning. Over and over. She would have tossed and turned last night if he hadn't held her safely in his arms. She'd even bought herself a new dress. Pale pink with tiny flowers. It was ridiculous. She didn't need it. But she'd wanted to wake up this morning and feel like everything was new.

More than anything, she wanted to be prepared.

Florence was alive. She'd forgotten how much she loved this city. Chattering voices were all around them, tourist parties bustling past and Italian voices mixing with a multitude of other languages.

She slid her hand into his, clutching her pink and lilac flowers in her hand. 'I'm ready,' she said with a certainty she hadn't known she possessed.

The walk through the streets took around fifteen minutes, the crowds lessening the further out they went. No one else was going where they were.

It was a pleasant walk with a few shopkeepers nod-

ding at Logan as they passed by and him pointing out
a few changes to the city since she'd left.

As the green archway of the cemetery came into
view her footsteps faltered. Logan slipped his hand
around her waist. As their bodies pressed against each
other she fell into step with him. It felt natural and gave
her the added reassurance to continue.

The cemetery was quiet, bathed in warm sunlight,
with only a few people dotted around in quiet condo-
lence.

Her throat was closing up as they walked along the
white paved path. Like most cemeteries this one had a
special section for children and babies. It was tucked
away at the back, next to the white wall that separated
the cemetery from the rest of the city.

There was a white bench in the middle, with lots
of green grass and flower beds erupting with colour.
Something inside her clenched. She hadn't allowed herself to think about this. She hadn't allowed herself to
realise the beauty of the surroundings.

Within the cemetery walls she couldn't even hear
the noise of the city outside. It was like their own private sanctuary.

She squeezed her eyes closed as they passed rows
of little white headstones. So many little lives lost. So
many other people who'd experienced the same pain
that she had.

Had she maybe even met some of them? She'd been
so immersed in her own grief that she hadn't stopped
to think about anyone else's.

Their footsteps slowed. She'd only been here once
and Logan had been numerous times but she still knew

exactly where Ariella Rose was buried—it was imprinted in her brain.

They stopped and stood for a second, looking down at the little white headstone.

Beloved daughter.
Ariella Rose Cascini.
Born asleep.

Apart from the date, there was nothing else on the stone.

Lucia laid her head on his shoulder as silent tears fell down her cheeks. She needed this. She'd needed to do this for so long.

A dove swooped in the air above them, landing on the grass at their feet. Lucia gave a little nod of her head as it eyed her suspiciously then walked away. She put her pale pink and lilac flowers into the little white vase at the graveside then leaned over to touch the stone.

It was odd. Any marble headstone she'd ever touched before had been cold. But Ariella's wasn't. It was bathed in the bright light and warmed by the sun.

The horrible closed-in feeling that had been around her heart for so long was gone. The terrible weight and the dark cloud that had pressed on her shoulders for the last twelve years was finally gone.

Today she didn't feel despair all around her. Today she saw a beautiful memorial and resting place for her darling daughter. A place where she could come and sit sometimes if she needed to.

She'd been so afraid for so long. But with Logan by her side she didn't need to be.

'I love you, Ariella Rose,' she whispered. 'I'm sorry

I haven't been here and I promise to visit in the future.' She stroked her hand along the stone and stood up, taking the few steps to Logan and wrapping her arms around his waist.

'Thank you,' she said quietly. 'Thank you for bringing me here.'

'Any time. Any time at all.'

He threaded his fingers back through hers. 'Do you want to take some time? How do you feel?' His voice was cautious.

She tilted her head up towards the sun and the face of the man that she loved and adored. The man she wanted to grow old with.

'I feel as if I've taken that step. The one that I've needed to for so long. I'm ready now.'

He clasped both her hands in his. 'Ready for what?'

She met the gaze of his steady green eyes. 'Ready to move forward. Now I can love the man I want to without feeling overcome with grief.' She smiled up at the sun. 'Now I can look towards the future.'

There was a swell in her chest. A confidence she hadn't felt in so long.

He reached up and slid his hand through her hair as he pulled her to him.

'Then let's start now.'

And he kissed her.

And she kissed him right back.

She was laughing. She was running through the cobbled streets of Monte Calanetti in her impossibly high heels.

He loved it. He loved every second of it. 'Watch out!' he shouted. 'You'll break something!'

'Keep up, slowcoach!' she shouted over her shoul-

der as she made the final dash towards the fountain.
He walked up behind her and slid his hands around her
waist. He could feel her rapid breaths against his chest
wall.

'Do you have them?' she asked.

He unfurled his fingers, revealing the shiny euro
coins in his hand. He eyed the clamshell the nymph
held above her head in the centre of the fountain. 'First
time?' He was smiling. She'd tried this a hundred times
before and had never managed to hit the mark—the
clamshell that would make your wish come true.

Her deep brown eyes met his. 'First time,' she repeated. Her index finger moved the coins in the palm
of his hand as if she was looking for just the right one.
After a few seconds she smiled. 'This one,' she said,
weighing the coin in her hand.

'That one? You're sure?'

'Oh, I'm sure.' She spun around to face the nymph.
His hand was on her abdomen and she pressed her right
hand over his, as she took a deep breath, pulled back
her left hand and let the coin fly.

His eyes stayed on the coin as it caught the sunlight
as it arced through the air, but his left hand was flicking
something else into the fountain at their feet.

The coin was on a direct path and landed squarely
in the middle of the clamshell. Lucia let out a shriek.
'I've done it! I've finally done it!' She spun around and
flung her arms around his neck. 'I've finally done it.'

He picked her up and spun her around, her hair
streaming out behind her. 'You've done it,' he cheered
as he set her back down. 'Now, what did you wish for?'

For the first time his stomach wasn't in knots around
Lucia. Slowly but surely she was turning back into the

woman he loved. The dark shadows were going from her eyes. Her steps were lighter. She laughed more. She cried more. And she still loved to dance.

'Isn't the wish supposed to be a secret?' she said coyly.

He swallowed. He'd never felt more nervous, or surer about anything in his life. 'Look down,' he said quietly.

She blinked. It obviously wasn't what she had expected to hear. A frown creased her brow as she stared down, taking a few seconds to see the glint of gold under the clear water.

Her eyes widened and she bent down, putting her hand into the water and pulling out the ring.

'Logan?' she asked as a smile spread across her face.

It wasn't a traditional flashy engagement ring. He didn't want to waste any time. It was a gold wedding band studded with diamonds and rubies. It was a ring of promise. A ring of hope.

He didn't hesitate, just got down on one knee in front of the woman he loved. 'Lucia Moretti. You're the woman of my dreams. The woman I love with my whole heart. You are my perfect match. The person I want to laugh with, cry with, play with and grow old with. I believe this was meant to happen. I honestly believe we were meant to meet again and mourn our daughter together. I don't care where you want to make a life. I don't care if it's Venice, Florence, Rome or anywhere else. All that matters to me is that home is with you.' He pressed his hand against his heart. 'As long as I'm with you, I don't care where we are. You're the person I call home. You're all that I need. Will you make me the happiest man alive and marry me?'

She was still staring at the ring, watching the sun

glint off the little diamonds and rubies. The smile was permanently etched on her face.

She wrapped one arm around his neck and sat down on his knee. She didn't hesitate to slip the ring on her finger. 'How on earth could any woman refuse such a romantic proposal at Burano's fountain?' Her eyes were twinkling. She put her hand over his. 'There's no one else I ever want to be with. You're the only man for me.'

He pulled something out from behind his waist. 'I've brought you something else.'

She stared at the wrapped package. It wasn't big, small enough to tuck into his waistband. Plain canvas tied with string. She pulled the string and let the package unfurl. It was new paintbrushes and some oils. Her mouth fell open.

'How…how did you know?'

'That you'd want to take up painting again?'

She nodded as her eyes glistened with tears. 'Because we've come such a long way, Lucia. We've both moved on. You used to love painting and I know that you've found that little piece in your heart again that makes you ready to start again.'

She nodded her head slowly. 'You're right. I have. But I'd only just started to think about it.' She looked around. 'We're in such beautiful surroundings I can't help but feel inspired.'

He leaned forward to kiss her. 'Which leads me to my next question. Where do you want to live?'

She smiled and looked around. 'This might surprise you, but I've kind of grown fond of these Tuscan hills. I like the peace. I like the quiet. Maybe I'm not the city girl I thought.' She bit her bottom lip. 'How would you feel about finding somewhere to live around here?'

He stood and pulled her to her feet, holding her close. He ran his fingers through her hair. 'I think that this is a good place, a healing place. And I'm sure there's a Tuscan villa somewhere in these hills just waiting for us to renovate it. A villa where we can build you your own studio.'

She smiled again, 'All work and no play makes Logan a dull boy.'

She was teasing and he knew it. 'Who says anything about working?' he murmured.

She pressed a little kiss against his lips. 'Do you want to know what I wished for?'

'Are you going to tell me?'

She nodded. 'Someone must have been listening. When I threw that coin I wished for new beginnings.'

His eyebrows rose. 'You did?' It was perfect. It was as if everything was just meant to be.

'I did,' she said with confidence, and with that she rose up on her toes to kiss him. 'To new beginnings,' she whispered.

'New beginnings,' he murmured, and he kissed her right back.

* * * * *

UNFINISHED
BUSINESS WITH
THE DUKE

HEIDI RICE

A special thanks to my Florentine specialists, Steve and Biz, to Katherine at the terrific Kings Head Theatrein Islington, and Leonardo, who answered my daft questions about architecture.

CHAPTER ONE

THE six-inch stiletto heels of Issy Helligan's thigh-high leather boots echoed like gunshots against the marble floor of the gentlemen's club. The sharp rhythmic cracks sounded like a firing squad doing target practice as she approached the closed door at the end of the corridor.

How appropriate.

She huffed and came to a stop. The gunshots cut off, but her stomach carried right on going, doing a loop-the-loop and then swaying like the pendulum of Big Ben. Recognising the symptoms of chronic stage fright, Issy pressed her palm to her midriff as she focussed on the elaborate brass plaque announcing the entrance to the 'East Wing Common Room'.

Calm down. You can do this. You're a theatrical professional with seven years' experience.

Detecting the muffled rumble of loud male laughter, she locked her knees as a thin trickle of sweat ran down her back beneath her second-hand Versace mac.

People are depending on you. People you care about. Getting ogled by a group of pompous old fossils is a small price to pay for keeping those people gainfully employed.

It was a mantra she'd been repeating for the past hour—to absolutely no avail.

After grappling with the knot on the mac's belt, she pulled the coat off and placed it on the upholstered chair beside the door. Then she looked down at her costume—and Big Ben's pendulum got stuck in her throat.

Blood-red satin squeezed her ample curves into an hourglass shape, making her cleavage look like a freak of nature. She took a shallow breath and the bustier's underwiring dug into her ribs.

She tugged the band out of her hair and let the mass of Pre-Raphaelite curls tumble over her bare shoulders as she counted to ten.

Fine, so the costume from last season's production of *The Rocky Horror Picture Show* wasn't exactly subtle, but she hadn't had a lot of options at such short notice—and the man who had booked her that morning hadn't wanted subtle.

'Tarty, darling. That's the look I'm after,' he'd stated in his cut-glass Etonian accent. 'Rodders is moving to Dubai and we plan to show him what he'll be missing. So don't stint on the T and A, sweetheart.'

It had been on the tip of Issy's tongue to tell him to buzz off and hire himself a stripper, but then he'd mentioned the astronomical sum he was prepared to pay if she 'put on a decent show'—and her tongue had gone numb.

After six months of scrimping and saving and struggling to find a sponsor, Issy was fast running out of ways to get the thirty grand she needed to keep the Crown and Feathers Theatre Pub open for another season. The Billet Doux Singergram Agency had been the jewel in the crown of her many fund-raising ideas. But so far they'd had a grand total of six bookings—and all of those had been from well-meaning friends. Having worked her way up from general dogsbody to general manager in the last seven years, she had everyone at the theatre looking to her to make sure the show went on.

Issy sighed, the weight of responsibility making her head hurt as the corset's whalebone panels constricted around her lungs. With the bank threatening to foreclose on the theatre's loan any minute, feminist principles were just another of the luxuries she could no longer afford.

When she'd taken the booking eight hours ago she'd been determined to see it as a golden opportunity. She'd do a tastefully suggestive rendition of 'Life Is a Cabaret', flash a modest amount of T and A and walk away with a nice healthy sum to add to the Crown and Feathers's survival kitty, plus the possibility of some serious word-of-mouth business. After all, this was one of the most exclusive gentlemen's clubs in the world, boasting princes, dukes and lords of the realm, not to mention Europe's richest and most powerful businessmen among its membership.

Really, it should be a doddle. She'd made it quite clear to her booker what a singing telegram did—and did not—entail. And Roderick Carstairs and his mates couldn't possibly be as tough an audience to crack as the twenty-two five-year-olds tripping on a sugar rush she'd sung 'Happy Birthday' to last week.

Or so she hoped.

But as Issy eased the heavy oak panelled door to the East Wing Common Room open, and heard the barrage of male hoots and guffaws coming from inside, that hope died a quick and painful death.

From the sound of it, her audience were primed and ready for her—and not nearly as old and fossilised as she'd assumed. The corset squeezed her ribcage as she stayed rooted in the doorway, shielded from view.

Putting on 'a decent show' didn't seem such a doddle any more.

She was staring blankly at the rows of bookcases lining the wall, mustering the courage to walk into the lions' den, when she caught a movement on the balcony opposite. Silhouetted by the dusky evening light, a tall figure strode into view, talking into his mobile phone. It was impossible to make out his features, but *déjà vu* had the hair on the back of Issy's neck standing to attention. Momentarily transfixed by the stranger's broad-shouldered build, and the forceful, predatory way he moved in the small space, Issy shivered, thinking of a tiger prowling a cage.

She jumped at the disembodied chorus of rowdy masculine cheers and dragged her gaze away.

Focus, Issy, focus.

She straightened her spine and took a step forward, but then her eyes darted to the balcony again. The stranger had stopped moving. Was he watching her?

She thought of the tiger again. And then memory blindsided her.

'Gio,' she whispered, as her breath clogged in her lungs and the corset constricted like a vice around her torso.

She gasped in a breath as heat seared up the back of her neck and made her scalp burn.

Ignore him.

She pulled her gaze away, mortified that the mere thought of Giovanni Hamilton still made all her erogenous zones do the happy dance and her heart squeeze painfully in her chest.

Don't be ridiculous.

That guy could not be Gio. She couldn't possibly be that unlucky. To come face to face with the biggest disaster of her life when she was about to waltz into another. Clearly stress was making her hallucinate.

Issy pushed her shoulders back and took as deep a breath as the corset's stays would allow.

Enough with the nervous breakdown, already. It's showtime.

Striding into the main body of the room, she launched into the sultry opening bars of Liza Minnelli's signature song. Only to come to a stumbling halt, her stomach lurching back into Big Ben mode, as she rounded the door and got an eyeful of Rodders and his mates. The mob of young, debauched and completely pie-eyed Hooray Henries lunged to their feet, jeers and wolf whistles echoing off the antique furnishings as the room erupted.

Issy's throat constricted in horror as she imagined Little Red Riding Hood being fed to a pack of sex-starved, booze-sodden wolves while singing a show tune in her underwear.

Suddenly a firing squad looked remarkably appealing.

Go ahead and shoot me now, fellas.

What in God's name was Issy Helligan doing working as a stripper?

Gio Hamilton stood in the shadows of the balcony, stunned into silence, his gaze fixed on the young woman who strutted into the room with the confidence of a courtesan. Her full figure moved in time with her long, leggy strides. Sequins glittered on an outfit that would make a hooker blush.

'Gio?' The heavily accented voice of his partnership manager crackled down the phone from Florence.

'*Si, Gio.*' He pressed the phone to his ear and tried to

get his mind to engage. 'I'll get back to you about the Venice project,' he said, slipping into English. 'You know how the Italian authorities love red tape—it's probably just a formality. *Ciao.*' He disconnected the call—and stared.

That couldn't be the sweet, impulsive and impossibly naïve girl he'd grown up with. Could it?

But then he noticed the pale freckled skin on her shoulder blades and he knew. Heat pulsed in his groin as he recalled Issy the last time he'd seen her—that same pale skin flushed pink by their recent lovemaking and those wild auburn curls cascading over bare shoulders.

The smoky, seductive notes of an old theatre song, barely audible above the hoots and jeers, yanked Gio out of the past and brought him slap-bang up to date. Issy's rich, velvety voice sent shivers rippling up his spine and arousal flared—before the song was drowned out by the chant of 'Get it off!' from Carstairs and his crowd.

Gio's contempt for the arrogant toff and his cronies turned to disgust as Issy's singing stopped and she froze. Suddenly she wasn't the inexperienced young temptress who'd seduced him one hot summer night, but the awkward girl who had trailed after him throughout his teenage years, her bright blue eyes glowing with adoration.

He stuffed his phone into his back pocket, anger and arousal and something else he didn't want to acknowledge coiling in his gut.

Then Carstairs lunged. Gio's fingers clenched into fists as the younger man grabbed Issy around the waist. Her head twisted to avoid the boozy kiss.

To hell with that.

The primitive urge to protect came from nowhere.

'Get your filthy hands off her, Carstairs.'

The shout echoed as eleven pairs of eyes turned his way.

Issy yelped as he strode towards her, those exotic turquoise eyes going wide with astonishment and then blank with shock.

Carstairs raised his head, his ruddy face glazed with champagne and confusion. 'Who the…?'

Gio slammed an upper-cut straight into the idiot's jaw. Pain ricocheted up his arm.

'Ow! Dammit,' he breathed, cradling his throbbing knuckles as he watched Carstairs crumple onto the carpet.

Hearing Issy's sharp gasp, he looked round to see her eyes roll back. He caught her as she flopped, and scooped her into his arms. Carrying her against his chest, he tuned out the shouts and taunts coming from Carstairs's friends. Not one of them was sober enough—or had enough gumption—to cause him a problem.

'Kick this piece of rubbish out of here when he comes to,' Gio said to the elderly attendant who had scurried in from his post in the billiards room next door.

The old guy bobbed his head. 'Yes, Your Grace. Will the lady be all right?'

'She'll be fine. Once you've dealt with Carstairs, have some ice water and brandy sent to my suite.'

He drew a deep breath as he strolled down the corridor towards the lifts, caught the rose scent of Issy's shampoo and realised it wasn't only his knuckles throbbing.

He gave the attendant a stiff nod as he walked into the lift, with Issy still out cold in his arms. She stirred slightly and he got his first good look at her face in the fluorescent light.

He could see the tantalising sprinkle of freckles on her nose. And the slight overbite which gave her lips an irresistible pout. Despite the heavy stage make-up and the glossy coating of letterbox-red lipstick, her heart-shaped face still had the tantalising combination of innocence and sensuality that had caused him so many sleepless nights a lifetime ago.

Gio's gaze strayed to the swell of her cleavage, barely confined by dark red satin. The antique lift shuddered to a stop at his floor, and his groin began to throb in earnest.

He adjusted her dead weight, flexing his shoulder muscles as he headed down the corridor to the suite of rooms he kept at the club.

Even at seventeen Issy Helligan had been a force of nature. As impossible to ignore as she was to control. He was a man who loved taking risks, but Issy had still been able to shock the hell out of him.

From the looks of things that hadn't changed.

He shoved opened the door to his suite, and walked through into the bedroom. Placing his cargo on the bed, he stepped back and stared at her barely clad body in the half-light.

So what did he do with her now?

He hadn't a clue where the urge to ride to her rescue had come from. But giving Carstairs a right jab and knocking the drunken idiot out cold was where any lingering sense of responsibility both started and stopped. He was nobody's knight in shining armour.

He frowned, his irritation rising right alongside his arousal as he watched her shallow breathing.

What was that thing made of? Armour-plating? No

wonder she'd fainted. It looked as if she was struggling to take a decent breath.

Cursing softly, he perched on the edge of the bed and tugged the bow at her cleavage. Issy gave a soft moan as the satin knot slipped. He loosened the laces, his eyes riveted to the plump flesh of her breasts as the corset expanded.

She was even more exquisite than he remembered.

The pain in his crotch increased, but he resisted the urge to loosen the contraption further and expose her to his gaze. Then he spotted the red marks on her pale skin where the panels had dug into tender flesh.

'For heaven's sake, Issy,' he whispered as he smoothed his thumb over the bruising.

What had she been thinking, wearing this outfit in the first place? And then prancing around in front of a drunken fool like Carstairs?

Issy Helligan had always needed a keeper. He'd have to give her a good talking-to when she came round.

He stood and walked to the window. After flinging open the velvet drapes, he sat in the gilt chair beside the bed. This shouldn't be too hard to sort out.

The reason for her disastrous charade downstairs had to be something to do with money. Issy had always been headstrong and foolhardy, but she'd never been promiscuous. So he'd offer her an injection of capital when she woke up.

She'd never have to do anything this reckless again— and he'd be free to forget about her.

His gaze drifted to the tantalising glimpse of one rosy nipple peeking over the satin rim of the corset.

And if she knew what was good for her, she'd damn well take the money.

Issy's eyelids fluttered as she inhaled the fresh scent of clean linen.

'Hello again, Isadora.' The low, masculine voice rumbled across her consciousness and made her insides feel deliciously warm and fuzzy.

She took a deep breath and sighed. Hallelujah. She could breathe. The relief was intoxicating.

'Mmm? What?' she purred. She felt as if she were floating on a cloud. A light, fluffy cloud made of delicious pink candyfloss.

'I loosened your torture equipment. No wonder you fainted. You could barely breathe.'

It was the gorgeous voice again, crisp British vowels underlaid with a lazy hint of the Mediterranean—and a definite hint of censure. Issy frowned. Didn't she know that voice?

Her eyes opened, and she stared at an elaborate plaster moulding on the ceiling. Swivelling her head, she saw a man by her bedside. Her first thought was that he looked far too masculine for the fancy gilt chair. But then she focussed on his face, and the bolt of recognition hit her, knocking her off the candyfloss cloud and shoving her head first into sticky reality.

She snapped her eyelids shut, threw one arm over her face and sank back down into the pillows. 'Go away. You're a hallucination,' she groaned. But it was too late.

Even the brief glimpse had seared the image of his harsh, handsome features onto her retinas and made her heartbeat hit panic mode. The sculpted cheekbones, the square jaw with a small dent in the chin, the wavy chestnut hair pushed back from dark brows and those thickly-lashed chocolate eyes more tempting than original sin. Pain lanced into her chest as she recalled how those eyes had looked the last time she'd seen them, shadowed with annoyance and regret.

Then everything else came flooding back. And Issy groaned louder.

Carstairs's sweaty hands gripping her waist, the rank whiff of whisky and cigars on his breath, the pulse of fear replaced by shock as Carstairs's head snapped back and Gio loomed over her. Then the deafening buzzing in her ears before she'd done her 'Perils of Pauline' act.

No way. This could not be happening. Gio had to be a hallucination.

'Leave me alone and let me die in peace,' she moaned.

She heard a husky chuckle and grimaced. Had she said that out loud?

'Once a drama queen, always a drama queen, I see, Isadora?'

She dropped her arm and stared at her tormentor. Taking in the tanned biceps stretching the sleeves of his black polo shirt and the teasing glint in his eyes, she resigned herself to the fact this was no hallucination. The few strands of silver at his temples and the crinkles around the corners of his eyes hadn't been there ten years ago, but at thirty-one Giovanni Hamilton was as devastatingly gorgeous as he had been at twenty-one—and twice as much of a hunk.

Why couldn't he have got fat, bald and ugly? It was the least he deserved.

'Don't call me Isadora. I hate that name,' she said, not caring if she sounded snotty.

'Really?' One eyebrow rose in mocking enquiry as his lips quirked. 'Since when?'

Since you walked away.

She quashed the sentimental thought. To think she'd once adored it when he'd called her by her given name. Had often basked for days in the proof that he'd noticed her.

How pitiful.

Luckily she wasn't that needy, eager-to-please teenager any more.

'Since I grew up and decided it didn't suit me,' she said, pretending not to notice the warm liquid sensation turning her insides to mush as he smiled at her.

The eyebrow rose another notch and the sexy grin widened as he lounged in his chair. He didn't look the least bit wounded by her rebuff.

His gaze dipped to her cleavage. 'I can see how grown up you are. It's kind of hard to miss.'

Heat sizzled at the suggestive tone. She bolted upright, aware of how much flesh she had on display as the bustier drooped. She drew her knees up and wrapped her arms around her shins as the brutal blush fanned out across her chest.

'I was on a job,' she said defensively, annoyed that the costume felt more revealing now than it had in front of Carstairs and all his mates.

'A job? Is that what you call it?' Gio commented dryly. 'What sort of *job* requires you to get assaulted by an idiot like Carstairs?' His eyes narrowed. 'What exactly do you think would have happened if I hadn't been there?'

She heard the sanctimonious note of disapproval—and the injustice of the accusation made her want to scream.

In hindsight, she should never have accepted the booking. And maybe it had been a mistake to walk into that room once she'd known how plastered her audience was. But she'd been under so much pressure for months now. Her livelihood and the livelihood of people she loved was at stake.

So she'd taken a chance. A stupid, desperate, foolish chance that had backfired spectacularly. But she wasn't going to regret it. And she certainly wasn't going to be criticised for it by someone who had never cared about anyone in his entire life but himself.

'Don't you *dare* imply I'm to blame for Carstairs's appalling behaviour,' she said, fury making the words louder than she'd intended.

Surprise flickered in Gio's eyes.

Good.

It was about time he realised she wasn't the simpering little groupie she'd once been.

'The man was blind drunk and a lech,' she continued, shuffling over to the other side of the bed and swinging her legs to the floor. 'Nobody asked you to get involved.' She stood and faced him. 'You did that all on your own. I would have been perfectly fine if you hadn't been there.'

Probably.

She marched across the lavishly furnished bedroom—keeping a death grip on the sagging costume. What she wouldn't give right now to be wearing her favourite jeans and a T-shirt. Somehow her speech didn't have as much impact while she was dressed like an escapee from the Moulin Rouge.

'Where do you think you're going?' he said, his voice dangerously low.

'I'm leaving,' she replied, reaching for the doorknob.

But as she yanked the door, all set to make a grand exit, a large, tanned hand slapped against the wood above her head and slammed it shut.

'No, you're not,' he said.

She whipped round and immediately realised her mistake. Her breath caught as her bare shoulders butted the door. He stood so close she could see the flecks of gold in his irises, taste the spicy scent of his aftershave, and feel the heat of his body inches from hers.

She clasped her arms over her chest as her nipples puckered, awareness making every one of her pulse-points pound.

'What?' she snapped, cornered. The last time she'd been this close to Gio she'd been losing her virginity to him.

'There's no need to go storming off.' The rock-hard bicep next to her ear tensed before his arm dropped to his side. Her breath released in an audible puff as he eased back.

'You misunderstood me,' he said, heaving an impatient sigh.

'About what, exactly?' She tilted her head, thrust her chin out.

How infuriating.

At five foot six, and with six-inch heels on, she ought to be able to look him in the eye. No such luck. Gio had always been tall—tall and lanky—but when had he got so...solid?

She tried to look bored. No easy feat, given her limited acting skills and the fact that her heart felt as if it were being ripped out of her chest all over again. She pushed the memory back, locking it back in the box marked 'Biggest Mistake of your Life', while his gaze roamed over her, the chocolate-brown giving nothing away. To think she'd once believed that bleak expression was enigmatic, when all it had ever been was proof Gio had no soul.

'Carstairs deserved everything he got, and I enjoyed giving it to him,' he said coldly, shoving a fist into the pocket of his trousers. 'I'm not blaming you. I'm blaming the situation.' His eyes met hers and she saw something that stunned her for a second. Was that concern?

'If you needed money you should have come to me,' he said with dictatorial authority, and she knew she'd made a stupid mistake. That wasn't concern. It was contempt.

'There was no need for you to become a stripper,' he remarked.

Her heart stopped and the blush blazed like wildfire. *Did he just say stripper?*

He cupped her cheek. The unexpected contact had her outraged reply getting stuck in her throat.

'I know things ended badly between us, but we were friends once. I can help you.' His thumb skimmed across her cheek with the lightest of touches. 'And, whatever happens, you're finding another job.' The patronising tone did nothing to diminish the arousal darkening his eyes. 'Because, quite apart from anything else, you're a terrible stripper.'

CHAPTER TWO

Issy wasn't often rendered speechless. As a rule she liked to talk. And she was never shy about voicing her opinion. But right now she couldn't utter a single syllable, because she was far too busy trying to figure out what outraged her the most.

That Gio thought she was a stripper. That he thought she was terrible. That he actually thought it was any of his business. Or that he should have the audacity to claim he had been her friend...

'We're not friends,' she spluttered. 'Not any more. I got over that delusion a long time ago. Remember?'

His hand stroked her nape, making it hard for her to concentrate. 'Perhaps friendship's not the right word.' His eyes met hers, and what she saw made her gasp. His pupils had dilated, the chocolate-brown now black with desire. He was turned on. Seriously turned on. But what shocked her more was the vicious throb of arousal in her own abdomen.

'How about we kiss and make up?' he said, purpose and demand clear in the husky voice.

Before she could respond he brushed his lips across hers, then dipped his head and kissed the swell of her left breast. Raw desire assailed her, paralysing her tongue as he nipped at the sensitive flesh. Her breath gushed out and her head bumped against the door, shock and panic obliterated by the swift jolt of molten heat.

Stop him. Stop this.

The words crashed through her mind. But the only thing that registered was the brutal yearning to feel his mouth on her breast. She could still remember the way his insistent lips had once ignited her senses. Her arms relaxed their death grip on the corset, and the ripe peak spilled out.

She sobbed as he circled the rigid nipple with his tongue, then captured it between his lips and suckled strongly. Vivid memory and raw new sensation tangled as she arched into his mouth. Her thigh muscles clutched and released as she surrendered. He pushed the sagging bodice down, cupped her other breast. She moaned as he tugged at the swelling peak.

The firestorm of need twisted and built. Dazed, she clasped his head, gripping the silky waves—and felt the sharp knock on the door rap against her back.

Her eyes popped open as he raised his head.

'Hell, ten years isn't enough,' he murmured, the sinful chocolate gaze hot with lust and knowledge.

She scrambled away, shame shattering the sensual spell. Drawing in a ragged breath, she grasped the sagging corset, covered herself, wincing as the cool satin touched tender flesh.

The knock sounded again, and panic skittered up her spine.

What had just happened? What had she let happen? How could he still have this effect on her?

'Excuse me, Your Grace.' The tentative voice, muffled by the door, broke the charged silence. 'Would you like me to leave the tray here?'

'Just a minute,' Gio shouted, his eyes fixed on hers. 'Stand over there,' he murmured, nodding to a space behind the door that would keep her out of sight.

She bristled at the note of command, but stepped back. She had to get out of here. Before this got any worse.

'I have your brandy and iced water, Your Grace,' the footman announced as Gio swung open the door. 'And the lady's coat. It was on the hall chair downstairs.'

'Great,' Gio said curtly as he took the coat from unseen hands. Glancing her way, he passed it to her.

She stuffed her arms into the sleeves. Hastily tying the corset laces, she belted the mac as she watched Gio hand over a large tip and take the tray from the invisible footman.

He scowled as he pushed the door shut. 'Let's talk,' he said, sliding the tray onto the table beside the door.

'No, let's not,' she said, pleased that she'd stopped shaking long enough to cover some of her modesty.

She stepped forward and gripped the door handle, but she had wrestled it open less than an inch before his hand slapped against the wood, holding it closed.

'Stop behaving like a child. Surely after ten years you're over that night?'

She flinched at the impatient words. Then straightened, his casual reference to the worse night of her life forcing her pride to finally put in an appearance. Better late than never.

'Of course I'm over it,' she said emphatically, ignoring the ache under her breastbone. 'I'm not a child any more. Or an imbecile.'

She'd rather suffer the tortures of hell than admit

she'd cried herself to sleep for over a month after he'd gone. And lived with that pointless spurt of hope every time the phone rang for much longer. It was pathetic. And all completely academic now.

She might still have a problem controlling her body's reaction to him. But thankfully her heart was safe. She wasn't that overly romantic child any more—who'd believed infatuation was love.

But that didn't mean she was going to forgive him.

'I may have been young and foolish.' She tried not to cringe at the memory of *how* young and foolish. 'But luckily I happen to be a fast learner.'

Fast enough to know she would never fall that easily again. And especially not for a man like Gio, who didn't understand love and had no idea what it was worth.

'What's the problem, then?' He shrugged, as if that night had never happened. 'There's still a powerful attraction between us.' His eyes lowered to her lips. 'The way you just responded to me is proof of that. So why get upset because we acted on it?'

'I'm not upset!' she shouted. She paused, lowered her voice. 'To get upset, I'd actually have to give a damn.'

She turned to make her getaway again, but his hand slammed back against the door.

'Will you stop doing that?' she said, exasperated.

'You're not leaving until we sort out your situation,' he said, with infuriating patience.

'What situation?'

'You know very well what situation.'

His mouth had flattened into a grim line. What on earth was he on about?

'In case you haven't noticed, Your Dukeship, this is a free country. You can't hold me here against my will.'

'Nothing's free—and you know it.' His eyes raked over her outfit. 'Let me spell it out. I'm here in the UK having Hamilton Hall renovated, which means I can transfer the money you need by the end of today.'

What?

Her tongue went numb. Good God, he'd rendered her speechless again.

'And don't tell me you *like* working as a stripper,' he continued, clearly oblivious to her rising outrage, 'because I saw how petrified you were when Carstairs put his paws on you. My guess is this was your first job. And I intend to ensure it's also your last.'

'I'm not a stripper,' she all but choked. Of all the arrogant, patronising, overbearing... 'And even if I were, I would never be desperate enough to ask *you* for help.'

She'd always stood on her own two feet, had worked hard for her independence and was proud of what she'd achieved—even if it *was* all about to belong to the bank.

'If you're not a stripper,' he said, scepticism sharpening his voice, 'then what on earth were you doing downstairs?'

'I was delivering a singing telegram.'

His brow furrowed. 'A what?'

'Never mind.' She waved the question away. Why was she explaining herself to him? 'The point is, I don't need your help.'

'Stop being stupid.' He gripped her arm as she tried to turn. 'Whatever you were doing, it's obvious you must be desperate. I'm offering you a way out here. No strings attached. You'd be a fool not to take it.'

She tried to wrestle free, glaring at him when his fingers only tightened. 'I'd be an even bigger fool to take anything from you.' Anger and humiliation churned, bringing back the feeling of defeat and inadequacy that had dogged her for years after he'd walked away. And she hit back without thinking. 'Haven't you figured it out yet, Gio?' she said, hating the bitterness and negativity in her voice. 'I'd rather do twenty stripteases for Carstairs and his whole entourage than accept a penny from you. I happen to have a few principles, and I would never take money from someone I detest.'

His fingers released as the words struck home.

She fumbled with the door and darted out of the room, determined not to care about the shock on his face.

'Your body may be all grown up, Isadora.' The deep voice taunted her as her booted heels clicked on the polished parquet. 'What a shame the rest of you still has a way to go.'

She squared her shoulders as the door slammed at her back, and plunged her fists into the pockets of the mac, battling the blush burning her scalp. As she rushed down the hallway she played her parting shot over in her mind.

If only she *did* detest him.

Unfortunately, where Gio was concerned, nothing was ever that simple.

Gio strode into the living room of the suite and dumped the tray on the coffee table. Sitting on the fussy Queen Anne chaise-longue, he kicked off his shoes, propped his feet on the equally fussy antique table, and for the first time in years fervently wished for a cigarette.

Reaching for the generous glass of vintage cognac, he chugged it down in one punishing swallow. The burn in his throat did nothing to alleviate the pain in his groin, or the frustration making his head start to throb.

Issy Helligan was a walking disaster area.

He stared at the thick ridge in his trousers.

If that didn't go down in a minute he'd be forced to take a cold shower. Dropping his head against the sofa's backrest, he gazed at the ceiling. When had he last been stuck with an erection this persistent?

The vivid memory of Issy, her lithe young body moulded to his as he rode his motorcycle through the leafy country lanes to the Hall, instantly sprang to mind. And the blood pounded even harder.

Unbelievable. He could still recall every detail of that twenty-minute trip. As if it had happened ten seconds ago instead of ten years. Her full breasts flattening against his back, her thighs hugging his backside, her arms clinging to his waist—and the earlier shock to his system when she'd first strolled out of the school gates and climbed aboard the reconditioned Harley.

He'd expected to see the plump, cute tomboy he remembered—not a statuesque young woman with the face and figure of a goddess.

At twenty-one, he had been far more experienced than most men his age, and lusting after a girl of seventeen—a girl who had once been his only friend—had seemed wrong. But he hadn't been able to control his reaction to her then any more than he had today.

He cursed. If it hadn't been for the footman's welltimed interruption five minutes ago things would have gone a great deal further.

The second his lips had tasted her warm, fragrant flesh, and he'd heard her breath catch and felt her shudder of response, instinct had taken over—as it always did with Issy. His mouth had closed over her breast and he'd revelled in the feel of her nipple swelling and hardening under his tongue.

He blew out a breath and adjusted his trousers.

But Issy had changed. She wasn't the sweet, passionate teenager who had once adored him, but a vibrant, self-aware and stunningly beautiful young woman—who detested him.

Gio placed the brandy glass back on the tray, frustrated by the strange little jolt in his chest. He pressed the heel of his hand against his breastbone. He didn't care what she thought of him. Why should he?

Women tended to overreact about this stuff. Look at most of the women he'd dated.

He always made it crystal-clear he was only interested in recreational sex and lively companionship but they never believed him. And recently the triple whammy of career success, reaching his thirties and inheriting a dukedom had only made them harder to convince.

Angry words had never bothered him before when the inevitable breakup occurred. So why had Issy's?

Gio frowned and pushed the hair off his brow.

Why was he even surprised by his odd reaction? Nothing made sense where Issy was concerned, for the simple reason that he stopped thinking altogether whenever she was around. He was probably lucky the sudden rush of blood from his head hadn't left him with permanent brain damage.

Gio brought his feet off the table and rested his elbows on his knees. He poured himself a glass of the iced water and gulped it down. Much more concerning was his idiot behaviour this afternoon.

He'd decided at an early age never to be controlled

by his lust or his emotions—yet he'd been controlled by both as soon as he'd spotted Issy downstairs.

But then, this wasn't the first time Issy had torpedoed his self-control.

Images swirled of Issy at seventeen, her eyes brimming with adulation, her beautiful body gilded by moonlight, the scent of fresh earth and young lust in the air.

She'd caught him in a moment of weakness ten years ago, but he still didn't understand why he'd given in to her innocent attempts to seduce him. The way things had ended had been messy and unnecessary—and he had to take the lion's share of the blame.

He rolled the chilled glass across his forehead. Damn Issy Helligan. At seventeen she had been irresistible. How could she be even more so now?

Standing, he crossed to the window and peered out at the tourists and office workers jostling for space on the pavement below.

Why was he even worrying about this? He would never see Issy again. He'd offered her money, and she'd declined. End of story.

But then his gaze caught on a familiar shock of red curls weaving through the crowd. With her raincoat barely covering her bottom, and those ludicrous boots riding halfway up her thighs, she stood out like a beacon.

As he studied her, striding away disguised as a high-class hooker, a picture formed of Issy ten years ago, with the vivid blue of her eyes shining with innocence and hope and a terminal case of hero-worship. He heard the echo of her voice, telling him she would love him forever.

And the jolt punched him in the chest again.

* * *

'Iss, I've got dreadful news.'

Issy glanced over as her admin assistant Maxi put down the phone, peering over the teetering pile of papers on her desk. Maxi's small pixie-like face had gone chalk white.

'What is it?' Issy asked, her heart sinking. Had one of the company broken a leg or something equally catastrophic? Maxi was exceptionally calm and steady. Panicking was Issy's forte.

Issy steeled herself for very bad news. But, really, how much worse could it get?

After her aborted singergram a week ago, the singing telegram business had dried up completely. The three grants they'd applied for had been awarded elsewhere, and all her sponsorship requests had come back negative. She'd spent the week frantically cold-calling a new list of potential but even less likely donors, while also arranging the schedule for a season of plays that would probably never go into production. And the boiler had sprung another leak. Not a problem in the height of summer, but come autumn it would be another major expenditure they couldn't afford. Assuming they still had a theatre to heat.

'That was the bank manager,' Maxi muttered.

Issy's heart sank to her toes. Okay, that was worse.

'He's demanding payment of the interest in ten working days. If we don't find the thirty thousand to cover the payments we've missed, he's calling in the bailiffs.'

'What the—?' Issy shouted.

Seeing Maxi flinch, she held on to the swear word

that wanted to fly out of her mouth and deafen the whole of Islington.

'That toerag,' she sneered. 'But we *paid* something. Not the full amount, I know, but something.' Her fingers clenched so tightly on her pen she felt as if she were fighting off rigor mortis. 'He can't do that.'

'Apparently he can,' Maxi replied, her voice despondent. 'Our last payment was so low it amounts to defaulting on the loan. Technically.' She huffed. 'Toerag is right.'

'Remind me not to send Mr Toerag any more complimentary tickets,' Issy replied, trying to put some of her usual spirit into the put-down. But her heart wasn't in it, her anger having deflated like a burst party balloon.

This wasn't the banker manager's fault. Not really. The theatre had been skirting the edge of a precipice for months; all he'd done was give it the final nudge into the abyss.

Issy crossed to the office's single dust-covered window and stared at the back alley below, which looked even grottier than usual this morning.

Maybe a broken leg wouldn't have been so bad. Three weeks laid up in bed on a morphine drip with excruciating pain shooting through her entire body couldn't make her feel any worse than she did at this moment.

She'd failed. Utterly and completely. How was she going to break the news to everyone? To Dave their principal director, to Terri and Steve and the rest of their regular crew of actors and technicians, not to mention all the ushers and front-of-house staff? They'd worked so hard over the years, many of them offering their time and talent for free, to make this place work, to make it a success.

They'd have to stop all the outreach projects too, with the local schools and the church youth group, and the pensioners' drop-in centre.

She pressed her teeth into her bottom lip to stop it trembling.

'Is this finally it, then?'

Issy turned at the murmured question to see a suspicious sheen in her assistant's eyes.

'Are we going to have to tell Dave and the troops?' Maxi asked carefully. 'They'll be devastated. They've worked so hard. We all have.'

'No. Not yet.' Issy scrubbed her hands down her face, forced the lump back down her throat.

Stop being such a wimp.

The Crown and Feathers Theatre wasn't going dark. Not on her watch. Not until the fat lady was singing. And until Issy Helligan admitted defeat the fat lady could keep her big mouth shut.

'Let's keep it quiet for a bit longer.' No point in telling anyone how bad things were until she absolutely had to. Which would be when the bailiffs arrived and started carting away crucial parts of the stage. 'There must be some avenue we haven't explored yet.'

Think, woman, think.

They had two whole weeks. There had to be something they could do.

'I can't think of any,' Maxi said. 'We've both been racking our brains for months over this. If there's an avenue we haven't tried, it's probably a dead end.' Maxi gave a hollow laugh. 'I even had a dream last night about us begging Prince Charles to become our patron.'

'What did he say?' Issy asked absently, eager to be distracted. Her head was starting to hurt.

'I woke up before he gave me an answer,' Maxi said dejectedly, giving a heartfelt sigh. 'If only we knew someone who was loaded and had a passion for the dramatic arts. All our problems would be over.'

Issy swallowed heavily, Maxi's words reminding her of someone she'd been trying extra hard to forget in the past seven days.

Not that. Anything but that.

She sat back down in her chair with an audible plop.

'What's the matter?' Maxi asked, sounding concerned. 'You've gone white as a sheet.'

'I do know someone. He's a duke.'

'A duke!' Maxi bounced up. 'You're friends with a duke, and we haven't approached him for sponsorship yet?' She waved the comment away as she rushed to Issy's desk, her eyes bright with newfound hope. 'Does he have a passion for theatre?'

'Not that I know of.' And they weren't exactly friends either.

Heat rose up her neck and her nipples pebbled painfully as the memory she'd been trying to suppress for a week burst back to life.

No, they definitely weren't friends.

'But he is loaded,' she added, not wanting to extinguish the excitement in Maxi's gaze.

Or she assumed Gio was loaded. She had absolutely no idea what he did for a living, or even if he did anything. But he was a duke. And he kept a room at the swanky gentlemen's club. And hadn't he said something about renovating Hamilton Hall? Surely it made sense to assume he must be loaded?

Issy crossed her arms over her chest as her breasts began to throb. Something they'd been doing on a regular basis for days, every time she thought about Gio and his hot, insistent lips… She shook her head. Those thoughts had been coming a lot thicker and faster than she wanted to admit. And not just those thoughts, but other ones—which involved his lips and tongue and teeth and hands on the whole of her naked body, driving her to untold…

Issy squeezed her pulsating breasts harder as all her nerve endings started to tingle.

'When are you going to see him again? Can you contact him today?'

She tensed at Maxi's eager question.

'What's wrong?' Maxi asked, the light leaving her eyes. 'You don't look all that enthusiastic.'

'It's a long shot, Max. At best.'

More than a long shot, if she were being totally honest. She'd told Gio she detested him, for goodness' sake. Like a spoilt child. And, while it had given her some satisfaction at the time, and she doubted he cared *what* she thought of him, it wasn't going to make begging him for money any easier.

Maxi cocked her head to one side, looking concerned. 'Exactly how well do you know this duke? Because you've gone bright red…'

'Well enough.' Maybe too well.

She needed a strategy before she saw Gio again. A foolproof strategy. If she was going to have any hope of winning a stay of execution for the theatre—and keeping even a small part of her dignity intact.

Issy felt as if she'd travelled back in time as she stepped off the train at the tiny Hampshire station of Hamilton's

Cross and walked down the platform. It was a journey she'd done dozens of times during her childhood and adolescence when her widowed mother Edie had been housekeeper at the Hall.

Seeing her reflection in the glass door of the ticket office—which never seemed to be open then and wasn't now—Issy congratulated herself on how much her appearance had changed from that dumpy schoolgirl with the fire-engine red hair. The chic emerald silk dress with matching pumps, accented with her favourite chunky necklace and designer sunglasses, looked a good deal more sophisticated than the ill-fitting school uniform, for starters. Teased into a waterfall of corkscrew curls instead of the unruly fuzzball of her childhood, even her vivid red hair now looked more Rita Hayworth than Little Orphan Annie.

The thought gave her a confidence boost as she headed for the newspaper booth which doubled as a mini-cab office. A boost she desperately needed after spending half the night struggling to figure out a workable strategy for her meeting with Gio.

If only she hadn't told him she detested him!

Unfortunately the strategy she'd settled on—to be businesslike and efficient and not lose her cool—seemed disappointingly vague and far from foolproof as zero hour approached.

She tucked the stray curls behind her ear and gripped the shoulder strap on her satchel-style briefcase. Full of paperwork about the theatre—including details of the loans, financial projections, the stunning reviews from their summer season and her plans for next season—the briefcase put the finishing touch on her smart, savvy career-woman act.

Not that it was an act, *per se*, she corrected. She *was* smart and savvy and a career woman—of sorts. Unfortunately she was also a nervous wreck—after a sleepless night spent contemplating all the things that could go wrong today.

Having discarded the idea of informing Gio of her visit beforehand—fairly certain he would refuse to see her—she had surprise on her side. But from what she'd learned about Gio after scouring the internet for information, surprise was about all she had.

The startling revelation that Gio was now a world-renowned architect, with a reputation for striking and innovative designs and a practice which was one of the most sought-after in Europe, hadn't helped with her nervous breakdown one bit.

Okay, Gio was definitely rich. That had to be a plus, given the reason why she was here. But the discovery that the wild, reckless boy she had idolised had made such a staggering success of his life had brought with it a strange poignancy which didn't bode well for their meeting.

And that was without factoring in the way her body had responded to him a week ago. Which, try as she might, she still hadn't been able to forget.

She was here for one reason and one reason only, and she was not going to lose sight of that fact. No matter what. Or the theatre's last hope would be dashed for good.

She had to stick to her plan. She would promote the theatre and do her absolute utmost to persuade Gio that investing in a sponsorship would give his company added profile in the British marketplace. If all else failed she'd remind him that he had offered her financial help. But under no circumstances would she let their history—or her hormones—sway her from her goal. No matter what the provocation—or the temptation.

'Good Lord, is that you, Issy Helligan? Haven't you grown up!'

Issy beamed a smile at the short, balding man sitting in the mini-cab cubicle. 'Frank, you're still here!' she said, delighted to see a familiar face.

'That I am,' the elderly man said bashfully, as his bald patch went a mottled red. 'How's your mother these days? Still living in Cornwall?'

'That's right, she loves it there,' Issy replied, grateful for the distraction.

'Awful shame about the Duke's passing last summer,' Frank continued, his smile dying. 'Son's back you know. Doing up the Hall. Although he never saw fit to come to the funeral. 'Spect your mother told you that?'

Edie hadn't, because her mother knew better than to talk to her about Gio after that fateful summer.

But the news that Gio hadn't bothered to attend his own father's funeral didn't surprise Issy. He and his father had always had a miserably dysfunctional relationship, evidenced by the heated arguments and chilly silences she and her mother had witnessed during the summers Gio spent at the Hall.

She'd once romanticised Gio's troubled teenage years, casting him as a misunderstood bad boy, torn between two parents who hated each other's guts and used their only child as a battering ram. She'd stopped romanticising Gio's behaviour a decade ago. And she had no desire to remember that surly, unhappy boy now.

It might make her underestimate the man he had become.

'Actually, I don't suppose you know whether Gio's at the Hall today? I came to pay him a visit.'

According to the articles she'd read, Gio lived in Italy, but his office in Florence had told her he was in England. So she'd taken a chance he might be at the Hall.

'Oh, aye—yes, he's here,' said Frank, making Issy's pulse skitter. 'Came in yesterday evening by helicopter, no less—or so Milly at the post office says. I took the council planners over to the Hall for a meeting an hour ago.'

'Could I get a lift too?' she said quickly, before she lost her nerve.

Frank grinned and grabbed his car keys. 'That's what I'm here for.'

He bolted the booth and directed her to the battered taxi-cab parked out front.

'I'll put your journey out on the house, for old times' sake,' he said cheerfully as he opened the door.

Issy tensed as she settled in the back seat.

No way was she going to think about old times. Especially her old times with Gio.

She snapped the seat belt on, determined to wipe every last one of those memories from her consciousness.

But as the car accelerated away from the kerb, and the familiar hedgerows and grass verges sped past on the twenty-minute drive to the Hall, the old times came flooding back regardless.

CHAPTER THREE

Ten Years Earlier

'I CAN'T believe you're really going to do it tonight. What if your mum finds out?'

'Shh, Melly,' Issy hissed as she craned her neck to check on the younger girls sitting at the front of the school bus. 'Keep your voice down.'

As upper sixth-formers, they had the coveted back seat all to themselves, but she didn't want anyone over-hearing the conversation. Especially as she didn't even want to be *having* this conversation.

When she'd told her best friend about her secret plan to loose her virginity to Giovanni Hamilton two years before, it had been thrilling and exciting. A forbidden topic they could discuss for hours on the long, boring bus ride home every day. And it had had about as much chance of actually happening as Melanie's equally thrilling and exciting and endlessly discussed plan to lose her virginity to Gary Barlow from *Take That*.

Gio had been completely unattainable back then. When she'd been fifteen and he'd been nineteen the four years between them had seemed like an eternity.

But it hadn't always been that way.

When Issy and her mother had first come to live at the Hall, and Gio had appeared that first summer, the two of them had become fast friends and partners in crime. To a nine-year-old tomboy who was used to spending hours on her own in the Hall's grounds, Gio had been a godsend. A moody, intense thirteen-year-old boy with brown eyes so beautiful they'd made her heart skip, a fascinating command of swear words in both English and Italian, and a quick, creative mind with a talent for thinking up forbidden adventures, Gio had been more captivating than a character from one of Issy's adventure books.

Best of all, Gio had needed her as much as she'd needed him. Issy had seen the sadness in his eyes when his father shouted at him—which seemed to be all the time—and it had made her stomach hurt. But she'd discovered that if she chatted to him, if she made him laugh, she could take the sad look away.

At fifteen, though, when she'd first formulated her plan to lose her virginity to him, her childhood friendship with Gio had slipped into awkward adolescent yearning.

She'd been gawky and spotty, with a figure her mum had insisted on calling 'womanly' but Issy thought was just plain fat, while Gio had been tall, tanned and gorgeous. A modern-day Heathcliff, with the looks of a Roman god and a wildness about him that drew every female within a twenty-mile radius like a magnet.

At nineteen, Gio already had a formidable reputation with women. And one night that summer Issy had seen the evidence for herself.

Creeping down to get a glass of water, she'd heard

moaning coming from the darkened dining room. Getting as close as she could without being spotted, she had watched, transfixed, as Gio's lean, fully-clothed body towered over a mostly naked woman lying on her back on the Duke's oak table. It had taken Issy a moment to recognise the writhing female as Maya Carrington, a thirty-something divorcée who had arrived for the Duke's weekend house party that afternoon.

Issy hadn't been able to look away as Gio's long, tanned fingers unclipped the front hook of Maya's black lace push-up bra, then moulded her full breasts. Issy had blushed to the roots of her hair at the socialite's soft sobs as Gio traced a line with his tongue over her prominent nipples, then nipped at them with his teeth as his hand disappeared between Maya's thighs.

Issy had dashed back to bed, her glass of water sloshing all over the stairs with her palm pressed against her pyjama bottoms to ease the brutal ache between her legs as her ragged breathing made her heart race.

She'd dreamt about Gio doing the same thing to her that night and for many nights afterwards, always waking up soaked in sweat, her breasts heavy and tender to the touch, her nipples rigid and that same cruel ache between her legs.

But Gio had never stopped treating her like a child. During that last visit two years ago, when he'd paid so much attention to Maya, he'd barely even spoken to her.

Then, the day before, something magical had happened.

He'd appeared at the school gates on his motorbike, looking surly and tense, and told her the school bus had been cancelled and her mother had asked him to give her a lift home. She hadn't seen Gio in two long years, and the feel of his muscled back pressing into her budding breasts had sent her senses into a blur of rioting hormones. She'd spent today reliving the experience in minute detail for her starstruck classmates, but in reality she'd had to make most of it up, because she'd been so excited she could barely remember a thing.

And then this morning she'd caught him looking at her while he was having breakfast with her and her mother, and just for a second she'd seen the same awareness in those turbulent brown eyes that she had always had in her heart.

She didn't have a schoolgirl crush on Gio. She loved him. Deeply and completely. And not just because of his exotic male beauty and the fact that all the other girls fancied him too. But because she knew things about him that no one else knew. Unfortunately, her attempts to flirt with him that morning had been ignored.

It was past time to take matters into her own hands.

What if Gio didn't come back again for another two years? She'd be an old woman of nineteen by then, and he might have got married or something. Tonight she would make him notice her. She would go to his room and get him to do what he'd been doing to Maya Carrington two years ago. Except this time it would be a thousand times more special, because she loved him and Maya hadn't.

But the last thing she'd wanted to do was discuss her plans with Melanie. It made Issy feel sneaky and juvenile and dishonest. As if she was tricking Gio. When she really wasn't. She should never have mentioned the motorcycle ride. Because Melly had latched on to the information, put two and two together and unfortunately made four. And now she wouldn't let the topic drop.

'What will your mum say?' Melanie asked in a stage whisper.

'Nothing. She's not going to find out,' she whispered back, pushing aside the little spurt of guilt.

Up till now she'd told her mother everything. Because it had been just the two of them for so long Edie had been a confidante and a friend, as well as her mum. But when Issy had tried to bring up the subject of Gio as casually as possible after breakfast her mother had been surprisingly stern with her.

'Don't hassle him. He has more than enough to deal with,' Edie had said cryptically while she pounded dough. 'I saw you flirting with him. And, while I understand the lure of someone as dashing and dangerous as Gio Hamilton, I don't want to see you get hurt when he turns you down.'

The comment had made Issy feel as if she were ten years old again—sheltered and patronised and excluded from all the conversations that mattered—and still trailing after Gio like a lovesick puppy dog.

What did Gio have to deal with? Why wouldn't anyone tell her? And what made her mum so sure he would turn her down? She wanted to help him. To be *there* for him. And she wanted to know what it felt like to be kissed by a man who knew how, instead of the awkward boys she'd kissed before.

But everyone treated her as if she was too young and didn't know her own mind. When she wasn't. And she did.

She'd wanted to tell her mum that, but had decided not to. Edie had looked so troubled when they'd both heard the shouting match between Gio and his father the night before, coming through the air vent from the library.

'Do you have protection?' Melanie continued, still talking in the stupid stage whisper.

'Yes.' She'd bought the condoms months ago, just in case Gio visited this summer, and had gone all the way to Middleton to get them, so Mrs Green the pharmacist in Hamilton's Cross wouldn't tell her mum.

'Aren't you worried that it'll hurt? Jenny Merrin said it hurt like mad when she did it with Johnny Baxter, and I bet Gio's…' Melanie paused for effect. 'You know…is twice the size. Look how tall he is.'

'No, of course not,' she said, starting to get annoyed.

Yes, it would probably hurt a bit, she knew that, but she wasn't a coward. And if you loved someone you didn't worry about how big their 'you know what' was. She'd read in *Cosmo* only last week that size didn't matter.

The bus took the turning into the Hall's drive and she breathed a sigh of relief. She wanted to get home. There was so much to do before dinnertime. She needed to have a bath and wash her hair, wax her legs, do her nails, try on the three different outfits she had shortlisted for tonight one last time. This was going to be the most important night of her life, and she wanted to look the part. To prove to Gio she wasn't a babyish tomboy any more, or a gawky, overweight teenager.

She felt the now constant ache between her legs and the tight ball of emotion in her throat and knew she was doing the right thing.

As the bus driver braked, she leapt up. But Melanie grabbed her wrist.

'I'm so jealous of you,' Melanie said, her eyes

shining with sincerity. 'He's so dishy. I hope it doesn't hurt too much.'

'It won't,' Issy said.

Gio wouldn't hurt her—not intentionally—of that much she was certain.

So much had changed in the last few years, but not that. Before she'd fallen in love with him he'd been like a big brother to her. Teasing her and letting her follow him around. Listening to her talk about the father she barely remembered and telling her she shouldn't care if she didn't have a dad. That fathers were a pain any way. Things had been difficult, tense between her and Gio since she'd grown up—partly because they weren't little kids anymore, but mostly because he'd become so distant.

His relationship with his father had got so bad he hardly ever came to visit the Hall any more, and when she did see him now his brooding intensity had become like a shield, demanding that everyone—even her—keep out.

But tonight she would be able to get him back again. That moody, magnetic boy would be her friend again, but more than that he'd be her lover, and he'd know he could tell her anything. And everything would be wonderful.

Issy crept through the darkness. Feeling her way past the kitchen garden wall, she pushed the gate into the orchard. And eased out the breath she'd been holding when the hinge barely creaked. She sucked in air scented with ripe apples and the faint tinge of tobacco.

Kicking off her shoes, she stepped off the path onto the dewy grass. It would ruin the effect slightly, but she didn't want to trip over a root in her heels. After waiting for nearly three hours for Gio to come home she was nervous enough already, falling on her face would not be the way to go.

She pressed the flat of her hand to her stomach and felt the butterfly flutter of panic and excitement. Squinting into the shadows, she saw the red glow of a cigarette tip and her heart punched her ribcage. He'd always come to the orchard before whenever he argued with his father. She'd known he would be here.

'Gio?' she called softly, tiptoeing towards the silent shape hidden beneath a tree burdened with summer fruit.

The red glow disappeared as he stamped the cigarette out.

'What do you want?' He sounded edgy, dismissive. She ignored the tightening in her chest. He was upset. He didn't mean to be cruel.

She didn't know what his father and he had been shouting about this time, but she knew it had been bad— worse than the night before.

'Is everything all right? I heard you and the Duke—'

'Great,' he interrupted. 'Everything's great. Now, go away.'

As she stepped beneath the canopy of leaves her eyes adjusted to the lack of light and she could make out his features. The chiselled cheekbones shadowed with stubble, the dark brows, the strong chin and jawline. He stood with his back propped against the tree trunk, his arms crossed and his head bent. The pose might have been casual but for the tension that crackled in the air around him.

'No, I won't go away,' she said, surprised by the forcefulness in her voice. 'Everything's not great.'

His head lifted and the hairs on her nape prickled.

She could feel his eyes on her, even though she couldn't make out his expression, could smell his distinctive male scent, that heady mix of soap and musk.

'I mean it, Iss,' he said, the low tone brittle. 'Go away. I'm not in the mood.'

She stepped closer, feeling as if she were encroaching on a wild animal. 'I'm not going anywhere,' she said, her voice trembling but determined. 'What did he say, Gio? Why are you so upset?'

She placed a palm on his cheek, and he jerked back.

'Don't touch me.' The words were rough, but beneath it she could hear panic.

'Why not? I want to touch you.'

'Yeah?' The snarl was wild, uncontrolled. But before she could register the shock he grabbed a fistful of the silk at her waist and hauled her against him.

Her breath gushed out, adrenaline coursing through her body as he held her hips. She could feel every inch of him. The thick ridge of something rubbed against the juncture of her thighs, and she squirmed instinctively.

He swore. Then his mouth crushed hers. The faint taste of tobacco made all the more intoxicating by heat and demand.

He cradled her head, held her steady as his tongue plunged. She gasped, her fingers fisting in the soft cotton of his T-shirt as she clung on. She opened her mouth wider, surrendered to a rush of arousal so new, so thrilling, it made her head spin.

He lurched back, held her at arm's length. 'What the hell are you doing?'

'Kissing you back,' she said, confused by the accusatory tone.

Why had he stopped? When it had felt so good?

'Well, don't,' he said, his voice sharp. His fingers released her and he crossed his arms back over his chest.

'Why not?' she cried. She wanted him to carry on kissing her, to keep kissing her forever.

'Issy, go away.' The anger sounded almost weary now. 'You don't know what you're doing. I'm not some kid you can practise your kissing technique on. And I don't take little girls to bed.'

'I'm not a little girl. I'm a woman, with a woman's desires,' she added, hoping the line she'd read in one of her romance novels didn't sound too cheesy.

'Yeah, right.' Her confidence deflated at the doubtful tone. 'How old *are* you?'

'I'm nearly eighteen,' she said with bravado. Or rather she would be in six months' time. 'And I do know what I'm doing.' Or at least she was trying her best to know. Surely he could teach her the rest?

The silence seemed to spread out between them, the only noise the pummelling of her own heartbeat and the hushed sound of their breathing.

He reached out and traced his thumb down her cheek. 'For God's sake, Issy, don't tempt me,' he murmured. 'Not unless you're sure.'

'I am sure. I have been for a long time,' she replied. He needed her. She hadn't imagined it. The thought was so thrilling she locked her knees to stay upright.

He cradled her cheek. She leant into his palm.

'I want you, Gio,' she whispered, covering his hand with hers. 'Don't you want me?'

It was the hardest question she'd ever had to ask. If he said no now she would be devastated. She caught her breath and held it.

He pushed his fingers into her hair, rubbed his thumb against the strands. 'Yeah, I want you, Isadora. Too damn much.'

Her breath released in a rush as he pulled her close and his lips slanted across hers. The kiss was sensual, seeking this time, his tongue tracing the contours of her mouth with a tenderness and care that had her shuddering.

He leaned back. 'Are you sure you know what you're doing?' he said, searching her face, his hands framing her cheeks. 'I don't want to hurt you.'

'You won't hurt me. You couldn't.'

Dropping his hands, he linked his fingers through hers. 'Let's take this inside.'

Nervous anticipation made her stumble as he led her through the moonlit gardens and the gloomy shadows of the house's back staircase, his strides long and assured and full of purpose. She took the stairs two at a time, the first tremors of doubt making her legs shake. When he shoved open the door to his room on the second floor her heart beat so hard she was convinced he would hear it too.

He reached to switch on the light and she grasped his wrist.

'Could you leave the light off?' she blurted. She let go of his arm, desperate to disguise the quiver in her voice.

'Why?' he asked.

She scoured her mind for a viable excuse. If he knew how inexperienced she was he might stop, and she couldn't bear that. 'It's…it's more romantic,' she said.

He seemed to study her in the darkness for an eternity before he crossed the room and opened the drapes, letting the moonlight flood in.

'Issy, I don't do permanent,' he said as he came back to her. He brushed a kiss on her forehead. 'You know that, right?'

She nodded, not trusting herself to speak. That would change, she was sure of it, once he had the proof of how much she loved him. She draped her arms over his shoulders, calling on every ounce of her fledgling skills as an actress. She'd told him she wasn't a little girl. It was time to stop behaving like one.

'Yes, I know.' Driving her fingers into the short hair at his nape, she took a deep breath of his scent, revelled in the feel of him as he pressed her back against the door, captured her waist in hot palms.

'Good,' he muttered, as his teeth bit into her earlobe.

She shuddered, letting the delicious shiver race down her spine as his lips feasted on the pulse-point in her neck. The hot, vicious ache at her core throbbed in time with her deafening heartbeat. She reminded herself to breathe as he drew the zipper on her dress down, tugged her arms free. The shimmering silk puddled at her feet. She clung to his neck, the heady thrill making her dizzy as he bent and lifted her easily into his arms.

This was really happening at last. After years of fantasising, her dreams were coming true.

Silvery light gilded his chest as he cast off his T-shirt. He unfastened his belt and she looked away, suddenly overwhelmed. He looked so powerful, so strong, so completely male. The mattress dipped as he joined her on the bed. His hand settled on her midriff, drew her towards him. She felt the heat of his big body, the thick outline prodding her thigh.

His face looked hard, intent in the shadows, as his deft fingers freed her breasts from the confining lace of her bra.

'You're beautiful, Issy' he said, his voice low and strained as one rough fingertip traced over her nipple. 'I want to look at you properly. Let's turn on the light.'

She shook her head, mute with longing and panic. 'Please—I like it dark,' she said, hoping she sounded as if she knew what she was talking about.

'Okay,' he said. 'But next time we do it my way.' Her heart soared at the mention of *next time*, and then he bent his head and captured the pebble-hard nipple in his teeth.

A sob escaped as sensation raw and hot arrowed down to her core. She arched up, bucked under him as he suckled. Damp heat gushed between her thighs.

Her hands fisted in the sheets as she tried to cling to sanity. Tried to stop herself from shattering into a billion pieces.

'Open your legs for me, *bella*.' The urgent whisper penetrated, and her knees relaxed to let his palm cup her core.

Strong fingers probed, stroked, caressed, touching and then retreating. She cried out, begged, until he stayed right at the centre of ecstasy. The wave rose with shocking speed, and then slammed into her with the force and fury of a tsunami.

She struggled to find focus, to claw her way back to consciousness as hot hands held her hips. He loomed above her in the darkness. 'Dammit, Issy, I can't wait. Is that okay?'

She couldn't register his meaning, but nodded as he

fumbled with something in the darkness. Then she felt it—huge, unyielding but soft as velvet, spearing through her swollen flesh. A heavy thrust brought sharp, rending pain. She strained beneath him, a choking sob lodged in her throat.

He stopped, tried to draw out. 'Issy, what the—?'

'Please, don't stop.' She gasped the plea, gripping shoulders tight with bunched muscle. 'It doesn't hurt.' And it didn't. Not any more. The overwhelming pressure, the stretched feeling, had become a pulsing ache, clamouring for release.

He swore, but pressed back in slowly, carefully. Her hands slipped on slick skin, hard sinew, her jagged breathing matching the relentless thrusts. She heard his harsh grunts, her own sobs of release as the tsunami built to another bold crescendo, threatening so much more than before. Her scream of release echoed in her head as the final wave crashed, exploding through her as she hurtled over the top.

'For God's sake, Issy. You were a bloody virgin.'

Her eyelids fluttered open—and the bedside light snapped on, blinding her.

'I know.' She threw her arm up to cover her eyes, registering his temper. What had she done?

Tremors racked her body as afterglow turned neatly to aftershock.

'Shh. Calm down.' The hammer-beats of his heart thudded against her ear as he settled her head on his chest, gathered her close. 'I'm sorry, Iss. Stop shaking.' He brushed the locks from her brow. 'Are you okay? Did I hurt you?'

She opened her eyes. The soft light illuminated his features clearly. Love swept through her, more intense, more real than ever before as she saw the worry, the concern.

A smile spread as euphoria leaped in her chest. 'Yes, I'm okay.' She snuggled into his embrace and sighed. Despite the soreness between her legs, she'd never felt more complete, more wonderful in her life. 'I never dreamed it could be that amazing.'

He shifted back. Holding her chin, he lifted her face. 'Wait a minute. I asked you.' His eyes narrowed. 'Why didn't you tell me the truth?'

'I don't…I don't understand,' she stammered, chilling as he took his arm from around her and sat up.

Whipping back the sheet, he turned his back to her and stood up. As he paced across the room, the sight of his naked body had the heat between her thighs sizzling back to life. But then she noticed the sharp, irritated movements as he yanked on his jeans, pulled on the T-shirt.

'Is something wrong?' she asked, her pulse stuttering. She clasped the sheet to her chest. This wasn't right. This wasn't how it was supposed to be. This was the moment when they were supposed to declare their undying love for each other.

He twisted round, sent her a look that had colour rising in her cheeks.

'I asked you if you were a virgin.' The harsh tone made her flinch. 'Why did you lie?'

'I…' Had he asked? She gave her head a quick shake. 'I don't…I didn't mean to lie.'

'Sure you did.' He flung the words over his shoulder as he grabbed a bag from the closet, swept the few personal items on top of the dresser into it. He ripped open the top drawer, scooped out his clothes, shoved them in too. The tense movements radiated controlled anger.

Tears stung her eyes, swelled in her throat. 'Please, Gio, I don't understand. What are you doing?'

'I'm leaving. What does it look like?' He slashed the zipper closed.

Facing her at last, he slung the holdall over his shoulder. 'I'm sorry if I hurt you. I should have stopped once I realised what was going on. But I couldn't. And that's on me. But whatever game you were playing, it's over now.'

'It's not a game.' She clung to the sheet, kneeled on the mattress, desperate to hold on to her dream. This was a silly misunderstanding. He loved her. He needed her. She needed him. Hadn't they proved that together?

'I love you Gio. I've always loved you. I always will. We were meant to be together.'

He went completely still, and then his eyebrow rose in cynical enquiry. 'Are you nuts? Grow up, for heaven's sake.'

The cruel words made her shrink inside herself. She sank back, her body quaking as she watched him stamp on his boots and walk to the door.

He couldn't be leaving. Not now, not like this, not after everything they'd just done.

'Don't go, Gio. You have to stay.'

He turned, his hand on the door handle. She braced herself for another shot. But instead of anger she saw regret.

'There's nothing for me here.' His voice sounded

hollow, but the bitterness in the words still made the agonising pain a thousands times worse. 'There never was.'

A single jerking sob caught in her throat and the tears streamed down her cheeks.

'Don't cry, Issy. Believe me, it's not worth it. When you figure that out, you'll thank me for this.'

CHAPTER FOUR

The Present

Issy released her fingers to ease their death grip on the handle of her briefcase.

How could every damn detail of that night still be so vivid?

Not just the anguish and the pain, but the euphoria and the hope too—even the intense pleasure of their lovemaking. How many times had she played it over in her head in the months and years that had followed? Hundreds? Thousands?

Way too many times, that was for sure.

She forced herself to ignore the pressure in her chest at the thought of Gio's parting words that night. They couldn't hurt her. Not any more. All her tears had dried up a long time ago.

Gio had been right about one thing. She should thank him. He'd taught her an important lesson. Never open your heart to someone until you're positive they're the prince and not the frog. And don't be fooled by fancy packaging.

'Nearly there,' Frank called cheerfully from the front

seat. 'Wait till you see what the lad's done with the place. Amazing, it is. Must have cost a fortune by my reckoning.'

Issy drew a deep breath, eased it out through her teeth. No more ancient history. She had enough of a mountain to climb just concentrating on the here and now.

She glanced out of the window. Only to have her fingers tighten on the briefcase again.

Amazing wasn't the word. More like awe-inspiring, Issy thought as she stepped out of the cab onto the newly pebbled driveway and gaped at the magnificent Georgian frontage of her former home. Gio hadn't just restored the Hall, he'd improved upon it. The place looked magnificent. The bright sand-blasted stone gleamed in the sunshine. The columns at the front of the house had always looked forbidding to her as a child, but a terrace had been added which gave the house a welcoming Mediterranean feel.

Having failed to persuade Frank to take a fare for the journey, she bade him goodbye.

As the cab pulled away, she gazed up at the Hall. Why did Gio's transformation of the place make her feel even more daunted?

She adjusted the strap of her briefcase and slung it over her shoulder.

Don't be silly. Remember, this isn't about you, or Gio, or the Hall. It's about the theatre—and shutting the fat lady up long enough to see out another season. Absolutely no more trips down memory lane allowed. The past is dead, and it needs to stay that way.

'Hey, can I help you?'

She glanced round to see a young man strolling towards her. Her fingers locked on the strap.

Curtain up.

'Hi, my name's Isadora Helligan.' She thrust out her hand as he approached. 'I'm here to see Giovanni Hamilton.'

Stopping in front of her, he ran his fingers through his sandy-blond hair and sent her a quizzical smile. 'Hi, Jack Bradshaw.' He took her hand and gave it a hearty shake. 'I'm Gio's PA.' He put his hand back in his pocket. 'I'm sorry, I keep Gio's diary, but…' He paused, looking a little perplexed. 'Do you have an appointment?'

Not quite.

'Yes,' she lied smoothly. 'Gio made it himself a week ago. He must have forgotten to tell you.'

If Gio was going to kick her out, he would have to do it personally.

'No problem,' Jack replied. 'It won't be the first time. Creative geniuses rarely pay attention to the little details.' He extended his arm towards the Hall. 'He's finishing up with the planners on the pool terrace. Why don't you come through?'

As Jack led the way, Issy found herself too busy gazing at all the changes Gio had made to get any more nervous thinking about what she had to do.

How had he managed to get so much light into the interior of the building? And how come the place looked so spacious and open whereas before it had always seemed poky and austere?

The nerves kicked back in, though, as she stepped out onto the pool terrace and saw Gio. Tall and gorgeous and effortlessly commanding in grey linen trousers and an open-necked shirt, he stood on the other side of the empty pool, chatting with a couple of men in ill-fitting suits who were several inches shorter than him. Almost as if he sensed her standing there, staring at him, he turned his head. She could have sworn she felt the heat of his gaze as it raked over her figure.

Her stomach tensed as an answering heat bloomed in her cheeks.

She watched as he shook hands with the two men and then walked towards her over the newly mown grass. And was immediately thrown back in time to all the times she'd watched him in the past.

She'd always adored the way Gio moved, with that relaxed, languid, confident stride, as if he was completely comfortable in his own skin. He'd always been the sort of man to turn heads, even as a teenager, but age had added an air of dominance to that dangerous sex appeal. Unfortunately, the full package was even more devastating now. Tanned Mediterranean skin, the muscular, broad-shouldered physique and slim hips, that sharply handsome face and his rich chestnut-brown hair which had once been long enough to tie in a ponytail—to annoy his father she suspected—but was now cut short and fell in careless waves across his brow.

Was it any surprise she'd idolised him once—and mistaken him for the prince? Thank God she didn't idolise him any more. Unfortunately, the assertion didn't seem to be doing a thing for the heat cascading through her as he took his own sweet time strolling towards her.

Her heartbeat spiked, her nerve endings tingled and adrenaline pumped through her veins. She fidgeted with the bag's strap, trying to bring her breathing back under control.

Good grief, what on earth was happening to her? Had the extreme stress of the last few months turned her into a nymphomaniac?

Her knees wobbled ever so slightly as he drew level, a sensual, knowing smile tilting his lips.

'This is a surprise, Isadora,' he said, pronouncing her full name with the tiniest hint of Italy. 'You're looking a lot more...' His gaze flicked down her frame. Her knees wobbled some more. 'Sophisticated today.'

'Hello, Gio,' she said, being as businesslike as she could with her nipples thrusting against the front of her blouse like bullets.

Trust Gio to remind her of their last meeting. No way was he going to make this easy for her. But then she hadn't expected easy.

'I'm sorry to arrive unannounced,' she said, looking as meek as she could possibly manage. 'But I have something important I wanted to discuss with you.'

His gaze drifted to her chest. 'Really?'

She crossed her arms over her chest to cover her inappropriate reaction. Why hadn't she worn a padded bra? 'Yes, really,' she said, a little too curtly. 'Do you mind if we discuss it in private?'

If he was going to humiliate her, she'd rather not have an audience. Several of his employees were already staring at them from the other side of the pool.

'There are workmen all over the house,' he said calmly, but the challenge in his eyes was unmistakable as they fixed on her face. 'The only place we'll be able to have any privacy is in my bedroom.'

What? No way.

Her mind lurched back as the memories she'd been busy suppressing shot her blood pressure straight into the danger zone. But then she noticed the cynical curve of his lips and knew it wasn't a genuine invitation. He expected her to decline. Because he thought she couldn't handle the past, couldn't handle him.

Think again, Buster.

'That'd be great,' she said, even though her throat was now drier than the Gobi Desert. 'If you're sure you don't mind?' she added with a hint of defiance.

'Not at all,' he replied, not sounding as surprised as she'd hoped. He lifted his arm. 'I believe you know the way,' he said, every inch the amenable, impersonal host.

Blast him.

They climbed the back staircase without a word. His silent, indomitable presence starting to rattle her. How could he be so relaxed, so unmoved?

She cut the thought off. Of course he could be. What had happened in his bedroom all those years ago had never meant a thing to him. She pushed the residual flicker of hurt away, clinging to being businesslike and efficient. If he could be, so could she.

But even as the rallying cry sounded in her head he opened his bedroom door, and she had to brace herself against the painful memories. She caught his scent, that dizzying combination of soap and man, more potent this time without the masking hint of tobacco, as he held the door for her to walk in ahead of him.

Colour flooded up her neck as she stepped into the room where he had once stolen her innocence. And destroyed her dreams.

The walls were painted utilitarian white now, the bed a brand-new teak frame draped with pale blue linen, but the memories were all still there, as vivid and disturbing as yesterday. She could see herself kneeling on the bed, the sheet clutched to her chest, her heart shattering.

'So what exactly is it that's so important?'

She whirled round to see him leaning against the door, his arms folded over his chest, his expression indifferent. She held the briefcase in front of her, tried to control the rush of emotions. He was goading her deliberately. She had no idea why, but she wasn't going to let it mean anything.

'You offered me money. A week ago.'

His brows arrowed up. Seemed she'd surprised him at last.

'I wanted to know if the offer's still open,' she added.

'You came here to ask me for money?'

She heard the brittle edge and took a perverse pleasure in it. Good to know she could rattle him too.

'That's correct.'

'Well, now,' he said, pushing away from the door and strolling towards her. 'So what happened to the woman who has principles and wouldn't dare lower herself to take anything from me?'

He stopped in front of her, standing so close she could feel the heat of his body.

'It *was* you who said that? Wasn't it?'

'I apologise for that.' She lifted her chin to meet his gaze, refusing to take a step back. She knew perfectly well he was trying to intimidate her. She should never have said those stupid things, but he had provoked her. 'But I didn't think you cared what I thought,' she finished, knowing perfectly well her comments hadn't bothered him in the slightest.

He ran a finger down her cheek and she stiffened, shocking desire coiling in her gut at the unexpected touch.

'You'd be surprised what I care about,' he murmured.

She stepped back. Forced into retreat after all. How was he still able to fan the flames so easily?

'I should go,' she said hastily, her courage suddenly deserting her.

What on earth had possessed her to come here? He would never give her the money. All she'd done was humiliate herself for no reason.

But as she tried to step around him and make a dash for the door he grasped her upper arm.

'So it wasn't *that* important?' he said, a challenging glint in his eyes.

Spurred on by desperation and an unreasonable panic, her temper snapped. She yanked her arm out of his grasp. This wasn't a game. Not to her anyway. 'It *was* important. Not that you'd ever understand.'

She'd always been willing to fight for what she believed in. He'd never once done that. Because he'd never believed in anything.

He laughed, the sound harsh. 'Why don't you show me, then?' Holding both her arms, he hauled her closer. 'If you want the money so much, what do I get in return?'

'What do you want?' She hurled the words at him, angry, upset, and—God help her—desperately turned on.

His fingers flexed on her arms. 'You know what I want.' His jaw tightened. 'And you want it too. Except you always had to sugar-coat it with all that nonsense about love.'

The barb hit home, but did nothing to quell the flames licking at her core.

'Sex?' She huffed out a contemptuous laugh. Not easy when she was about to spontaneously combust. 'Is that all?' She pressed closer, rubbed provocatively against the thick ridge in his trousers. Past caring about pride, or maturity, or scruples, as temper and desire raged out of control.

He thought she was still the fanciful naïve virgin who expected love and commitment. Well, she wasn't, and she could prove it.

'If that's all you want, why don't you take it?' she goaded, revelling in the rush of power as his eyes darkened. 'You don't have to worry. I won't sugar-coat it a second time.'

His lips crushed hers. He tasted of fury and frustration and demand, his fingers caressing her scalp as he invaded her mouth. She clutched his shoulders and kissed him back, all thoughts of revenge, of vindication, incinerated by the firestorm of need.

He broke away first, only to swing her up in his arms. She fell back on the bed, feeling as if she were careering over Niagara Falls in a barrel—terrified and exhilarated, her body battered by its own sensual overload. He struggled to get the dress over her head, the sibilant hiss of rending fabric drowned out by their laboured breathing. She grasped his shirt, popping buttons, reached for the firm silky flesh beneath as he grappled with her bra, exposing her breasts.

He pushed her back on the pillows, kneeled over her. Unlike that first night, when she'd hidden herself from his sight, she basked in the intoxicating rush of desire as her nipples swelled and hardened under his assessing gaze.

He cupped the heavy orbs, rubbed his thumb over the engorged peaks.

'Dammit, you're even more beautiful than I remember.'

The stunned words touched her somewhere deep inside, but the fanciful emotion was lost as he bent forward and captured a nipple with his teeth. A staggered moan escaped as fire blazed down to her core. Grasping his cheeks, she pushed into his mouth. The rasp of stubble against her soft palms as primal as the crude heat burning at her centre.

She watched spellbound and desperate as he scrambled out of his own clothes. Kicking off his loafers, he wrestled out of the torn shirt, and dropped trousers and briefs in a crumpled heap to the floor.

Where once she'd been afraid to look at him, this time she devoured the dark male beauty of his body. Tanned skin, muscled shoulders, a lean ridged abdomen and powerful flanks all vied for her attention. But then her gaze fixed on the long, thick erection, and the tantalising bead of moisture at its tip. Her breath clogged in her lungs as he climbed onto the bed, caging her in.

Reaching, she closed her fingers around the hard, pulsing flesh. Vicious desire coiled as the magnificent erection leapt in response.

He pulled out of her grasp, deft fingers probing beneath the lace of her panties and finding the slick furnace at her core. Sensation assaulted her as he toyed with the hard nub. She sobbed, hurtling towards that brutal edge, but he withdrew.

Her eyes flew open, her senses straining. 'Don't stop!' she cried.

He laughed, the sound raw, and dragged off the thin swatch of lace, casting it over his shoulder. Leaning forward, he whispered against her ear. 'I'm going to be deep inside you when you come.'

She wanted to make a pithy comeback, but she could barely think let alone speak. All thoughts of caution, of consequences, were lost in the frantic hammer of her heartbeat as he grabbed a foil package from the bedside dresser and rolled on a condom.

He stroked her thighs, held her hips wide. Staring into her eyes, he gripped her bottom and pressed within. She gasped, quivered, stretched unbearably as he eased in up to the hilt.

He was a big man, and the fullness was as overwhelming and shocking now as it had been a decade ago. But this time she didn't panic. She held on, angling her hips as the pleasure intensified, battering her senses as he paused, allowing her to adjust to the brutal penetration.

She tensed, panting, her skin glowing with sweat as he began to move. She tried to hold back, to make it last, her body buffeted by rolling waves of ecstasy, but the rhythmic thrusts drove her towards orgasm at breakneck speed.

'Stay with me, *bella*,' he grunted, the molten chocolate of his eyes locking hot on her face.

But the tight coil exploded in a blast of raw, delirious sensation.

She screamed out her fulfilment as he shouted his own release, and collapsed with her into oblivion.

'I've never come that fast in my life.'

Issy stiffened at the muffled words next to her ear, the hazy afterglow shattering.

He was still buried deep inside her. Still firm, still semi-erect. His large frame anchoring her to the mattress.

She shoved his shoulder, tried to lower her legs— next to impossible with her thighs clasped tight around his hips. 'Let me up. I need to leave.' Now.

He lifted himself off her, and she stifled the groan as her swollen flesh released him with difficulty.

'What's wrong?' he murmured.

Was he joking?

They'd just had sex! Make that wild monkey sex. And they didn't even like each other. She closed her legs, curled away from him, the aching tenderness between her thighs a shameful reminder of the way they'd just ravaged each other.

It wasn't just wrong, it was insane. Forget ten years ago. This now classified as the biggest, most humiliating mistake of her life.

'Absolutely nothing,' she said caustically, the scent of sex suffocating her as she scooted over to the corner of the bed.

She sat up, ready to make a swift getaway, but one strong arm banded round her waist and dragged her back against a solid male chest.

Panic constricted around her throat. 'I really have to leave.'

'Settle down. Why are you in such a rush? You haven't got what you came for yet.'

'I…' She stuttered to a halt, his words slicing through the panic and cutting straight to the shame. 'I didn't…' She stopped, cleared her throat. The conversation they'd had before ripping each other's clothes off replaying in her mind at top volume.

She cringed. She hadn't meant to tell him she'd have sex with him for money, but somehow the desire, the need, the resentment had got all tangled up. And she had. Sort of.

Wild monkey sex had been bad enough, but adding in the money took things to a whole new level of sordid. 'The money wasn't the reason I…' She paused. Tried again to explain the unexplainable. 'I don't expect you to pay…'

His arm tightened. 'I know that, Issy. After what almost happened at the club, sex was inevitable.' He gave a rough chuckle. 'And, frankly, I'm insulted. I don't pay women for sex. Even you.'

She blinked. Furious at the sting of tears. 'Good, I'm glad you understand that,' she said, trying to regain a little dignity while she was stark naked and blushing like a beetroot.

She struggled. He held firm.

'Will you let go?' she demanded.

'What's the big hurry?' he said, his reasonableness starting to irritate her. 'Now we've got the sex out of the way, why shouldn't we talk about the money?'

Because I'd rather die on the spot.

She swung round, astonished at his blasé attitude. Was it really that easy for him to dismiss what they had done? Chalk it up to inevitability and forget about it?

She'd never had sex just to scratch an itch. Not until now anyway. She felt dreadful about it. Didn't he feel even a little bit ashamed about their behaviour?

Apparently not, from the easygoing look on his face.

She gripped the sheet in her fist. 'Yes, well, now we've got the sex out of the way…' How could he reduce everything to the lowest common denominator like that? 'I don't want to discuss anything else.' Because she, at least, had scruples. 'I need to get dressed. I'm getting a chill.'

Which was a blatant lie. She was the opposite of cold. The sun was blazing through the windows, and she could feel something that was still remarkably hard pressing against her bottom.

His hands stroked her tummy through the thin linen sheet, sending a shiver through her that had nothing to do with being chilled either.

'You can get dressed on one condition.' His breath whispered past her ear. 'That you don't run off.'

She nodded, so aroused again she would agree to tap dance naked to get out of his arms. Having to endure a conversation with him was by far the safer option, she decided as she dashed out of the bed.

To her consternation, he made no effort to get dressed himself, but simply relaxed back against the pillows, folded one arm behind his head and watched her. Ignoring him, she raced round the room in a crouch, with one arm banded across her breasts and the other covering what she could of her sex. Unfortunately she soon discovered that left her one crucial hand short to pick her bra and panties off the floor.

'Issy, what exactly are you doing?' Gio's amused voice rumbled from the bed.

She glanced round to find him staring at her, a puzzled smile on his face. 'I'm trying to maintain a little modesty. If that's okay with you,' she snapped.

Something he conspicuously lacked, she thought resentfully. With the sheet slung low on his hips, barely covering the distinctive bulge beneath, he looked as if he were auditioning for a banner ad in *Playgirl*.

'Isn't it a little late for that?' he said casually.

The blush burned as she concentrated on stepping into her knickers and fastening her bra behind her back one-handed.

She glared at him, having finally completed the tricky manoeuvres. 'Yes, I suppose it is. Thank you so much for pointing that out.'

Why did men always have to state the bloody obvious?

She turned away as he chuckled. Scouting around for her dress, she spotted it peeking out from under the bed. She whipped it off the floor and climbed into it, trying not to notice the torn seam caused by his eagerness to get the dress off her.

She then spent several agonising seconds trying to fasten the zip, with her arm twisted behind her back like a circus contortionist.

'Want some help with that?' His deep voice rumbled with amusement.

She huffed and gave in. The sooner she got dressed, the sooner she could get out of here.

She perched on the edge of the bed and presented her back to him. But instead of fastening the zip he swept the heavy curtain of hair over her shoulder and ran the pad of his thumb down the length of her neck.

'That's not helping,' she said, squeezing her thighs together as awareness ricocheted down her spine.

He chuckled as he tugged up the zip. He rested a warm palm on her bare shoulder. 'So how much money do you need?'

The softly asked question had a blast of guilt and despair drowning out her embarrassment.

The theatre!

What was she going to do now? Gio had been her last hope. Admittedly it hadn't been much of a hope, but she couldn't even ask him for the sponsorship now—it would make her look like a total tart, and anyway he wouldn't give it to her. Why should he?

'None,' she said, her mind reeling. How could she have been so reckless and irresponsible? 'Really, it'll be fine,' she murmured, her bottom lip quivering alarmingly

Don't you dare fall to pieces. Not yet.

She'd have to find another way. Somehow.

But as she went to stand he held her wrist. 'Why do I get the feeling you're lying?'

She looked down at the long, tanned fingers encircling her wrist. And suddenly felt like a puppy who had been given a good solid kick in the ribs.

'I'm not lying,' she said, alarmed by the quake in her voice. 'Everything's fine.'

He gripped her chin, forced her eyes to his. 'Issy, if you say everything's fine again I'm going to get seriously annoyed.' He pressed his thumb to her lip. 'I was there when you broke your wrist. Remember? You were twelve, and in a lot of pain, and yet you refused to shed a single tear. You look a lot closer to tears now. So there has to be a reason.'

She dipped her eyes to her lap, disturbed by the admiration in his voice—and the memory he'd evoked.

She hadn't cried that day, but she hadn't been particularly brave. The pain had seemed minimal once the sixteen-year-old Gio had discovered her in the grounds. He'd carried her all the way back to the Hall in his arms, the experience fuelling her fantasies for months and making her forget about her sore wrist as soon as he'd plucked her off the ground.

She brushed at her eyes with the heel of her hand. Gio's brusque tenderness that day was not something she needed to be thinking about right now.

'Maybe things aren't completely fine,' she said carefully. 'But I'll figure something out.'

He lifted a knee and slung his arm over it—edging that flipping sheet further south.

'That had better not mean more strip-a-grams,' he said.

'It *wasn't* a strip-a-gram,' she said, not appreciating the dictatorial tone. 'It was a singing telegram. There's a difference.'

'Uh-huh.' He didn't sound convinced. 'What's the money for? Are you in financial trouble?'

'Not me,' she murmured, her indignation forgotten. Strip-a-grams could well be the next step. 'It's the Crown and Feathers. The theatre pub I work for. I'm the general manager. I have been for the last four years. And we're about to be shut down by the bank.'

She stared at her hands, the enormity of the situation overwhelming her.

'All the people who work there and everyone in the local community who's helped us make the place a success will be devastated.' She blew out an unsteady breath, the truth hitting her hard in the solar plexus. 'And it's all my fault.'

She'd made a mess of everything. The fat lady was singing her heart out and, barring a miracle, there would be no shutting her up now.

* * *

Gio stared at Issy's pale shoulders rigid with tension, and at her slender hands clasped so tight in her lap she was probably about to dislocate a finger.

And wanted to punch his fist through a wall.

Why couldn't she have wanted the money for herself?

Of course she didn't. Issy didn't work that way. She'd always had too much integrity for her own good.

Now he didn't just feel responsible, he felt the unfamiliar prickle of guilt.

He shouldn't have goaded her. Made the money an issue.

But he hadn't been able to stop himself. The minute he'd spotted her waiting by the empty pool the desire he'd been trying and failing to handle for well over a week had surged back to life like a wild beast.

And he'd instantly resented it. And her.

She'd told him she detested him. Why did he still want her so much?

Suggesting she come up to his bedroom had been a ploy to humiliate her. He'd been sure she would refuse. But she hadn't. And her forthright acceptance had made him feel like a jerk.

Then she'd asked him for money. And resentment had turned to anger.

He'd seen the unconscious flare of desire in her eyes and decided to exploit it. She wasn't here for his money, and he could prove it.

The sex had been incredible. Better even than the first time. Explosive. Exhilarating. A force of nature neither of them could control.

And she'd enjoyed it as much as he had. So he'd been well and truly vindicated.

But her financial problems had ruined the nice buzz of triumph and spectacular sex, stabbing at his conscience in a way he didn't like.

'Exactly how much of a hole is your theatre in?' he asked.

'The interest on our loan is thirty thousand. And we've got less than two weeks to raise it.'

Her damp lashes made her turquoise eyes look even bigger than usual. And his conscience took another hit.

'Is that all?' he prompted.

She shook her head, looked back at her lap. 'We'd need over a hundred to be safe for the rest of the year.' She gave a jerky shrug, as if a huge weight were balanced on her shoulders. 'We've been trying to find sponsors for months now,' she continued. 'The two grants we got last year have been withdrawn. The pub revenue was hit by the smoking ban, and…' She trailed off, sighed. 'It was a stupid idea to come to you. Why should you care about some bankrupt theatre?' She brushed a single tear away. 'But I was desperate.'

He covered her clasped hands with one of his, surprised by the urge to comfort. 'Issy, stop crying.' He'd always hated to see her cry. 'The money's yours. All of it. It's not a problem.'

Her head lifted and she stared at him as if he'd just sprouted an extra head. 'Don't be silly. You can't do that. Why would you?'

He shrugged. 'Why wouldn't I? It's a good cause.' But even as he said it he knew that wasn't the reason he wanted to give her the money.

He'd never really forgiven himself for the way he'd stormed out on her all those years ago.

He didn't regret the decision to walk away. Issy had been young, romantic and impossibly sweet. She'd had a crush on him for years and didn't have a clue what he was really like. But he'd been much harder on her than he needed to be.

He'd accused her of keeping her virginity a secret. But he'd realised in hindsight that had been a stupid misunderstanding. She'd been too innocent to know they were talking at cross-purposes. But at the time he'd felt trapped and wary—and furious with himself for not withdrawing the instant he knew he was her first—and he'd taken it out on her.

Then she'd told him she loved him, and for one fleeting second he'd actually wanted it to be true—making him realise how much he had let his argument with the Duke get to him—and he'd taken that out on her too.

He wasn't about to explain himself now. Or ever. It was too late to apologise. But giving her the money would be a good way to make amends.

But as he looked into those luminous blue eyes the blood pounded back into his groin. And he realised he had a bigger problem to handle than any lingering sense of guilt.

Why hadn't the mind-blowing orgasm been enough?

'But you can't give me a hundred grand.' She pulled her hand out of his. 'That's a lot of money.'

'Do you want to save your theatre or not?' he replied impatiently. He wanted the money out of the way, so he could deal with the more pressing problem of how to re-establish control over his libido.

'Yes—yes, I do. But…' She trailed off.

'Then why are you trying to talk me out of this?'

'Because it's a hundred thousand pounds!'

'Issy, I spent close to that on my last car. It's not that much money. Not to me.'

Her eyebrows rose. 'I didn't know architecture was that lucrative.'

'It is when you do it right,' he said. And had to stifle the foolish desire to say a lot more.

He'd qualified two years early, beaten off a series of more experienced applicants to win a huge design competition, and then worked his backside off. And in the last three years it had paid off.

The Florence practice had won kudos around the world. He'd opened another office in Paris. Won a slew of prestigious architectural awards. And best of all he didn't have to bother entering competitions any more. The clients came to him. He was proud of how he'd managed to tame the destructiveness that had ruled his teenage years and turn his life around.

But he resisted the urge to launch into a list of his accomplishments. He didn't boast about his achievements. He didn't need anyone's approval. So why should he need Issy's?

'If it makes you feel better,' he began, 'I've been thinking of opening an office in London for a while.' Which wasn't exactly the truth. 'The Florence practice donates over a million euros to worthy causes every year. It's great PR and it keeps Luca, my tax accountant, happy.' Which *was* the truth. 'Sponsoring your theatre makes good business sense.'

She pressed her hands to her mouth, her eyes widening to saucer size. 'Oh. My. Lord. You're serious!' she shrieked, the decibel level muffled by her hands.

'You're actually going to give us the money.' She grasped his hand in both of hers. 'Thank you. Thank you. Thank you. You have no idea how much this means to me. And all the people who work at the Crown and Feathers.'

But he had a feeling he *did* know. And it made him feel uncomfortable. His reasons weren't exactly altruistic. And they were getting less altruistic by the second.

'I wish I knew how to thank you,' she said.

He almost told her it wasn't her thanks he wanted. But stopped himself because he'd just figured out what it was he did want.

He wanted Issy Helligan out of his system.

The girl and now the woman had been a fire in his blood for well over ten years. Why not admit it? He didn't fixate on women, but somehow he'd got fixated on her.

He'd tried walking away. He'd tried denial. And neither had worked.

Sorting out her financial troubles would finally put the guilt and responsibility from their past behind them. So why not take the next step? He had to return to Florence this afternoon, and he wanted Issy with him. So he could burn the fire out once and for all. Forget about her for good.

'There's only one snag,' he said, the white lie tripping off his tongue without a single regret.

No need to tell Issy about his plans yet.

She had a tendency to overreact, she was totally unpredictable, and she had a terrible track record for complicating sex with emotion. Better to get her to Florence first, and then deal with any fall-out.

'Oh, no—what?' she said, her face crumpling comically.

'You'll have to come to Florence with me. This afternoon.'

'To Florence?' She looked even more astonished than she had by the offer of money. But when he saw the flash of interest in her eyes he had a tough time keeping the smile of triumph off his face.

She needed this as much as he did. The only difference was she hadn't figured it out yet.

Issy tried to ignore the bubble of excitement under her breastbone. She had to get a grip on this thing... whatever it was. Now.

Maybe she could justify giving in to her hormones once, in the circumstances. She'd been stressed to the max in the last few months, hadn't dated in over a year, and Gio had always been able to short-circuit her common sense and make her yearn for things that weren't right for her. But she was *not* about to do the wild thing with him again. No matter what her body might want.

Gio was now officially the answer to the theatre's prayers. Which would make sex with him even more indefensible than it was already.

'Why?' she asked, hoping he wasn't about to suggest what she thought he was about to suggest.

'You need the money by next week, right?'

She nodded, still unable to believe that the theatre's problems could be solved so easily. And so completely.

'There's a ton of paperwork to sign, plus you may have to give a presentation to the board before I can release the money. It makes sense for you to come over. It shouldn't take more than a couple of days. The snag is, I'm leaving this afternoon. The helicopter's due here at two to take me to London City Airport, and then I'm taking the company jet back to Florence.'

'Oh, I see,' she murmured, disconcerted by the way the bubble had deflated at his businesslike tone. 'I'll ring my assistant Maxi. She can pack me a bag and meet us at City Airport. Don't worry. It's not a problem.'

This was good news. Fantastic news, in fact. Gio had committed to sorting out the theatre's financial situation. And she could think of worse things than spending a few days in Florence—especially after the hideous stress of the last few months. She had earned a break. And they could spare some of the theatre's money on a guesthouse now they were going to have plenty. She might even find time for some sightseeing.

'Arranging leave will be fine,' she said, managing to be businesslike and efficient at last. 'The sooner we can make it official the better.'

She and Gio probably wouldn't see that much of each other, she thought, dismissing the prickle of disappointment. 'Is it okay if I have a shower?' she asked, keeping her tone polite and impersonal.

'Go ahead and use the *en suite*,' he said, just as impersonally. 'I'll take the bathroom down the hall.'

But as she stepped into the bathroom she caught a glimpse of Gio's naked behind as he walked to his dresser, and realised her pheromones weren't being nearly as businesslike and efficient as the rest of her.

Gio grinned as the door to the *en suite* bathroom clicked closed. The offer to scrub her back had been close to irresistible. But he wasn't twenty-one any more—and he didn't plan to rush into anything he couldn't control. He would have to make sure Issy understood exactly what their little trip to Florence meant, and what it didn't, before he made his next move.

And once they'd got that settled he planned to indulge himself.

He pulled jeans and a T-shirt out of the dresser, listened to the gush of water from the shower and imagined Issy's lush, naked body slick with soapsuds.

After ten years, and two bouts of mind-blowing sex, he was finally going to get the chance to seduce Issy Helligan without anything between them. No guilt, no responsibility, no hurt feelings and preferably no clothes.

And he intended to savour every single second.

CHAPTER FIVE

'THAT guy's your Duke?' Maxi whispered loudly, as she passed Issy her battered wheel-around suitcase. Her eyes remained glued to Gio's retreating back as he disappeared into the sea of passengers at the airport's security checkpoint. 'How could you have kept *him* a secret all this time? I mean, look at that backside.'

'Max, close your mouth. You look like a guppy,' Issy said testily. After the strain of the last few hours she was feeling more than a little out of sorts—and she didn't want to deal with Maxi's regression into a fourteen-year-old schoolgirl.

Frankly, she was having enough trouble dealing with her own vivid fantasies about Gio. They'd done the wild thing. Once. And that had been quite enough. For both of them. So why couldn't she stop thinking about doing it again? Especially given that Gio had made it crystal-clear he wasn't in the market for a repeat performance.

After a twenty-minute shower she'd arrived downstairs, to find Gio in a meeting with the landscape architects and Jack Bradshaw assigned as her chaperon.

Jack had graciously invited her to share a buffet of

delicious antipasti dishes with the group of young architects and engineers working on the Hall project. But
her stomach had tied itself in tight little knots as she'd
fielded a barrage of questions from Gio's team about
their shared childhood at the Hall. Did they all know
about her private appointment in his bedroom earlier?
If only he could put in an appearance so she didn't have
to deal with their avid curiosity all on her own.

But Gio hadn't appeared. Thankfully Jack had
whisked her off on a tour of the Hall after lunch, so she
hadn't had too much time to examine why she felt so
disappointed.

It hadn't stopped the strange and inexplicable feelings that had sprung to the surface as she and Jack had
strolled through her childhood home and he'd pointed
out all Gio's improvements. She hadn't needed Jack's
running commentary. She'd seen for herself the remark-
able changes he'd made. And the tight little knots of disappointment and embarrassment had quickly turned to
giant knots of confusion as she marvelled at the bril-
liance and artistry of Gio's redesign.

The forbidding, cramped and suffocating rooms had
been turned into light, airy spaces by knocking down
partition walls and reinstating windows that had been
boarded up. Old carpets had been ripped out to reveal
beautiful inlaid mosaic flooring, a new staircase had
been constructed using traditional carpentry to open up
the second floor, and the grimly unappealing below
stairs kitchen had been turned into a state-of-the art
catering space any master chef would have been proud
of by digging out the basement and adding yet more
light with a domed atrium.

Gio had brought the Hall back from the dead. But, more than that, he'd given it a new lease of life. And she couldn't help wondering why he would have gone to all this trouble.

He'd left the Hall all those years ago, and to her knowledge had never come back. Not once bothering to contact his father or even attend the Duke's funeral. She'd always thought he hated this place, so why had he restored it so sensitively? Had he wanted to prove something?

And why couldn't she shake the odd feeling of pride in his achievements? What Gio had done to his father's house had nothing whatsoever to do with her.

The helicopter ride to London had gone smoothly enough; the noise in the cabin making it impossible for them to speak without shouting. Gio had worked on his laptop and she hadn't disturbed him, even though a million and one questions about the Hall and what he'd done to it had kept popping into her head.

This was a business trip. And she had to keep it that way. Asking Gio questions about his motivations for restoring the Hall felt too personal.

Unfortunately, every time his thigh had brushed against the silk of her dress, or his elbow had bumped hers on the armrest, business was the last thing on her mind. And by the time they'd arrived at City Airport and been whisked into the terminal building, Issy's hormones had been cartwheeling like Olympic gymnasts.

She'd only had a moment to introduce Gio to Maxi, and watch her friend gush all over him, before he'd excused himself again, explaining that he had a few calls to make and would meet her on the plane.

The ludicrous thing was, she was starting to get a

bit of a complex about how eager he seemed to ignore her. Which was totally idiotic. She didn't need his attention. Or want it. It would only encourage her cartwheeling hormones.

Maxi's excited chatter wasn't helping. Reminding her of all the giggly conversations she'd once had about Gio in her teens.

'How do you know him?' Maxi asked, still gushing like his number one fan. 'It's obvious there's a connection between you. Is that why he offered to fund the theatre?' Maxi turned wide eyes on her. 'You're having a fling, aren't you?'

Colour flushed into Issy's cheeks. 'We are not,' she said, pretty sure one bout of wild monkey sex didn't count. 'We grew up together. He's an old friend.'

Maxi's eyes narrowed. 'Then why are you going to Florence with him? And why are you blushing?'

'I'm not blushing,' she lied, cursing her pale skin. 'And I have to go to Florence to sign the sponsorship papers. It's just a formality. I told you that.'

'Iss, don't get me wrong,' Maxi said, putting on her sincere face and grating on Issy's nerves even more. 'I think it's fab that he's taking you to Florence. You absolutely deserve a break. Especially with someone as tasty as that. You don't have to pretend with me. We're mates.' She nudged Issy's shoulder. 'And I'll give Dave and the troops the official story, I promise.' She smiled. 'So, how long have you two been an item?'

Good grief.

Issy yanked up the handle on her suitcase. 'It's not an official story. It's the truth.'

'Oh, come on,' Maxi scoffed. 'Let's examine the

evidence here,' she said in her no-nonsense voice. The one Issy usually appreciated. 'First off: no one needs to travel anywhere to sign a few papers these days, because it can all be done by e-mail.' She began to count off points on her fingers. 'Second: it's obvious you've had a shower in the last few hours, because your hair has started to frizz at the ends.'

Issy touched her hair self-consciously, remembering how observant Maxi was.

'And then there's the rip in the back of your dress to account for.'

Far *too* observant.

'And, last but by no means least,' Maxi continued, 'there's the way he looked at you just now.'

'What way?'

'Like he wanted to devour you in one quick bite.'

Okay, that was an observation too far. Gio had gone out of his way to avoid her for the last two hours. She ought to know. She had the inferiority complex to prove it.

'No, he didn't.'

'Yes, he did.' Maxi's quick grin had Issy blinking. 'I saw him. Those dreamy brown eyes went all sexy and intense, and he stared at you so long even I started to get excited. And I'm just an innocent bystander. If you aren't already having a hot, passionate fling with that guy, you should be.'

'But that's…' She sputtered to a stop, embarrassingly excited herself now. 'That's not possible.'

'Why not?'

'Because…' Her mind went totally blank as her hormones cartwheeled off a cliff.

'Miss Helligan? Mr Hamilton has asked me to escort you through Security.'

Issy turned to find a man in a flight attendant's uniform hovering at her elbow.

'Right. Fine.'

Please, God, don't let him have heard any of that.

She gave Maxi a quick hug. 'I've got my mobile if you need to call. But I'll check in tonight when I know where I'm staying. Give Dave and the troops the good news. And see if you can't locate the—'

'Issy, stop organising and go. Everything's under control.' Maxi squeezed her extra hard. 'Be sure to give His Grace my extra special thanks,' she whispered wiggling her eyebrows suggestively. 'And please feel free to do anything I wouldn't do.'

Issy shot her a hard stare, but couldn't think of a thing to say that would sound remotely convincing. It seemed she had some serious thinking to do—because her trip to Florence had just got a great deal more dangerous.

'This way, Miss Helligan. Mr Hamilton is waiting for you on the plane.'

Issy tried to take stock of the situation as the flight attendant led her past the endless queue snaking towards the security checkpoint.

'But what about passport control and security?' she asked, trailing behind him.

Did none of the usual headaches of air travel apply to a man with Gio's lifestyle?

But as she followed her battered suitcase through the door the attendant held open, and watched it being whisked through an X-ray machine by her own personal security official, it occurred to her that Gio's wealth and success were the least of her worries.

Mounting the metal steps of a sleek silver jet with the GH Partnership logo emblazoned on its tail, she tried to think rationally.

She'd planned to be in complete control here. But she wasn't. This was supposed to be a business trip. Plain and simple. Nothing more. Nothing less. But what if it wasn't?

Gio stepped out of the pilot's cabin as she boarded the plane—and she felt a traitorous thrill shoot through her. He looked relaxed and in control as he leaned against the metal portal, folded his arms over his chest and let his eyes wander over her figure. His casual attire of jeans and a faded T-shirt were at odds with the jet's luxury leather seats and thick pile carpeting, but they reminded her of the reckless, rebellious boy.

But he wasn't that boy any more. He was a man. A wildly successful, dangerously sexy man she'd agreed to go to Florence with. His gaze drifted back to her face. Make that a wildly successful, dangerously sexy man with a very predatory gleam in his eye.

How could she not have spotted that earlier?

'Hello, Isadora,' he said, his voice a husky murmur. 'Ready for lift-off?'

Her nipples puckered into bullet points, her toes curled in her pumps—and she wondered if he was talking in euphemisms just to annoy her.

Ignoring the flush working its way up her neck, she decided to wrestle back some control. He'd bulldozed her into this. It was about time she found out exactly what was going on.

'Is there really any paperwork to sign in Florence?'

He rubbed his jaw. 'Now, why would you ask that?'

he said as the predatory gleam went laser-sharp. And she knew she'd been had.

'This has all been a set-up, hasn't it? But why…?' Her indignation cut off as the blood drained out of her face. 'The sponsorship? That wasn't a joke too, was it?'

'You can cut the drama queen act.' He chuckled, stepped towards her. 'I've already spoken to Luca and the money will be transferred tomorrow, once you give him your bank details.'

Her relief was short-lived as indignation surged back. 'So why am I going to Florence?'

He placed his hands on her hips, his eyes darker than the devil's. 'Why don't you take a wild guess?'

'I've got a better idea.' She braced her palms against his chest. 'Why don't you give me a straight answer?'

'All right, then,' he said, not remotely chastened. 'I plan to spend a few days ravaging you senseless.'

'Ravaging…' Her jaw went slack as fire spiked her cheeks and roasted her sex. 'Are you insane?'

The smug smile got bigger. 'Stop pretending to be outraged. Once wasn't enough. And you know it.'

A sharp reprimand rose up in her throat, but got choked off when his fingers sank into her hair and his lips covered hers in a hungry, demanding kiss.

She pushed him away, clinging onto the last edge of sanity. 'I'm not doing this. It's…' *What?* 'A very bad idea.'

'Why?'

'It just is.' If he gave her a moment she could probably come up with a thousand reasons. Just because she couldn't think of any right this second…

His hands caressed her scalp, making it hard for her

to think straight. 'Issy, the past's over,' he murmured. 'But if you're still hung up on—'

'Of course I'm not,' she cut in. 'This has nothing to do with our past.' She pulled out of his arms. 'And everything to do with your unbelievable arrogance. How dare you trick me into coming to Florence? When exactly were you going to tell me about your plans to ravage me senseless?'

His lips quirked some more. 'I'm telling you now.'

'Well, that's not good enough. What if I want to say no?'

He drew a thumb down her cheek, his eyes black with arousal. 'And do you?'

Even as the denial formed in her mind, it was muted by the long, liquid pull low in her belly. 'No…I mean, yes,' she said, scrambling to keep a firm grip on her indignation.

His palm settled on her nape. 'Let's finish what we started.' His thumb stroked her throat, stoking the fire at her core. 'Then we can both move on.'

Could it really be that simple? Was this thing between them just left-over sexual chemistry?

But even as she tried to make sense of her feelings he tugged her towards him and took her mouth in another mind-numbing kiss.

Her fingers curled into the cotton of his T-shirt, but this time she couldn't find the will to push him away. The pent-up hunger of only a few hours ago burst free as her tongue tangled with his.

He drew back first, the slow smile melting the last of her resistance. 'No ties. No strings. Just some great sex and then we go our separate ways. It's your choice. If you can't handle it, we part now. I'm not interested in anything serious.'

'I'm perfectly well aware of your commitment problems,' she countered.

Not only did she have personal experience, but when she'd been Googling him yesterday she'd found numerous paparazzi shots of him with supermodels and starlets and society princesses on his arm. And not one photo of him with the same woman twice. The man's track record when it came to relationships sucked. Any fool could see that.

'As long as that's understood,' he said easily, clearly not insulted in the least, 'I don't see a problem.' The sensual smile made the heat pound harder. 'Florence is spectacular at this time of year, and I have a villa in the hills where we can satisfy all our prurient sexual fantasies. And, believe me, after ten years I've stored up quite a few.' He threaded his fingers into her hair, pushed the heavy curls away from her face. 'We had fun together when we were kids, Issy. We could have more fun now.'

Issy swallowed, the rough feel of his palm on her cheek making the promise of pleasure all but irresistible. 'And the theatre's sponsorship will be okay either way?' she clarified, desperate not to get swept away on a sea of lust too soon.

He gave his head a small shake. 'I already told you—'

'Okay. Yes,' she interrupted, placing her hands on his shoulders. 'I accept.'

Gio was dangerous. Yes. But danger could be thrilling as well as frightening. And right now the thrill was winning. Big-time. She felt like Alice, tumbling head first into Wonderland. Exhilarated, excited, and totally terrified.

His arms banded around her waist. 'Good.'

Issy had bounced up on her toes, eager to seal their devil's bargain, when she heard a gruff chuckle from behind them.

'You'll have to save that for later, Hamilton,' said an unfamiliar voice.

She jerked round, spotting a stout, older man in a pilot's uniform.

'Our slot's in ten minutes,' the man said, sending her an indulgent smile. 'I'm sorry, miss, but we need to do the final equipment check.'

Gio swore softly, touched his forehead to hers, then stepped to one side. 'Issy, this is James Braithwaite,' he said, keeping his arm round her waist. 'Co-pilot and all-round killjoy.'

Issy shook the man's hand before her foggy brain registered the information. 'Did you say co-pilot?'

'That's right,' Gio said nonchalantly, giving her a quick kiss on the nose and letting her go. 'You'd better get strapped in.'

'Wait a minute.' Issy held his arm, her fingers trembling. 'You're not flying this thing yourself?'

The sleek jet suddenly morphed into a metallic death trap. Images flashed through her mind of Gio as a teenager after he'd totalled his father's vintage Bentley, or Gio on his motorbike with her clinging on the back, shooting around blind bends at twenty miles above the speed limit.

Okay, maybe she could risk a quick fling with Gio, to finish what they'd started this afternoon, but she wasn't about to risk her life letting him fly her anywhere. The boy had always had a need for too much speed and far too little caution. On the evidence so far, she wasn't convinced the man was any less reckless.

Gio grinned at her horrified expression. 'Oh, ye of little faith,' he murmured. 'I happen to be a qualified pilot, Isadora. With a good solid one hundred hours of flying time under my belt.' His smile widened as he stroked her cheek, weakening her resolve, not to mention her thigh muscles. 'Trust me. You're perfectly safe in my hands.'

As she strapped herself into her seat and watched him duck into the pilot's cabin, Issy knew she'd be mad to trust Gio Hamilton with anything.

But forewarned was forearmed. And, given how well aware she was of Gio's shortcomings, she was more than capable of keeping herself safe this time.

After a smooth take-off, and an even smoother touch down in Pisa two hours later, Issy had to concede Gio could be trusted to pilot an aircraft without plummeting her to earth. But when he ushered her just as smoothly into an open-topped Ferrari at the airport, then sped her through miles of glorious sun-drenched Italian countryside, her pulse continued to thump like a sledgehammer and she knew she shouldn't trust him with anything else.

The noise of the wind and the rush of the heart-stopping scenery meant they couldn't talk during the drive. Which gave Issy more than enough time to think.

Was what she had agreed to do demeaning? After all, what self-respecting smart, capable career woman agreed to be ravaged senseless?

But after examining their arrangement Issy came to

the conclusion she didn't have a choice. Because Gio was right. She needed to get over the dirty trick her hormones had been playing on her for years.

She'd had a measly two proper boyfriends since Gio had introduced her to the joys of sex. And both relationships had ended with a whimper rather than a bang. At the time she'd told herself it was because she wasn't ready, because the timing hadn't been right, because the two guys she'd dated hadn't been right for her. But now she knew the truth.

That special spark, that frisson of sexual energy that had exploded in her face today had always been missing. Sex wasn't the *most* important thing in a relationship. She knew that. But it wasn't unimportant either. She'd compared Johnny and Sam to Gio in bed without even knowing it, and found them wanting. Maybe it was some sort of natural selection, a mating instinct thing—after all Gio was the ultimate alpha male in the sack—or maybe it was just that Gio had been her first. But whatever the problem was it needed to be dealt with.

Because if she didn't deal with it she might never be able to form a long-term committed relationship with anyone, ever. The sort of relationship she'd spent her girlhood dreaming about. The sort of relationship her parents had shared before her father's early death. The sort of relationship she'd almost given up hope of ever being able to find for herself.

This wasn't about letting Gio ravage her senseless—it was about releasing her from the sexual hold he had always had over her, ever since that first night, and allowing her to forget about him so she would be free to find the *real* one true love of her life.

Convinced she'd satisfied all her concerns about the trip, Issy couldn't understand why her pulse refused to settle down during the drive. In fact it was still working overtime when Gio steered the Ferrari off a narrow cobbled road in the hills around the city and onto a tree-lined drive.

The scent of lemon trees perfumed the air as he braked in front of a picture-perfect Florentine villa constructed of dusky pink terracotta stone. A grand fountain with two naked water nymphs entwined at its centre tinkled quietly in the circular forecourt.

Issy gawped as Gio leapt effortlessly out of the low-slung car.

She wasn't a stranger to wealth and privilege, for goodness' sake. She'd spent the formative years of her life living below stairs in a stately home. So why had her pulse just skipped into overdrive?

He opened the car door. As she stepped onto the pebbled drive she had to remind herself to breathe.

The carved oak entrance door swung open as they approached. A middle-aged woman with a homely face and a pretty smile bowed her head and introduced herself in Italian as Carlotta. Gio introduced Issy in turn, and then had a conversation with the housekeeper before she excused herself.

Hearing Gio speak Italian had Issy's heartbeat kicking up another notch.

How strange. Even though he spoke English with barely a hint of an accent, Issy knew he was fluent in Italian. But there was something about hearing the language flow so fluidly, watching him use his hands for emphasis, that made him seem very sophisticated and

European—as far removed from the surly boy she remembered as it was possible to get.

She tried to shake off her uneasiness and calm her frantic heartbeat, but as Gio led her through a series of increasingly beautiful rooms the unsettled feeling only got worse.

The house's furnishings were few, but suited the open Mediterranean layout and looked hand-crafted and expensive. The minimalist luxury should have made the place seem exclusive and unapproachable, but it didn't. As they walked into a wide, open-plan living area, the brightly coloured rugs, the lush, leafy potted plants and the stacks of dog-eared architectural magazines on the coffee table gave its elegance a lived-in feel, making the house seem unpretentious and inviting.

Gio held open a glass door at the end of the room and beckoned her forward.

Issy stepped on to a balcony which looked across the valley past a steeply terraced garden. At the bottom of the hill in the distance the sluggish Arno River wound its way through Florence, the city laid out below them like a carpet of wonders. She could make out the Ponte Vecchio to her right, probably heaving with tourists in the sweltering afternoon heat, and appreciated the citrus-perfumed breeze even more. Walking to the low stone wall that edged the terrace, she spotted a large pool in the lawned garden one level below, its crystal blue waters sparkling in the sunshine.

'Goodness,' she whispered, as her heartbeat pounded in her ears.

Who would have expected the wild, reckless boy

whom she had assumed would never settle anywhere to make himself a home almost too beautiful to be real?

'So what do you think?' he asked.

She turned to find him standing behind her, studying her, his hands tucked into the back pockets of his jeans. She thought she saw a muscle in his jaw tense. As if he were anxious about what she might say.

Don't be an idiot.

He didn't care what she thought. That had to be a trick of the light. He knew how amazing this place was. And she knew perfectly well she was only one in a very long line of women he'd invited here.

Don't you dare start analysing every little nuance of his behaviour, you ninny. Reading things into it that aren't there.

She cleared her throat. 'I think you have incredible taste.' She stared out at the breathtaking view. 'And calling this place a villa doesn't do it justice. I think paradise would be more appropriate.'

'It'll do for now,' he said casually.

His palms settled on her waist. Tugging her back against his chest, he nuzzled the sensitive skin below her ear. 'Although, given what I'm thinking right now, paradise lost would be the best choice.'

She gasped out a laugh, finding it hard to breathe as brutal realisation hit her. Being in Gio's home would involve an intimacy she hadn't bargained on during all her careful justifications.

'Why don't we go check out the master bedroom?' he said, the humour doing nothing to mask his intentions. He folded his arms around her waist, making her breasts feel heavy and tender as he drew her into a hard hug. 'I'd love to know what you think of the...' He paused provocatively, nipping her earlobe. 'View...'

She pictured the view the last time they'd been naked together. And the hot, heavy weight in her belly pulsed. Panic spiked at the vicious throb of desire.

I'm not ready for this. Not yet.

She whipped round to face him, breaking his hold. 'Could we go sightseeing?' she said, trying not to wince at the high-pitched note in her voice.

She couldn't dive back into bed with him. Not straight away. Sex was one thing, intimacy another, and she couldn't afford to confuse the two.

His brows rose up his forehead. 'You want to go sightseeing? Seriously?'

'Yes, please. I adore sightseeing,' she said, keeping her voice as firm as possible to disguise the lie. She could feel his arousal against her hip and eased back a step. 'I've never been to Florence. I'm dying to see as much of it as I can. Could we eat in the city tonight?' A couple of hours to establish some distance. That was all she needed. She was sure of it. 'I've never been to Italy before,' she rattled on, pretending not to notice the frown on his face. 'And I've heard Florence has some of the best *trattorias* in Italy.'

What the...?

Gio knew a delaying tactic when he heard one. And Issy's sudden transformation into super-tourist definitely qualified. He spotted the rigid peaks of her breasts beneath her dress, the staggered rise and fall of her breathing—and almost howled with frustration.

Hadn't they settled all this on the plane?

He was ready to get to the main event now. More than ready. In fact, if he hadn't been co-piloting the plane he would have got to it sooner, giving in to the temptation to initiate her into the Mile-High Club.

Thrusting his hands into his pockets, he kept his face carefully blank. Her cheeks were a bright rosy pink but he could see the alarm on her face.

He should have guessed things wouldn't be that straightforward, because nothing ever was with Issy. She'd been jumpy ever since they'd walked into the house. He'd enjoyed her nerves at first. Keeping Issy off-kilter was a good way to handle her. And it hadn't done his ego any harm to see how impressed she was with his home.

But when she'd turned round, her eyes wide with surprise, he'd had the strangest sensation she could see right through him. And for the first time in his life he'd wanted to ask a woman what she was thinking.

Not that he intended to do it. For one thing, straight answers were not Issy's forte. And for another, he had a golden rule against asking women personal questions. Once you opened that floodgate it was impossible to slam it shut again.

He'd already broken one golden rule by inviting her into his home. He generally avoided getting into any kind of routine with the women he dated.

'Sure. No problem.' He forced his shoulders to relax.

If Issy wanted to play hard to get for an evening, why not let her? He could slow the pace for a few hours. If he had to.

'I know a place not far from the Piazza della Repubblica. Their *bistecca fiorentina*'s like a religion.'

And Latini had the sort of low-key, unpretentious atmosphere that should relax her while still being classy enough to impress her.

He would ply her with a couple of glasses of their Chianti Classico, comfort-feed her the Florentine speciality and indulge in a spot of light conversation. Maybe he'd even show her a few of the sights. Keep things easy. He could do that. For an evening.

'Are you sure?' she said, sounding surprised but looking so relieved he smiled.

'Yeah. It'll be fun,' he said, forcing down his frustration. He could wait a while longer to get her naked. He wasn't *that* desperate.

Then a thought struck him, and he realised he could make it more fun than he'd figured. He smiled some more. 'We can take the Vespa. My mechanic Mario gave it an overhaul recently, so it's running fairly well for once.'

'A scooter?' She had the same shocked look he'd seen on the plane. 'You ride a scooter? That sounds a bit incongruous for a duke.'

'Now, Isadora.' He brushed a thumb across her cheekbone. 'I hope you're not saying I'm a snob?' he teased as her cheeks pinkened prettily. 'No Florentine with a brain takes a car into the city. A scooter is the only way to go.'

And, like all natives, he drove his Vespa at breakneck speed. Which meant she'd have to glue herself to him to stop from falling off.

His grin got bigger as his gaze flicked down her outfit. 'If you've got some jeans, you might want to put them on. The staff will have put your suitcase in the master bedroom.' Placing his hands on her shoulders, he directed her towards a wrought-iron staircase at the end of the terrace. 'Take those stairs and the door's at the end of the balcony. I'll get the Vespa out of the garage and meet you out front.'

By the time they got back here, he'd have her naked soon enough.

Mounting the stairs to the upper balcony, Issy watched Gio stroll across the terrace, those damn denims hugging his gorgeous butt like a second skin.

She dragged her gaze away and took a moment to admire the almost as phenomenal view of Florence at dusk. In the enormous bedroom suite she slipped into jeans and a simple white wraparound blouse, and stared at the king-size mahogany bed dominating the room. The reckless thrill cascading through her body at the thought of what the nights and days ahead would hold had the hot, heavy feeling turning to aching need.

She huffed out a breath.

Okay, abstinence had never been an option. Not where Gio was concerned. He was too irresistible. And trying to distract him from the inevitable would only end up frustrating them both.

But that did not mean he got to have everything his own way. He'd railroaded her into boarding that plane, then exploited the hunger between them to get exactly what he wanted. Mindless sex with no strings attached.

Well, fine, she didn't want any strings either. But it wasn't as easy for her to simply dismiss their past. And she wasn't quite as adept at separating sex from intimacy, the way he was. And the reason why was simple. She'd never had sex with a stranger before. Or not intentionally. But she could see now that was exactly what Gio was. Now.

Finding a lavish *en suite* bathroom, she spent a few extra minutes brushing out her hair, washing her face and reapplying her make-up. And struggling to slow the rapid ticks of her heartbeat.

She'd once believed she knew Gio and understood him. And from there it had been one short step into love.

After that first night she'd always thought the reasons why she'd been so foolish were simple. She'd been young and immature and in desperate need of male approval. She'd lost her father at an early age, and it had left an aching hole in the centre of her life that couldn't be filled. Until Gio had appeared, a sad, surly but magnetic boy, who had seemed to need her as much as she needed him.

But now she could see there had been another, less obvious reason why she'd fallen in love with a figment of her own imagination.

Even when they were children there had been an air of mystery about Gio. He'd always been so guarded and cautious about any kind of personal information.

She had talked endlessly about her hopes and dreams, about her mum, about her schoolfriends, even about the shows she liked to watch on TV. Gio had listened to her chatter, but had said virtually nothing about his own life, his own hopes and dreams in return. She'd never even had an inkling he was interested in design. No wonder she had been so surprised about his success as an architect.

And then there had been the wall of silence surrounding the ten months of the year he spent in Rome, with his mother.

As a teenager, Issy had been totally in awe of Claudia Lorenzo—like every other girl her age. A flamboyant and stunningly beautiful bit-part actress, who had fought her way out of the Milan slums, Gio's mother had reinvented herself as a fashion icon, gracing the pages of *Vogue* and *Vanity Fair* while on a merry-go-round of affairs and marriages with rich, powerful men. Not all that surprisingly, Issy had quizzed Gio mercilessly about 'La Lorenzo' in her early teens.

But Gio had always refused to talk about his mother. So Issy had eventually stopped asking, conjuring up all sorts of romantic reasons why he should keep his life in Rome a secret.

Issy squared her shoulders and ran unsteady palms down the stiff new denim of her jeans. Why not use this week to dispel that air of mystery. To finally satisfy her curiosity about Gio? She'd always wanted to know why Gio kept so many secrets and why he seemed so determined never to have a permanent relationship. Once she had her answer, his power to fascinate her, to tantalise her, would be gone for good.

Gio was unlikely to co-operate, of course—being as guarded now as he had ever been—and it would be hard not to get sidetracked while indulging in all the physical pleasures and revelling in the sights, sounds and tastes of the beautiful Tuscan capital.

But luckily for her she was a master at multi-tasking, and she never backed down from a challenge. Skills she'd perfected while running the theatre and handling everything from actors' egos to imminent bankruptcy. Why not put those skills to good use?

So she could enjoy everything the next few days

had to offer. Get over her addiction to Gio's superstar abilities in bed. And finally get complete closure on all the mistakes of her past.

CHAPTER SIX

'So why arc you so petrified of commitment?'

Gio choked on the expensive Chianti he'd been sipping, so surprised by Issy's probing question he had to grab his napkin to catch the spray. He put the glass down on the restaurant's white linen tablecloth, next to the remains of the mammoth T-bone steak they'd shared. 'Issy, I've just eaten about a half pound of rare beef. What are you trying to do? Give me indigestion?' he said, only half joking.

Where had that come from?

Everything had been going surprisingly well till now. Their sightseeing trip had been less of a chore than he'd expected. Issy had always been sexy as hell, but he'd forgotten how refreshing, funny and forthright she was too.

Perhaps because she was still a little jumpy, she'd hardly stopped talking since they'd left the villa, but rather than annoying him the mostly one-sided conversation had brought back fond memories from their childhood. For a boy who had been taught as soon as he could speak that it was better to keep his mouth shut, listening to Issy talk had made him feel blissfully normal. Having her chatter wash over him again tonight had reminded him how much he'd once enjoyed just listening to her speak.

The only time she'd been silent was when he'd whipped his classic Vespa through the streets of Florence with her clinging on like a limpet. Which had brought back another more visceral memory of that first wild ride aboard his motorbike.

After that he'd needed a distraction. Her warm breasts pressing against his back had not done a great deal for his self-control. So he'd had the inspired idea of taking her on a private tour of the Uffizi while he cooled off. But as they'd walked hand in hand through the darkened Vasari gallery and she'd peppered him with questions, a strange thing had happened. He'd watched Issy's face light up when she took in the Renaissance splendour of Boticelli's *Primavera*, heard her in-drawn breath at the ethereal beauty of Titian's *Venus*, and he'd really started to enjoy himself.

He'd taken a few dates here before, but none of them had been as awestruck and excited by the beauty of the art as Issy.

When they'd got to Latini for a late dinner, Issy had devoured the rich, succulent Tuscan speciality with the same fervour. But, as he'd watched her lick the rich gravy from her full bottom lip, enjoyment and nostalgia had turned sharply to anticipation.

As much as he'd enjoyed Issy's company over the last few hours, her avid appreciation of the art and her entertaining abilities as a conversationalist, he didn't want to talk any more. And especially not about his least favourite subject.

But before he could think of a subtle way to change the subject, she started up again.

'You're always so adamant you don't do permanent. You don't do the long-haul,' she said, looking him straight in the eye. 'Don't you think that's a bit peculiar? Especially for a man of your age?'

'I'm only thirty-one,' he said, annoyed. It wasn't as if he were about to pick up his pension.

'I know, but isn't that when most men are thinking of settling down? Having kids?'

That did it. Forget subtle—he wasn't having this conversation. No way. 'Why do you care? Unless you're angling for a proposal?' he said, a bit too forcefully.

Instead of looking hurt or offended, she laughed. 'Stop being so conceited. A man with your commitment problems is hardly the catch of the century.'

'That's good to know,' he grumbled, not as pleased as he would have expected by the off-hand remark.

Propping her elbow on the table, she leaned into her palm and gazed at him. 'I'm just really curious. What happened to make you so dead set against having a proper relationship?'

'I *have* proper relationships,' he said, not sure why he was defending himself. 'What do you call this?'

She giggled, her deep blue eyes sparkling mischievously in the candlelight. 'An *improper* relationship.'

'Very funny,' he said wryly as blood pounded into his groin.

Signalling the waiter, he asked for the bill in Italian. As the man left, laden with their empty plates, Gio topped up their wine glasses. 'Let's go back to the villa for dessert,' he said. Time to stop debating this nonsense and start debating which part of her he planned to feast on first. 'And discuss *how* improper.'

Seeing the heat and the determination on his face, Issy struggled to keep the simmering passion at bay that she was sure he'd been stoking all evening.

Every time his fingers cupped her elbow, every time his palm settled on the small of her back, every time his breath brushed across her earlobe as he whispered some amusing story or anecdote in her ear, or his chocolate gaze raked over her figure, her arousal had kicked up another notch. And she was sure he knew it.

But she wasn't going to be distracted that easily. Not yet anyway.

'What's the matter, Gio. Don't you *know* why you can't maintain a relationship?'

He drummed his fingers on the table, the rhythmic taps doing nothing to diminish the intensity in those melted chocolate eyes. 'It's not that I can't,' he replied. 'It's that I don't want to.' He leaned forward, placed his elbows on the table, a confident smile curving his lips. 'Why would I bother if it will never work?'

'What makes you think that?' she asked, stunned by the note of bitterness.

'People get together because of animal attraction,' he said, adding a cynical tilt to his smile. 'But that doesn't last. Eventually they hate each other, even if they pretend not to.' He took her wrist off the table, skimmed his thumb across the pulse-point. 'It's human nature. Relationships are about sex. You can dress it up with hearts and flowers if you want. But I choose not to.'

Issy sucked in a breath, shocked by the conviction in his voice and a little hurt by the brittle, condescending tone.

The evening so far had been magical. So magical she had been lulled into a false sense of companionship to go with the heady sexual thrill.

From the moment Gio's vintage scooter had careered down the steep cobbled hill into the city, his rock-hard abs tensing beneath her fingertips and the wind catching her hair, the sexual thrill had shot into her bloodstream like a drug. She was in Florence with a devastatingly handsome man who knew how to play her erogenous zones like a virtuoso. Why not ride the high?

But as the evening wore on it wasn't just the promise of physical pleasure that excited her.

Their first stop had been the world-famous Uffizi art gallery, where an eager young architectural student who worked as a night-guard and obviously idolised Gio had ushered them into a veritable cave of wonders of Italian art treasures.

Gio had taken courses in art history as part of his degree, and hadn't seemed to mind answering her endless questions. He'd regaled her with fascinating stories about the paintings on display, and talked about his love of art and architecture with a knowledge and passion so unlike the reticence she remembered about him as a boy it had captivated her.

When they'd stepped out of the gallery, darkness had fallen, the cloaking spell of evening giving the city a new and enchanting vibrancy. The tourists had all but disappeared, no doubt retiring to their hotels after a day spent sightseeing in the merciless August heat, and the locals had reclaimed their streets. Crowds of young,

stylish Florentines, posing and gesticulating, spilled out
of bars and cafés into cramped alleyways and grand
piazzas, illuminated by neon and lamplight. As she'd
clung on to Gio and watched Florence and its inhabi-
tants whip past, Issy had been assailed by a powerful
sense of belonging. Tonight, with Gio beside her, it
didn't seem to matter that she didn't speak a word of
Italian and couldn't have looked less Mediterranean if
she tried. She knew it was a fanciful notion, conjured
by the city's enchanting allure, but it had brought with
it a buzz of anticipation to complement the desire
coursing through her veins.

What if she and Gio could become friends again, as
well as lovers, during their weekend of debauchery?

The meal had been equally glorious. The small but
packed *trattoria* wore its centuries-old history on its
smoke-stained walls and in the sensational tastes and
textures of its signature dish. Gio was clearly a regular.
The head waiter had clapped him on the back and led
them to the only table which wasn't communal as soon
as they'd arrived.

Issy suspected Gio had entertained hundreds of other
women here before, but she refused to care. This was a
few days out of time for both of them. A chance not just
to indulge in the intense physical attraction between
them, but maybe also to renew the precious childhood
companionship they'd once shared before misunder-
standings and maturity—and one night of misguided
sex—had destroyed it.

But how could they do that if Gio insisted on shutting
her out and treating her as if her view on love and relationships was beneath contempt?

Maybe she'd been young and foolish at seventeen, and she'd certainly made an enormous mistake picking Gio as her Mr Right, but she intended to carry on looking—and she resented him implying that made her an imbecile.

She tugged her hand out of his. 'That's all very interesting, Gio. But what about love? What about when you find the person you want to spend the rest of your life with?'

'You don't still believe that's going to happen, do you?' he said with an incredulous laugh.

'Yes, I do. It happens all the time. It was exactly like that for my parents,' she said with passion, her temper mounting. 'They adored each other. My mum still talks about my dad, and he's been dead for twenty-one years.'

'If you say so,' he said, sounding sceptical. 'But that would make *your* parents the exception, not the rule.'

She heard the tinge of regret, not quite drowned out by his condescension, and her temper died. 'What makes you think your parents aren't the exception?'

He stiffened at the quiet comment, and she knew she'd hit on the truth. Gio's cynicism, his bitterness, had nothing to do with his opinion of her but with the terrible example his own parents had set.

Although the Hamiltons had divorced three years before she and her mum had come to live at the Hall, lurid stories about the split had fed the rumour mill in Hamilton's Cross for years afterwards.

Two impossibly beautiful and volatile people, Claudia Lorenzo, the flamboyant Italian socialite, and Charles Hamilton, the playboy Duke of Connaught, had indulged in years of vicious infighting and public spats, before Claudia had finally stormed out for good, taking their nine-year-old son back to Italy with her. The brutal custody battle that followed had made headlines in both the local and national press. Although Issy had never understood why the Duke had fought so hard for his son when he'd treated Gio so harshly during his court-ordered summer visits.

As a teenager, Issy had found the concept of Gio as a tug-of-love orphan both fabulously dramatic and wonderfully tragic, like something straight out of *Wuthering Heights*, but she could see now it must have been a living hell for him as a child. And could easily have warped his view of relationships ever since.

'Your parents were selfish, self-absorbed people,' she said. 'Who didn't care about love or each other.' *Or you*, she thought. 'But you shouldn't let that make you give up on finding a loving relationship for the rest of your life.'

Gio groaned, dumping his napkin on the table. 'Will you give it a rest? You don't know what you're talking about.'

It wasn't quite the reaction she'd been hoping for, but she wasn't going to give up that easily.

'I know enough,' she countered. 'My mother and I heard how your father shouted at you and belittled you. And I saw for myself how much it upset you,' she persevered, despite the rigid expression on his face. 'On that last night, when I found you in the orchard, you'd just had a massive row with him. You looked so upset. So…' She trailed off as he turned away, a muscle in his jaw twitching. And she realised something she should have figured out years before.

'*That's* why you needed me that night. *That's* why we made love,' she said softly, her heart punching her throat. 'Because of something he said to you.'

His head swung back, his eyes flashing hot, and she knew she'd touched a nerve.

Whatever his father had said that night had made him reach out to someone, anyone, to ease the pain. And, thanks to circumstance, that someone had been her.

The revelation shouldn't really matter now. But it did. She'd believed for ten years that their first night had been a terrible mistake, brought about by her immature romantic fantasies. But what if he really *had* needed her—just not in the way she'd thought?

'We didn't make love,' he said flatly. 'We had sex.'

She didn't even flinch at the crude words. 'What did he say?' she asked, her heart melting at the anguished frown on his face.

'Who the hell cares what he said? That was a million years ago.'

It wasn't a million years ago, but even if it had been it was obvious it still hurt.

'Dammit, you're not going to let this go, are you?'

She shook her head. 'No, I'm not.'

'Fine.' He dumped his napkin on the table. 'He told me I wasn't his son. That Claudia had screwed a dozen other men during their marriage. That I was some other man's bastard.'

Shock reverberated through her body at the ugly words. 'But you must have been devastated,' she murmured. How could the Duke have harboured that nasty little seed in his head all through Gio's childhood? And then told his son? 'But what about the custody battle. Why would he…?'

'He needed an heir.' Gio shrugged. 'And he enjoyed dragging Claudia through the courts, I suspect.'

The words were delivered in a gruff, deliberately contemptuous monotone. But underneath it she could hear a plea that he couldn't quite disguise, of the little boy who had been so easily hurt by the two people who should have cherished him the most.

'Gio, I'm so sorry.' She covered his hand where it lay on the table, and squeezed.

'Why should you be sorry?' he said, pulling his hand out from under hers. 'It didn't matter to me. In fact, it was a relief. I'd always wondered why I could never please the man.'

He was lying. It *had* mattered. He'd brooded for days every time the Duke had reprimanded him as a teenager. She'd seen the hurt and confusion he'd tried so hard to hide behind surly indifference. And she'd seen how unhappy, how volatile he'd been that night.

And still mattered now.

No wonder he found it so hard to believe that love existed. That relationships could last.

His eyes narrowed sharply. 'Bloody hell,' he said. 'Stop that right now.' Standing up he threw a fistful of euro notes on the table.

'Stop what?' she gasped as his fingers locked on her wrist and he hoisted her out of her chair.

'Stop psychoanalysing me.' He shot the clipped words over his shoulder as he walked out of the restaurant, tugging her behind him.

'I'm *not* psychoanalysing you,' she panted, trying to keep up with his long strides. 'I'm just trying to understand why…'

'There's nothing to understand.' He stopped on the street outside, his voice stiff with frustration. 'I wanted you and you wanted me. There wasn't anything significant about that night except you were a virgin. And if I'd figured that out sooner, believe me, I wouldn't have touched you no matter how tempted I was.'

The fervent denial made her emotion swell to impossible proportions. Why did he find it so hard even now to admit he'd needed someone? Even fleetingly?

'All right,' she said placatingly. 'But I still find it moving that—'

'Well, don't.' He cut her off as he marched down the street again. 'Because it's not.' They reached the scooter. 'That night was about animal passion.' Lifting the spare helmet off the handlebars, he thrust it at her. 'Climb aboard, because I've got some more animal passion for you.'

Great. She wasn't feeling that moved any more. 'Stop ordering me about.' She shoved the helmet on her head. Damn, he'd made her pout—and she hated to be a cliché. 'How about if I said I didn't *want* your animal passion?'

'You'd be lying,' he said with infuriating certainty as he mounted the scooter and jammed the key into the ignition. 'Now get on. You've got exactly ten seconds.' He stamped his foot on the start pedal. 'Or we're going to be doing it against the back wall of Latini instead of in the privacy of my bedroom. Your choice.'

'I will *not* get on your scooter!' she shouted, as colour flooded her cheeks at the sensual threat—and her traitorous nipples pebbled beneath the thin silk of her blouse.

'Ten…'

'How dare you talk to me like that?' she cried, flustered now, as well as outraged.

'Nine…'

He's kidding. He has to be.

'Eight…'

'I am not your personal floozy!'

One dark brow arched. 'Seven…'

Her knickers got moist.

'Six…'

'And, frankly, you've got an awfully high—'

'Five…'

'—opinion of your powers of seduction,' she tried to scoff, but rushed the words.

'Four…' He slung his arm across the handlebars of the scooter, looking relaxed but ready—like a tiger waiting to pounce. 'Three…'

'As if you could get me to *do it* with you in a public place,' she hedged desperately, her voice rising. Time was running out.

'Two…' He stood up on the scooter, looming over her.

She slapped her hands on her hips. 'Now, listen here—'

'One.'

Oh, hell.

She scrambled onto the seat behind him and grabbed two fistfuls of his T-shirt.

'All right. All right.' She yanked. 'You win. For now,' she said, sighing with relief as he sank back with a triumphant chuckle.

'I'm so not finished talking about this, though,' she continued, fighting a rearguard action as he revved the engine and she wrapped her arms around his waist. 'You arrogant, oversexed...'

The protest was lost in the roar of the Vespa's engine as it careered away from the kerb.

Issy clung on, her mind spinning, her tender breasts vibrating against the muscled sinews of his back.

As they sped over the Ponte Vecchio she caught sight of a couple embracing in the shadows of the ancient bridge. And agonising desire flooded between her thighs.

She held on for dear life. What were the chances she was going to be in any fit state to conduct a conversation, let alone an argument, once they got back to the villa?

Not a lot, actually.

After the fifteen-minute journey up the hill, Gio clasped her hand in his and walked through the darkened house. He didn't utter a word. And neither did she. Too preoccupied by the thought of the animal passion they had already sampled to remember why she'd objected to sampling some more.

Within seconds of slamming his bedroom door, he had her naked.

As he flung off his own clothing she stood shaking, mesmerised by the hard, masculine beauty of his body gilded in the moonlight. Then her eyes snagged on the powerful erection jutting out as he sheathed himself.

And the animal passion that had smouldered all evening leapt into flame.

'No more delaying tactics.' He lifted her easily in his arms. 'There's nothing to understand.' Gripping her thighs, he hooked her legs around his waist. 'All we need is this.'

'Why can't we do both?' she asked, as her back

thudded against the door. But she knew she was fighting a losing battle as the head of his erection probed at the folds of her sex.

His eyes met hers in the half-light. 'Later, Isadora.' He planted a possessive kiss on her lips. 'We're busy.' And impaled her in one powerful thrust.

She sobbed at the fullness of the penetration.

Okay, later works, she thought vaguely, as he sank in to the hilt.

A long time later, her body aching from an overdose of physical activity and sexual pleasure, they finally collapsed onto his huge *bateau* bed.

'Do you think we'll ever get to slow and easy?' she mumbled, curling against his side and pillowing her head on his shoulder, so tired she would happily beg for oblivion.

She heard his chuckle, felt the soft rumble in his chest before his arm drew her close and his hand caressed her bottom. 'That would be next time. Now, go to sleep.'

Her eyes fluttered closed as his lips brushed her hair, and she heard him take a deep breath before releasing it.

'Issy. What the hell am I going to do with you?' he murmured.

Despite the fuzziness of exhaustion, she heard the confusion in his voice and felt her heart stutter in response.

Become my friend again.

She nestled deeper into his embrace as the warm, languid afterglow of sensational sex pulled her into a dreamy sleep.

CHAPTER SEVEN

'WAKE UP, Sleeping Beauty, you need to get out of the sun before you end up with third degree burns.'

Issy shaded her eyes to see Gio standing by her sun-lounger, looking tall and delicious in chinos and an open-necked shirt.

'You're back already?' She stretched lazily, ignoring the persistent flutter beneath her breastbone at the sight of him. He'd left for a meeting in town after breakfast, and she'd taken a swim in the pool. It was a surprise to see him back so soon.

He crouched down on his haunches until they were eye to eye. 'I've been gone for over two hours.' He rested his arm across his knee and touched her nose. 'And you're looking a little pink.'

'What's the time?' she asked groggily, determined not to read too much into how her spirits lifted at his look of concern.

Despite Gio's assertions that all they had was animal passion, they had drifted into friendship again as easily as breathing. After only a few days the companionship they shared had become as exciting as their sexual relationship.

If the first day's sightseeing had been magical, yesterday's had been even more so. They'd brushed shoulders with businessmen and market traders alike in a *trattoria* at the Mercado Centrale, while Gio had chuckled at her pathetic attempts to order in Italian. He'd taken her to see the stunning golden mosaics in the Romanesque basilica of San Miniato al Monte, then cuddled with her under the stars as they watched *La Dolce Vita* in flickering black and white on the ten-foot open-air screen in a nearby park.

In the last twenty-four hours she'd seen a man emerge who was cultured and charismatic, had a decidedly mischievous sense of humour, and was passionate about his work and the beautiful city he lived in.

Maybe they hadn't talked about their past or anything else too personal again—something she knew was deliberate on Gio's part—but she hadn't pushed. Taking the sweet, steady glide into friendship and getting an enchanting glimpse of what that unhappy boy had made of his life had been enough. Frankly, friendship didn't get much better than this. Why ruin the mood?

Gio glanced at his watch. 'It's after one,' he replied. 'And about the hottest time of the day.'

'Oh.' She'd been asleep for over an hour. And would probably be a bit sore tomorrow as a result. Thank goodness she'd slathered factor fifty sunscreen on before she'd dozed off.

She gave a jaw-breaking yawn and sighed. 'I don't know why you're looking at me like that. This is all your fault.'

'How?'

'You're the one who hasn't let me sleep since I got here,' she teased, although it wasn't far from the truth.

This was a friendship with some exceptional benefits, she thought, as her pulse spiked at the sight of his trousers stretching across muscled thighs.

They'd done hard and fast, slow and easy, and everything in between. Gio's powers of recovery had proved to be Herculean, and she'd never been more satisfied, more sated—or more exhausted—in her life. When she'd woken up snuggled in his arms that morning, inhaling the familiar musk of his scent had sent shockwaves through her oversensitised flesh, but her hunger had been as insistent as ever when his morning erection had brushed her bottom.

Okay, so she'd felt a strange dragging sensation when he'd left her to shower alone this morning because he had an important meeting. But she hadn't let it bother her. The let-down feeling was to be expected. They were having a fabulous time, but it would be over soon. The ennui was probably just to do with endorphins, or something.

'Exactly how long have you been out here?' he asked. 'Did you even put on any cream?'

Her grin widened. 'Yes, boss.'

'It's not funny,' he said, all serious and intense. 'You've got very fair skin. Sunburn's no joke.'

'Spoken by a man who's probably never had it.' She ran her fingernail over one tanned bicep, enjoying the way the muscle bunched. 'Honestly, Gio. You sound like my mum.'

'Oh, yeah?' His eyebrow lifted, the frown replaced by a slow smile.

'Yes, yeah,' she said, desire curling anew in her belly. 'Just for that…'

She shrieked as he thrust one hand under her knees and the other behind her back.

'What are you doing?' she said, gripping his neck as he straightened with her wriggling in his arms.

'Helping you cool off.'

She started to wriggle in earnest when she saw his direction. 'No. No way. I've already had a swim today.' And the water would feel freezing after she'd been lying in the sun.

Ignoring her protests and her struggles, he hefted her towards the pool. 'Yes, but I haven't,' he said, and stepped off the edge fully clothed.

'So, is that sunburn or are you still blushing?' Gio asked, a teasing smile lurking on his lips.

'I don't know what you're talking about.'

He sat at the terrace table, his wavy hair furrowed into slick rows, damp wisps of chest hair visible through the open lapels of his robe.

'I had no idea you could move that fast.' He poured a glass of lemonade from a pitcher on the table and passed it to her. 'I think you may have set a land-speed record.'

She took a swallow of the icy drink to calm the giddy beat of her pulse. 'It's not remotely funny,' she said dryly, trying to control her flush. 'Your housekeeper will think I'm a tart.'

If she doesn't already.

They'd been about to ravage each other during their impromptu dip when Carlotta had interrupted them to announce that lunch had been set out on the terrace. Issy had scurried off to the bedroom wrapped in a towel and dying of embarrassment. Gio's laughter had echoed behind her. She still hadn't quite managed to get over her mortification.

'No, she won't,' he said lazily, slicing into the veal *parmigiana* on his plate. 'She's Italian. They don't get as hung up on social niceties as you Brits.'

'You Brits? Aren't you half-British?'

He grinned. 'When it comes to social niceties, I'd say I'm more Italian.'

'So would I,' she said emphatically.

He chuckled.

Issy smiled back. But as she crossed her legs and smoothed her robe over her knees the heat continued to burn in her cheeks.

How could she not have noticed Carlotta beside the pool?

And how could she have got carried away like that, knowing there was a houseful of servants who could interrupt them at any minute? Gio had turned her from nun to nymphomaniac in the space of a few days—and it was starting to concern her.

Shouldn't the passion have begun to fade a little by now?

Gio lifted her hand off the table and linked his fingers with hers. 'In deference to your British sensibilities, I suggest we retire to the privacy of the bedroom after lunch.'

The familiar thrill shot through her as he pressed his lips to her knuckles. Concerning her even more. Why couldn't she say no to him? Ever?

Carlotta stepped onto the terrace, holding a small silver tray, and Issy tugged her hand free.

Gio took a large envelope off the tray and thanked the housekeeper. Issy sent Carlotta what she hoped was a friendly smile and the woman smiled back, apparently unperturbed by what she'd almost interrupted in the pool.

As Issy watched the housekeeper leave, she wondered how many more of Gio's sexual escapades Carlotta had witnessed. The instant prickle of jealousy made her frown. This was temporary—with no strings attached. Gio's other women didn't matter to her in the least.

'Dammit.'

At the whispered curse, she turned to see Gio dump a large magnolia card into the wastepaper bin and throw the torn envelope on top.

'What was that? It's not bad news, is it?'

'No, it's nothing,' he said as he picked up his knife and fork.

The movement made his robe gape open. Issy pulled her gaze away from the sprinkle of dark hair that arrowed down his abdomen.

It wasn't nothing. That much was obvious from the tense, annoyed expression on his face.

Brushing off the torn envelope, she lifted the card out of the bin. The fancy gold lettering was in Italian, but she could make out today's date.

Why had he reacted so violently to something that looked so innocuous?

'Who is Carlo Nico Lorenzo?' she asked, reading out the name printed in the centre of the card.

He glanced up, his eyes stormy. 'I threw that away for a reason. It's rubbish.'

'Is he a relative of yours?' she asked, pretending she hadn't heard the rude comment as curiosity consumed her. 'Did your mother have brothers and sisters?' She trailed off, waiting for him to fill in the blanks.

'Carlo is the baby they're baptising,' he said curtly, then leaned forward and plucked the invitation out of her hand. 'He's the grandson of Claudia's oldest brother. Who's also called Carlo.' He dumped the card onto the table, face down. 'Now, can we finish our lunch?'

'You mean he's your uncle's grandson?' she prompted. Why had he never mentioned his Italian family before? She'd had no idea he had relatives in Italy.

'I guess.' He bent his head to concentrate on his food. The tactic so deliberate, her curiosity only increased.

Picking up the invitation, she scanned the contents again, then flipped it over. 'What does this say?' She pointed to the spidery handwriting scrawled across the back.

He chewed, swallowed, his eyes narrowing. 'You know, Issy, sometimes your persistence can be very annoying.'

She waited calmly for a proper answer.

He huffed, snatched the card and read aloud. 'It says: "We miss you, Giovanni. You are family. Please come this time."' He flicked the card back into the bin. 'Which is insane, because I hardly know the man—or his family.'

'This time? How many times have they invited you to a family event?' It went without saying that he'd never attended any—had probably never even bothered to RSVP.

'I don't know. Hundreds.' He blew out a frustrated breath. 'There's a lot of them. Claudia had five older brothers, and they all had tons of kids. There's an event every other week.'

'Where do they live?' Maybe they lived on the other side of Italy? Maybe that was why he had never bothered to visit them?

'About an hour's drive,' he said. 'The family owns an olive farm near San Giminiano. Most of them still live around there, I guess.' He sent her a bored look. 'So, do you want to tell me why you're so interested?'

A spurt of temper rose up.

Her own family had only consisted of her and her mother. She'd always dreamed of having more. Of having brothers and sisters, cousins and aunts and uncles. She knew perfectly well Gio was an only child too—and from what he'd already told her she knew he'd been a lot more alone than she had as a child. So why hadn't he embraced the chance to get to know his own family?

'For goodness' sake, Gio,' she said, riding the temper. 'Why haven't you been to see them? They're your *family*.'

'I don't have a family. I don't even know them,' he continued. 'They disowned Claudia before I was even born. Cut her out of their lives.'

'Is that why you dislike them?' she asked, confused now, and a little appalled by his indifference. 'Because they treated your mother badly?'

'Of course not!' He sounded annoyed now—annoyed and something else she couldn't quite define. 'I expect she made their lives a misery. I can testify to the fact that she was a nightmare to live with, so I don't blame them for kicking her out.'

She heard the contempt in his voice. So that was why he never talked about his mother.

'Are you upset that they never got to know you as a boy, then?' Issy asked carefully, still trying to understand his hostility towards the rest of his family. *Why* was he so determined to have nothing to do with them?

He pushed his plate away and reached for the pitcher of lemonade. 'Issy, in case you haven't realised yet—'

he poured himself a glass, gulped some down '—this conversation doesn't interest me.'

'Well, it interests *me*,' she said, determined not to back down—not this time. 'I think you *do* blame them. But you shouldn't. It doesn't—'

'I don't blame them.' He shoved his chair back, walked to the balcony rail. 'Why should they care about me? I'm nothing to them.'

Her temper died as she heard the defensiveness in his tone, saw his knuckles whiten where they gripped the terrace rail.

'That's clearly not true,' she said, feeling desperately sad for him. 'Or why would they have invited you to this christening?' She watched his shoulders tense, but he didn't say anything. 'There must be a reason why they didn't try to get to know you as a child. Maybe they—'

'They did try,' he interrupted her. 'I met Carlo. Once. He came to our apartment in Rome.' He paused, his voice barely audible above the breeze. 'Claudia wasn't there. She'd been out all night at some party, and I was in the place alone.'

'How old were you?' she asked gently. She'd tried not to think of him as a boy too much since their first night in Florence. Had tried not to make the mistake of reading too much into his parents' behaviour and its effect on him. But now she wanted to know. How bad had it been?

'Ten,' he said, as if it weren't particularly significant.

She bit down on her lip, tried not to let the thought of that neglected boy get to her.

But then another shattering thought occurred to her, and she felt tears sting the back of her throat.

As long as she had known Gio he had always called his parents Claudia and the Duke. Even as a boy he had never referred to them as Mum or Dad. And now Issy knew why. Because in all the ways that counted they had never been his mother and father. Just people who had battled over him and then rejected him.

'What happened?' She asked. 'With Carlo?'

Gio shrugged, the movement stiff. 'Not a lot. He asked to see Claudia. We waited together for her to come home. He told me who he was, asked me about myself. How old was I? What did I like doing? My Italian wasn't great then, and his questions confused me.'

He sounded so puzzled, even now, and her heart ached. No wonder Gio had no faith in relationships, in family. He'd never been part of one. Not one where people cared for you and about you and were interested in what you did and said.

'She came home eventually,' he said, derision edging his voice. 'Coked up to the eyeballs as usual. They had a massive row, she called the police, and he had to leave. He never came back. But the invitations started to come a few months later. Always addressed to me. She threw them away—wouldn't let me open them. After her death I replied to a few, giving excuses why I couldn't come, but they didn't get the hint so now I throw them away.'

'I think you should go.' Taking the card back out of the bin, she crossed the balcony, placed a hand on his back. 'I think you should go to this christening. See your family. See Carlo again.' Suddenly it seemed vitally important.

He turned round, stared down at the card she held but didn't take it.

'Issy, for God's sake.' He cupped her cheek in his

palm, his eyes shadowed. 'Haven't you heard a word I've said? I don't want to go. I don't belong there,' he murmured.

She rested her hand on his heart, felt the rapid beats. 'Yes, you do. You don't have to be scared of them, you know.'

'I'm not scared. Don't be idiotic.'

But she could hear defensiveness behind the irritation.

He was scared. He was scared to let them get too close. To trust them. To trust anyone.

Her heart clutched as he looked away.

Every child deserved to be loved unconditionally, supported in whatever they chose to do. She thought of the way her own mother had loved and supported her in every mad decision she'd ever made in her life. Edie had always been there. Praising her as if she'd been Sarah Bernhardt when she'd played a tomato in her first school play. Providing a shoulder to cry on when she'd bawled her eyes out over Gio. Even nagging her into admitting that her lifelong dream of becoming an actress needed some serious tweaking after she'd begun her job at the Crown and Feathers and discovered that she preferred bossing people about to angsting about her motivation.

For all his apparent confidence and charisma, Gio had never had any of that as a child. He'd been entirely alone—criticised and rejected by his father, or neglected and ignored by his mother. Even though he'd made a staggering success of his life, he'd survived emotionally by closing himself off and convincing himself he didn't need love.

He'd persuaded himself it wasn't important, that it didn't matter to him, when obviously it did.

Gio had needed a friend as a boy, and he still needed one now. To show him there was another way.

'They can make your life so much richer, Gio. Can't you see that?'

He gave a harsh laugh. 'You've still got a romantic streak a mile wide, haven't you?' He leaned back against the rail, his stance deliberately casual. 'I'm not interested in meeting Claudia's family. I've got nothing to offer them. And they've got nothing to offer me.'

She stared at him, saw stubborn refusal, but she knew it wasn't true. He had so much to give. And he could get so much back in return.

'There's only one thing I need.' He took the invitation from her. 'And it's got nothing to do with this.' He flicked the card onto the table behind her.

He grasped her waist, tugged her close, then slanted his lips across hers.

She curled her fingers into his hair and kissed him back, not caring that he was trying to make a point. Not caring any more what the point was. Because she could taste his desperation right alongside his desire.

He bracketed her waist, boosted her into his arms. 'Wrap your legs around me.'

She did as he commanded, feathering kisses over his brow, his chin, his cheeks, as he strode through the French doors into the master bedroom.

He took her mouth again as he lay beside her, his hard, beautiful body covering hers. The kiss was so deep and dangerous and full of purpose she wanted to scream.

They wrestled their robes off together.

He delved into the curls at her core with clever, insistent fingers.

'I love the way you're always wet for me,' he murmured as she bucked beneath him, cried out, the twist and bite of arousal so vicious it stunned her.

She peaked in a rush of savage sensation. Before she had a chance to draw a steady breath he gripped her hips and settled between her thighs.

She grasped his shoulders, opened for him as he plunged.

The fullness of the strokes had her building to a crescendo again with staggering speed, the harsh grunts of his breathing matching her broken sobs. But instead of cresting this time she cruised the brutal orgasm for an eternity, shooting up and then clawing back until she felt trapped in a vortex of pleasure too intense to survive.

Straining, desperate, she crashed over into the abyss at last, and heard his roar of fulfilment as he crashed and burned behind her.

Issy combed the damp curls at his nape with shaking fingers, her body still quivering from the aftermath of the titanic orgasm.

Had that been sex? She felt as if she'd just survived an earthquake.

He lifted his head. But he didn't speak. He looked as stunned as she felt. Easing out of her, he flopped down by her side.

Then cursed. 'I didn't wear a condom. Is that going to be a problem?'

The flat words took a moment to penetrate her fuzzy brain. 'Sorry. What?'

'No condom.' He cleared his throat. 'I forgot.' He propped himself up on his elbow, leaned over her. 'When's your next period?'

'I…' She tried to grasp the meaning, the rigid tone.

'You're not in the middle of your cycle, are you?'

'No. No, I'm not. I'm due soon.' She did a quick mental calculation. 'Tomorrow, I think.'

He lay back on the bed. 'Thank God.' The relief in his voice made her cheeks burn.

'What about emergency contraception?' she whispered, her mind trying to cling to practicalities. 'Is there somewhere near here we could get it?' The thought of taking the morning-after pill, something she'd never had to do before, made her stomach clench.

'You'd probably need a prescription,' he said, so matter-of-factly it made her heart pound.

'Oh.' She sat up, disorientated. 'It doesn't matter. It'll probably be fine,' she said, the words catching in her throat. 'I can get it from a pharmacy in the UK— perhaps I should arrange a flight just in case.' They hadn't talked about when she would leave. Why hadn't they talked about it? It suddenly seemed vitally important. 'I'll look into that now.' She swung her feet off the bed, struggling for calm as she pulled on her robe.

He caught her arm as she tried to stand. 'You're being irrational. There's no need to book a flight.' He paused. 'I'll get the jet to take you.' He caressed the inside of her elbow with his thumb. 'But let's wait till tomorrow.'

The quiet comment brought with it a rush of excitement that made no sense at all.

This was silly. She should leave—sooner rather than later after their little accident—so why was she so pleased with the casual offer?

'But we only agreed to a couple of days.' She should go. Why didn't she want to?

He brushed her hair behind her ear. 'We did something stupid, that's all. You said yourself it probably won't lead to anything.' He tucked his index finger under her chin.

She tried to rein in her galloping heartbeat. His eyes were full of an intensity she'd never seen before.

'Don't worry. We'll sort it out if we need do.' His deep, steady voice was reassuring, the stroke of his hand on her hair making her heart-rate slow to a canter.

Why did it feel as if everything had spun off its axis and nothing made any sense any more?

He took her shoulders, held her at arm's length to look into her eyes. 'Let's not think about it today. Tomorrow is soon enough. Go and get dressed. Wear something fancy. We'll go somewhere special.' He brushed a kiss across her brow, making her smile despite her confusion. 'It'll take our minds off it.'

'Do you really think—'

'We can go anywhere you want,' he interrupted her. 'Your choice.'

'Okay,' she said, more pleased than she probably should be at the thought that she didn't have to go today.

She hurried into the bathroom, shut the door and leaned back against it, letting the excited little hammer-beats of her pulse drown out the doubts. Everything was fine. More than fine. They'd made a silly mistake, but it didn't have to mean anything.

She'd always found it hard to hold back as a teenager, to weigh and judge and interpret other people's feelings properly. It was the reason she'd fallen so easily for Gio, and she'd worked long and hard in the decade since at keeping her emotions in check and never letting them get the better of her again. But maybe she'd held on too hard, turned herself into someone she really wasn't.

It didn't have to be a bad thing that she had such strong feelings for Gio. They had a shared history, and now she'd spent time with him, and understood the extent of his parents' neglect and what it had done to him, it made sense that she would feel their friendship more keenly.

She twisted the gold-plated taps on the large designer tub.

She'd come here to get over her past mistakes, but surely the best way to do that was to heal the part of herself she'd lost that night. She didn't have to be frightened of her feelings for Gio any more.

When their fling was over they would go their separate ways, having reclaimed the good things from their childhood and left behind the bad.

As the water gushed out, and she sprinkled bath salts, another thought occurred to her and she smiled.

Gio had said she could pick their destination for this afternoon. And she knew exactly where she wanted to go. She wasn't the only one who needed to heal.

But as Issy slipped into the steamy, scented water, and let the lavender bubbles massage her tired muscles, she couldn't quite shake the suspicion she had failed to grasp something vitally important.

* * *

What the hell had he done?

Gio lay on the bed, his arm folded under his head, as he stared at the fan on the ceiling.

He'd taken her without a condom. He turned his head to stare at the bathroom and heard the reassuring hum of running water.

Except he wasn't feeling all that reassured.

Had he totally lost his mind?

He never, ever forgot to wear condoms. Partly for personal safety reasons, but mostly because he had absolutely no desire to father a child. Even if the woman said she was on the pill. No matter how hot he got, or how desperate he was to make love, he always used protection.

But Issy got him hotter and more desperate than any woman he'd ever met—and for the first time ever the thought of contraception hadn't entered his head.

She'd made him feel raw and vulnerable with all that nonsense about getting to know Claudia's family, until he'd been desperate to shut her up. But the minute he'd tasted her, the minute he'd touched her, the usual longing had welled up inside him and all he'd been able to think about was burying himself inside her. Before he knew what was happening he'd been glorying in the exquisite clasp of her body and shooting his seed deep into her womb without a thought to the consequences.

It hadn't been a mistake, or an oversight. It had been sheer madness.

Getting off the bed, he shrugged into his robe, then scraped his fingers through his hair.

How the hell had this happened? He felt more out of control than ever now.

What if she actually got pregnant? He knew Issy. She

would never consider an abortion. But he didn't want a child. He knew what it was like to be an afterthought, an inconvenience, a mistake.

And why had he asked her to stay? By rights he should have been breaking the speed limit to race her to the airport even now, and then piloting the plane back to England to make sure she got whatever she needed to ensure there was no chance of a baby.

Temporary insanity had to be the answer. He slumped into a chair by the terrace table and frowned at the remnants of their aborted lunch. Although he wasn't sure how temporary it was any more.

The woman was driving him nuts. In the last few days he'd become addicted to everything about her.

The fresh, sweet scent of her hair when he woke up beside her in the morning, the sound of her voice as she chatted away about everything and nothing, even the stubborn tilt of her chin and the compassion in those deep blue eyes when she had tried to insist he go to that stupid Christening.

He'd become so enthralled he'd gone to the office this morning just to prove he could. But the plan had backfired—because he hadn't been able to stay away. And then he'd found her on the sun-lounger, her skin pink from too much sun, and he hadn't been able to keep his hands off her.

They'd nearly made a spectacle of themselves in front of Carlotta. And, while he'd found Issy's outraged dignity amusing at the time, it didn't seem all that funny any more.

But the worst moment had come when she'd announced she was going to book a flight home. He'd actually felt his stomach tighten with dread. And it had taken a major effort not to let the panic show.

He never got worked up about women. But he'd got worked up about her.

He walked towards the guest suite, steadfastly resisting the urge to join Issy in the master bath. He needed to take a break, because ravaging Issy senseless wasn't turning out to be the cure-all he'd been hoping for.

He frowned as he entered the bathroom of the guest suite.

Maybe that was the problem. He wasn't used to sharing his home with the women he dated, having unlimited sex on tap. As soon as the novelty wore off he'd be able to let Issy go with no trouble at all. And everything would be back to normal. Getting her out of his system was just taking longer than originally planned.

He reached for the shower control. A trip into town might be just what he needed.

He never would have believed it, but maybe you really could have too much of a good thing.

'You want to go *where*?' Gio's fingers clenched on the Ferrari's steering wheel as all his positive feelings about their afternoon out crashed and burned.

'I have the address right here.'

He watched, stunned into silence, as Issy pulled the christening invitation out of her handbag and reeled off the address.

'You were right,' she chirped. 'It is in San Giminiano. And I've got my posh frock on, just like you suggested. So we're all set.' She smiled, looking deceptively sweet as she pressed the button on the dash to bring up the car's inbuilt navigation system. 'Shall I programme the GPS?'

He shoved the panel back into the dash. 'We've already had this conversation. We're not going,' he said firmly, prepared to argue the point if she decided to sulk.

But instead of the expected pout she simply stared at him. 'You said I could choose. I choose to go to your cousin's christening.'

There was that stubborn little chin again. And it wasn't enchanting him any more.

'He's *not* my cousin.' Why couldn't she get that through her head? 'He's nothing to me. None of them are.'

'If that's the case, why are you so frightened of paying them a visit?'

'I'm *not* frightened.' She'd accused him of that before, and it was starting to annoy him.

'Then prove it,' she said softly.

He opened his mouth to tell her to go to hell. He wasn't ten any more, and he didn't take dares. But then he saw the sympathy, the understanding in her eyes, and the words wouldn't come.

He cursed under his breath. 'Okay, we'll go to the christening.' He flipped up the GPS. 'But you're going to be bored out of your brain. I guarantee it.'

As he stabbed in the co-ordinates, she leaned across the console and kissed his cheek.

'No, I won't be. And neither will you.' Her fingers touched his thigh, stroked reassuringly. 'It's going to be an experience you'll never forget.'

I know, he thought grimly, as he gunned the engine.

CHAPTER EIGHT

'*GIOVANNI, mio ragazzo. Benvenuto alla famiglia.*'

Issy blinked away tears, hearing the gruff affection in the elderly man's voice as he threw his arms wide to greet his long-lost nephew.

Stiff and hesitant in the designer suit he'd worn for a different occasion entirely, Gio leant down and accepted the kisses Carlo Lorenzo placed on his cheeks. The old man chuckled, then clasped Gio's hand with gnarled fingers, talking all the time. Issy hadn't a clue what was being said, but she could guess from the confusion on Gio's face and his short, monosyllabic answers that Carlo was as overjoyed to see him as the rest of his family.

She huffed out a breath, so relieved she had to reach into her purse and find a tissue.

As the Ferrari had swung round the twisting mountain roads to the Lorenzo farm, she'd begun to doubt her decision to make Gio come to the christening.

What if she'd been wrong to suggest he come? What if the family didn't welcome him as she expected?

With each mile that passed Gio had become more tense and withdrawn, answering her questions in curt

sentences and handling the car with none of his usual
skill. It was the first time she'd ever seen him nervous,
and his reaction had forced her into admitting an un-
pleasant truth.

What had made her think she had the right to meddle
in his life? He'd never shown any interest in meddling
in hers. They'd been in an intimate relationship for a
grand total of three days. An intimate relationship that
would be over very soon. Yes, they were friends, but that
was all they were. Did that really give her the right to
make assumptions about what he needed in his life?

Now, as Carlo continued to chat away to Gio, she let
her pleasure at the wonderful way Gio's family had
greeted him push the doubts away. This could have gone
so horribly wrong. But it hadn't—which counted for a lot.

'You are Giovanni's *ragazza*, yes?'

Issy glanced round to see a petite, pretty and heavily
pregnant young woman dressed in a colourful summer
dress smiling at her.

Issy stuffed the tissue back into her bag and held out
her hand. 'I'm Issy Helligan,' she said quickly, not quite
sure how to reply to the question.

Didn't *ragazza* mean girlfriend? Was she Gio's girlfriend? Not really. Not in any permanent sense.

'I'm a friend of Gio's,' she said, feeling oddly dis-
pirited. 'I'm so sorry, but I don't speak much Italian.'

'It is good I speak excellent English, then,' the
woman said, her brown eyes—which were the exact
shade of Gio's—alight with mischief. 'Or we would
not be able to gossip about my long-lost cousin. My
name is —after La Loren.' She wrinkled her nose.
'Sadly, I only got her name and not her body.'

Issy laughed, liking Sophia instantly. 'When is your baby due?' she asked.

Sophia looked down at her bump, her eyes glowing as she stroked it. 'In two weeks. But my husband Aldo says it will be sooner. Our two boys were early, and he will not let me forget it.'

'That's sweet,' she said unable to deny the whisper of envy.

Hearing the love and contentment in Sophia's voice made Issy want to reach for her tissue again. This woman looked younger than her, and she already had two children and another on the way—and a man who loved her.

What on earth have I been doing with my life?

'Come.' Sophia deftly linked her arm with Issy's. 'I have been told to fetch you by my sisters, my aunts and all my girl cousins.' She drew her away from Gio, who looked shell-shocked and a little hunted as Carlo introduced him to more relatives he had never met.

'They all want to know about you and Giovanni,' Sophia added, dropping her voice to a conspiratorial whisper. 'He is like the prodigal son, no? You are very beautiful.' She gave Issy an appreciative once-over. 'And we are very nosy.'

'Oh, Gio and I aren't really…' Issy hesitated. 'We're not exactly…' She paused again. She didn't want to mislead Sophia, but how did she describe what she and Gio were, exactly? 'There isn't that much to gossip about,' she said lamely, glancing over her shoulder. 'And I feel like a traitor leaving Gio alone. I'm the one who suggested he come today.'

Gio glared at her as he was kissed and hugged by a group of older men she assumed were his other uncles.

'Giovanni is a big boy,' Sophia said, patting Issy's arm and tugging her towards a huge trestle table on the farm's flagstone terrace, laden with an array of mouth-watering dishes. 'And he will not be alone.'

A large group of women and girls, ranging in age from twelve to ninety, clustered around the table, watching Issy with undisguised curiosity—making her feel like even more of a fraud.

'My father has been waiting for over twenty years to see *il ragazzo perduto* again,' Sophia added. 'He will be showing him off for hours. But when the dancing starts we will get him back for you.'

Dancing? Issy smiled at the thought. Funny to think she'd never danced with Gio before.

She allowed Sophia to lead her away, ignoring the panicked plea in Gio's eyes. It would do him good to be fêted by his family. That was exactly why they were here. So that he could reconnect with what really mattered in life. And it wouldn't do her any harm to stay out of his way. To absorb the wonder of this large, happy and loving family—and reconnect with her own pri-orities in life.

'What does *il ragazzo perduto* mean?' she asked absently.

Sophia sent her a warm smile. 'Carlo calls Giovanni "the lost boy". He has worried about him ever since he went to Rome years ago and met him. Carlo said without the family he had no one to love him, to care for him.' Sophia's smile turned knowing. 'But, seeing the way you look at him, I don't think he's lost any more.'

Issy's pulse jumped at the softly spoken words. *Pardon me?*

* * *

'Let's dance, Isadora.'

Issy's head turned at the deep, commanding voice as strong fingers gripped her elbow. 'Oh, hi, Gio.' Her lips tilted up in an instant smile.

He looked confused, harassed and exhausted.

'So you finally escaped from your uncle?' she said brightly.

'Don't you dare laugh.' He skewered her with a quelling look. 'The man has been talking my ear off for two solid hours. And he's introduced me to more people in one afternoon than I've met in my entire life. All of whom he insists I'm related to.'

He treated Sophia and the other women to a quick greeting in Italian, but before any of them could reply, he clamped his hand round Issy's arm and directed her towards the wooden dance floor that had been constructed in the middle of the olive grove.

Dusk was falling, but fairy lights had been hung from the heavily burdened olive trees, casting a magical glow on the couples already slow-dancing in the twilight.

'I've had my cheek pinched by not one but two grannies,' he continued, his voice pained as they stepped onto the uneven boards and he swung her into his arms. 'I've been made to recite my life story about twenty times.' He wrapped his arm round her waist and pulled her flush against his lean, hard body. 'I've been force-fed my Aunt Donatella's *fusilli ortolana* and my second cousin Elisabetta's rabbit *cacciatore*.' He twirled her round in time to the slow, seductive beat of the music before holding her close in his arms. 'And come within a hair's breadth of getting peed on by the guest of honour.'

Issy stifled a laugh as her heart kicked in her chest.

Beneath the confusion and the fatigue she could see the creases around his eyes crinkling and hear the amusement in his voice.

The day had been a success. He looked tired, but happy.

She rested her cheek on his chest, gripped his hand. There had been no need to panic. All the questions she'd been fielding from Sophia and her family had unsettled her, but coming to the christening had been an unqualified success.

'I'm shattered,' he said, leaning down to whisper in her ear, his hands flattening on the bare skin of her back. 'And the only thing that's kept me going is the thought of all the ways I'm going to make you pay for this later tonight.'

Issy pulled away to lay a palm on his cheek. 'Poor Gio. It's tough being loved, isn't it?'

He stopped in the middle of the dance floor. 'What did you say?' His face was masked by the lights behind him, but she could hear his wariness, his sharpness.

'I said it's tough being loved,' she said, wishing she hadn't seen him tense. The emotional stability she'd been working so hard on in the last few hours started to wobble again.

'They don't love me. They're just good people doing what they consider to be their duty.'

They did love him. How could he not see it?

She wanted to argue the point, but knew from the rigid line of his jaw he would refuse to believe it. The ripple of disappointment had her shivering, despite the sultry evening air.

'My father wants me to translate for him.' Sophia stood beside Carlo as the old man clasped Issy's hands.

'Because Giovanni has told him your Italian is not so good. Yet.'

'Oh, has he now?' Issy joked, although her emotions felt perilously close to the surface.

Sophia smiled back as Carlo began to speak in a sober, steady voice, before lifting Issy's hand to his lips and giving it a chivalrous kiss.

Sophia translated. 'My father says that his heart is full with gratitude to you for making Giovanni come today, after being lost to his family for so many years. He says that you are a beautiful woman both inside and out and he hopes that Giovanni can see this too.'

Issy felt herself blush, dismayed by the old man's words.

Carlo turned to Gio and took his hand. Issy felt Gio tense beside her as his uncle spoke. He dipped his head, spots of colour rising on his cheeks beneath his tan as Carlo patted his cheek, his voice rough with pride.

Tears pricked the back of Issy's eyes as Sophia translated.

'My father says that the Lorenzo family is very proud of Giovanni.' Even Sophia's voice sounded more sober than Issy had ever heard it before. 'For all he has made of his life, despite a mother who did not know how to be a mother. Carlo says that Giovanni has made strong, important and beautiful buildings that will stand for a long time.' Sophia swallowed, her voice as thick with emotion as Issy felt. 'But he must not forget that the only thing that lasts forever is a man's family.' Sophia gave a half-laugh as Carlo finished his speech. 'And that Giovanni is getting older and shouldn't waste any more time getting started.'

Issy laughed too, at the old man's audacity and the

roguish sparkle in his eyes. As Gio replied in Italian Issy noticed the measured tone, devoid of his usual cynicism, and felt her heart lift. He wasn't completely blind to what these people had to offer, whatever he might think.

As they said their goodbyes to everyone, Issy's hand strayed automatically to her belly.

What if their mistake ended in a pregnancy?

To her surprise, the question didn't bring the panic she might have expected. But she forced the thought away anyway. A pregnancy was highly unlikely. And today had been quite emotional enough already.

The last to say her goodbyes was Sophia, who gave Issy a final hug as Gio climbed into the Ferrari.

'You must both come to the next *battesimo*, as it will be for my baby,' she whispered, before standing back and winking at Issy. 'And if Giovanni does as he is told, maybe the one after that will be yours.'

Issy waved furiously as Gio reversed the car down the farm track, sniffing back tears and trying not to take Sophia's little joke to heart.

What she and Gio had was fleeting. That had always been understood.

But as the whole family shouted salutations at them, and a group of children raced after the car, a few tears slipped over her lids. This was what it felt like to belong, to be part of something bigger than yourself—and she'd never realised how much she wanted it until now.

'That wasn't so bad,' Gio said, resting his palm on Issy's knee as he turned the car onto the main road.

Issy sank into the leather seat and watched the dark shapes of San Giminiano's fortress walls disappear into the night as Gio accelerated. Leaning her head against the door, she rested her palm on her belly, the emotion of the day overwhelming her.

'Will you go back again?' she asked.

He said nothing for several seconds. 'I doubt it.'

Despite the murmured reply, a tiny smile touched the corners of Issy's mouth. Was it wishful thinking, or did he sound less sure of himself than usual?

Easing up the handbrake, Gio stared at the woman fast asleep beside him in the car. She'd been incredible today. So beautiful, so captivating and so important to his peace of mind. He'd needed her there in a way he never would have anticipated.

All through the afternoon and evening, whenever the impact of being introduced to his family had become too much, his gaze had instinctively searched her out. As soon as he'd spotted her—chatting to Sophia and the other women, or playing games with some of the younger children, or charming his elderly uncles with her faltering Italian—and their eyes connected, his heartbeat had levelled out and the strangling feeling of panic and confusion had started to ease.

At one point she'd been cradling baby Carlo in her arms. He'd marvelled at how she could look so relaxed and happy, as if she were a part of this family, even though these people were strangers and she didn't even speak their language. When his uncle had whispered in his ear, 'She will make an excellent mother for your children, Giovanni. She is a natural.'

The old man was hopelessly traditional and senti-mental. It hadn't taken Gio long to realise that. But the foolish words had still made Gio's heartbeat pound, just as it was doing now.

He continued to stare at her in the moonlight—her rich red hair framing that pale heart-shaped face and her hand lying curled over her belly. A picture of her lush body heavily pregnant with his baby formed in his mind. He imagined her full breasts swollen with milk, the nipples large and distended, and her belly round and ripe, ready to give birth. Desire surged to life so fast he had to grit his teeth.

Okay, this was more than temporary insanity. This was becoming an obsession. An obsession he was beginning to fear he had no control over whatsoever.

Adjusting his trousers, he waited in the darkness until he'd finally calmed down enough to scoop Issy up and carry her to their bedroom without causing himself an injury. She barely stirred. But as he undressed her and tucked her into bed the visions of her body ripe with his child refused to go away.

It wasn't the desire that bothered him, though, as he climbed into bed beside her. Their livewire sexual attraction had always been as natural as breathing. It stood to reason a pregnant Issy would turn him on too.

What disturbed him much more was the irrational need and the bone-deep longing that went right along with the lust.

Sweat trickled down his back as the fear he'd been holding onto with an iron grip all day kicked him in the gut.

Issy squinted at the pre-dawn light filtering through the terrace doors, then moaned softly as cramping pain gripped her abdomen. Gio's warm hand stirred against her hip as she listened to the low murmur of his breathing, and tears caught in her throat. The familiar pain could mean only one thing. She was about to start her period.

She bit down hard on her bottom lip, lifting his hand and laying it down behind her. She didn't want to wake him up and have him see her in this state. Slipping out of bed, she made a beeline for the bathroom.

After taking care of the practicalities, she donned one of Gio's bathrobes and sat on the toilet seat, feeling utterly dejected. Which was ridiculous.

The fact that there was no baby was good news.

She'd have to be an idiot to want to get pregnant under these circumstances. She wasn't ready for motherhood yet. And Gio certainly wasn't ready to be a father. Yesterday's trip had proved that beyond a shadow of a doubt. The man was deeply suspicious of love and families and relationships in general. And even though that may have started to change, it would take a lot more than an afternoon spent with his extended family to repair the damage his parents had done.

But, despite all the calm common-sense justifications running through Issy's mind, she felt as if a boulder were pressing against her chest, making it hard for her to breathe.

She got off the toilet seat and reached for some tissues, swiped at her cheeks to catch the errant tears. She blew her nose, brushed her fingers through her hair and stared blankly into the mirror, but the boulder refused to budge.

As she stared at her reflection she thought of Gio the evening before, his cheeks flushed a dull red while his uncle bade him farewell.

Tenderness and longing and hope surged up. And the boulder cut off her air supply.

'Oh, God!'

She collapsed onto the toilet seat, her fist clutching the tissue, her knees trembling and every last ounce of blood seeping from her face.

'I can't have,' she whispered. 'It's only been a few days.'

But she sank her head into her hands and groaned. Because there was no getting away from it. She'd let her emotions loose and now look what had happened? She'd only gone and fallen hopelessly in love with Giovanni Hamilton. Again.

She wanted to deny it. But suddenly all those wayward emotions made complete sense.

Her Pollyanna-like obsession to get Gio to embrace his family. Her blissful happiness at their renewed friendship. Her relentless attempts to understand the traumas of Gio's childhood and then help him fix them. Even her bizarre anguish at the discovery that she wasn't pregnant.

Her fabulous holiday fling had never been about sex, or friendship, or putting the mistakes of her youth behind her. That had been a smokescreen generated by lust and denial.

She groaned louder.

Fabulous. She may well have just made the biggest mistake of her life. Twice.

It took Issy a good ten minutes to get off the toilet seat. But in that time she'd managed to get one crucial thing into perspective.

Falling in love with Gio again didn't have to be a disaster.

The man she'd come to know wasn't the surly, unhappy boy she'd once fallen for. He was more settled, more content and much more mature now. And so was she.

She hadn't imagined the connection between them in the last few days. The power and passion of their love-making. The intensity of their friendship. Or the astonished pride on Gio's face when his uncle Carlo had welcomed him into the bosom of his family.

All of which meant Gio wasn't necessarily a lost cause.

But she also knew that the spectre of that boy was still there. And, given all the casual cruelty that boy had suffered, it wasn't going to be easy for the man to let his guard down and accept that she loved him. Especially not in the space of three days!

After splashing her eyes with cold water, Issy practised a look of delighted relief in the bathroom mirror for when she informed Gio of her unpregnant state.

She mustn't give Gio any clues about how she felt. Not until she'd worked out a strategy. She needed to be calm and measured and responsible this time. The way she *hadn't* been at seventeen. Which meant taking the time to gauge Gio's feelings before she blurted out her own.

Putting her hand on the doorknob, she took a steadying breath—and decided not to dwell on the fact that her strategies so far hadn't exactly been a massive success.

Stepping out of the bathroom, she closed the door behind her, grateful for the darkness.

'What's going on? You okay?'

The deep, sleep-roughened voice made her jump.

'Yes. I'm absolutely fine,' she said, forcing what she hoped was a bright smile onto her face.

'You sure?' He paused to rub his eyes. 'You've been in there forever.'

Propped up on the pillows, the sheet draped over his hips, Gio looked so gorgeous she felt the boulder press on her chest again. She made herself cross the room.

'Actually, I'm better than fine. I've got some good news.' She shrugged off the bathrobe and slipped under the sheet. 'I've started my period.'

He frowned, and something flickered in his eyes, but the light was too dim to make it out. 'So you're not pregnant?' he said dully, as his hand settled on her hip, rubbed.

She snuggled into his arms, pressing her back against his chest.

'What a relief, right?' she said, swallowing down the words that wanted to burst out.

Don't say anything, you ninny. It's far too soon.

'Which means there's no need for any emergency contraceptives,' she continued. 'Here or at home. Thank goodness,' she babbled on, the mention of home making the boulder grow. He'd asked her to stay another night. Did that mean he would expect her to leave today?

He said nothing for a long time. His hand absently circling her hip. The only sound was the deafening hum of the air conditioner.

Would he say something? Give her a sign that he'd like her to stay a little longer? She needed more time.

Eventually he moved. Warm palms settled over her belly and stroked gently, easing the ache from the dull cramps.

'That's good,' he said at last, the murmured words devoid of emotion.

Issy placed her hands over his and breathed in his scent. 'Yes, isn't it?' she said, trying to ignore the now enormous boulder.

He hadn't asked her to stay. But he hadn't asked her to leave either. That had to be a good sign. Didn't it?

'*Buongiorno, signorina.*'

Issy blinked at Carlotta's greeting as she pushed herself up in bed, gripping the sheet to cover her nakedness. She pushed her hair out of her eyes and watched the older woman place a tray on the terrace table, put out a plate of pastries, a pot of coffee and one cup.

She felt achy and tired, as if she hadn't slept at all. Probably because she hadn't. All the questions she didn't have answers for had made her emotions veer from euphoria to devastation during the pre-dawn hours as she'd tried to sleep.

'*Scusami, Carlotta. Dové Signor Hamilton?*' she asked, doing her best to pronounce the question correctly.

The housekeeper smiled and replied in Italian, speaking far too fast for Issy to catch more than a few words. Then Carlotta took a folded note out of her apron pocket, passed it to Issy, bobbed a quick curtsy and left.

Issy waited until the door had closed, a feeling of dread settling over her, before glancing at the clock on the mantelpiece. It wasn't even nine o'clock yet. Where could Gio have gone?

She opened the note, her hands trembling. But as she read it her breath gushed out in a shaky puff.

Sorry, Issy.
Had business at the office. You'll have to survive
without me today.
Back around dinnertime. Ask Carlotta if you
need anything.
Ciao, Gio

A lone tear trickled down her cheek as the hope she'd
been clinging to dissolved.

How could he have gone to the office without waiting
for her to wake up? She sniffed heavily. Well, she
wouldn't have to worry about blurting out her feelings,
seeing as he wasn't even here.

It was only after she'd read it three more times that
the full import of the curt dismissive note dawned on her.

What had Gio really been hoping for when he'd left
this morning? The veiled message in the cursory note
seemed obvious all of a sudden. When he returned home
tonight, he hoped to discover the sticky business of
ending their affair had been dealt with in his absence.
He hadn't said anything about her leaving last night
because he'd hadn't felt he needed to. It had always been
understood that she would go once her period started.

The agony threatened to swamp her as she choked
down breakfast and got dressed, but she refused to let
any tears fall. There would be time enough for that
when she got home.

After breakfast, Issy packed her bag and arranged a
flight home via the computer terminal in Gio's study.
She rang Maxi and told her she would be at the theatre
tomorrow, ready to get back to work. The conversation
fortified her. She needed to return to her own life. To

start grounding herself in reality again. But as she disconnected the call and keyed in the number Carlotta had given her to book a cab to the airport, her fighting spirit finally put in an appearance.

Her fingers paused on the buttons.

Why was she making this so easy for Gio? Why was she letting him call all the shots, even now?

By keeping quiet about her feelings earlier, by trying to be mature and sensible and take things slowly she'd played right into his hands.

She'd been prepared to give Gio everything—not just her body, but her heart and her soul too. And even if he didn't want them, or the family and the life they could build together, didn't she at least owe it to herself to tell him how she felt?

After getting an address for Gio's office out of Carlotta, Issy booked a cab to take her to the airport. But when the cab arrived twenty minutes later she handed the driver the piece of notepaper with the Florence address scribbled on it, explaining in her faltering Italian that she needed to make a quick stop first.

She had four hours before her flight. More than enough time to see Gio one last time and let him know exactly what he was chucking away.

CHAPTER NINE

EXHAUSTED, but determined, Issy walked into the domed reception area of the stunning glass and steel building on the banks of the Arno.

She'd figured out exactly what she was going to say to Gio and exactly how she was going to say it during the drive into the city. She would be calm, poised and articulate, and would keep a tight grip on her emotions. Under no circumstances would she dissolve into a gibbering wreck as she had at seventeen and let Gio see her utterly destroyed.

Because she wasn't. She'd matured over the last ten years—enough to know that she had to accept the things she couldn't change. However much it hurt. Because she couldn't afford to spend another ten years pining over a man who had nothing to offer her.

'*Mi scusi*, *parle inglese*, *signor?*' she asked the perfectly groomed young man at the reception desk, praying he did speak English.

'Yes, signorina. What can I do for you?' he replied in heavily accented English.

'I would like to see Giovanni Hamilton.'

'Do you have an appointment?'

'No, I'm...' She stuttered to a halt, the heat spreading up her neck. 'I'm a friend of his.'

The young man didn't show by a single flicker of his eyelashes what he thought of that statement, but the heat still hit Issy's cheeks as her hard-fought-for composure faltered. How many other women had come to his offices like this? Looking for something he wasn't going to give them?

'I need to see him if at all possible,' she soldiered on. 'It's extremely important.'

To me, at least.

She wasn't sure if the receptionist believed her or simply took pity on her, but he sent her a sympathetic smile as he reached for the phone on his desk. 'I will contact his office manager. What is your name?'

'Isadora Helligan.'

After conducting a brief conversation in Italian, the receptionist hung up the phone.

'His office manager says he is at a site meeting, but if you would like to go up to the top floor she will contact him.'

The stylish young men and women working on state-of-the-art computers and at large drawing easels stopped to watch as Issy walked through the huge open-plan office on the sixth floor—and her composure began to unravel completely.

What was she doing here? Was this another of her hare-brained ideas that was destined to end up kicking her in the teeth? And how the hell was she going to stop herself dissolving into tears with a boulder the size of Mount Everest already lodged in her throat?

Given her tenuous emotional state, she was extremely grateful when Gio's calm, matronly officer manager, who also spoke English, ushered her into Gio's office and informed her that Signor Hamilton had interrupted his meeting at the site office and would be with her in about ten minutes.

Well, at least he wasn't avoiding her.

Unfortunately Gio's office, which took up one whole corner of the floor, was made completely of glass. As she sat down on the green leather sofa adjacent to his desk, and stared out of the floor-to-ceiling window at the Florence cityscape, she could feel the eyes of all his employees burning into the back of her neck.

After suffering from goldfish-in-a-bowl syndrome for an endless five minutes, she paced to the window and stared out at the Florence skyline, the enormity of the task ahead hitting her all over again.

Did she really want to do this? If Gio dismissed her feelings, the way he had done ten years ago, how much harder would it be to pick up the pieces of her shattered heart?

'Issy, this is a nice surprise. Why don't I take you to lunch?'

She lifted her head and saw Gio standing in the office doorway, his shirtsleeves rolled up and his suit trousers creased and flecked with mud. He looked rumpled and ridiculously pleased to see her. His impossibly handsome face relaxed into a sexy, inviting smile.

Mount Everest turned into the Himalayas.

How could she love him so much and not know whether he was even capable of loving her in return?

'I don't have time for lunch,' she said, glad when her

voice hardly faltered. 'I dropped by to tell you I'm catching a flight home this evening.'

The smile disappeared, to be replaced by a sharp frown. He closed the door and walked towards her. 'What the hell for?'

Tell him now. Tell him why.

She tried to find the words, but the dark fury in his eyes shocked her into silence.

'You're not getting a flight home tonight…or tomorrow.' He grasped her arm, hauled her against him. 'You're staying at the villa even if I have to tie you to the bloody bed.'

'You can't do that.' She was so astonished the words came out on a gasp.

'Don't bet on it. This isn't over. And until I decide it is you're not going anywhere. So you'll have to call your people and let them know.'

'My…? What?' she stammered, her mouth dropping open.

'*Dio*!' He let go of her arm and stalked past her, a stream of what she assumed were swear-words in Italian coming out of his mouth.

Flinging the door open, he shouted something at a colleague. It was only then that she noticed every one in the office beyond was standing up at their desks and gawking at them. Some were whispering to each other, others were gaping in open curiosity. They'd all heard every word. And, knowing her luck, they probably all spoke perfect English.

But as she stood there being stared at, while Gio's office manager made an announcement to the staff, she simply didn't have it in her to blush. So she and Gio had made a spectacle of themselves? So what? Frankly, she was past embarrassment and past caring what anyone else thought.

She was too busy trying to figure out Gio's temper tantrum.

Clearly he hadn't intended his note to be a thinly veiled invitation for her to go before he got home, as she had suspected.

The news should have pleased her. But it didn't.

Why was he so angry with her? And what right did he have to order her about like that? Had she really been that much of a push-over that he thought he could treat her like his personal possession? This didn't feel like good news. Had they ever really been friends? Or had that been an illusion too?

She waited by the desk, folding her arms across her midriff to stop the tremors racking her body as she watched Gio's employees troop off towards the lifts. Most of them glanced over their shoulders as they left, to get one last juicy look at the crazy lady.

Five long minutes later they were entirely alone, the whole floor having been evacuated.

He propped his butt on the desk, braced his hands on the edge. 'Now, I want to know what's going on.' The stiff tone suggested he was making an effort to keep hold of his temper. 'Why do you want to go home?'

The question had the Himalayas rising up in her throat to choke her. But she couldn't tell him she loved him now. Not until she knew whether she had ever meant more than all the others.

'Why do you want me to stay?'

* * *

I want you to love me.

The plea formed in Gio's mind and he recoiled.

He couldn't say that. Now now. Not ever. He didn't want her love. He didn't want anyone's love.

After lying awake for hours this morning, listening to her sleep, he'd forced himself to leave the house in a desperate attempt to put the whole fiasco out of his head.

Unfortunately burying himself in work hadn't had the effect he'd hoped. Instead of forgetting about her, he'd missed her even more than yesterday. To the point where, when his manager had called to say she'd arrived to see him, he'd broken off an important site meeting to rush back and take her to lunch.

And then she'd told him she was leaving and he'd lost it completely.

He was behaving like a lovesick fool. Which was preposterous. He wasn't in love. He couldn't let himself be in love.

'What do I want?' he replied. 'I want what I've always wanted.' He sank his fingers into her hair, drew her mouth close to his, vindicated by the flash of arousal in her eyes.

Her lips parted instinctively, but as he plundered she dragged her mouth away, staggered back.

'That's not good enough,' she said, the deep blue eyes turbulent with emotion. 'Not any more. I can't stay just for the sex.'

'Why not? It's what we do best,' he said, unable to prevent the bitter edge in his voice.

She'd tricked him into this—just as she'd tricked him into going to that christening yesterday. And now he was paying the price.

She flinched as if he'd struck her. 'Because I want more than that.'

'There isn't any more.'

'Yes, there is. I love you.'

He heard the words, and felt panic strangle him as the great gaping wounds he'd kept closed for so long were ripped open. 'Don't worry, you'll get over it.'

'I don't want to get over it,' Issy stated, the sharp, searing pain at his dismissal ramming into her body like a blow. It had taken every last ounce of her courage to say the words. Only to have them thrown back at her with barely a moment's hesitation.

How could he be so callous? This was worse than the last time—much worse.

'Doesn't it matter to you at all how I feel?' she whispered.

'I told you right from the start I'm not looking for…that.' He couldn't even bring himself to say the word. 'You chose to misinterpret that. Not me.'

She felt numb. Anaesthetised against the pain by shock and disbelief. How could she have been so wrong about him? How could she have been so wrong about everything?

She crossed her arms over her chest, forced her mind to engage. 'I see,' she said dully, her voice on autopilot. 'So this is all my own fault? Is that what you're saying?'

Suddenly it seemed vitally important that she understand. Why had she made so many mistakes where he was concerned?

'Issy, for God's sake.' He stepped close, tried to take

her hand, but she pulled back. 'I never meant to hurt you. I *told* you what I wanted—'

'Why does it always have to be about what *you* want?' she interrupted, allowing resentment through to quell the vicious pain. But as she looked at his handsome face, tense with annoyance, she suddenly understood what it was he had always lacked. And the reality of how he'd played her—of how she'd *let him* play her—became clear.

'I never realised what a coward you are,' she said softly.

He stiffened as if she had slapped him. 'What the hell does that mean?'

She scrubbed the tears off her cheeks with an impatient fist. 'You say all you want is sex, that relationships don't matter to you, because you're too scared to want more.'

'That's insane!' he shouted. But his angry words couldn't hurt her any more.

He'd never wanted what she had to offer—and that was something she would have to learn to live with. But he hadn't needed to be so cruel.

They *had* been friends. She hadn't imagined that. And maybe one day they could have had more—but he'd thrown it away because he didn't have the guts to try. And she knew why.

'Your parents hurt you, Gio. They treated you like a commodity and never gave you the love you deserved. You survived. But you'll never be truly free until you stop letting what they did rule your life.'

'This has nothing to do with them,' he snapped, with the same closed-off expression on his face she had seen so many times before. He still didn't get it—but, worse than that, she knew now he never would.

'Doesn't it?' she said wearily as she walked past him towards the door.

'Come back here, dammit.'

She didn't turn at the shouted words. Didn't have the strength to argue. What would be the point when she could never win?

'I'm not going to come chasing after you, Issy, if that's what all this is supposed to achieve.'

She carried on walking, her heart breaking all over again at the defiant tone.

She had never been the enemy. Why couldn't he see that?

CHAPTER TEN

'DO YOU think our new sponsor will want his company's name on the cover page?'

Issy's fingers paused on the computer keyboard at Maxi's enquiry. 'Sorry? What?' she asked, even though she'd heard every word.

'I'm putting the finishing touches to the new programmes. Shouldn't we add your Duke's company name to it?'

'Yes, I suppose so,' she replied, as the all-too-familiar vice tightened across her torso. 'That's a great idea,' she added, with an enthusiasm she didn't feel.

She'd left Florence over two weeks ago. And she couldn't even talk about the sponsorship without falling apart.

When was she going to get over this?

She didn't want to think about it any more, go on re-playing every little nuance of Gio's behaviour during the hours she had spent in his house. Apart from the fact that it was exhausting her, it wasn't going to change a thing.

She'd thought she'd made a major breakthrough a week ago, when she'd come to the conclusion that she hadn't been crazy enough to fall in love after only three short days. She knew now she'd never stopped loving him. In all the years they'd been apart her love had lurked in some small corner of her heart, just waiting to be rediscovered.

But now she knew how hopeless it was, shouldn't she be able to move on?

To start rebuilding her life?

Gio would have moved on the minute she'd walked out the door. And, however sad that made her, she should be grateful. At least his indifference meant his company hadn't pulled the theatre's sponsorship.

She'd allowed herself to get so wrapped up in Gio she'd completely forgotten about the theatre. Which had added a nice thick layer of guilt to the heartache and recriminations in the weeks since her return.

Taking a professional attitude now was essential. And if she had to deal with Gio in the future, as a result of his donation, it would be a small penance to pay. The theatre was now her number one priority.

'Why don't you give the Florence office a call and see what they say?' she said to Maxi, not quite ready to take the next step.

'Are you sure you don't want to ring them?' Maxi asked, a quick grin tugging at her lips. 'They might put you through to the Dishy Duke.'

'No, that's okay,' she said tightly. 'I'm busy doing Jake's bio.' She turned back to her keyboard.

She hadn't told Maxi what had happened in Florence, despite a lot of probing, and she didn't intend to. Talking about it would only make it harder to forget.

She continued to type, glad when the hammer thumps of the keys shut out Maxi's call to Florence. But

as she tapped in the final piece of biographical information from Jake's scribbled notes she couldn't miss the
sound of Maxi putting the phone back in its cradle.

'Everything go okay?' Issy asked, as casually as she
could.

'Better than okay,' Maxi said excitedly. 'Thank God
I happened to call them. The e-mail must have got lost.'

'What e-mail?' Issy asked, a strange sinking feeling
tugging at the pit of her stomach.

'The e-mail informing us about his visit.' Maxi
glanced at her watch. 'His plane touched down over an
hour ago, according to his PA. He could be here in less
than an hour.' Springing up, Maxi began stacking the
files on her desk. 'We should get this place cleared up.
I expect he'll want to come up here and check out the
office before he catches the afternoon show.'

The sinking feeling turned to full-on nausea. All her
erogenous zones melted and a vicious chill rippled
down her spine.

'Who are you talking about?' Issy asked, but her
voice seemed to be coming from a million miles away.
All her carefully constructed walls were tumbling down,
to expose the still battered heart beneath.

'The Dishy Duke,' Maxi said confidently. 'Who else?'

'When did you say she'd be back?' Gio lifted the ale
glass to his lips, but the lukewarm beer did nothing to
ease the dryness in his throat as he glanced round the
mostly empty pub.

He noticed the autographed photos on the wall, the
yellowing playbills under glass. Issy had talked about
this place often during their time together in Florence.

But had he ever really listened, or even bothered to ask her about it? While her assistant had showed him round this afternoon, and he'd been introduced to all the people who worked here and clearly adored Issy, he'd come to realise how much work she'd put into the place and how much it meant to her—and yet he'd been too self-absorbed, too wrapped up in his own fears to notice.

He'd been a selfish bastard about that, as well as about everything else. How could he even begin to make amends?

Issy's assistant sent him a puzzled look, probably because he'd asked her the same damn question approximately fifty times since he'd arrived at the tiny theatre pub two hours ago.

'I'm really not sure. Would you like me to try her mobile again?' she replied, polite enough not to mention that she'd given him the same answer ten minutes ago.

He put his glass down on the counter.

How the hell had Issy got word of his arrival? He'd been careful not to tell anyone but his PA of his plans, just in case she did a vanishing act.

He stared at the girl, who was looking at him with a helpful smile on her face. He couldn't wait any longer. Which meant he'd have to throw himself on this girl's mercy.

It made him feel foolish, but any humiliation was likely to be minor compared to what he would face when he finally got Issy alone again.

Don't go there.

He forced the panic back. That was exactly what had got him into this mess in the first place.

'I need to ask you a favour,' he said, hoping he didn't

sound as desperate as he felt. If she said no, he'd have to find out where Issy lived, which could cost him another night. Now he'd finally built up the courage to do this thing, he needed to get on with it.

The girl's eyebrows lifted. 'Of course, Your Grace.'

'Call me Gio,' he said, straining for the easy charm which had once come so effortlessly. 'I didn't come here to see the theatre. I came to see Issy.'

The girl didn't say anything, her eyes widening.

'We had a disagreement in Florence.' Which was probably the understatement of the millennium. 'I think she's avoiding me.'

'Oh?' the girl said. 'What's the favour?'

'Call her and tell her I've left. I can wait in your office until she gets back, and then say what I need to say.' Although he didn't have a clue what that was yet.

The girl stared at him.

The murmured conversation of the pub-goers got louder, more raucous, and the musty smell of old wood and stale beer more cloying as he waited for the girl's answer.

How had he managed to screw things up so badly?

Ever since he'd returned home from the office that day he'd known he'd made a terrible mistake. But he had refused to admit it.

Anger had come first. Just as it had all those years before. He'd spent a week furious with Issy. How *dared* she delve into his psyche and tell him what he'd made of his life wasn't enough? He'd thrown himself back into work. Determined to prove it was all he needed.

But as the days had dragged into a week the anger had faded, leaving a crushing, unavoidable loneliness in its wake. She'd been at the house for only a few short days—how could he miss her so much?

He'd tried to persuade himself the yearning was purely sexual. And the mammoth erections he woke up with every single morning seemed like pretty good proof. But even he had to accept, as the days had crawled past and the yearning had only got worse, that this was more than just sex.

Whenever he had breakfast he imagined her smiling at him across the terrace table, and felt the loss. Whenever he woke up in the night he reached for her instinctively, but she was never there. He couldn't even visit any of the galleries and churches he loved, because without her there he couldn't see the beauty any more. But what he missed most was the simple pleasure of listening to her talk. The silence had become acute, like a suffocating cell that followed him about, just as it had during his childhood, before he'd met her.

He'd been sitting in his office that morning when he'd finally acknowledged the truth. The only way to remedy the problem was to get Issy back.

He didn't kid himself it would be easy. But he had to try.

He studied her assistant, trying to hold on to his patience. What was taking the girl so long?

Finally she pulled her mobile out of her pocket, began keying in a number. As she lifted it to her ear she sent him an astute look. The helpful smile had vanished.

'Just so you know, I don't care if you are a duke. Or if you're the theatre's angel. If you hurt her, I'll have to kill you.'

He nodded, knowing the reckless threat wasn't the worst that could happen.

'Is Maxi still here?' Issy shouted above the pub crowd to Gerard, one of the barmen.

'Think she's backstage,' he replied, pulling a pint of Guinness. 'Dave had a wardrobe emergency with one of the trolls. I can send Magda to get her.'

'No, that's okay.' She was being ridiculous. Maxi had told her over an hour ago that Gio had left. She needed to stop being such a wuss.

Dipping behind the bar, she sent Gerard a quick wave and started up the narrow staircase to the office. It was after seven, and she still had all the ticket sales from the matinee and evening shows to put on the computer and bank. Staying away all afternoon meant she was going to be here till gone midnight, finishing up, but she didn't care as she pushed open the door. Maybe she'd be able to face Gio again one day, but why pile on the agony before she was ready?

'Hello, Isadora.'

She whipped round at the husky words, her heart ramming full-pelt into her ribcage.

He sat at her desk, looking exactly like the man who had haunted her dreams. One leg was slung over his knee, his hand gripping his ankle, and his hair was combed back from his brow.

She turned back to the door. Staccato footsteps stamped on the wooden floor as her frantic fingers slipped on the knob. She dragged the door open but a large hand slapped against the wood above her head and slammed it closed.

His big body surrounded her as she continued to struggle pointlessly with the handle. She breathed in the spicy scent of his aftershave and her panic increased to fever pitch. The ripple of sensation tightening her nipples and making her sex ache.

'Don't run away, Issy. We need to talk.'

Hot breath feathered her earlobe. They had been in the same position all those weeks ago at the club. Her response to his nearness had been just as immediate, just as devastating then. But why couldn't her body be immune to him even now?

'I don't want to talk,' she said, her voice shaking with delayed reaction. 'Leave me alone.' Her knees buckled.

His arm banded around her midriff, held her upright. 'Are you okay?'

She shook her head. His prominent arousal evident even through their clothes. She tried to pry his arm loose. She couldn't afford to fall under his sensual spell again.

'If you've come here to have sex, I'm not interested,' she said, the melting sensation at her core making her a liar.

'Ignore it,' he said as he let her go, stepped back. 'I came to talk, Issy. Nothing else. I don't have any control over my body's reaction to you.'

She forced herself to face him. 'Once you've said what you have to say, do you promise to leave?'

Regret flickered in his eyes, and his jaw tensed, but he nodded. 'If that's what you want.'

She edged away from the door, moved to stand behind her desk, needing the barrier between them. 'Go on, then,' she prompted.

He said nothing for what seemed like an eternity. The only sound was the muffled noise from the pub downstairs.

'I want you back.'

The irony struck her first. A few short weeks ago she would have given anything to hear him say that. But then anger seeped in. How pathetic. To think she would have settled for so little. 'What do you expect me to say to that?'

He ducked his head, sank his hands into his pockets. When he lifted his head she saw something she hadn't expected. 'I want you to say you'll give me another chance.'

It almost made her weaken. The plea in his voice, the look of raw need darkening the chocolate brown. But she knew she couldn't give in—not after everything he'd put her through.

'I can't.' She pressed her lips together, swallowed the ball of misery back down. 'I've already given you too many chances. I've loved you ever since we were kids. I don't want to love you any more.'

He stepped forward, braced his hands against the desk. 'That's not true,' he countered. 'You didn't love me when you were a girl. That was infatuation.'

'No, it wasn't,' she cried, temper strengthening her voice. How could he ask her for another chance and still belittle her feelings?

'You fooled yourself into believing it, Issy. Because you were young. And sweet.' He turned away.

She shook her head. 'That's not true. I was immature. I know in many ways I was still a child. But I did love you. Because when I met you again the feelings were all still there.'

He swung back. 'No, they weren't. You detested me,' he said. 'You said so yourself.'

Despite the off-hand remark she could see the anguish in his eyes, and she realised the rash words had hurt him.

She'd assumed he couldn't be hurt, that she had never meant that much to him. But what if she had misjudged the strength of his feelings all along? In the same way as she'd misjudged her own.

'Why did you push me away?' she asked, tentative hope flickering to life. 'Why didn't you believe me when I said I loved you?'

He gave a deep sigh. 'You're going to make me say it, aren't you?'

She heard the turmoil, the resignation in his voice, and hope blossomed. 'Yes, I am.'

His eyes met hers. 'Because I'm not the man you think I am.'

'And what man is that?' she asked simply.

He dipped his head, the gesture weary. 'One that deserves you.' His voice broke on the words and she realised that finally, after all these years, all the heartache and confusion, the barriers were at last crumbling away.

'Gio, you idiot,' she murmured. 'What makes you think you don't deserve me?'

'I spent my whole childhood trying to make them care about me. And they never did. I knew there had to be a reason. Then you came along and filled up all those empty spaces. And I never even had to ask.'

'But you kept shutting me out.' He'd done the same thing when they were children, as soon as she'd got too close. 'Why would you do that?'

'Because I was petrified,' he murmured. 'I didn't

want to need you and then have you figure out you'd made a mistake.'

Stepping out from the desk, she wrapped her arms round his waist, laid her head on his chest. And the last of the chill burned away as his hands settled on her shoulders.

'You were right, Issy. I've let what they did control my life. I'm not doing that any more.' His lips brushed her hair. 'Give me another chance. I know you probably don't love me any more, but...'

'Gio, be quiet.' She squeezed him and then looked up. Resting her hand on his cheek, she felt the rough stubble and saw the tired smudges under his eyes she hadn't noticed before. 'Love doesn't work like that. I couldn't stop loving you even when I wanted to. And believe me, I gave it a really good try.'

The realisation that now she wouldn't have to brought with it a surge of euphoria.

'I'll give you another chance,' she said, knowing all her hopes and dreams were written on her face, 'as long as you promise not to shut me out ever again.'

'You've got your promise,' he said, kissing her. But then he pulled back, framed her face, his eyes shadowed. 'Wait a minute—don't you want me to say I love you back?'

She almost laughed at the look of bewilderment on his face. 'When you're able to do that, that will be lovely.' And she knew he would be able to one day— once he'd become completely secure in the knowledge that she meant everything she said. 'And my romantic heart will cherish the moment. But in the end they're just words, Gio. What really matters is how you feel. And whether you want to be with me and make a commitment that matters.'

Ten years ago she would have demanded he say the words. But she wasn't going to pressure him into it now. He'd come such a long way already.

'That's really noble of you, Issy,' he said, the amusement in his eyes puzzling her. 'But it may surprise you to know I'm not that much of a coward. Not any more.'

'I know,' she replied, not sure where this was leading. To her surprise, he took a step back and got down on one knee. 'What are you doing?'

'Be quiet and let me do this properly.'

'But I told you, it's not necessary.'

'I know what you told me,' he said, his lips quirking as he squeezed her hands tight. 'And you probably even believe it at the moment. Because you're sweet and generous and you never think anything through before you open your mouth.'

'Gee, thanks,' she said, pretty sure that wasn't a compliment.

'Stop pouting and let me say what I've got to say,' he said, his voice sobering. 'Maybe you don't need to hear the words, but I sure as hell need to say them. I owe you this, Issy—for what I said to you ten years ago, and for the things I said a fortnight ago.' He cleared his throat, took a deep breath. 'So here goes.' His eyes fixed on her face as excitement geysered up her chest and made her knees tremble.

'*Ti amo*, Isadora Helligan. I love your sassy wit, the smell of your hair, the feel of your body next to mine when I wake up in the morning. I love that you are always ready to fight for what you think is right and you never back down. I love your passion for life and your spontaneity, and I especially love that drama queen tendency that makes you so damn easy to tease.'

'Hey!' she said, grinning like a fool.

'But most of all, Issy,' he continued, chuckling at her mock outrage, 'I love your courage and your tenacity and your ability to always see the best in people, and that because of all those qualities you gave me all the chances I needed till I finally got it right.'

She flung her arms around his shoulders, almost toppling him over. 'I love you, Gio. So much I'm not even going to make you pay for that drama queen comment.'

He laughed, standing up with her arms still wrapped around his neck. Holding onto her waist, he lifted her easily off the ground, then kissed her with the passion and purpose she adored.

Setting her down at last, he held her face in his hand, brushed a thumb over the tears of joy rolling down her cheeks. 'Don't cry, Issy. This is where the fun starts.'

She smiled up at him, her body quivering with need as his hand stroked under her T-shirt.

'Is that a promise, Hamilton?' she said, lifting a coquettish eyebrow.

'Pay attention, Helligan,' He hugged her close, his lips hovering above hers. 'That's not a promise, it's a guarantee.'

And then he proved it—in the most delicious way possible.

EPILOGUE

'I MAY have to hate you.' Sophia smiled cheekily as she settled beside Issy on one of the comfortable upholstered chairs that had been set out among the olives groves. 'How did you get your figure back so quickly?'

Issy smiled, weary but blissfully happy. It had been a very long day—she and Gio had been woken up at three that morning by their baby son—but she wouldn't have missed a moment of it. 'Are you joking?' she scoffed. 'Haven't you noticed? My boobs are the size of two small hot-air balloons!'

Sophia laughed. 'Hasn't anyone ever told you? Here in Italy, big is beautiful.'

Colour rose to Issy's cheeks as she spotted Gio making his way towards them across the makeshift dance floor. The loose languid gait she adored made even more beguiling by the tiny baby perched on his shoulder.

'Aha!' Sophia said. 'Someone *has* told you, I think.'

Issy didn't even attempt to hide the blush as her smile spread.

'Someone may have mentioned it,' she replied demurely, enjoying Sophia's delighted giggle as she watched her husband being stopped and kissed by an elderly woman whose name she couldn't remember. There had to be at least a hundred people gathered at the Lorenzo farm to celebrate their son's birth—and even with her greatly improved skill in Italian she was struggling to keep all the names and faces and family connections straight.

As she observed Gio, he took the baby off his shoulder to show him off to the cooing lady, and Issy's grin grew. All the anxiety and confusion of their first visit a year ago had gone. Gio had been relaxed and completely comfortable today—and she suspected it was mostly their son's doing.

One more thing to thank little Marco Lorenzo Hamilton for, whose unexpected arrival had deepened and strengthened their relationship in ways she could never have imagined.

To think she'd agonised for weeks about how to break the news to Gio when she'd fallen pregnant ten months before. Their relationship then had seemed so precious, and yet so vulnerable.

Neither of them had spoken about children since that first early pregnancy scare, and, as much as Issy might have fantasised about having Gio's baby, the abstract romantic dream had swiftly turned into a downward spiral of doubt and panic when that little pink plus sign had appeared in the window of the home pregnancy test.

How would Gio respond to the prospect of becoming a father? How could she ask him to make more changes in his life when he'd already made so many? And how would they both cope with adding yet more pressure to an already difficult domestic situation?

For, once the romance of that mutual declaration of love had worn off, they'd soon discovered that living together was a logistical nightmare. They both had homes they loved and careers they were passionate about in two different cities, hundreds of miles apart.

To solve the problem Gio had insisted on buying a penthouse apartment in Islington, and flying between the two cities three or four times a week. But the long hours Issy put in at the theatre and the nights Gio was forced to spend in Italy meant that even with the exhausting commute they had hardly any quality time together.

Which was how she had managed to get pregnant in the first place, Issy thought wryly, her face flushing as she recalled the many frantic and shockingly explosive encounters they'd snatched together, often in the most preposterous places. She still hadn't quite worked out how she was going to tell her son, if he ever asked, that he had been conceived on the stage of the Crown and Feathers's Theatre Pub late one night after Gio had flown back unexpectedly from Florence and caught her as she locked up.

In the end she would have waited a lot longer to tell Gio about the pregnancy than just a couple of weeks. She'd still been trying to second-guess his reaction and formulate a viable strategy when morning sickness had struck with a vengeance, exactly a month into her pregnancy.

Gio had patted her back while she retched. Made her nibble some dry toast and sip peppermint tea and then insisted she sit down. He had something to tell her. To her total shock he'd announced that they were getting married. That he'd planned to wait until she told him about the baby, but that he couldn't wait any longer. And that he knew the reason she hadn't told him was because she thought he would make a terrible father, but it was way too damn late to worry about that now.

Issy had promptly burst into tears, feeling miserably guilty and totally ecstatic and extremely hormonal—all at the same time. When she'd finally got over her crying jag she'd accepted his proposal, apologised for being such a ninny, and told him she'd never doubted his abilities as a father.

She'd seen he didn't believe her, and it had crucified her, but in the months that had followed the agonising guilt had faded as their relationship changed and developed in new and exciting ways.

Their marriage had been immediate, at Gio's insistence, and necessarily low-key, but still impossibly romantic to Issy's mind. They'd said their vows together one wintry afternoon at Islington Town Hall, with only Issy's mum, Edie, in attendance and had been thrown a surprise reception party by Maxi and the gang at the Crown and Feathers. The baby's first ultrasound scan the day before had only added to the magic of the evening's festivities. Issy had watched, dizzy with happiness, every time Gio whipped out the scan photo— which had looked to her very much like a picture of a large prawn—and showed it to anyone who stood still long enough.

No longer prepared to commute, Gio had announced two days after the wedding that he was relocating his architectural practice to London. The announcement had caused their first major row as husband and wife— because Issy had refused point-blank to let Gio do such an idiotic thing, explaining that *she* was giving up her job at the theatre instead and moving to Florence.

Gio had huffed and puffed, then cajoled and shouted, and eventually sulked for over a week. But Issy had got her way in the end—and enjoyed every minute of his irritation and anger and exasperation.

Gio had been prepared to give up everything for her, and, even though she hadn't been consciously aware of her doubts, when he'd blithely informed her he was moving to London those last nagging doubts about his commitment to their life together had disappeared.

Once he'd informed her of his plans in that matter-of-fact way, and the more strenuously he'd tried to convince her it was the right thing to do, the more Issy had known it wasn't. Her body was ripening more each day with their child, the weight of his ring on her finger made her feel content and secure, and she could see the enthusiasm and excitement on his face when he kissed her growing bump each morning and wished their baby *buongiorno*.

The time was right to give up one dream and concentrate on another.

The ease with which she'd handed over control of the theatre to Maxi and supervised the move to Florence had confirmed her decision. And then to top it all had been that heady rush of love when the Ferrari had pulled up outside her new home and Gio had insisted on carrying her over the threshold—even though she knew she weighed more than a small semi-detached house.

They had begun an ever more exciting phase of their lives as they'd spent those last two months together waiting for the baby's arrival. And she hadn't had a single regret about what she'd left behind.

Not that she had left it entirely behind. She'd kept in touch with Maxi and the gang, and she'd even found some voluntary work at a small children's theatre in the Oltarno before she'd got too huge to move.

But she was more than happy to put her career on hold for now, and enjoy the fruits of her labour. Watching Gio blossom into a warm, loving and ludicrously proud papa had been the sweet, gooey icing on a very large cake. The last of the barriers had dropped away, the last of his insecurities had disappeared. He hadn't just given his whole heart to her and their son, but also to his huge extended family. And being there to witness his transformation had been so intoxicating Issy could feel tears stinging her eyes even now as she observed him chatting easily with the old woman he'd never met before today—as comfortable and relaxed in her company as if he'd known her for years.

She sighed, contentment settling over her like a warm blanket. They both had a place to belong and a future so bright with exciting challenges it was hard not to want to rush to the next one.

As Gio approached, having bade goodbye to his latest friend, Sophia bounced up and kissed him on both cheeks.

'So, how is the proud father holding up?' she asked.

'I'm exhausted.' He sent his cousin a quelling look. 'Next time you and your father and my wife concoct one of these "little get-togethers" my son and I are going to demand full disclosure of the numbers involved.'

Sophia gave an impish giggle. 'Stop pretending you haven't enjoyed showing off your *bambino*,' she said, brushing her hand down the baby's downy black curls. 'I've never seen a man's chest puff up so much.'

The *bambino* in question gave a tired little cry and began to wriggle in Gio's arms. Feeling the instinctive dragging sensation in her breasts, Issy knew what the problem was. She reached for her son. 'How's he holding up to being adored?'

Gio lifted the baby off his shoulder, and kissed his son's cheek before passing him over.

'He's been a superstar. He didn't even grumble when Uncle Carlo lectured him about the intricacies of olive oil production and the importance of carrying on the family tradition.'

Both women laughed.

'Don't panic, Gio,' Sophia said. 'My father has been giving that speech to every baby born in the last forty years. So far only Carmine's son Donato has fallen for it.'

Issy settled back into the chair and eased her breast out of the nursing bra. The baby latched on to the nipple like an Exocet missile and began sucking voraciously.

Sophia patted the baby's head. 'I should find my own *bambino*, before Aldo comes looking for me.' She leaned down to kiss Issy's cheek, then gave Gio a hard hug. 'If I don't catch you later, we'll see you next month for Gabriella's first Holy Communion, yes?'

Gio nodded. 'Wouldn't miss it for the world,' he said, and meant it as he watched his cousin leave. Who would have thought that one day he'd actually be looking forward to these insane gatherings?

He sat beside his wife and child, the feeling of pleasure and contentment and pride that had been building all day making his throat burn. Slinging his arm over the back of Issy's chair, he played with the ends of her hair. Staring at his young son feasting on her lush breast in the gathering twilight he wondered, not for the first time in the last year, how the hell he had ever got so lucky.

'Slow down, fella,' he murmured as the baby's cheeks flexed frantically. 'Anyone would think you hadn't been fed in months.'

'Your uncle Carmine calls it the Italian appetite for life,' Issy said, her throaty giggle sending heat arrowing down to Gio's groin.

He shifted in his seat to ease the pressure, and brushed the curtain of hair behind her ear so he could see her face. 'That sounds like the sort of daft thing Carmine would say. What he means is, our son's greedy.'

Issy turned, her lips curving, and his heart thumped his chest wall. 'Apparently it's a Lorenzo family trait, though, so that's okay,' she said, laughing.

Unable to resist a moment longer, Gio cupped her cheek and touched his lips to hers.

He hadn't meant to be too demanding, hadn't meant to take the kiss any deeper, but when she shuddered and her lips parted his tongue swept into her mouth of its own accord. His hand gripped her head as their mouths fused. He feasted on her, the hunger clawing at his gut like a wild thing.

The little wiggle against his chest and the grumpy little wail had him springing back, so ashamed of himself he felt physically sick.

'Issy, I'm sorry. I don't know what the hell got into me.'

Seeing the look of horror on Gio's face, Issy didn't know whether to laugh, or cry, or scream with frustration. It had been six weeks now since their son's birth. And that brief moment had been their first proper kiss!

'Why are you apologising?' she said, deciding to go

with exasperation as she noticed the large bulge in his loose-fitting suit trousers.

She'd been ready and eager to resume their sex life for weeks now. And she'd seen Gio's almost constant state of arousal recently, so she knew he had to be as frustrated as she was. Still, she'd waited patiently for him to tell her what the problem was. But he hadn't. And her patience had finally run out.

'I want to make love again,' she said, annoyance sharpening her voice. 'And I'm getting a bit tired of you pulling back every time we get intimate.'

His eyebrows rose, and then he frowned. 'I'm being considerate,' he said tightly. 'You've just given birth.'

'I gave birth six weeks ago,' she shot back. 'And I was lucky enough not to need any stitches, so I'm completely healed.'

He paled beneath his tan and winced.

Lifting the now dozing Marco off her breast, Issy readjusted her clothing and placed the baby on her shoulder. She kept her eyes fixed on Gio.

'What exactly is the problem?' she said, her voice rising. 'Are you squeamish about having sex with me because I've had a child? Because if that's the—'

'For God's sake, Issy,' he interrupted, his tone rising to match hers. 'You know perfectly well that's not true. I've been sporting erections Superman would have been proud of in the last month.'

He looked so embarrassed, sounded so frustrated, her bubble of amusement burst out without warning.

'What's so funny?' he asked, his frown deepening.

'Gio,' she said, placing her hand on his cheek as she

tried to stifle the giggles, 'what on earth are you waiting for then?'

His lips quirked. 'Good question.'

Putting his hand on her nape, he rested his forehead on hers, blew out a frustrated breath. 'As much as I love my family, let's sneak out. I'm liable to explode if we have to say goodbye to all these people. And I don't fancy walking around with an erection the size of the Leaning Tower of Pisa while I'm doing it.'

Issy had trouble keeping her mirth under control as they crept furtively through the olive trees to their car. As Gio strapped the sleeping baby into his seat, swearing softly in Italian in his haste, Issy felt desire curl low in her belly and a thrilling surge of heat make her head spin.

Issy rested her palm on her husband's thigh, slid it up seductively as the low-slung car jolted down the rough farm track,

'There's no need to hurry, Gio,' she said, smiling cheekily as his harsh handsome face turned towards her in the shadowy light. 'We've got the rest of our lives.'

He gripped her hand and drew it deliberately off his thigh. 'I know,' he murmured, kissing the tips of her fingers. 'And as soon as we get home I plan to make the most of every single second.'

The cheeky smile turned serene as a rush of love overwhelmed her.

'Well, good.' She sighed. 'That makes two of us, then.'

THE ITALIAN'S
BLUSHING
GARDENER

CHRISTINA HOLLIS

CHAPTER ONE

SHADOWS rippled over Kira's slight form. She stood on the lookout of ancient pine trees guarding the Bella Terra estate, all her attention focused on the other side of the valley. Far away across the rolling grassland a white streak scarred the distant hillside. It was a road, and Kira was waiting. She was watching for the telltale cloud of white Tuscan dust that meant the end of her solitude.

Her little patch of paradise was about to be changed for ever. The land surrounding her house was up for sale. And according to Bella Terra's estate agent, the most fantastic man in the world was interested in buying it.

Kira could not have cared less. She had moved to Italy to get away from all that. Everything she had heard so far about Signor Stefano Albani hadn't done anything to improve her general opinion of men. He had been due to view the Bella Terra villa and estate earlier that afternoon, but he hadn't shown up. The female estate agent had called in at Kira's cottage, looking for him. She had been breathless with excitement and full of this charming billionaire's flirty telephone manner, but Kira wasn't impressed. She guessed this rogue Albani was probably more interested in women than he was in buying a big country estate.

As time went on and he still never showed up, the estate agent's interest dwindled. She began to worry about missing her next appointment. Eventually, feeling sorry for her, Kira offered to take care of the villa's keys and details. Dealing with strangers tied her in knots, but it didn't look as though Signor Albani was coming, and her offer was only a ploy anyway. All she really wanted to do was get rid of the estate agent.

It worked. Her unwelcome visitor dashed off, leaving Kira alone once more.

That was exactly how she liked it.

And there were much worse ways of spending an afternoon than enjoying this view of the Bella Terra estate.

The scorching sun eventually slid behind a bank of clouds, heading for the wooded ridge on the western side of the valley. Kira began to relax. She felt more and more confident that Stefano the Seducer wouldn't come. That was a relief to her, in more ways than one. The fewer people who viewed the estate, the longer it would take to sell. Kira didn't care if the rambling old place stayed empty forever. Her small home was nicely isolated from the villa, although each building could see the other in the distance.

Bella Terra's last owner, Sir Ivan, had been as reserved as Kira. They had waved to each other across the valley every day, and she had looked after the estate gardens, but that was pretty much the extent of their friendship. It had suited them both, but now Sir Ivan was dead. It was odd: in the two years since she had bought La Ritirata Kira had rarely spoken to the man except on business, yet she missed him. And now she was faced with the unknown. Whoever bought La Bella Terra was unlikely to be as peaceful and unobtrusive as the old man. She hated that thought.

She wondered if the future would seem quite so threatening if she had someone to talk to. A letter had arrived from England the previous day. Kira knew she should have sent a curt reply by return, but couldn't bear to do it. The envelope lay where she had dropped it, unopened, on the kitchen table. She would have to release its tentacles of emotional blackmail sooner or later, but not just now.

With an effort, she tried to concentrate on the beautiful scene in front of her. The valley was a patchwork of flowery grassland and ancient woods. She strolled as far as the cool green shadows of the sweet chestnut wood. Thunderheads were forming over the hills. There would be a storm soon. That would cool everything down. She smiled. Rain would transform the single-track road leading to the Bella Terra villa into a quagmire. If Signor Albani was still on his way, that was almost guaranteed to put him off. The prospect of fighting a prestige sports car upstream like a salmon was sure to turn him back. Her little retreat would be safe for a while longer.

As Kira counted her blessings, she became aware of a subtle change in the air. All the birds fell silent. She looked around. The landscape was poised, waiting for something to happen. Then she felt a vibration. Faint at first, it rose from the ground beneath her feet like an earthquake. She started forward as a roe deer bounced through the trees behind her. With one bound it crossed the track and was gone. Still the shuddering increased, rising up through Kira's ribcage until she looked around for somewhere to run. Instinctively, she headed out into the summer-rich pasture. The trees surrounding it had been still in the oppressive heat. Now they swayed and bucked like a wild green sea. It wasn't an earthquake, but something even more alarming. A helicopter was sweeping in from above, and tearing Kira's peaceful valley apart.

'I'm going off-message for a couple of hours,' Stefano Albani announced into his hands-free phone. 'I've got the Milan project back on track, and if Murray's people ring, tell them the publishing tie-in is off, unless they come up with something that can really appeal to me.'

Closing the call, he sat back in his seat. There was no question of relaxing; his spine remained rigid. Flying a helicopter took a lot of concentration. He never inspected any property from ground level without making a low-level pass over it first. The Bella Terra estate looked perfect, and its aspect was a dream. Cool, shady woodlands offered sanctuary from the roasting heat of summer, while beautifully planned terraces around the house offered plenty of space for entertaining in the golden sunshine. Talking of which…

A movement at the edge of the trees caught his eye. It was a girl. She was flinging her arms about, and waving papers at him. Stefano's sensuous mouth lifted in a half-smile. He had only spoken to the estate agent by phone so far, but from where he was sitting she looked as good as she sounded.

His dark features eased as he thought back to that long, teasing telephone conversation with her. Taking up where they had left off would be a good way to wind down after a high-pressure day.

He gazed down on the pretty little ragazza, and gave her a wave. As he did so, a corresponding ripple of relief passed up his arm and across his shoulders. His muscles were tense from working for far too long without a break. What he needed was distraction. A few hours in a place like this would take his mind off all those boardroom battles and investment decisions. The company of a pretty girl was a bonus he had half forgotten in all the chaos.

Stefano smiled as he set his helicopter down on the far side of the house. His few precious hours of freedom were off to a great start.

Kira was in no mood for games. Bella Terra was supposed to be a private valley, and the helicopter's racket was shockingly intrusive among all that usually undisturbed beauty. Worst of all, it felt like an omen of things to come.

'I've seen pheasants fly higher than that!' she shouted after the helicopter as it swept overhead. Her voice was totally swamped by the thundering rumble of its rotors, but it hardly mattered. Simply putting her anger into words made Kira feel better.

As she watched, hands on hips, the machine swung its nose around and dropped down behind the beautiful old villa. If the pilot's antics hadn't made her so annoyed, she might have been nervous. Instead, she saw it as a chance to catch up with him. She sprinted along the track, heading for an overgrown entrance to the Bella Terra gardens. Squeezing in through a gap in its rusty ironwork, she marched up the path.

She found the helicopter parked as neatly as a saloon car, very close to the main house. It was deserted, and silent apart from the click of cooling metalwork. There was absolutely no sign of the pilot. Confused, she circled the villa buildings in the sultry heat. From every side, ornamental broom and gorse set off their exploding pods like gunfire. Anyone with any sense would have headed straight for shade. She made for the yew walk. Reaching the north end, she glimpsed a tall, masculine figure disappearing through a gap in the hedge that led into the fountain garden. She was about to call out to him, but something about the decided, athletic grace of his movements made her pause, and when she came out into the sunlit square of the fountain garden, it was empty.

Turning her head, she strained to hear any signs of life. Only the quiet rustle of air through pine trees and the constant sniper fire of genista seeds disturbed the peace. Then, as she listened, she heard something that might have been footsteps. It was only one tiny sound, and all the interconnecting yew hedges made it difficult to decide from which direction it came. She looked around, but there was no one.

Then two strong hands slipped around her waist, and in one smooth movement she was drawn into an inescapable embrace.

'We meet at last, Miss Barrett!' a deep, delicious Italian voice purred in perfect English. 'I have been searching for you. I felt sure you would be waiting for me at Bella Terra's front door!'

His teasing words reverberated into the curve of Kira's neck. She froze, shrinking from the whisper of warm breath against her skin. The movement only drew her closer to his hard, masculine body. He was holding her so perfectly, she could barely breathe.

'When we spoke on the phone you said you were looking forward to meeting me. Remind me—exactly where did you want to have dinner tonight?' There was a soft, low chuckle in his voice as he murmured, pulling her around to ravish her with a kiss.

Before he could make contact, Kira burst from his grasp with reflexes that astonished them both.

'I'm not Amanda Barrett, and I'm not very happy!' she confronted him, breathing fast. 'Please keep your hands to yourself!'

The visitor recoiled instantly, but he was far too professional to give his horror free rein. Instead, his features became a mask. With a slow, careful dip of his head, he addressed her gravely. 'Scusi, signora.'

Glaring, Kira took two steps backwards. His assault had been so swift and sure she hardly expected him to stop so suddenly. She had no idea what to do next. If this was Signor Stefano Albani, billionaire, then he was nothing like any of the rich men she had worked with in the past. They were predictable, humourless and would never have dreamed of such a stunt. In contrast, Stefano Albani looked ready for anything. He was fit and he was handsome in a tense, distracted way. Standing straight and tall before her, he seemed quite unfazed by her rebuff. He brushed his shirtsleeves down over his bare brown arms and fastened his unbuttoned cuffs.

'I mistook you for someone else, I'm sorry. It was arranged that I should meet the property agent here. Do you know where I can find her?' he asked in his softly accented English.

'She's probably at home by now, having dealt with

at least two more clients in the time it took you to get here,' Kira snapped, still unsettled by the unexpected embrace. Stefano's face remained expressionless, but his eyes glittered, and suddenly Kira regretted her rudeness to this rather formidable man. Then his mouth curled with sudden humour.

'Dio—it's been a long time since anyone spoke to me like that!'

In that puzzled instant, years fell away from his face and he looked much younger. Kira was momentarily thrown off balance. His beautiful eyes and quizzical expression were almost too much to bear. She had to swallow hard before she spoke again, but she'd be damned if she'd let him walk all over her just because she couldn't stop staring at his mouth.

'I'm sorry, *signore*, but you have turned up over three hours late—without any apology—and flown ridiculously low over this valley, terrifying the wildlife and ruining a beautiful evening,' she said firmly, quailing slightly inside as his expression turned stormy. Someone like this didn't hear enough straight talking in his working life. He had just said as much himself.

'If I have caused offence, I apologise,' he said, slightly stiffly. 'Not having the neighbours flying in overhead all the time is a big selling point as far as I am concerned.' Then his features softened. 'I am Stefano Albani, by the way. I'm interested in buying the Bella Terra estate. That's why I assumed you were Miss Barrett, the agent. I thought you were welcoming me with cries of delight!' he joked, searching her expression as he spoke, his mocking eyes somehow piercing her outraged manner and making it irritatingly difficult to stay angry.

'Well, I wasn't,' Kira said, biting back everything

else she felt like telling him. She had to tread carefully. Stefano Albani might have arrived late and lascivious, but there was, unfortunately, a chance he would become her new neighbour and there was no point in making it more difficult than it had to be.

Stefano compressed his lips at the note of accusation in her voice.

He has a really beautiful mouth, Kira caught herself thinking, before his frown dragged her attention back to the Mediterranean depths of his eyes.

'A delay put me behind schedule, and I wanted to get here as fast as I could. That meant flying. Besides, the disturbance was over in a few seconds. I'm sure the valley has recovered from much worse over the years. People always try to imprint themselves on the countryside. The land shakes them all off, sooner or later.'

Kira's alarm must have shown in her face. He quickly softened his tone and added, 'You have my promise that it won't happen again. There will be no low flying in this valley after I move in.'

His words were quite definite, but the essence of a smile still hovered around his lips. When he looked like that, it was impossible for Kira to look away. There was plenty to see. With the air cleared between them, his eyes were now the untroubled blue of a perfect Italian sky. His dark hair was a riot of soft curls, short enough to be neat but long enough to move slightly in the warm air rising from the parched earth at their feet. He was undoubtedly powerful, but it was the strength of steel hawsers rather than unsophisticated animal bulk. Unlike the millionaires Kira had worked for in the past, this man looked as though he used his body as hard as his brain. She could never imagine him parked behind a computer console. She wished she had paid more attention when Amanda Barrett had been rabbiting on about the wonderful Signor Albani. At the time, Kira had shut her ears. Thank goodness the estate agent wasn't here now. She would have fallen for this man like a lead weight.

It's all too easy to see how women must do that, Kira thought darkly. With bewildered fascination, she wondered why they didn't see him for what he must really be—a rich pleasure seeker with no thought for anyone but himself. She could tell exactly the sort of man he was, simply by the way he brimmed with self-assurance. Kira watched him looking up at the grand old building as though he already owned it. She tried to ignore a shiver of apprehension, and told herself looks meant nothing. He hadn't stepped over the villa's threshold yet. How could he be so sure this was the place for him?

'We'll see—if you move in,' she replied grimly, wondering if she held any influence over his purchase. Maybe it's time to forget what I think about Stefano Albani, and start wondering what he might be thinking about me, Kira told herself. Stefano seemed like the kind of man who might actually thrive on opposition rather than avoid it. She decided to try and muffle her objections, for as long as it took this man to make up his mind about the villa and estate. She told herself sharply that this had nothing to do with not wanting to appear like an angry shrew in front of such a gorgeous man.

'The fact is, *signore*, I was only waiting here with the estate details and keys, because I was confident you would never turn up,' she told him. 'I had my whole evening planned until you dropped out of the sky—'

'And wrecked all your plans?'

Kira's scowl returned. 'I was going to say you gave me the fright of my life and apologise for the way I reacted,' she replied frostily.

Stefano said nothing. Instead, he reached out his hand. Kira stared woodenly at his smooth, pale palm until she realised what he was after. She pushed the property details at him. They had been turned around in her nervous hands for too long, and he had to smooth out some creases before he could begin to read.

'What did I stop you doing this evening?' he asked after a few moments' study. His eyes never left the printed page, so the question caught Kira off guard.

'Nothing, as usual,' she replied instantly, before remembering what she had said to him in the heat of her anger.

He looked up from the brochure with a smile that glittered like pearl against his golden skin.

'In that case, why don't you show me around this old place?'

The offer was so unexpected, Kira replied without thinking. 'Oh, I'd love to!'

She regretted the words in an instant. This wasn't her job. She had no business here. She had simply offered to hand over the details and keys, before disappearing. That was the deal—nothing more. She tried to backtrack. 'Yes, I'd love to, Signor Albani, although I'm only a neighbour.' She looked up at the lovely old house and heaved a long, heartfelt sigh. 'I don't really know anything about the place. I've only seen inside one or two rooms before—'

'"It has been owned by an Englishman for many years,"' Stefano read aloud from the notes. 'Do you know him?'

'Sir Ivan was my client. I was his landscape consultant. That's all,' she added hurriedly.

'I suppose you two English people both "kept yourselves to yourselves," in that well-worn phrase?' Stefano's wry smile made Kira feel defensive. However right he may be, she didn't like that he assumed so much about her. Piqued, she ignored her impulse to refuse him.

'I'll gladly show you around outside, *signore*. There's no one who knows more than I do about the estate and the gardens here, but you'll be better off with the brochure when it comes to viewing the house.'

'You're a landscape consultant, you say?' His smile dimmed as he looked her over with a different intensity. Kira reddened as he studied her working clothes of dusty jeans and simple white shirt. Seeing her reaction, his generous mouth lifted in a grin.

'But why are we wasting time out here talking, when we could be looking around this beautiful house? If I know English women—which I do,' he said in a way that needed absolutely no explanation, 'I'm sure you are as keen as I am to get inside the villa and have a good look around. So come with me now. What do you say?'

There was nothing Kira could say. He was talking about a tour of the house she had spent two years dreaming and wondering about. She had been trying to pluck up the nerve to have a peek inside before he arrived, but couldn't bring herself to do it. Now he was inviting her in....

Without waiting for her answer, he started forward. Holding the Bella Terra brochure in one hand, he touched her waist lightly with the other. Kira found herself drawn gently towards the big old building. His pat of encouragement was enjoyable in a way she did not want it to be. Putting on a little more speed, she moved fractionally ahead of his hand. She reached the steps of the house just in front of him. Then there was a pause as Stefano used the great iron key to unlock the door. Standing aside, he let Kira enter first. Still she hesitated. She was desperate to poke around the villa, but on her own. Quite apart from him possibly becoming the villa's next owner, exploring such a beautiful place with Stefano Albani felt somehow much too intimate.

Stefano had none of her misgivings. His hand connected with her waist again, gently urging her to enter. A little sigh left Kira's lips. It felt dangerously like the sound of her scorn softening around the edges. He stayed where he was, but inclined his head politely. 'After you. I need to see everything, so I'm afraid this may take some time.'

He spoke softly, but with absolute authority. He was acting as though the house already belonged to him. Kira coloured guiltily. She had enjoyed the run of this valley for so long she considered it to be her own private haven. Now she finally had a chance to look around the villa at its heart, but the company of such a man added an extra frisson of excitement. If she was honest, it was the surprising intensity of this feeling which was making her hesitate.

What if she couldn't think of enough to say? She had got out of the habit of small talk. Flustered, she looked around wildly for help. Why, she had no idea. There was no one for miles. She had never felt so alone. This man scrambled her brains. He had totally blown away all her common sense. She looked into his eyes and saw things she recognised from the reflection in her bathroom mirror each morning. His blue eyes spoke words that never reached his lips, and she knew that look. Aside from his dangerously smooth assurance, there might be a deeper, darker reason to beware. He might have secrets like hers hiding beneath that sophisticated surface. Unaccountably, she felt the need to peel away his seductive veneer and find out the truth beneath the image.

The weight of Stefano's hand began to rest against her a little more noticeably. At first it had been the merest brush of his fingertips. Now his palm settled gently in the hollow of her back, like falling snow.

With terrifying clarity, Kira imagined it sliding around to encircle her waist again. It felt so good, it had to be wrong. Swallowing hard, she suppressed every wild, unfamiliar instinct and announced quietly, 'Please don't touch me, Signor Albani.'

His hand fell away. He stepped back, surprised.

'Are you sure?'

'I'm positive.'

He stared at her, trying to puzzle out her expression. Kira willed herself to return his look blandly.

'That's interesting,' he murmured at length.

After studying her face, he let his gaze drift at leisure over her body.

'First you answer me back, but now you're as nervous as a kitten,' he mused, his eyes hooded with thought. 'I came to look at property. It seems that's not the only thing around here that might be worth investigating.'

CHAPTER TWO

'DON'T flatter me, or yourself,' Kira muttered, beginning to fuss with the belt of her jeans. It felt wrong to be exploring such a place in her dusty work clothes; somehow she felt that the villa demanded a sense of occasion. He was standing so close to her that the temptation to study him was next to irresistible. Instead, she concentrated on brushing herself down, removing any stray grass seeds before she crossed the threshold of the grand house.

'Don't worry. It's a villa, not the Vatican!' He chuckled, again exhibiting a disquieting ability to read her thoughts. 'You look fine. You're one of those women who look good in anything.'

Kira glanced up sharply at his unexpected compliment. He laughed as their gazes connected. She couldn't stop staring at him, and when he caught her eye it sent a confusion of signals through her body.

'You're right. I'm only looking around a house, that's all. It's nothing more than that,' Kira murmured, trying to stake her claim to innocence. This Stefano Albani was strangely magnetic. Leaving him to investigate on his own might mean she never saw him again. If she followed him, she would delay the moment of parting and get to view the property of her dreams, too.

'So if you are ready, *signore*, shall we make a start?' she added with a bit more confidence.

He laughed again. 'Suddenly so businesslike! I'm making the effort to leave the world behind for a while. Why don't you do the same? I suspect it would do us both good to live a little, for once.' His gaze was uncomfortably direct and Kira shifted under it. 'In fact, it occurs to me that I don't even know your name. So, as we begin, why don't we start with some simple introductions? You know who I am, but who are you?'

Kira had often wondered that herself. 'That isn't important, Signor Albani.' She shook her shoulders irritably.

'Of course it is!'

'No, really. I'm nobody.'

'Don't be ridiculous.' His smile showed signs of fading. 'Everybody is somebody. Your name is your own. You can give it to me.'

Kira stopped. Ignoring this danger sign, Stefano didn't.

'Go on. You know you want to, and it won't hurt!' he teased her gently.

His question revived all Kira's pain. The isolation of Bella Terra meant she didn't have to introduce herself more than once or twice a year. That suited her. Every time she spoke her name, it reminded her of the shame she had left behind in England.

'It's Kira Banks,' she muttered. Head down, she tried to cross the threshold but Stefano blocked her retreat.

'You don't sound very happy about it.' His air

was light, but she saw interrogation in his relentless blue gaze.

Blast him, what was wrong with the man? Kira was used to people backing off, becoming bored when met with her reluctance to talk about herself. In her experience most people preferred to be talking about themselves in any case. It appeared Signor Albani was used to having his questions answered.

'Why is that?' Stefano persisted quietly in the face of her continued silence.

Kira wanted to stare him out but her features lost the struggle. They were moving of their own accord. Her lids would not obey. She lowered her lashes, unable to struggle against the depth of his gaze. Making up some excuse for any other person would have been easy enough, but Stefano Albani was looking down at her with a fiction-piercing stare that demanded nothing less than the truth.

She gritted her teeth and muttered, 'I came here to escape. I wanted to live in a place where no one knows my name.'

He drew back from her a little.

'Okay, I'll let it go at that…' he relented, although his face told a different story. 'For now…' he added with a smile.

Kira mastered her features and managed a bland smile.

'Don't say I have stumbled on a master criminal, living in her bolthole in Italy?'

He was teasing her again. She managed to lift her eyes to challenge him, but knew she couldn't afford to rise to his bait. Her pain hovered too close to the surface.

She didn't need him to aggravate her injuries. There were other people only too willing to do that.

'Why I'm here is nobody's business but my own.' She tried not to snap, but it was difficult. Only his steady gaze softened her reaction. 'In any case, the reasons would take far too long to explain, Signor Albani. Some things are best kept private. Why don't we stop wasting time, and start looking around this lovely house?'

Purposely keeping her voice casual, she jerked herself out of his grasp. She could not escape his expression so easily. It was like a caress. It took all her determination to break eye contact with him. She managed it by concentrating on the breathtaking photograph on the cover of the property brochure in his hand. It was the only sure way she could distract herself from the delicious dangers of this man. Stefano gestured for her to walk across the entrance hall first. It was large, cool, and it echoed with his slow footsteps as he followed her across the cracked marble tiles.

Kira took a good look around. She had only ever entered the villa by one of the back doors. This was her first time in the grand public areas, and she didn't want to miss a thing. While she was daydreaming, Stefano strolled past her. Pulling a pearl-handled penknife from his pocket, he pushed the blade against the woodwork of the nearest door. Kira gazed in wonder at the ornate plasterwork, and the beautifully worked banisters on the great double staircase, but he was busy with more practical things. He worked his way methodically around the entrance hall, testing, checking and inspecting.

'This is the most beautiful house I have ever seen,' she said wistfully. Stefano was not so easily impressed.

'My town house in Florence is more practical, and in

better condition,' he observed, before flashing another brilliant smile at her. 'But you're right. The setting and space here can't be beaten.'

Kira nodded. 'It's a lovely house. Oh, yes, there are bound to be things about it that must be altered, updated or replaced. It's old. But I'd like nothing better than the chance to give it some homely touches. Couldn't you just imagine the scene in December, with a fifteen-foot Christmas tree standing in that bay between the staircases?'

Stefano looked over to where she pointed. He studied the space, tipping his head first one way, and then the other.

'Yes, the proportions would be exactly right. That's important with these old houses. Everything must be in scale,' he said firmly.

Kira's heart gave a strange flutter. She had been half joking, hardly expecting the big-shot billionaire to consider Christmas trees with such seriousness. That might be a glimmer of hope. Even if he might fill the place with rowdy celebrity friends, he clearly had an eye for the important things in life.

'A tree like that in a place like this will need to hit exactly the right note. When I host my first Christmas party I want everyone to be speechless with delight— because I'm all for a quiet life.' He smiled, and gave her a look of undisguised interest. 'So that's the festive season sorted out. What do you suggest for my house-warming extravaganza?'

It was a totally unexpected question. Kira looked to see if he was trying to wind her up. He gazed back innocently. Smiling in spite of herself, she decided to answer in the same spirit.

'Actually, I'm the last person you should ask about entertaining. I'm a garden designer. I prefer to work with plants rather than people.'

'What is a Christmas tree, if it isn't a plant?' He shrugged. 'And I shall need all sorts of those. When we become neighbours I shall want your advice, sooner or later.'

Kira shot him a look of pure disbelief. 'You can have exactly what you like, *signore*. You don't need anyone to advise you, let alone me!'

'There are times when everyone can do with a little help,' he slung straight back at her. 'By employing skilled people, I can spend my time and effort on all the things I really want to do. In this instance, it gives me plenty of time to plan for Christmas.' He stopped inspecting the paintwork and turned an acute gaze on her. 'I know— you must have a good eye for colour. How would you like the task of co-ordinating all the decorations?'

Kira nearly laughed out loud. It felt truly bizarre to be standing in a vast Tuscan villa in the heat of summer, talking about something that was months away.

'Why on earth would you want someone else to decorate your Christmas tree? It's something I've looked forward to every year for as long as I can remember! It's the chance to be a child again, I suppose, without all the pressure.'

It was Stefano's turn to look askance. 'I know all about pressure.' His voice darkened with meaning.

Kira groaned under the weight of memory. 'That's why it's so good to get away from it all, to a place like this. I can enjoy Christmas my way. No rehearsing recitals in Gloucester cathedral, dashing between carol services and amateur dramatics, torturing tons of holly, ivy and mistletoe into wreaths and swags. When I was a child, it was never ending.'

He pursed his lips, and then said drily, 'It's a wonder you had any time to yourself.'

'I didn't. That's the penalty you pay for being a trophy child, isn't it?'

'I wouldn't know. I missed out on all that. I skipped it, and went straight from sleeping in a box under the table, to earning a living.'

'Gosh, you must have had a deprived childhood!' she joked.

He stared at her, unimpressed. His eyes were suddenly chill with all the hidden feelings she recognised from her own reflection. She stopped laughing.

'Yes. Yes, I did.' He grazed his lower lip with his teeth for a moment, and then added, 'But that's behind me now. The future is all that matters.'

There was iron-hard determination in his voice. His eyes were everywhere. She wondered what havoc he would wreak on this beautiful old house when he took possession of it. The thought worried her. A few moments ago, she had been annoyed by the way he talked as though the villa was already his. Now she was thinking about it in the same way. He was checking every inch of the building like the rightful owner. If ever a man was made to lord it over the Bella Terra valley, it's Stefano Albani, she thought, with a shiver of apprehension.

'You're cold. Why don't you step outside into the evening sun and warm up?' he murmured.

His words surprised her. She thought all his attention was riveted on the villa's sales brochure, and hadn't expected him to notice.

'No, I'm fine,' she said quickly, unwilling to miss this

chance to look over the grand villa she gazed at every day from her favourite viewpoint on the other side of the valley.

His eyes glittered with sudden fire. 'As long as you're sure.'

Kira began to feel uneasy. Every time he looked at her, he smiled as he spoke. It was an unusual expression, caressing the most secret parts of her. As she tried not to shrink beneath his gaze, she felt the peaks of her nipples push against the smooth profile of her thin shirt. They stiffened still more to know he was looking at her. It was no longer the chill of the cool marble hall affecting her body. He must have realised it, too, but looked away sharply as obvious appreciation flared for a moment in his eyes.

Kira didn't know what to do. Putting her head down, she scuttled off towards the nearest door.

'Let's see what's through here, shall we?' she said, bursting into the first room beyond the entrance hall. Within half a step she stopped. It was the reception room that time forgot. Sunlight streamed through tall, graceful windows but its beams danced with dust motes. The design of the room was in a typically grand Italian style, although its furnishings wouldn't have been out of place in an English country house.

'Oh, my goodness!' Kira exclaimed. 'A little bit of England overseas!'

Following close behind her, Stefano clicked his tongue when he saw her shudder.

'My stepparents have spent a lifetime collecting stuff like this. Cane-back chairs, chintz upholstery and Goss china. Sir Ivan must have shipped everything over here from England. Why on earth would you move to Italy, then recreate England in your new home?'

'I don't know.' Stefano was equally put out at the sight. His mouth was a stern line of disapproval. 'Some foreigners buy up these properties claiming to love Italy. In reality, Toscana is nothing more to them than England with better weather. They are more interested in worshipping their own land from a safe distance.'

'I'm not. I love it here,' Kira told him. 'I couldn't wait to leave England behind, decorations and all...' She paused, wondering whether to push her luck, and decided she had nothing to lose.

'If we're going to be neighbours, I'd feel happier if I knew you were going to treat this old place well,' she went on. 'It would be such a shame to see it spoilt.'

'It won't matter to you for a few weeks a year, surely?' He shrugged.

Kira was puzzled. 'So you're going to be away a lot?'

'No, but you'll be leaving with the summer, won't you?'

Kira coloured up angrily. 'Why should I?'

'So you won't be flitting between here and your home in England?' He looked surprised.

She shook her head defiantly. 'No! I thought I'd made it clear—I don't have a home in England any more. In any case, I couldn't bear to leave at the end of summer, as the holiday-home owners do. How could I abandon my home here? The Bella Terra valley is everything I want—peace and beauty.'

Stefano's dark brows lightened a little. 'I assume that means you could find no peace in England, so you brought your beauty here?'

His voice was low and melodious but his eyes shone with mischief. Drawn to look straight at him again, Kira could not help lifting her lips in the ghost of a smile, but she said nothing.

'I don't know of many people who would willingly hide away in such an isolated spot,' he murmured. 'You're not afraid to stand up for yourself, you work for your living and you love this place as much as I intend to. How could anything make such a forthright, independent woman leave England under a cloud?'

Kira lifted one hand and began to fiddle with a skein of her dark auburn hair.

'It was a combination of things,' she said, hoping to stop him asking any more awkward questions.

He lifted his brows still higher, encouraging her to unburden herself. She shifted from foot to foot. Her fingers moved from her hair to toy with the thin gold chain around her neck. Stefano watched her. He seemed genuinely interested, and ready to listen. Suddenly she was tired of bottling everything up, and keeping herself to herself. She wanted to talk. She needed someone who might sympathise, or at least answer back. It hardly mattered about the words. She had never seen Stefano Albani before today, and might never see him again. He had already proved himself to be sympathetic. If she explained the whole miserable business to him, as an impartial third party, it might make her feel better.

It was on the tip of her tongue to tell him the whole sorry story. She pushed the guilty words against her teeth, trying to force them out. It was no good. She had kept silent for so long, she didn't know where to begin. Finally, she shook her head.

'It's nothing.'

He considered her gravely. 'I think it is. Something is obviously weighing heavily on your mind.'

He took a step towards her. Kira knew he moved almost silently, but the brush of his leather-soled shoes sounded loud in the peace of the reception room. She stared at the floor. She winced when his feet appeared in her field of view, but it was still a shock to feel the gentle touch of his hand on her shoulder.

'There's no need to jump. I'm only offering a little support,' he said.

'I don't need it,' she said staunchly, but he took no notice and never moved. His touch was warm, reassuring…seductive. In spite of herself, Kira relished the feeling. Then he spoiled the effect. His touch vibrated slightly. She looked up, and saw laughter in his eyes.

'One day, I would really enjoy the chance to discuss sins with you, Miss Kira Banks. Whatever you may have done, I'm sure I can top it!'

With a sharp twist of her head, Kira looked away. She could not bear to let him see her misery. Squeezing her lids tightly closed, she battled to stop the tears falling. She was so lost in her own despair she was completely unprepared for what happened next. Stefano closed the gap between them. His arms glided around her. She was drawn into his body again, and it felt so natural she let it happen without a word. For a few heart-stopping seconds she leaned against him. The sensation of his shirt pressed against her cheek and the enveloping male fragrance of him closed her eyes.

'Is there anything I can do?' His voice echoed around the unloved caverns of the villa.

Kira shook her head. 'I'd be grateful if you could

just drop the subject,' she managed, with a trace of steel showing through her muttered words.

'Okay.'

He took his time in releasing her. Kira normally disliked physical contact, but this was different. Stefano seemed to specialise in the sort of touch she might like to experience again.

He obviously wasn't going to give up on her. Kira sensed he couldn't resist a challenge any more than she could. However, she also knew her fragile self-esteem couldn't stand too many questions. Her reaction to unwarranted attention was usually to snap first, and apologise later. It appeared that this hadn't dissuaded Stefano in the slightest. The most disconcerting thing about that was how ready she'd been to indulge in the comfort he offered. *Pull yourself together!* she ordered herself silently. This man was clearly used to getting his own way and she was embarrassed how easily she had mistaken his charm for anything more permanent.

A hint of her old defiance returned. It allowed her to face him calmly, but it didn't stop her cheeks flaming red at how much she had nearly revealed. 'I'm sorry, *signore*. That was a momentary lapse, but now you'll see that I really don't want to talk about it. So I'd be grateful if we could leave it at that. Okay?' she finished crisply.

Stefano's gaze ebbed away from her as she spoke. He said nothing. Instead, he tightened his lips, and bobbed his head once in silent agreement. In the pause that followed, he glanced around. His eyes, like his body, were restless.

'Everyone has parts of their lives they're not proud

of,' he conceded. 'I can relate to that. So if we agree on a truce, can we continue with the tour?'

He had been almost teasing as he tried to extract her secret, but now he had retreated again behind that impenetrable mask. Kira felt a strange pang of loss. She wondered if he ever experienced the sort of social unease that tortured her. It seemed unlikely. What could ever make such a man feel inadequate?

She nodded and gave him a fleeting smile. 'Of course.'

What would it feel like to unburden herself to him? She was certain he would listen. Really listen, and not simply humour her because he wanted something. Life would take on a different dimension. It was something she had never bothered about before, but a few seconds in Stefano's arms had opened up a whole new world of possibilities for her. It almost tempted her out of her shell, but not quite. If he couldn't be on time for a business appointment, he was hardly likely to treat a casual acquaintance any better. She gave up on the idea. At least when she was on the defensive, she couldn't be hurt.

'If you are really interested in buying the Bella Terra estate, Signor Albani, you should be making the most of your visit. You mustn't stand around here with me.'

Without waiting for his reply, she turned her back on him and walked out of the sunlit room. The vast, gloomy hall beyond was supposed to cool her feelings.

'There's no need to run away from me, Kira.'

She stopped.

'You might be surprised,' she said finally.

Her darkening attitude didn't bother Stefano at all.

He stuck one hand casually in his pocket, and grinned at her.

'So what are you waiting for, then? Surprise me.'

His words made her uncertain. Until a short time ago, endless surprises—none of them good—had been the story of her life. Then she had escaped, and moved to Italy. For a couple of years she had experienced wonderful freedom. And now, with the loss of Sir Ivan, her foremost client, she was faced with the threat that happiness might soon be snatched away from her again. Unconsciously, her shoulders began to sag. Then she sensed his gaze was still on her. She looked up. He was still quizzing her with his eyes.

She shrugged. 'I'm afraid there's nothing more to me than you see here, *signore.*'

His face was totally impassive but he went on watching her as he said quietly, 'Then it's a good job I came here to see the Bella Terra estate, rather than anything else. My journey won't have been entirely wasted,' he announced before setting off across the hall again. 'Now, down to business. I want to look around this house. Would you like to come with me?'

CHAPTER THREE

TOGETHER, they began to walk.

'Why did Bella Terra's owner—the English gentleman—leave you alone here?' Stefano was looking at her in a new way. Kira preferred the old one, but still felt her cheeks flare.

'He died.'

For the first time, the smile left Stefano's eyes. 'Then I'm sorry.'

His sympathy looked genuine. Kira decided to give him the benefit of the doubt. 'He was eighty-five, *signore*, so it was hardly unexpected.'

He shrugged. 'But it must have been a shock, all the same. Deaths are always tragic.' His last words grated uncomfortably in the marble-lined hall. Kira recognised a dangerous flash in his eyes. She couldn't help noticing the length and thickness of his soot-dark lashes. *He* probably knows they are one of his best features, she warned herself abruptly. It can be the only reason he keeps looking at me like that.

'I'm sorry you lost a friend, Kira. I know what that is like.' His voice was distant and regretful. Something about the tone hinted that he had his own secrets.

He shook his head suddenly, as if discarding old

memories and turned to her, a playful smile again curving the corners of his mouth, taking refuge in flirtation.

'Kira—that is a beautiful name for a lovely woman. Coupled with your shining auburn hair, jade-green eyes and magnolia skin, what more could any man want?'

That broke the spell.

'Nothing—until his wife finds out.' Sidestepping him smartly, Kira headed back across the shady hall towards the only parts of the house she had seen before. That way she could put a little distance between them, without losing contact entirely. People made her uneasy, and that feeling fed on itself. Every time she began to warm towards Stefano, she felt bound to pull herself back into line. Yet increasingly, his every move held her hypnotised. When he started sweet talking her, it was too tender a reminder of how things could turn sour all too soon.

'I have no worries on that score, Kira. I don't have a wife.'

She heard his footsteps fall in beside her, but did not look at him.

'That's what they all say—to begin with, Signor Albani.'

'Call me Stefano.'

'They all say that, too.'

Walking over to the glazed door at the rear of the building, she unlocked it. When open, it would give him a view into the courtyard garden beyond. The fresh air and perfume of flowers always soothed her. Kira had designed this entire quadrangle garden. Originally, it was nothing more than cracked concrete and stagnant slime. Now it was one of her triumphs. Stefano was sure to be distracted once he got out there. She was looking forward to seeing what he thought of her work. It would be good to get an unbiased opinion. She knew that would help take her mind off her troubles, more than anything else.

It had always been a struggle to free the warped woodwork of the garden door. Although the interior paintwork was smart brown gloss, Kira knew it was a different story on the other side. The Tuscan sun had roasted away the shine within months. Now sunburnt flakes speckled the steps and sills. She tugged at the door, but it was only when Stefano came to help that it could finally be dragged back over the uneven tiles.

The large rectangular courtyard was paved with local cream-coloured stone. Around its boundary ran a deep, shady colonnade. In the centre was a raised fish pool. The air beyond the hall was still and hot. It hung over the threshold like a heavy curtain. Kira stepped outside, and Stefano followed her into the stormy sunshine. His hair glittered like jet as he looked around the garden. A large ceanothus had been planted in one corner. It hummed with bees, their sound joining the quiet splash of water trickling over wet stones. Ornamental ferns grew in the shadiest areas. The ones with smooth, satiny leaves enjoyed the damp soil and mosses in deepest shadow. Those with leaflets like lace rippled in the slightest breeze, patterning the old riven flagstones with light and shade. The coping stones around the pool were wide and warm. Stefano strolled over, and sat down. Leaning on one hand, he looked into the water.

'This is spectacular. Come and join me,' he drawled, his voice languorous in the heat.

Kira took her time. She didn't want to seem too eager;

being close to him seemed to rob her of her usual self-composure. She walked over and perched on the opposite side of the pool.

'I love this place already. What a beautiful oasis!' For the first time since she'd met him, Stefano seemed to relax completely, breathing in the fragrant air and gazing around with unaffected pleasure.

'Thank you. I wanted to give old Sir Ivan somewhere on the ground floor that he could enjoy, whatever the weather.'

'You are responsible for this?' His brows lifted appreciatively.

'Yes—and all the other recent work you'll see when you inspect the grounds. Sir Ivan saw one of my garden designs on display at the Chelsea Flower Show, several years ago. He commissioned me to create a roof garden for his town house in London. After that, I did more and more projects for him and his friends, before relocating here permanently two years ago.'

Stefano's beautiful mouth twitched in appreciation. 'So you're a self-made woman? Congratulations.'

'I'm only doing my job.' Kira shrugged.

'Don't be so modest! Word of mouth may have brought you a long way in business so far, but with the death of your friend Sir Ivan, you must have lost a major client. You'll need to find a replacement. Have you got anyone lined up?' he asked suddenly.

Kira shook her head. She had been trying not to think about that. She really hated having to publicise her business. The more people who contacted her because they had seen and enjoyed her work through their friends, the better.

'If I'm honest, all I enjoy is the work. Dealing with people is a nightmare I wish I could avoid for ever.'

Stefano cleared his throat. Kira wondered if he was as surprised as she was by how honest she was being with him. At least he liked her garden, which was a good sign. Standing, she brushed off her memories of working in this peaceful sanctuary. Once Stefano Albani came to live here, she might never see inside this place again. She ought to make the most of this tour.

It was a poignant moment. As Stefano stepped out of the stark sunlight and back into the shadows, Kira hesitated. The shade should have been a wonderful relief from the hot afternoon. Instead, she felt the chill of abandonment, and not for the first time. It was the story of her life. She had been given up as a lost cause by her stepparents. Then her place on the sidelines of their life became permanent when their unexpected natural child arrived. Now she was doing much the same to the garden she had cherished. In a few weeks or months, she would have to turn her back on this place and leave it in the hands of others. She shuddered.

Stefano noticed, and smiled at her in a way calculated to immediately warm her up.

'It sounds as though you will be my perfect neighbour.'

Kira shot him a look that said she didn't share his view.

'I promise the experience will be an unforgettable one,' he added quietly.

She ignored that, and told him the simple truth. 'I'm afraid anyone who buys this house automatically gets on the wrong side of me. Sir Ivan and I used to co-exist in this valley very well. I can't imagine anyone else being a better neighbour than he was.'

She thought it would be safer to warn Stefano what she was like, right from the beginning. Instead of sympathising, he laughed.

'I'll try,' he said mischievously. 'Let's hope I can play the part as well as you act the role of estate agent!'

His refusal to take her statement seriously was infuriating. 'I'm not acting. I'm here to make sure nothing happens to the villa keys,' she said stiffly. 'You're here to view the place. We've got nothing in common, and we're never going to see each other again after today.'

Stefano said nothing, but smiled at her with an assessing look in his meltingly dark eyes. The dappled sunshine played on his clean, beautiful features and suddenly the thought of never seeing him again wasn't quite as comforting as she had expected.

As they continued their tour of the house, Kira began to wonder if she had misjudged the captivating Signor Stefano Albani. They did have one thing in common. It was obvious the moment they reached the first floor. He strode straight to the nearest window and looked out. Only when he had inspected the vista with its avenue of sweetly scented lime trees did he begin his careful study of the floors, walls and furnishings. Watching him, she noticed he carried out the same ritual with each new room they entered. He paid no attention to the high ceilings and airily beautiful rooms until he had studied what was on show outside. Finally, she couldn't stay silent any longer.

'I see you like the view,' she said with satisfaction.

There was a pause before he answered. It gave her

strange pleasure to see that he carried on drinking in the scenery before he replied. 'Is it so obvious?'

'You make a beeline for the windows each time we enter a room.'

He frowned, seeming uncomfortable that she had noticed his simple enjoyment of their beautiful surroundings.

'I'm simply checking to see where the nearest neighbours are. I value my privacy.'

Kira nodded, covering a smile. 'I understand. This valley is perfect for that. You won't be disturbed. Let's hope you don't disturb me!'

He gave her a sharp look, then paced on towards the next room. As he walked, he compared what he was seeing with the beautifully produced brochure. Kira decided to get a copy of the booklet for herself. It would be a permanent reminder of this day, and the house. She was seeing it for the first and last time, and that made her happy to wander along in Stefano's wake. He needed no commentary, and took his time. While he judged and estimated distances and sizes, Kira simply enjoyed herself. The old house was beautiful. Its corridors and great rooms had a quiet grace, despite all the grime and dust. Sir Ivan couldn't have visited the upper storeys of his house in years. There were worm-eaten long-case clocks on plinths, dusty carriage clocks on equally dusty coffee tables and delicate little china clocks on every mantelpiece. There wasn't so much as a tick or a tock between them. All were silent. All were sad. Only the sound of a golden oriole warbling from the lime trees outside and swifts screaming overhead broke the thick summer silence.

'Ah, perfetto,' Stefano breathed, with a look of total

satisfaction. Kira was entranced. As he strolled on into the final room on the top floor, she stopped. There was no point in going any further. The small, square box room was no competition for her last uninterrupted viewing of Stefano Albani. She watched as he finished inspecting the house that might become his own. He moved with the self-assured grace of a man who would be at home anywhere. His gestures were expansive as he waved the brochure in her direction, drawing her attention to some fact or another. He only became still when he returned to his favourite position, at the window. Kira felt somehow relieved to see him at rest, if only for a short while. He gave the impression of continuous movement, no matter how slight. She found that unsettling. When he was still like this, lost in thought, she could almost imagine he was at peace. Almost…but not quite. There was always a trace of tension lingering around those eyes. When he forgot to try and charm her, they held the thousand-mile stare of a troubled man.

She found herself drawn inexorably towards him. Silently, she moved across the bare floorboards, past anonymous, dust-sheeted furniture. The need to reach out and touch him again before he was lost to her forever was irresistible.

And then he moved. The moment was broken. He turned to her in surprise, but then a slow smile warmed his features, and she realised she had raised a hand as though to touch him.

'Go ahead. Be my guest. As we're going to be neighbours, it's a good idea for us to get to know each other better, wouldn't you say?'

Kira pulled her hand back as though she had been burned. 'I—I was going to brush a cobweb from your shoulder. You know how dusty these old houses can be...' She faltered, convincing neither of them.

Stefano was intrigued. Kira was full of contradictions. Half of her seemed to be yearning towards him, but something kept pulling her back. With another woman, he might have taken advantage of the situation straight away, but he wasn't about to push his luck with Miss Kira Banks—not for a while, at least. She interested him.

In the short time they had been together, he recognised the pain in her. It was too close to home. He wondered how deep the similarities ran between him and this privileged young Englishwoman. Once, when he was young, he had come face to face with tragedy. He could have let it crush him to powder. He dodged that, but paid a heavy price. From that moment, he had spent his whole life on the run. He was afraid of nothing but his conscience. This woman didn't need to draw pictures when she spoke to him. She had escaped from somewhere and ended up here. That was enough information for him—for the moment. He knew what it felt like to be goaded by guilt.

The fact we've both decided on this hidden valley is somehow comforting, he thought, and then cursed sharply. What did he need with comfort? All he wanted was somewhere he could withdraw from his hectic business life and enjoy some quality time. The Bella Terra estate offered everything he wanted. And it had the added advantage that at least one of the neighbours shared his love of solitude.

* * *

'I really enjoyed that,' Kira said as they reached the front doors again after the grand tour.

'You sound surprised?' He raised his eyebrows.

'I am! I only agreed to stand in for that estate agent because I was sure you wouldn't turn up this afternoon. I tend to try and avoid people, when I can.'

'You couldn't avoid me,' Stefano reminded her, stepping out of the house and striding off across the terrace. He was intent on seeing the grounds. That made Kira nervous. The bulky clouds rising up over the far ridge of hills were backlit by a blood-red sun. Despite that warning, he kept heading away from his helicopter, and towards the storm. Kira didn't share his confidence.

'Shouldn't you be going, Stefano?' she called, needing to draw his attention to the threatening sky.

He turned. 'Anyone would think you were trying to get rid of me! I like this place, Kira. I want to see the rest of it.'

'But it's going to rain!'

He was unimpressed. 'Get wet, get dry again. That's my motto. I'm going to be living in this beautiful villa, so I should start thinking like a country person. Maybe I can learn to look on the trees as nature's umbrella.'

Kira wasn't sure if he was joking. She hated uncertainty, and followed him to find out. A growl of thunder prowled into the valley, which was something else she didn't like. She stopped dead.

'You're going to walk around the grounds in this weather? You might get struck by lightning! Are you mad?'

He paused. 'I've been called many things in my time, but never that!' After another second's thought, he started towards her as rapidly as the storm. As he reached her side, he narrowed his eyes. 'Are you scared? Is that it?'

'Of course not,' Kira said, raising her chin defiantly and determined to shadow him whatever the weather might throw at them. 'Nothing scares me.'

He didn't look convinced, but swung away across the terrace again.

'Come on, then. I've seen enough of your landscape work from the upper floors to know that I want you to work for me,' he announced, leaving her to run and catch him up. 'After hearing about what you did for Sir Ivan, I've decided my town house in Florence needs a new designer. I want more greenery, and a roof garden. When you're not busy with that, you can act as consultant to some inner-city work I'm funding. Currently, it lacks focus. Community projects have been successful elsewhere. Your input may be exactly what I need. I'll want you to design something to appeal to everyone, and then organise working parties to—'

'Wait!' Kira tried to halt the imperious flow of instructions. 'That all sounds good and important, but I can't simply drop everything on your say-so!'

He stopped, as the sun went behind a cloud.

'Why not?' He stared at her, uncomprehending.

'Because...I'll have to consult my schedule,' Kira replied with dignity. She decided that Stefano was clearly far too used to getting everything his own way. Still, a chance to design the roof garden for a no doubt exceptionally beautiful town house in Florence...

'With the loss of the Bella Terra's owner, you're one client down. You've already said as much. I can fill that gap for you,' Stefano announced affably. 'You've already told me you hate canvassing for jobs and courting publicity. I've seen what you can do, and I'm offering you a valuable, long-term contract working for me. Where's the problem?'

The problem, Kira thought desperately, is you.

'I'm not sure I want to work for you, Signor Albani,' she said a little stiffly. 'We're so different. We might not get on.'

He trapped her gaze for a long time. 'What you mean is, you're afraid we might get on too well. And remember—my name is Stefano...' he added with a tempting smile.

Kira stared at him. His self-confidence was astonishing, and yet somehow she could not bring herself to resent it. He could read her mind—how could she criticise him for that?

'I appreciate your concerns, but you don't have to worry,' he went on. 'I have so many properties and projects, my contractors are dealt with mainly by email and text. I wouldn't be there in person to tempt you.' With that, his smile came dangerously close to laughter.

Kira had to look away. His body wasn't the only thing tempting her. She tried not to think of the begging letter, waiting for her on the table at home. There were so many calls on her slender finances. She needed money. The fabric of her house was so old there was always something that required repair. The security of a long-term contract appealed to her cautious nature. Her problem was, whenever she earned more than she actually needed she always felt bound to send any extra money back to England.

Her natural generosity might feel right, but she knew in her heart it was wrong. She would soon live to regret it, as she had done every single time in the past. What she earned ought to be hers to keep. She tried to harden her heart. It was difficult, and that was why she was such an easy target. Emotional blackmail was an ugly thing. Kira knew a steady contract to work for a billionaire like Stefano Albani would be a perfect new start. With that security behind her, maybe she could manage to make a stand. It would give her some badly needed confidence, and she could make sure that anything she did for Stefano would be strictly on her own terms. Yes, of that she was certain.

Well…almost certain…

'Your projects sound pretty interesting,' she told him carefully. 'When I get back home I'll check my diary, and see if I can fit you in somewhere.'

He gave her a calculating look. Then he dug a hand into his pocket and drew something out. 'Of course, I appreciate you can't give me an answer straight away. Here—take my card. I'll have my office draw up all the documents, and you can give them a call when you've come to a decision.'

His wallet was immaculate dark brown leather. The blue silk lining was no match for the intensity of his eyes as he pulled out a business card and handed it to her. Trying not to stare at it like a souvenir, Kira slid it into the pocket of her jeans.

'Thank you. I'll give it some serious thought.'

Lightning crackled. Kira braced herself, but the explosion of thunder still made her jump.

'It's getting closer.' She looked up at the sky, and then across at the horizon. It was as dark as an overripe plum. 'Are you sure you want to risk a tour of the estate in this weather, Stefano?'

'It will be fine.' He smiled. 'Trust me.'

That was the last thing Kira ever did. People always used that phrase as casually as they said 'to be honest.'

From that moment, she knew in her heart things would go wrong. She tensed, retreating into the role of observer as Stefano roamed around the formal gardens. Not content with admiring her work from the upper storeys of the house, he wanted information from ground level, too. He asked intelligent questions and paid her compliments about her work, but Kira could only let herself believe a fraction of his kind words. She moved uneasily under the shadow of his praise and flinched as the thunder grew closer. Finally, when they were at the furthest point of the tour, the rain began. Warm drops the size of pound coins darkened the dust, first in ones and twos, then in a downpour of tropical proportions.

'We'll head for there!' Stefano shouted over the torrents of rain. He was pointing at her cottage. 'It's the only blot on my landscape. We might as well make use of it before my men clear it away.'

'What?' Kira shrieked, but her horror was drowned by thunder roaring right overhead. They dashed for the house, but as they got closer Stefano faltered at the sight of garden flowers spilling through the woven hazel fencing.

'So someone lives here?' he shouted over the downpour.

'Yes—me!' Kira raced past him and flung open the door of her little retreat.

Breathless and soaked, they tumbled into the house.

'I didn't realise this estate came with a tenant,'

Stefano said as Kira kicked off her sandals and padded, dripping and barefoot, into the kitchen.

'It doesn't. I own La Ritirata outright,' Kira told him proudly as she returned, carrying a couple of hand towels.

'I wasn't aware of that. How much do you want for it?' Stefano looked at her quizzically.

'Oh, it's not for sale!' Kira laughed, running lightly up the wide stone stairs to fetch some larger towels from the airing cupboard. Stefano followed her for a few steps. Leaning back against the cream-painted stone wall, he looked up at her as she stood on the landing.

'Of course it is. Everything is for sale at the right price. You could find yourself a nice little hideaway in this valley, well away from La Bella Terra. Then we could each pretend we were totally alone in the landscape.'

'That's the point. There are no other houses—not for miles. That's partly why I love it here so much.'

'You could build yourself another paradise anywhere, Kira!' he went on. 'I've seen the proof, remember. Go on—name a figure. Anything you want, and it's yours.'

'All right, then—a million pounds!' Kira called down with a giggle.

'Done. I'll have my staff draw up the paperwork as soon as I get back to the office.'

Kira waited for him to laugh, but he didn't. He was in deadly earnest.

'You're joking!' she gasped. 'This place isn't worth a fraction of that sort of money!'

'My peace of mind is beyond price,' he announced.

Taken aback by the determination in his voice, Kira shook her head.

'Well, you may not have been joking, but I was. My house means the world to me,' she told him firmly. 'No amount of money would tempt me to give it up. La Ritirata gives me what I've always wanted—independence and contentment. I've worked hard for my little home, and I feel safe here.'

A tremendous blast of thunder rattled the windows. Stefano smiled.

'I notice you aren't so nervous, now we are within your own four walls,' he observed. 'You've obviously made a real commitment to this place.'

'I have.' She nodded, glad he appeared to have accepted she wouldn't be moving.

'In that case, I can't wait to benefit from the Bella Terra effect. I own a lot of investment properties around the globe, but I can't honestly call any of them home. If I see a place with potential, I buy it,' he told her, looking around her neat and compact little home appreciatively. 'Yet none of my houses have ever developed the comfortable, lived-in feeling of this place.'

'I spend as much time as I can here. Maybe that's the secret of my success.'

'It really works,' he said as she started back down the stairs towards him, holding out a huge fluffy towel. 'Living alone in a place like this, you must be as brave and resourceful as you are talented and beautiful.'

He reached out to her. As he took the towel from her hands, their fingers brushed against each other. His touch was light as an angel's kiss, but it sent lightning coursing straight through Kira's body. She gasped.

A thunderbolt crashed directly overhead, but neither noticed.

Stefano was looking deep into her eyes, and nothing else mattered.

CHAPTER FOUR

THE universe held its breath. Kira gazed at the gorgeous man standing just out of her reach. Her body ached to touch him. She could think of a million and one reasons why she should take that single step down into his arms. Only one thing stopped her. There was already a monumental mistake in her past. Kira was no longer the innocent girl she had once been, long ago and far away. She had forged a new life since then and almost learned to trust her instincts again, but she had never been faced by a choice like this before. Every fibre screamed at her to fall into Stefano's arms. At the same time, every cruel word and accusation she had suffered in the past kept her nailed to the spot.

Stefano came up a step to join her. Taking the towel from her hands, he draped it over her head. Very gently, he began massaging her hair dry. His light, sure touches made Kira wonder how many other women he had treated in this way. It was impossible to know. That was the danger. She knew what powerful men were like. They acted with confidence, and never left any room for refusal. She had the horrible fear that once she was in his arms he would give her no time to think. It would be bed, and then treachery. It might take a day, a week or a month before he deceived her, but the result would be the same. He would carry on as though nothing had happened. She would be totally crushed. It had happened to her once before, and Kira was not about to let herself become a victim again.

She put up her hands, shrinking back and trying to intercept his movements. His fingers closed over hers and gently pushed the towel back over her head. The clip securing her tumble of auburn hair fell away. It clattered down the staircase. Kira barely noticed. She was completely absorbed by the look in Stefano's eyes as he drew the towel away from her hair. The appreciation she saw was all for her. She began to tremble, but now it was with anticipation, not fear. She had never known such a wild yearning before.

She swallowed hard. There was nothing in her mouth but the taste of temptation. His eyes levelled a steady, questioning gaze, willing Kira to read what she wanted in them. It was mesmerising, but she could not escape the feeling of being confined in her own home. To take a step forward would lead straight into his arms. Kira refused to repeat her mistakes, and the irresistible Stefano Albani showed all the signs of being a disaster waiting to happen—to her.

She couldn't allow herself to fall under his spell.

'This is dangerous,' she said, forcing a laugh when he showed no sign of moving. 'Didn't you ever get told not to fool about on stairs?'

'No. But then, if I had I wouldn't be where I am today.'

Turning, he headed back down the stairs.

Kira was torn between relief and disappointment. When he walked away it was because he was unwilling to open up about himself. They had that in common, she recognised. It gave her enough courage to follow him downstairs. Although unable to take that one momentous step into his arms, she did not want to lose touch with him altogether.

'It's still pouring out there, Stefano. Why don't you stay for a coffee?' she ventured.

He did not look at her. Instead, he went over to the open front door. There he stood with one hand on either side of the door frame. When he spoke, his voice was as light and careless as hers.

'That would be great. And I meant what I said about wanting you to work for me.'

They might as well have still been discussing the weather. His attention was riveted on the curtains of rain rippling over her drenched and glittering garden.

'And I'm equally determined to take my time over considering your offer,' Kira said firmly, fixing him the macchiato he requested. She poured herself an identical drink, keen to keep a clear head while he was under her roof. 'I need to know what strings are attached, Stefano.'

'There won't be any. I like to keep my affairs simple.'

He was still watching the rain. As Kira reached his side with the coffee, the downpour wavered and began to ease. A final flurry of thunder rattled away into the distance.

'I like to keep my affairs completely separate from my work,' she said, handing him his cup.

He was silhouetted against the doorway, surveying the land beyond her garden fence as though it was already part of his very own kingdom. At last he turned his head and looked at her. A man who took control so naturally would never expect a woman to refuse him anything. That thought made Kira fizz with an illicit thrill. Stefano Albani might be about to buy the Bella Terra estate, but the power he had over her had nothing to do with territory. She felt the need for him growing within her. That desire was reflected in his beautiful blue eyes. His gaze was as tempting as evening sunshine. Kira knew she held the key to her own escape from solitude, and that made her powerful. She could choose to satisfy the cravings he was awakening in her body, or tighten her armour of self-reliance. The choice was hers and she was glad, but it disturbed her. It would be so easy to give in, right here and now. She was afraid that if she did, Stefano would turn out to be no better than the last man she had learned to trust.

Some dreams needed to be kept at arm's length. That way they could last for as long as she wanted.

As she passed Stefano the coffee, his fingers made contact with hers again. It was only for a fraction of a second, but it would linger in her memory for the rest of her life. Their eyes met as he drained the small cup in one movement. Then he walked over and placed it on the coffee table.

'The rain has stopped, so I must go. Thank you for being such a delightful hostess, Kira. I don't like to mix women and work, but as you aren't quite on my payroll yet...'

Before Kira knew what was happening she was in his arms. He took complete control as his body spoke for them both. His lips were cool and totally irresistible. She dissolved under the pressure, and he was there to catch her. Despite all her good intentions, she let herself reach out to him. She delighted in the delicacy of the thin, smooth skin stretched taut over his finely drawn cheekbones. Her fingers ran through the silkiness of his dark hair as she drew him ever closer to her, hungry to experience every nuance of him. In response, his fingers stroked lightly over her bare arms, forming a prison she never wanted to escape. When he began to draw away, she instinctively tried to follow. Gently, he detached her arms from his neck. Holding her hands between his, he squeezed them lightly.

'No. After what you have said to me today, Kira, I know you would never forgive yourself for mixing business with pleasure,' he said, his expression carefully innocent, but a wicked sparkle in his eyes belying his words. 'I'll tell my staff to get a draft contract out to you as soon as possible. Until then, goodbye.'

Lifting his hand to his lips, he blew her one final kiss, and then strode right out of her house.

It was all Kira could do not to rush after him. Fighting every instinct, she forced herself to stay exactly where she was. She wanted go out and wave him off, but a man like Stefano would see that as his right. Women were probably doing it every day of the week. It would do him good to think there was one woman who didn't keep him at the centre of her universe. The thought gave Kira a funny twist of pleasure, and she almost smiled. The racket his helicopter made as it roared into life was almost as hard to ignore as its pilot.

Kira only went out onto the veranda when the throbbing engine sound had dwindled away. Stefano's helicopter was high in the sky, reduced to the size of a child's toy. It made several slow circuits overhead like a bird of prey, and then headed off swiftly in the direction of Florence. This time she really did allow herself to smile.

Kira had run from romance for years. After that first disastrous affair with Hugh, she vowed never to get entangled again. And now Stefano Albani breezed into her life, attacking the walls of her reserve. She told herself it didn't matter, as the way she was feeling had nothing to do with love. Her heart was not involved. That meant there was no danger she could be hurt a second time. Her response to Stefano was on a purely physical level, and that was how she intended to keep it. He aroused her body to a pitch she had never before experienced. It was unprecedented, startling, but at least it was simple.

It was love that would complicate matters, and Kira had absolutely no intention of allowing that.

Stefano was a happy man as he flew back towards Florence. He hummed a snatch of Don Giovanni to himself, revelling in the comfort of his air-conditioned cockpit. The Bella Terra estate was what life was all about. That was why he worked so hard, and put up with all the long hours and pressure. His features sharpened with their usual hawklike intensity. Memory was a savage goad. Whatever he had to put up with, he could do it in luxurious surroundings waited on by dozens of staff. As a teenager he had heard English tourists talk of their villas in Tuscany and vowed he would live like them one day. Whatever they could do, he would do better. It had taken him nearly twenty years, but he had managed it. He was going to own the most beautiful valley in all Italy.

His blue eyes veiled. It contained the most beautiful woman in the country as well. The enigmatic Miss

Banks might well prove a bigger challenge than he had at first anticipated. Her failure to be swayed by his wealth or reputation made her unique, in his experience. A slow smile spread over his face the more he thought about her. Novelty wasn't the only reason why she leapt into his mind. Kissing her senseless had kindled a need for her within his body. The temptation to carry on softening her resistance beneath his lips and hands had been difficult to resist. It had threatened to overcome him, but he had conquered it. There was no shortage of sex in Stefano's life, but his reactions to Kira Banks felt somehow different. For once in his adult life, he was wondering less about her beautiful body, and more about the woman within.

He found himself wanting to see her again. That thought made him feel uneasy.

Miles away and far below, Kira shared his feelings. It had taken her so long to get over the horror that had been Hugh Taylor, she was determined never to be taken in by a man again. Yet Stefano Albani made her feel weak at the knees. And weak in the head, she told herself crossly, but it was impossible to think about him and frown. That was a revelation. Her only experience of men so far had ended in tears. Now, for the first time in years, a man was forcing her to reconsider. Stefano hadn't made her cry. In fact, every time she thought about him, she smiled. That will have to stop, she told herself sternly.

Memories usually knocked all the daydreams out of her head. Thoughts about Stefano didn't. Instead, she was filled with a wonderful warm feeling. It was such an unfamiliar sensation it took her a while to recognise it as lust. Shy amusement engulfed her in a wave of embarrassment, but that vanished when she caught sight of the envelope lying on her table. Stefano had stroked all thoughts of it from her mind. She picked it up. Meeting him put this letter from her stepparents into perspective. If she could cope so well with a man like that, what was to stop her dealing with a call from home? Full of unusual optimism, she tore the envelope open. It was the usual tissue-lined affair, drenched in her stepmother's trademark perfume. Unfolding the stiff sheet of hand-made paper, Kira cut straight to the chase. Glancing at the foot of the letter, she read the words, 'All our love, Henrietta and Charles.'

She scowled. That was all she needed to know. Her stepparents only sent her their love when they wanted money. If things were going well, they conveniently forgot about the girl who had disappointed them in every way, except in her capacity as a cash cow.

She scanned the rest of the copperplate handwriting. Mr and Mrs Banks weren't stupid. They never came straight out with a request for cash. Hints were threaded through the glowing reports of their younger daughter Miranda's success as an actress, and her new romance with a millionaire. Of course, this meant the Banks family wanted to entertain on a grand scale. Kira chuckled, imagining her stepmother circling Miranda's boy-friend with canapés brought all the way from Fortnum and Mason. They were her preferred bait for a future son-in-law. The Bankses' mortgage was unpaid and their house was falling apart. Despite that, the expensive per-fume was still on draft and hopes of coming into money from somewhere or another were still high. Some things never changed.

Kira's face fell again as she read the final paragraph of the letter: 'When you ring each week, could you make it a little earlier? Six o'clock is such an inconvenient time as we're nearly always on the way out.'

Their instructions usually made her feel nine years old again, but today was different. Stefano Albani was stronger than all Kira's bad memories put together. Impulsively, she screwed up the letter and lobbed it towards the waste bin. It missed, but Kira was in good spirits as she got up to retrieve it. It was amazing what a little boost to the self-esteem could do.

And a kiss from Stefano Albani worked like rocket fuel.

Next day, Stefano's legal team presented him with a contract for the landscaping and design work he wanted done on his town house in Florence. His PA scheduled a call for him, summoning Miss Kira Banks to his office. While Stefano held meetings, Kira was pushed to the back of his mind. However, the moment he pulled her file from his in-box to make the call, things changed. At the sight of her name, he paused. One look at the neatly printed contract catapulted her to the front of his consciousness again. This wasn't some run-of-the-mill conquest. This was Miss Kira Banks, who had been funny and spiky and brought back powerful memories of the last time someone stood up to him. He found himself going back over every second of the previous day.

He inhaled deeply, bringing to mind the sweet lavender and lemon fragrance of her. She was perfumed by soap and fresh air. He spent a few moments revelling in her image. It was a mystery why she hid behind such a prickly attitude. He knew it was only a front. The warm surrender of her body beneath his hands when he touched her assured him of that. Her reactions were perfect. It was her mind he needed to explore. That idea made him uncomfortable.

Suddenly he leaned forward and snapped a button on his office intercom.

'Cancel that call, and the contract in the name of Kira Banks,' he growled. 'I need to do some more research.'

Stefano believed in being the best, and having the best. To keep up his high standards, he used only the top people. He wanted to employ Kira Banks because she really was the best person for the job, not just because he wanted to bed her.

Slumping back in his seat he gnawed the side of his thumb, deep in thought. Work and women were totally separate compartments of his life. He had fancied Kira from the first moment he saw her, but that was the very worst reason for giving anyone a job. Her work was great, but he had only seen one of her projects. For her body and spirit to haunt him like this, it could only be a bad thing. Emotion mustn't be allowed to affect his judgement. He ought to distance himself from the process, and get some other opinions. He needed to be absolutely sure she was the right person for this project.

Picking up his pen, he drew two careful lines through the name and address on the cover of the file in front of him. He liked speed, but not at the expense of perfection. Besides, that faint air of mystery surrounding Miss Kira Banks might erupt into some sort of scandal for Albani International. It didn't matter how Stefano wanted her, nothing could be allowed to taint the name of his company.

Not even the most beautiful Englishwoman in Italy.

Kira looked at Stefano's stark-white business card every day. Her heart fluttered with excitement. She ran her finger over the engraved wording until his telephone number was burned into her brain, but she never rang it. That smooth, self-assured man must never be in any doubt that Kira was her own woman, with other projects and a lot of things on her mind.

Finally, exactly two weeks after Stefano had grabbed her by mistake in the garden, she couldn't resist any longer. She sat down, cleared her throat and picked up the receiver. Then she put it down again. Maybe she should get her laptop up and running in case he started talking business straight away. She wanted him to think she was calm and efficient, even though she didn't feel it as she lifted the phone to try once more. This time she paused to fetch a glass of water. It would be terrible if her mouth dried before she could speak to him.

Eventually, her heart rattling like a touch typist's fingertips, she dialled the number.

'Signor Albani's office. How may I help you?' a sunny female voice enquired.

Kira had no idea. Naively, she'd thought the number on Stefano's own business card would have been a direct line to his desk.

'Who is speaking, please?' the voice asked as though she was only one among thousands.

'Kira Banks.' Kira made herself answer in the friend-ly, confident tone she reserved for clients. 'I'm ringing to check on a contract that Signor Albani was going to arrange for me.'

'Ah.'

That single sound was enough to bring her back to earth. While the receptionist went off to check, Kira was left to imagine exactly how many other women rang this number each day. Silver-tongued Stefano must make a million similar promises.

She was on hold for ages. The silence was almost as painful as piped music would have been. It gave her a long time to reflect on her foolishness. Finally, the receptionist returned, and Kira's heart fell still further.

'I'm sorry, Miss Banks, we have no record of a contract being issued in that name. Perhaps if you could give me a reference from the letter we sent you?'

'No...no. It's okay. I must have made a mistake,' Kira muttered indistinctly. And not for the first time, she thought bitterly as she put down the receiver.

Kira stared at the telephone for a long, long time. She felt totally deflated. In her daydreams, Stefano Albani couldn't wait to get back to her side. He would have paid cash for the Bella Terra estate, simply so he could move in as soon as possible. Instead, he must have forgotten about her the moment he climbed back into his helicopter. He had turned out to be no different from any of the other rich men she had worked for. All of them could spin a fine yarn. They couldn't make and hang onto big money without being able to charm investors. And women, she thought ruefully, touching her lips. Remembering the rasp of Stefano's cheek against her skin sent a tingle coursing through her body. She smiled, recalling the wonderful experience of being held and kissed until her worries spun away. The man was a rat, but why had she expected anything else?

She would cope. She had survived a worse disaster—and at least her brush with Stefano had happened in private. Her life was her own, and from now on that was how it would stay. She smiled sadly. Her single, unforgettable contact with him was a total one-off. It was destined never to happen again. *I should have known that from the start,* she told herself briskly.

She tried to smile again, but it was impossible.

Kira's disappointment over the contract squashed all her fantasies flat. No one did anything for nothing. Mentally she shrugged her shoulders, but Stefano refused to be forgotten. He had set such an exciting fire into her soul. Long ago, life had taught her to expect nothing when it came to men. She knew in her bones Stefano could be no different, but it had been a lovely fantasy. Those sweet memories of him refused to leave her. Whether drifting through her dreams or sending shock waves through her day when she thought she glimpsed his familiar figure in the street, Stefano would not let her go.

She was putting the finishing touches to a very chic project on the outskirts of Florence when her mobile rang.

'Miss Kira Banks?'

Kira couldn't recognise either the woman's voice, or the number that flashed up on her phone's screen. The only people who used this number were clients. Instantly on her guard, she hesitated.

'Who wants to know?'

'I work for Signor Albani. We understand you are on the point of completing a project for Prince Alfonse.

Signor Albani wants you to leave it and travel straight to his office. A car will pick you up in approximately—'

'Wait a minute!' Kira interrupted angrily. 'When I rang your office to check about this, you didn't even have any knowledge of a contract in my name!'

'When was this?'

'The day before yesterday.'

'Then perhaps you were a little impatient, Miss Banks.' The voice was cool.

Kira was in no mood to be treated like an idiot.

'If Signor Albani is clever enough to have found out where I'm working, then he ought to know better than to interrupt me when I'm busy. I don't have time to waste on idle chit-chat with an unreliable man.'

She heard a little gasp at the other end of the line. The voice became a shocked whisper.

'Miss Banks, what are you saying? No one refuses Signor Albani!'

'Well, I'm very sorry, but no one disappoints the person I'm currently working for, either. Especially not me,' Kira said firmly. 'And if you aren't willing to tell him that, maybe you could put me through to Signor Albani, direct?'

The woman wasn't happy, but put her on hold to see if the boss was taking calls. It gave Kira plenty of time to decide she had gone too far. She was being too emotional about this. Much as she hated to back down in any situation, where work was concerned she was a realist. She needed contracts. This one had the delightfully infuriating Stefano Albani at the other end, and that might make it more of a liability than a blessing. Autocratic behaviour was part of every billionaire's job description, but this particular man had got right under her skin. She wanted to be known for the quality of her work, not for making a fool of herself over a man.

Suddenly a voice purred in her ear.

'Kira, it's Stefano.' The sound was so deliciously accented, those few words were enough to wipe all the arguments from her mind.

'Hello,' she said, unable to think of anything else.

'You wanted to speak to me, Kira?'

'Yes.' Everything sensible and businesslike seemed to have been swept out of her head. She gave herself a mental shake. 'Thank you for having your secretary ring me, but I'm working on a very important project,' she snapped, hoping her brisk tone would put some distance between them again. 'I can't simply drop everything and rush to your side.'

'I know. You're a woman of spirit.' The laughter in his voice was infuriatingly engaging. 'Alphonse tells me you're practically finished at his place,' Stefano continued. 'I'm going to be out of the country for a while, and I wanted to discuss your contract with you, face to face, before I leave. I thought this would be a good opportunity for both of us,' he added.

Kira needed this job. She was also desperate to see Stefano again. After all, it does make good business sense, she told herself. There couldn't be any harm in a formal discussion. It would be like gazing at temptation through the window of a locked cake shop. Work would form an invisible shield between them, keeping her from disaster.

'You could be right...' She tried to sound grudging. 'How do I find you?'

She could hear his lack of surprise at her decision. 'Don't worry. I found you, don't forget. A car will be arriving to collect you…' There was a brief pause. Kira visualised him glancing at the designer watch clamped to his beautiful bronzed wrist as he added, 'In exactly fifteen minutes.'

And it was.

As her chauffeur-driven limousine glided to a halt at the main entrance of Albani International, Kira looked up at the grand old building with a hint of anxiety. It was enormous, and a constant stream of people flowed in and out of the revolving glass doors. A commissionaire stepped forward to open the car door for her. Thanking him, Kira took a few moments to compose herself before walking into the reception area. She had worked in palaces, villas and condos, but this place had something extra—Stefano Albani. Taking a deep breath, she went in to meet him.

To Kira's relief, there was no hanging around. That would have shredded her nerves beyond repair. She had been desperate to see Stefano again from the moment he left her house. Now she realised dreams were one thing, but reality was terrifying. The moment he spoke, her insides would turn to jelly. Her instinctive reaction was to keep her head down and pretend she was invisible, but that wasn't the way contracts were won. Instead, she lifted her chin, ready to meet his gaze with an equally bold stare. It took a huge effort.

The man of her dreams was lounging back in a big black chair. His feet were on his desk. He was dictating into a voice recorder and although his eyes instantly locked onto hers he did not stop speaking into it as she walked towards his visitor's chair.

Stefano looked every bit as intimidating as she

remembered. Despite his casual attitude, he was dressed in a beautifully cut dark suit. The formality of classically designed business wear suited him so well it was hard not to stare. Kira gave in to the temptation.

Completing his letter, Stefano switched off the recorder and tossed it aside.

'We meet again, Miss Banks.'

'Indeed we do.' Kira purposely kept her voice light and professional, but couldn't resist a question that had been tormenting her since he left her side. 'Did you buy the Bella Terra estate, *signore*?'

'Yes, but I've been too busy to visit since then. I suppose you've been wondering where I've been?'

'No, not at all,' Kira said coolly, determined not to betray any trace of the embarrassingly large amount of time she had spent wondering what he was getting up to while he was out of her sight.

She saw from a subtle change in his expression that the stony nature of her reply had given him pause. His reaction gave her a little lift, and added some real amusement to her smile.

'In fact, Signor Albani, when your assistant rang it took me a little while to remember who you were.' She batted the words easily across the desk at him.

He parried with a wicked smile. 'I knew you were one in a million, Kira. Now it seems you are unique.'

He took his feet off the desk and sat up straight in his chair, his suddenly businesslike attitude making him even more imposing. Kira fought to keep her expression impassive.

Don't overdo the flip answers! she thought. I might not want him to think he means anything to me, but he is a man who managed to borrow me from Prince Alfonse!

'I want you to work for me, Kira. Name your price,' he drawled, glancing down as he threaded a pair of solid-gold cufflinks into his cuffs.

'I'd rather find out what I'm letting myself in for first.' Kira was proud of the careful neutrality of her tone. It was a shame the rest of her being was entirely focused on the man she had been fantasising about for the past few days. 'I want to make sure I'm the right person for the job. I'd rather you offered the position to someone else if I thought I couldn't give you exactly what you wanted.'

'I agree completely,' Stefano said. 'However, I wouldn't have asked you here today were I not already certain. You, Kira Banks, are capable of giving me *exactly* what I want.' His face remained expressionless but the ambiguity of his words made her cheeks flush red and her breathing catch.

In a quick, carefully judged gesture he spun the file across the desk at her. 'So why don't you read that, and tell me what you think?'

Kira did not move, but regarded him coolly.

'What? Now?'

Stefano raised an eyebrow. 'Unless you have some objection?'

Kira had spent too many restless hours since their first meeting. After her roller-coaster ride of hope, disappointment and surprise, she did not find his words at all funny.

'No. This is so important to me, and it deserves to be studied carefully. I take my work very seriously,' she said slowly, trying to gauge his reaction.

Stefano nodded appreciatively. 'That's exactly the sort of attitude I expect from the people I employ. It's why I want you on board. I had my staff check out some of the other projects you've completed. I needed to make sure I was offering you work for all the right reasons, not simply the wrong one.'

His smile became enigmatic and Kira had to look away. She transferred her gaze back to the cover of the file in front of her. If he paid such careful attention to detail, she wondered what else his people might have found out about her.

'Could you give me an overview?' she said eventually. 'Isn't it simply a contract to work on the gardens at Bella Terra?'

'That, and my Florentine town house as well...'

It had been at the back of Kira's mind, but she'd hardly dared hope he would remember his casual offer.

'Words are cheap. Nobody knows that better than I do, Stefano. Men often say things they don't mean,' she said quietly.

He stared at her. 'Not when it comes to business. Honesty is the only policy there,' he said firmly. 'Since we met and I've had such favourable reviews of your work, I thought I'd raise the stakes. This contract offers you employment not only at Bella Terra, and Florence, but also on my new property in the Caribbean.'

Kira could have bounced straight up to the ceiling in sheer delight. It sounded like her dream contract. Instead, she frowned and bit her lip. 'I've never worked in the Caribbean.'

'Then you're in for a treat. It will be a wonderful experience,' Stefano assured her. 'Silver Island has everything. One hundred hectares of tropical wilderness surrounded by beaches as fine as sugar, set in a warm blue sea.'

Despite her determination to play it cool, Kira's eyes sparkled.

'It sounds lovely already,' she said wistfully.

Stefano had no illusions. He frowned. 'I thought so, too, when I first bought it. But despite all the luxury there's still something lacking. It'll be your job to make the whole place more—' he grimaced, so used to total satisfaction that he couldn't find the words to identify the problem '—user-friendly,' he said eventually, but looked no happier with the phrase than Kira felt.

'That doesn't give me much of a clue.' She shrugged.

'Silver Island is a perfect hideaway. No expense was spared in setting it up, and yet—' he ran his fingertip pensively across his lips '—for all its qualities, it lacks something. I want to import the magic you have worked on the Bella Terra estate. In the same way that you can live in the town house here in Florence while you're working on it, you could stay in the Caribbean while you restructure Silver Island. You'll be on the spot, all the time.'

And where will you be? Kira was appalled to find herself thinking.

'I don't suppose you noticed exactly how interested I was in your garden?' Stefano continued.

'I did,' Kira said, trying to concentrate on their moments of light, insubstantial chit-chat and forget the instant he took her in his arms. It was hopeless. The way she felt about him surged into her mind again. The force of his presence overwhelmed every other memory. A tiny tremble in her voice betrayed her. He noticed, and suddenly his devastating mouth curled up at the corners.

'Yes, I can see....'

All Kira's worries about the Bella Terra valley faded. The intensity of his stare focused on her to the exclusion of everything else. He looked like a tiger ready to pounce. The tremble extended throughout her body and she felt her self-control slipping away into warm arousal. It gathered in all her most feminine places, waiting for one word, one movement from him, to unleash its power.

'Good…so as soon as you're happy with your contract, we'll be on our way.'

'Where?' Kira asked faintly.

Stefano put his elbows on the desk and netted his fingers. 'To Silver Island—you'll need to experience the place in all its glory before you can hope to do it justice. The computer hasn't been built that can give you the experience of warm sand between your toes, and swaying palms beneath a tropical sky.'

The words flowed from him like the tropical breezes he spoke of—warm, gentle and so very seductive.

CHAPTER FIVE

KIRA wanted this job more than anything else in the world, but if she was honest with herself, working so closely with Stefano would be dangerous. How was she supposed to keep her mind on her job? Travelling around the world with him would be torture. It wouldn't simply be a case of storming off down the road if she felt herself weakening. She would be a long way from home and completely at the mercy of a man who held her spellbound. It was the same old story from her university days. Kira couldn't face falling into that trap again. A man like Stefano could never commit to just one woman—that much was obvious from his easy smile and delicious kiss. No woman with any sense should trust him with her heart.

Kira didn't know what to do. Surely if she was aware of the danger, that would make it easier to avoid? And a business contract was legally binding. It meant security. She rated that highly. The problem was, working for Stefano was bound to be a temptation too far. She had no confidence in her ability to resist him, and the man was trouble with a capital T. Her heart had spent the past few days on a helter-skelter of hope and gloom, and it was all his fault. Even if she kept her distance from him, working together would mean seeing exactly how faithless he could be from day to day. That would be a thousand times worse.

'I know—let's leave business behind and I'll take you to lunch first. We can discuss it further there, if you like?'

Kira put her hands on her chair and shifted her weight back a little in the seat. Her feelings were all over the place. She needed to draw some boundaries between the two of them, make it clear that she wouldn't simply fall into line. Everything was moving so fast. She blurted out, 'I won't be rushed. Please don't take me and my feelings for granted.'

He drew back across his desk, and stared at her. It wasn't often possible to read his expression, but Kira thought she saw a brief flash of astonishment.

'Is that what you think I'm doing? Is that how it feels to you?'

She braced herself for an explosion of rage, and answered him defiantly.

'Yes. Yes, it does.'

The expected outburst never came. Stefano simply looked at her thoughtfully. Kira gained a little confidence from that.

'What else would you call it?' she added, more boldly. 'Before you left my home, you promised me great things. It was a good job I didn't believe you, because all I got was radio silence. When I finally rang your office to check on whether there was a contract in the name of Kira Banks, there was no trace—'

Stefano couldn't resist interrupting. 'That was only because I wanted time to double-check your work, and to be completely sure you were the right person to—'

'Please! Let me finish.'

Surprised into silence, he met her scowl with raised eyebrows. Then, with a nod, he raised both his hands as a sign she would be allowed to carry on without any more interruptions.

'You seem to be expecting me to obey you without question, Stefano, and I won't have it,' she said bluntly.

His clear blue eyes watched her steadily, and then he suddenly nodded.

'I'll take that into consideration.' He frowned a little before continuing. 'That took courage. So that we both know where we stand, Kira, maybe I should tell you that no employee has ever got away with speaking to me like that before.'

She opened her mouth to say something, but the way he began to smile stopped her.

'My relationship with contractors, on the other hand, can be rather more—' he lowered his lids slightly, hooding those beautiful eyes '—easy-going, shall we say?'

She stared at him. When he looked at her like that, she couldn't have gone on scolding him if her life depended on it.

'You don't have to make any allowances for me,' she murmured, suddenly and mysteriously short of breath.

Stefano shook his head sagely. 'I admire you for making a fresh start in a new country. A heart in pain is too often the cause of endless trouble.'

He was probing. Kira could tell. When she thought of the research he had done on her, it made her edgy. Had he stuck to her work, or had he delved into more personal areas? The uncertainty made her nervous, so she refused to be drawn any further.

'I bet you've created a fair few broken hearts yourself!' she parried with a laugh. She thought he would do the same, but his reaction was quite different. Instead, he stood and roamed over to the window.

'You could say that. When I was younger, I saw too much abuse to put any faith in human relationships. Instead, I turned my back on all the fine old Italian bonds of family. Escape cost me so much, I'm never going there again.'

Standing at the window, hands on hips, he stared out over the busy cityscape like an eagle searching for prey. His words hinted at an inner pain of his own. Kira's heart went out to him, but it would take a lot of nerve to approach a man who so obviously shunned sympathy.

'I'm sorry,' Kira said softly, after a pause. 'It's terrible to grow up where you aren't wanted.'

Stefano's answer shrugged off her concern.

'That's why I made sure I didn't.' He spoke to the pane of glass in front of him. 'I kept right out of everyone's way. From that moment I started working, and never stopped. It was around the clock, and all year long. It saved me from having to go back home.'

Suddenly he clapped his hands with a loud report that made her jump. 'But what are you doing to me, Kira?' His easy smile returned as he swivelled around and strode back to his desk. 'I didn't bring you here to dissect my private life! I brought you here to talk business, and enjoy a working lunch. Then we'll go and see my town house.'

Kira's own experience of a loveless childhood made her wonder about his past. Then Stefano's eyes connected with hers and wiped the thought clean out of her head. She recognised a heart-stopping shadow of the longing she had seen when he left her. Confused, she picked up the file containing her contract. She wanted to sign, and yet such close contact with the gorgeous Stefano was bound to put her self-control under impossible strain. To her, surrender meant dangerous dependency. She had seen her stepmother and her stepsister fall prey to it. Once a man took over their lives, they stopped seeing themselves as individuals. Kira could not bear to lose a part of herself like that.

'Did you take Amanda the estate agent out to dinner when you signed the final paperwork on Bella Terra?' Her question was as mild as mustard.

There was silence. Made brave by it, she looked up at him sharply. Expecting to find him looking guilty, she was disappointed.

'Would it make any difference to you, Kira?'

His face was impassive. It was another probe. That only made her wonder all the more. He hadn't denied a liaison with the woman, although if he had, Kira would have assumed he was lying.

'Maybe,' she mused, trying to look and sound casual as she studied the closely typed document for snares and pitfalls. 'I don't like men who use their position in life as a lever for their sexual conquests. I like to keep my work and my private life strictly separate.'

'You told me as much the other day. I'll bear it in mind,' he said gravely, but then his mouth twitched. 'So in future, there will be absolutely no business talk whenever I visit your house after moving into La Bella Terra.'

The thought of inviting Stefano over the threshold of her home raised Kira's temperature in a frighteningly exciting way. She cleared her throat, trying not to squirm in anticipation. Her lips became dry, and she had to moisten them with her tongue before announcing, 'I think we ought to get one thing straight right from the start, Stefano. I'm a genuine loner. I don't fancy the idea of you dropping into my home at odd hours while I'm off duty, distracting me with…talk,' she finished awkwardly.

His reply was so simple, it shocked her. 'That's a shame.'

She looked up, waiting for him to try and persuade her otherwise. His face was as poker fit as her own as he added, 'Now come on, let's have lunch.'

Kira stood, mentally preparing herself. Lunch with Stefano was sure to be the stuff of fairy tales. That worried her. Powerful people liked to create a good impression—to begin with. They showered you with pixie dust until you were dazzled into falling in with their plans.

'I'd be delighted, but don't expect me to sign this contract on the strength of it. I'd rather my legal people had a good look at it before I make a final decision,' she said airily.

Kira's only advisers were her cynical nature and a glass of pinot grigio, so she was rather looking forward to that consultation.

'Good. That leaves us free to discuss much more interesting things over lunch.' He smiled, pulling on his jacket as he led her to the door. 'Although I'm rather surprised a forthright woman like you doesn't go through her own paperwork!'

She smiled as he strode across his office and opened the door to let her out.

* * *

Kira's journey to the ground floor couldn't have been more different from her trip up to the executive suite. Then, she had spent every second checking her appearance. Now she kept her eyes riveted on the thick cream carpet. It wasn't that she didn't know where to look. She desperately wanted to gaze at Stefano, but somehow she couldn't do it. She had to be content with hints of his aftershave or the jingle of change in his pockets as he stood so close to her, yet so distant.

A limousine was waiting for them outside the revolving doors of the office block. Its driver opened the door for Kira. She slid in, glad of the excuse not to have to look at Stefano as he exchanged a few words with his driver.

He was every bit as good as her fantasies. His first words to her when she walked into his office had been absolutely right. The past few days had tortured, tormented and distracted her with thoughts of what he had been doing, and with whom. Stefano was the only man who had ever moved her like this. It made her certain he must have a new girl every night. Who could possibly resist that clear-eyed gaze? Kira was terribly afraid she couldn't. Her pulse increased to dizzying levels each time he looked at her. As he took his seat beside her in the car it felt as though her heart was trying to jump into her throat. Her mouth went dry, and she felt heat pool in the pit of her stomach.

It had been hard enough not to reach out to him when he had been standing alone and aloof in his office stronghold. How much more difficult would it be to resist him when they were at lunch together?

'When it comes to that contract, you'll have no worries,' Stefano said as their car pulled out into the stream of traffic outside the headquarters of Albani International. 'I'm ruthless in business, but I'm always fair. That agreement is simple, straightforward and totally unthreatening. Working for me will be the smartest move you ever make. I've seen the design work and planting you did on the Bella Terra estate, and I've heard brilliant reports from your other clients. Your touch is exactly what I need. You'll bring your talents to my properties around the world. In return, I'll reward you well and give you free advertising among all my contacts. That will save you all the tiresome brown-nosing for business you hate so much. Think of it—all the work you could ever want, but none of the socialising.'

He slid a smile towards her. Kira thought of the man she had seen silhouetted against the cityscape. His expression tangled her heartstrings before her brain had time to intercept it.

'You don't know what that would mean to me,' she said, the relief of getting work without having to pitch for it filtering through her words. Whenever she was in Stefano's presence, her body refused to behave. It ignored all the warning signs. Her brain screamed *danger* but her soft, warm feminine core heard only *temptation* and remembered only their kiss.

'We're here,' he said, sounding slightly husky, and Kira wondered if he was struggling with similar memories, but he leapt out of the car before she could see his face. By the time he had arrived to open her door, he was back to business.

'This is one of my favourite restaurants,' he explained as he escorted her into a beautiful old building in the heart of the city. Its glamorous receptionist was all teeth and talons. She greeted Stefano by name, and led them to a spacious table for two. It was like no business lunch Kira had ever attended. As a respected professional she was used to being treated well. Stefano's idea of entertaining was in an entirely different league. The Michelin-starred restaurant was as perfect as its extensive menu, and Kira felt entirely uncomfortable. She looked down the list of tempting dishes, studying the menu intently, but it was no good. Eventually, she had to swallow her pride. It stuck in her throat, but as a regular Stefano was the best person to ask for help. 'I'm sorry. This is a cordon bleu restaurant and I'm a cucina povera girl at heart. All these exotic things are way out of my zone. Which do you recommend?'

'Definitely the lamb. It's a favourite of mine.'

Her mind made up, Kira ordered and handed her menu to the waiter.

Stefano ordered the same for himself, and a bottle of wine to accompany their meal. When they were alone again, he leaned towards her. His eyes were keen with interest.

'I would have thought a woman such as yourself would be entertained in restaurants like this all the time,' he said quietly. 'You deserve the best.'

Kira withdrew from the intensity of his gaze. 'I've told you—I enjoy plain Italian food.'

Stefano smiled suddenly. 'You are very much an Englishwoman. None of them are any good at truly indulging themselves.'

Clearly, thought Kira wryly, *he's never met my mother.*

'There aren't any fish-and-chip shops in the Bella Terra valley, so I've learned to adapt a little!' she said, relaxing in spite of herself as she looked around at their luxurious surroundings. 'It makes it easier when you bring me to a wonderful place like this. Everything is so beautiful, especially that dessert trolley over there. Mmm, I do so love my puddings!' She laughed, suddenly overcome with amazement at where she was and who she was with.

The waiter delivered their main course, and the glorious scent helped to relax her further. She ate a forkful and almost moaned in pleasure. Stefano watched her appreciatively. There was something suspiciously predatory in his eyes, but, overwhelmed and exhausted from fighting her attraction to him, when he held her gaze Kira didn't look away. He smiled slowly and she felt her hunger change into a more immediate desire.

'I wonder if this is a good time to tell you I haven't thought about another woman since we met,' he murmured slowly, in a voice silken with charm.

'It wasn't the thinking I was worried about!' Kira sighed reflexively before snapping her mouth shut and blushing bright red. Too late, she corrected herself. 'If I was worried at all, which I'm not.'

His voice became a caress. 'That's good. I wouldn't want to worry you, Kira. The fact is, you intrigue me. I've spent the time since I left your side wondering about you, pure and simple.'

'I'll bet there was nothing remotely pure or simple about it,' she retorted, although it was hard to stay angry with a man who gazed into her eyes with such intensity.

Her tone had definitely mellowed. Stefano picked up on it. He put down his fork. For a moment his hands spoke for him. The fingers spread wide, his wrists rolled from side to side on the edge of the table.

'Why block me when I'm trying to tell you something,

Kira?' His words were quiet, but intense. 'Let me into your life a little. You won't regret it. I can do things for you that you would never dream were possible. With your skill and my backing, there is no limit to what can be achieved. I want to start finding my pleasure much closer to home, and you are the one who can make it happen.'

Transfixed by his expression, Kira let him slide his hand over hers as it lay on the table. Incapable of resisting him, her fingers went limp. He began to stroke the back of her hand. His movements teased her with thoughts of how he had held her willing body against his only two weeks before. From the second he swept out of her front door, he left a yawning void in her life. She had spent so little time with him, and yet over those long, lonely days she had missed him so much. Kira felt every moment she didn't spend gazing into his eyes must be wasted.

A rising tide of emotion stirred her restlessly in her chair. Fine dining was nothing to the thought of Stefano making love to her. Suddenly she wanted him as urgently as she had desired him that day in her house. The colour of his eyes mirrored her needs. Beneath the long, flowing tablecloth she felt the slight movement of his foot as it slipped between hers. It happened as easily as his bare limbs might caress and possess her own.

'The moment you agree to work for me and sign that contract, I shall take you to Silver Island and show you my new paradise. Sun, sand and warm blue waters. It is everything you deserve, *cara mia...*' he whispered. His voice slipped over the words like a lazy tide lapping over land. Kira felt the last vestiges of her common sense slipping away. It was the powerful seduction in his eyes....

She passed the tip of her tongue over her parched lips.

'Stefano...I...'

The yapping of a pocket dog at the reception desk broke the spell. Kira blinked as though waking from a dream. As she came to her senses she saw an unmistakable look pass across Stefano's face. He might be a master at hiding his feelings, but he wasn't quite quick enough to conceal them from her. He was anticipating something. She looked across the busy restaurant. An impossibly tall, thin blonde was handing over her designer shoulder bag. The head of a noisy chihuahua poked out of it like a ripe russet apple. Relieved of the sum total of her responsibilities, the blonde turned around and surveyed the restaurant as though she was at the end of a catwalk. After jiggling a hand at several acquaintances, her eyes fastened on the table where Kira and Stefano were sitting.

In a cacophony of sleek designer fabric and six-inch heels she sashayed towards them. Kira tensed. Unconsciously her fingers went to her hair, then her smart but simple jacket, smoothing down its creases and fiddling with the buttons.

'Ah, Chantal!' Stefano turned as the woman got nearer.

Kira couldn't see his face, but heard his smile and could imagine the rest.

'Darling Stefano!'

With a winning smile especially for her, Stefano abandoned his plate and stood up. Greeting the blonde as though he was used to interruptions like this, he showed more style than Kira's one and only lover had ever done. She wondered how many times a seasoned philanderer had to run through this routine before it became second nature. Stefano had obviously put in the hours. He had turned it into an art form. Grasping his friend Chantal by the elbows, he air-kissed her with great pleasure.

'It's been a while, Stefano!' The blonde returned his gesture, running cool blue eyes over Kira's clothes and hair in a way that didn't simply give Kira a hint, it dug her savagely in the ribs.

Stefano was totally unfazed. Taking Chantal's hand, he pulled her fingers towards his lips for a real kiss. 'How was Biarritz?'

Chantal sighed theatrically. 'Nothing without you, darling, of course! Aren't you going to introduce me to your new friend? I haven't seen you about before, have I?' she said, giving Kira a bright, shiny look.

'Kira is a business associate,' Stefano said with barely a flicker.

'Pleased to meet you.' Chantal sent her a vague smile which failed to reach her eyes, before turning her attention back to Stefano.

Kira wasn't fooled for a moment. There was sympathy in that look. It told her—loud and clear—that Chantal didn't see her as any sort of threat. That made her feel more alone than she had ever done in her life. Chantal and Stefano, two of the beautiful people, chatted easily about friends she knew only as employers. Several times, Stefano tried to include Kira in their conversation, but she was simply too self-conscious and had nothing to say. She sat in mortified silence until Chantal left. When Stefano turned his full attention back to her again, she couldn't meet his eyes. She looked down hurriedly at her meal.

He introduced me as his 'business associate,' she thought, catching sight of herself in the glittering silver cutlery. *That really puts me in my place. I suppose I should be glad—it saves me having to worry about getting jumped on at every opportunity.*

At least it meant she could sign that contract safe in the knowledge nothing more than work would be on offer.

Somehow, having seen Stefano in action as he charmed Chantal, that didn't feel like such a good thing any more.

He went back to his meal as though nothing had happened. Kira was left to burn with embarrassment in silence. She tried to console herself that an affair with Stefano would be like this all the time. There would be constant interruptions from glamorous women in designer dresses. It would be Kira's idea of hell on earth.

After savouring another mouthful of lamb, Stefano looked up and smiled at her again.

'Now, where were we?' he said in a confiding murmur.

Kira put her heart and soul into a dazzling smile. It was the only way she could speak without screaming.

'I was about to tell you I wasn't in the ego-massaging business, Stefano. I've been fooled by a plausible rogue once before and I've got no intention of being caught out a second time, thank you!'

A look came into his eyes that she could not name, but it definitely wasn't remorse.

'I never for one moment imagined you would be,'

he said, looking so serious that she knew straight away he was telling the truth. 'Although you've touched on something I've been unable to get out of my mind since I met you at Bella Terra. When we were talking the other evening, it sounded as though you left England under a cloud. If you feel able, I would like to know more about what happened.'

Kira stared at him. His eyes hadn't left her since he said goodbye to Chantal. He had never once looked over his shoulder to see what the other woman was doing. *Whatever she might have been to him in the past, he's gazing at me now,* she thought in a desperate attempt to steady her nerves. She thought of everything that had happened over the past two weeks. Throwing away that begging letter from her stepparents had been a wonderfully freeing gesture. She remembered how close she had come to unburdening herself upon their first meeting. It was so tempting to let him in, to give Stefano a tiny insight into her problems. She took a deep breath, trying to summon up the courage to shed a little more light onto her murky past.

'Yes, I did—but the cloud wasn't of my making,' she began, but the memory of Chantal's contemptuous gaze and how separate a world Stefano came from shook her, and at the last moment she could not bring herself to go into details. 'Although I helped make it into the thunderstorm that sent me scuttling over here. I was escaping a disastrous affair. I abandoned the rat, and started all over again. I found myself a new life, and made a new start.'

Realising she would go no further, Stefano nodded. 'I might have guessed. There are two sorts of people—

those who crumble at the first hint of disaster, and those who conquer it and thrive.'

'I didn't exactly bounce back the next day,' Kira said ruefully, waving away his concern. 'But you're right— drawing a line under my mistake was the best thing I did. It let me move on. I took stock of my life, and then decided to apply for a course in horticulture. I've always liked working with plants, and it turned out I had quite a talent for it. One thing led to another so fast I was exhibiting before the world at Chelsea within three years. Shortly after that I found my home in La Ritirata. I've been here ever since.'

'And achieved wonders.' Stefano leaned forward and quietly pushed a strand of hair behind her ear. Kira melted. It would be so easy just to lean forward and kiss him…. In less than an hour he had delighted, infuriated and confused her, sometimes all at once. She could hardly think straight. Then, from the other side of the room, she heard Chantal's laugh and suddenly tensed.

Maybe she's laughing at me, she thought, hopelessly hypnotised by a consummate seducer. If they're not laughing now, then surely it's only a matter of time….

That was all it took. Her mind cleared, but her words were unsteady. 'I thought we came here to talk about work, Stefano?'

Lifting his glass of wine to her in a silent toast, he treated her to a devastating smile.

'Yes, but there's no need to restrict ourselves, Kira.'

Colour rushed into her cheeks. The days fell away and once again she was in his arms, her hands hungry for his perfectly formed body. The powerful bulk of him was so close she could have reached out and touched him.

Right now his body was hidden beneath the beautifully tailored lines of a white shirt and business suit, but the look in his eyes concealed nothing. He expected to take her to his bed. He demanded nothing less—and Kira wanted nothing more.

CHAPTER SIX

SHE fought to remain calm. Stefano wanted her, she wanted him—but she didn't need all the problems that would bring. He had affected her deeply from the moment they met. Bitter experience told her that was dangerous. She didn't want her illusions about him shattered by getting too close. He was bound to break her heart. She knew it. What happens when he dumps me—as he will, sooner or later? she asked herself. When he moved into La Bella Terra he would be living only a few hundred metres from her front door. Becoming the heartbroken doorstop of a faithless philanderer was definitely not on her 'to do' list.

Obviously deciding he'd let her suffer for long enough, Stefano seamlessly changed gear.

'How do you feel about house-hunting? With access to my contacts, the world really is your oyster. If you see anything that takes your fancy, let me know. There's no limit.'

Just as Kira felt herself taking off, Stefano's words brought her back to earth. Grateful for the chance to nail her feet back to the ground again, she interrupted him quickly.

'I hope you aren't trying to buy me out again. I'm

happy living right where I am, in the house I've made my own, in the perfect position.'

Stefano said nothing, but his slowly widening smile was enough to make her body move uneasily beneath its warmth.

'You are a stubborn woman. You have integrity and determination. Work with me and I can assure your future. It isn't only a matter of beautifying my own properties. My company, Albani International, has a charitable arm which is involved in all sorts of exciting projects. I was deeply impressed when I saw the work you have done at Bella Terra. Once you have finished working on my homes, you can start bringing your influence to bear in many other places.'

'I'm glad you've got such confidence in me.' Kira blushed, her clear skin for a moment matching the intricate strawberry meringue the waiter set before her.

Stefano's sensual lips parted in a half-smile as he saw Kira's delight in the summery confection of pinks and white on the dish laid in front of her.

'Look, why don't we visit my apartment after we finish here? You can see where you'll be working, if you decide to sign that contract. I told Prince Alfonse not to expect you back today.'

'Oh, you did, did you?' Kira said archly, inspired by a sugar rush. 'I hope you also told him we're out on business.'

Stefano didn't answer. His expression was telling Kira everything she didn't want to know, but her conscience was clear. For the moment, at least.

'As it happens, I think visiting the site is a very good idea,' she added coolly. 'I never accept a job until I have made a thorough study beforehand.'

'Good. I'm all for close scrutiny,' he said. With a nod of his head he summoned the head waiter, who brought a bottle of chilled champagne to their table. When it had been poured out, Stefano lifted his glass to her in another toast.

Kira remembered the last time he looked at her like that. It was in the split second before he kissed her. His eyes had a way of stripping away everything from her soul. She tried telling herself that he must size up every one of his female conquests like this, but a viper's nest of conflicting responses writhed within her body. His smile held out all sorts of possibilities. That was what made him so dangerous. At least she had no illusions, and could be on her guard.

'To our new partnership,' he said, his voice a sensual growl of anticipation which immediately created answering ripples in the pit of her stomach. Determined to quell them, she snapped

'Are you always so openly provocative?'

He broke the tension with a sudden laugh. 'I've never met another woman quite so woundingly honest! I can't help it, I'm afraid. Some men are born to it, while others need to be coaxed out of their shell by a loving, sensitive hand.'

Kira felt colour riot in her cheeks. Before she could explode, Stefano turned his statement into a warning.

'I am most definitely not one of those men.'

Stefano's town house was such a short distance from the restaurant he didn't bother calling up his driver. They walked. Kira had difficulty in keeping up with his long strides as he led her through the narrow streets. Without a word he fell back in step with her. Crossing a

sunlit square, he directed her into a narrow canyon between two impossibly high and ancient stone walls. Kira
looked around nervously as they left the sun-drenched
crowds and plunged into shady solitude. Suddenly she
realised he was no longer at her side. With a start, she
swung around. He stood beside a pair of large wooden
gates, let into the anonymous wall. With one hand he
turned the wrought-iron handle in a small pass door
and pushed it open.

'We're here. Go ahead.'

Kira cast one last apprehensive look up and down the
narrow alley.

'Why are you so nervous? This is the best part of
town.' He chuckled. 'Anyone would think I was trying
to abduct you.'

A crazy vision of Stefano sweeping her away into
the desert on a spirited Arab stallion flashed into Kira's
mind. That threw her into confusion, but her mind
cleared the instant she stepped into his courtyard. It
was like standing at the bottom of a dry well. High walls
irregularly perforated by small barred windows closed
in on every side. This was a place the sun only reached
when it was directly overhead. The building was ancient
and beautiful, but putting a garden here would require
imagination and skill. When he first mentioned a town
house, Kira's mind had started playing with the idea of
a private sun terrace. This place offered all the privacy
anyone could want, but none of the rays.

'Good grief,' she whispered to herself, before adding
aloud, 'This is going to be a challenge.'

He looked concerned. 'If you think it's going to be
too much for you, tell me. I'll get someone to steam
clean the whole place and leave it at that.'

'No!' Kira left his side and began pacing out the stark, stony area. 'There's nothing I enjoy more than a challenge. I'm not a quitter. If something can be imagined, it can be achieved.'

'Like a holiday home on Mars, maybe?'

Kira ignored him. Rummaging in her bag for a notebook and pencil, she began scribbling instead.

'I'll tell you what I like—' Stefano began, but she shook her head.

'This will only work if I tell you what is feasible first. Then you can choose which plants from my list you prefer.'

Stefano lodged his hands on his hips. 'What happened to "the client is always right"?'

Kira snapped her notebook shut, looked up and stared at him. He stared back. Despite her flinty expression, her mind was moving like quicksilver. This was one argument she could not afford to lose. Stefano could be infuriating, but he was offering her a series of lucrative contracts. He was also close to irresistible, and very easy on the eye. As long as she could harden her heart to stay out of his clutches, this would be a dream appointment. This site presented huge problems, but Kira would enjoy overcoming them. It gave her an unbeatable feeling to see a satisfied client, especially when it was a job other firms might consider too difficult. And she would be working for Stefano. The idea remained deliciously dangerous. She decided on a trial run.

'Fine. You're right—I'm not going to argue with you,' she announced. 'As long as you settle my bills, I'll do whatever you want. I can't guarantee you will be perfectly happy first time, though. The only plants that have a chance of surviving here are the sorts chosen specifically for these conditions. Unless you do as I say, you may end up with plants that have to be replaced every few weeks, because they die.'

'That's not a problem.' He shrugged.

'It is for me. I'm no tree hugger, but I can't stand the thought of all that waste. I'd rather we worked together as a team from the start and got this right straight away. Wouldn't you?'

'When you put it like that…' he reasoned.

Kira smiled. 'Great. My own website has a facility for choosing the right plant for the right place. I'll take you through the process, and then you'll be able to download the selection and spend as long as you like choosing what you want. The final decision will always be yours.'

His eyes narrowed. 'I know. That's why I'm looking forward to co-operating with you. Why don't we go inside? I can check out your suggestions, and try to soften a few of your rough edges at the same time.' He showed her towards the main door of his house.

Stefano ordered coffee and invited Kira into a stark, brightly lit office on the ground floor. It was full of the best and most expensive computing equipment, and the school-room stink of exam papers, solvents and printing ink. She recoiled. It was too sharp a reminder of the days when every exam success meant she was subject to more sneering at home.

With a computer logged in, Stefano stood to let her take his place at the keyboard. Kira called up her website. The moment he saw it, he looked impressed. That gave her confidence a big boost.

'I want to feel the same affection you have for your

own home,' he said, leaning over the back of her chair. 'I enjoy property, yet somehow it never turns out to be the pleasure I expect it to be. Whenever I buy anything, it is a rock-solid investment,' he said, but with an unusual lack of enthusiasm.

Kira was so surprised by the note in his voice, she swivelled her chair around to face him.

'You don't sound convinced, and I can't say I'm surprised. I don't care what my cottage on the Bella Terra estate is worth, but I suppose it will be a lot less than I paid for it.'

'You're right. For once, I don't seem to care about the money. It's something far more important that concerns me, Kira. I want Bella Terra to be much more than simply a run-of-the-mill investment.' He grimaced, and twitched a shoulder.

Kira turned back to the computer screen. He sounded like the typical spoiled billionaire, bemoaning his idle lifestyle.

'Ah, the curse of great wealth!' she muttered.

'I've told you—this isn't about money.' His retort was swift and sure. 'You are a case in point—the first time I looked across the valley from the Bella Terra villa I assumed your cottage would be nothing but a horrible reminder of everything I was trying to leave behind. And yet when you let me get closer, I got a different angle on your little garden and the homely touches inside. I envy you, Kira.' He stopped abruptly and straightened up. 'But maybe that was a case of giving you too much information.'

She felt the exact opposite. 'Why in the world would you envy me? I've got nothing, while you've got everything anyone could ever want!'

He modified his smile, and the angles of his fine face became acute. 'Is that what you think?'

Kira swung back to her screen. Tapping a few names over the keyboard, she accessed her file of planting suggestions for shady places. 'Pretty much.'

'Then I'll shut up. When I lived and worked on the streets, I spent too long listening to financiers and expats moaning. I was a tour guide, not an agony aunt—not that you would have believed it.' He put his coffee cup down beside hers.

'I'll bet you only guided the women!' Kira said with sly humour.

'That depended on where they wanted to be led,' he replied with an equally wicked grin. 'I gave a top-class service to everyone, whoever they were—every time. And that is how I got here.' He gestured around the IT suite of his impressive house. 'I saw that tour guides were always in demand, and they were invariably a rip-off. There was a gap in the market for a first-class service. I set myself up with a second-hand suit and the right attitude, and cleaned up. The sky was my limit, and it still is. My firm has branches all over the world, publishes travel guides—'

He stopped abruptly and frowned. 'And to think—I've had all that success, yet so little satisfaction.'

He leaned against the table beside the keyboard. Kira kept her eyes on her hands as she tapped over the keys.

'I want to be as happy in my houses as you are in your home, Kira,' he announced, and then chuckled. 'That's a tall order, but I believe you can give me answers to all my problems.'

Kira looked into his blue eyes and trembled to think

how much she wanted to do that. Attempting to sound crisp and businesslike, she said, 'Rest assured, I've never disappointed a client yet. If I work for you, I'll do my best to make all your dreams come true.'

CHAPTER SEVEN

KIRA blushed as she realised her words could so easily
hold another meaning. She held her breath. Once again
she had said exactly what she thought, and that was
the problem. Her words were intended to be a promise
to make all his desires for his properties come true.
Instead, she might as well have told him her deepest
feelings. He was watching her intently. Surely it was
only a matter of time before she betrayed herself to him?
She wanted to give this her best, but felt the need to hide
her true emotions. As usual, work came to her rescue.
She hit Return on the keyboard with all the force she
would have liked to use on herself. The screen leapt into
life again. Simulated raindrops falling on the surface of
water became a display of plant photographs.

'Almost as beautiful as you,' Stefano said.

Kira thanked him tersely. His words reminded her of
Chantal's patronising smile, and the way he could take
his pick from all the lovely women in the world.

'I'll key in the details of your courtyard—its aspect,
an estimate of the hours of sunshine it can expect—'

'There won't be much of that, I suspect.'

'I have a few ideas that can help,' Kira rallied. She
always felt more confident when she could bring the

subject around to the plants she loved. Dwelling on her own thoughts and feelings, and speculating on the way he might respond, made her uncomfortable. 'Some discreetly placed mirrors will bounce light into the shadowy places.'

'It sounds like the effect you have on me.'

He was leaning over her, only inches from where her fingers played on the keyboard. The subtle fragrance of his nearness was intoxicating. It was totally impossible to ignore. Kira felt her temperature rising as she logged all the details she had taken down so carefully. She tried to keep her eyes riveted on the screen, but within moments the effort was too much. They were constantly drawn back to Stefano's face. As though to prove he was able to ignore the effect he was having on her, he kept watching the rapidly developing images on the computer screen. Anticipation rose in Kira like a column of mercury. When she was almost at the point of screaming with need for him, he turned his clear blue eyes on her with a smile of sheer innocence.

'So you are confident you can give me what I want?'

His words were warm drops in a dipping pool of desire. He had chosen them with care. Knowing they were calculated for effect was the only thing that made it possible for Kira to resist him.

'While I'm working for you, that's all I'm interested in.'

Her voice was faint and strangely unsteady. Stefano continued to watch her, waiting for more signs that her resistance was weakening. Kira willed herself to return his gaze with equal candour, but she was powerless to stop a blush rippling over her skin. It was a firestorm of feeling. She needed distraction, and looked for it in a new computer image.

'Here's a mock-up of your quadrangle, with the rough shapes of some suggested plant groupings added.'

With one final flourish on the keyboard, she sat back and steadied her nerves with a sip of coffee. Stefano had drawn away slightly while she was typing, but now he leaned forward again. This time, Kira was strangely disappointed to find he was intent on the screen, rather than her.

'That's impressive.' He nodded slowly, his clear blue eyes flicking back and forth between the sidebars of text and the interactive graphics of the screen.

'It's only my first thoughts.' She basked in his approval, but tried not to show it. 'The final version will take a lot more work. And this is only the courtyard. I seem to remember you mentioned a roof garden?'

He nodded. 'There are some stark, flat areas resulting from repairs and building work done in the sixties. I like the idea of a hidden sanctuary that no one else knows about but me.'

'And me, as your designer,' Kira reminded him.

'The best secrets are those we are willing to share.'

Picking up on his enthusiasm, Kira smiled. 'Why don't we go up and inspect what you've got to offer?'

'I thought you'd never ask,' he said, already heading for the door.

Stefano's town house rambled over several floors. It was a warren of unexpected twists and turns. Kira always enjoyed the thrill of seeing how successful people ran their lives. She took in every detail when she visited their workplaces. This satellite branch of Albani International was no exception. Despite her solitary nature, whenever she took on a grand new job Kira spent her time idly wondering what she would tell her grandchildren. Today was different. There was nothing remotely idle about her thoughts. This wasn't just any grand house, owned by a faceless billionaire. It was where Stefano Albani lived. He worked and walked about here, and today he was strolling along beside her. The sensation was so powerful it had an immediate effect on all her dreams. Her fantasy grandchildren gained names, parents and inherited their grandfather's beautiful blue eyes and dark, dashing curls.

As Stefano piloted her along corridors scented by cream polish and fresh flower arrangements, she was torn. Admiring the modern, minimalist surroundings meant tearing her attention away from the gorgeous man at her side. He introduced her to everyone they passed by name. That was impressive. She wasn't quite so happy with the way he spoke to all the women in the same flirty fashion that set her own heart hammering.

'You're very quiet, Kira.' He smiled as they left the busy offices behind. Only the gentle burr of air conditioning followed them beyond a stained-glass door into his private quarters.

'I've been resisting the temptation to contradict you,' Kira said primly. 'You've asked everyone we met to welcome me onto your team. That ignores the tiny fact that I haven't actually agreed to sign your contract yet.'

Stefano's self-confidence shone through his reply. 'You will. You're an intelligent woman.'

His voice was as smooth as the glass elevator that took them up the final two storeys. Letting her out onto the roof, Stefano stood back to let her take in the whole breathtaking panorama. At this distance, the circling shoals of traffic sounded very faint and far away. The click of Kira's heels on the flat cement roof was loud, so she tried to make them sound efficient as well by striding straight over to the nearest parapet.

'This view is astonishing,' she breathed. 'You can see to the hills in almost every direction! We're so high I feel as though I could reach out and touch the dome of the cathedral. The light over the city is so beautiful. What do you suppose gives it that lovely golden glow?'

Stefano strolled to her side. Resting one hand against an ancient wall, he surveyed the scene with obvious pleasure. 'It is the Tuscan sun. It has mingled with the inspiration of poets, and matured over centuries.'

Pleased by the image, she turned to him with an unguarded smile, and found that he had switched his attention from the city to her.

'Do you think you can improve my situation?'

Kira considered her reply. She looked from the spectacular view to the dreary surroundings of his rooftop eyrie. Her mind went into overdrive. 'The beauty of beginning with nothing is that you can try whatever you like. Nobody could top an aerial view of Florence—but I can give you a better backdrop to it, Stefano. When you bring a beautiful woman like Chantal up here, she deserves something a lot better than bare cement and these pigeon prickles...' Patting the metal tangle that stopped birds perching on the parapet, Kira leaned out over the low wall. She was tempted to look straight down. It was a big mistake. Suddenly the events and emotions of the past two weeks rolled over her in a wave of dizziness.

'Ohh…'

She swayed for a terrifying moment, until Stefano seized her with his strong hands and pulled her back from the brink. Her eyes flew open, and she found herself looking up into his lean, intelligent face.

'It is never a good idea to stray too close to the edge,' he said brusquely.

His voice was wonderfully resonant. Kira felt so safe, but it frightened her.

'I—I know. I'm sorry, Stefano. I don't know what came over me.'

'This place can have a very strange effect.' His words were quiet and almost hesitant. They were in complete contrast to his iron grip as it crushed her against the solid security of his body.

'I'm beginning to realise that…' Kira's whisper rose between them like a dream.

'It makes me want to tell you again how beautiful you are, Kira,' he whispered.

She slowly shook her head. To her amazement, she felt Stefano contradict her with a definite nod. Neither of them moved for a long time. Then, in complete harmony, they came together in a kiss that made the world stand still.

After a long, long time, Stefano's lips left hers and he pressed his cheek hard against her hair.

'Come with me. Now,' he urged.

'I can't.'

'Why not?'

'I don't want to be hurt again.'

He stood back a little and looked down at her with a calm, forthright gaze. 'I would never do that.'

'I can't take that risk.' Desperation tore the words from her lips.

'I'm offering you nothing but good things, Kira. How can that bring you pain? Nothing lasts forever. We both know that. As long as we never forget it, there can be nothing but pleasure for us.'

He had been drawing her closer and closer. As his whisper died away, he kissed her with a power that held her long after he had drawn back from her lips.

'So let's enjoy that pleasure while we can....'

Wicked thoughts ran crazily through her mind. It's not as though he's married—no one will ever know, and if they do find out, it won't be like last time....

Her defences dissolved with the intensity of his smile. It was focused directly on her. There could be no resistance. Mirroring his expression, she nodded her head.

Stefano slid one arm around her shoulder and drew her back inside to the elevator. It took only seconds to reach his suite, but his hands were already dancing over the thin fabric of her clothes. He led her into the sophisticated setting of his private lounge. There he slid the jacket from her shoulders and flung it onto a glass-topped table.

'I know what you said about mixing business and pleasure, tesoro, but you would be the first to remind me you haven't actually signed my contract yet,' he murmured.

Kira veered between nervous tension and excitement at the thought of taking a leap into the unknown. For the first time in her life, temptation felt good. There was no need to wonder why. It was an opportunity to indulge in the fantasy that had been teasing her from the moment she first set eyes on him. A throaty chuckle rose up from somewhere deep within her.

'I think that's the perfect reason to make an exception.' Despite a tingle of fear, she wanted to find how far her body would go to quench this overriding fire for Stefano. She already sensed he would give her the ultimate in satisfaction. A strange combination of daring and desire unleashed all sorts of feelings deep in her body.

I know what I'm doing, she told herself. It'll be all right this time, because I'm watching for the danger signs. I can't resist him any more, but it doesn't matter because I don't want to try. I'm going into this with my eyes wide open. I'll enjoy Stefano while he satisfies my every need, but if he dares to try and get inside my heart, that's the end—no more.

From that moment on, there was no more thinking. She was aware of nothing but his touch on her arm and the movement of his body as he drew her into the silent sanctuary of his bedroom. The curtains were drawn against the afternoon sun. It was as cool and shadowy as an oasis at dusk, lit only by a narrow strip where the floor-length curtains were not quite fully closed. A tiny fragment of goose down spiralled upwards in the single shaft of sunlight. It looks as light as my heart feels, Kira thought. It was the last thing she remembered before a surge of need carried away all her inhibitions.

He was more gentle than even her fantasies had promised. His fingertips had a delicacy of touch that sent shivers of delight dancing over her skin. When his cheek brushed her face the roughness of his incipient stubble released a little cry of desire from her lips. It no longer mattered that he had travelled this route with one girl or a thousand. While she was in his arms, Kira felt like the only woman in the world. As the silk and lace of her slip slithered away, she was filled with the exuberance of being. Standing in a pool of sunlight beneath the warm appreciation of Stefano's haunting gaze, she felt the life force thunder through her body. This was where she wanted to be, now and forever.

'Carissima mia,' he breathed in a way that drew Kira's whole attention right back to him.

With a flutter of delight she saw a subtle change come over him. It wasn't so much a new look in his eyes, as the sudden loss of something she had not wanted to acknowledge before. Playful amusement no longer danced in his expression. Stefano was a changed man. For once he was not the flippant lover of thousands. All his attention was devoted to her and her alone.

'You don't mean that,' she murmured, while hoping with all her heart that he did.

'Would you like to put me to the test?' his voice rasped through the drowsy silence. It was thick with an emotion she had never heard from him before. He took one, two steps across the soft rug. Now they were so close, she could feel the warmth of desire radiating from him. His heat transformed her. With a moan of anticipation, her head fell back.

'You are so lovely.'

His voice was a whisper. Kira felt fingertips dance lightly over her face, and then dive into the rippling luxuriance of her coppery hair. His kiss was a long, thoughtful expression of delight. Pressing his forehead against hers, he slid his arms around her body, drawing it close. 'I've said that so many times, to so many different girls, but this is the first time it has been from the core of my being, mia tesoro.'

Kira opened her eyes. Another transformation swept over his face, and with delight she put her hand up to touch the uncharacteristic colour flushing his cheeks. He was holding her with a possessive strength as they sank into the yielding luxury of his bed. Stefano kissed his way down the curve of her neck, before lifting her arm to tease the delicate skin beneath. His lips pleasured her breasts and belly, encouraging her to stretch out languorously across his silken sheets. It was such a lovely, leisurely feeling that when he pulled away from her she tried to follow him, jealous of every second he spent away from her arms.

Stefano had no intention of disappointing her. He had only knelt up to strip off his clothes and give her the full benefit of his magnificent body.

'I want to feel my naked skin against yours.'

His demand was husky but his movements were smooth and unhurried. Watching the relish in his beautiful eyes as he twined his lithe golden limbs around hers was the most wonderful aphrodisiac. As his body glided over and around hers, she floated in the clear blue of his admiring gaze. His hands and lips brought her to the peak of pleasure, time after time, and he left no room in her mind for any doubts. She was his, and she could not get enough of him. Only when she was almost faint from this glorious pleasure overload did he turn to his own satisfaction. With a wild cry his body convulsed in the sheer pleasure of orgasm.

The physical release was absolute, but a new kind of torment was about to begin. Kira had never known her mind and body meld in such a way, but it could not last.

As Stefano enfolded her gently in his arms, she knew things could never be the same between them.

'That was beyond even what I had hoped for,' he murmured.

As he drifted off to sleep, he took Kira's sense of proportion with him. She lay in the gloom, unable to put her fears into words and unwilling to wake him. She had never been in exactly this situation before, but something about it was frighteningly familiar. Her mind reeled back the years to her only other intimate encounter. She had been swept off her feet then, too. Before, during and after sex she had been suspended in a make-believe world which almost instantly unravelled. Her illusions vanished with the cold light of an Oxford morning. The tutor she once idolised had only used her to relieve his midlife crisis. How long would it be before the younger, more virile Stefano wrecked her dreams in a similar way?

She lay awake through all the long dark hours of the night. She knew exactly how this would end. The pain and humiliation were all too familiar. Listening to Stefano's soft, regular breathing as he slept, it was agonising to think he would start taking her for granted from the moment he woke. The infatuation she felt would not survive the death of his sweet words and sensuous touch. She couldn't bear to think he would never look at her in the same way again. What had she done? She had ruined all her own dreams by fulfilling his desires. From the moment she succumbed to his charm, the doomsday clock began marking time on their relationship.

She turned her head. Outside, dawn was breaking. She looked back at him. In sleep, his brow was smooth and untroubled. His finely carved features were heart-breakingly handsome. Such a man would never stay with someone like her. She could not endure the thought of never seeing him again, but what was the alternative? If she didn't run away now, he would dump her. It was as simple as that.

As the sun crept above the distant rim of hills she agonised over what she should do. If she bolted now, she would lose everything—Stefano's respect, any chance for another blissful coupling and all those wonderful opportunities he had promised her. Work seemed a million miles away when she was still being cradled in his arms, but she could not live without it. Her job was her reality. The rhythm and routine of it endured, although everything around her might be falling apart. Stefano's starry list of contacts could ensure the survival of her business.

It took a long time, but Kira had plenty of experience in teasing out the good points of a bad situation. Eventually, she worked out a restless compromise. While Stefano was busy in Florence, she would make sure she was working on his Bella Terra estate. When he retreated to his country hideaway, she would turn her attention to his town house. That way, accepting his offer of a contract would give her the excuse to keep in touch while staying out of his hands.

Holding onto that thought like a lucky charm, Kira eased her way out of bed and headed for the bathroom. Stepping into the shower, she tried to blast away all her regrets. It was impossible. She couldn't have any. Then, to compound her sin, she saw the bathroom door open. Stefano walked in.

He was naked, and joined her in the shower as though

it was the most natural thing in the world. Already shamed by her complete lack of guilt, Kira squeaked and tried to cover herself with her hands. It didn't impress him for a second.

'There isn't a single centimetre of your body that I haven't admired and kissed, *cara*,' he said as the water coursed over him.

'Stefano, this has got to stop,' Kira announced, with as much force as she could against the warm, relaxing water and the tempting sight of his naked body.

'Of course. But not for a little while.' His voice fell as softly as the water.

Squeezing shower gel over his hands, he stroked it expertly over her shoulders and back. The warmth of him in the confined space of the shower cubicle intensified the lemony fragrance of the bubbles he caressed across her skin. Despite her determination not to weaken, Kira could not resist. She closed her eyes, and let her head fall back as he worshipped her body with hands and lips. As they stood beneath the powering torrent of hot water, she felt the urgency of his desire match hers. She moved in close to the sheltering power of his body, pressing herself eagerly against the growing ridge of his manhood. Reaching around, he cupped her bottom in his hands and lifted her off the ground. Kira instinctively twined her legs around his waist. He entered her with a guttural sigh of satisfaction that echoed her own cry of need. Water coursed over their naked bodies as they coupled with a fierce, animal urgency. Kira's orgasm clenched him with a grip as hard as iron, and with a gasp he stopped the water and carried her out of the cubicle. Pulling all the towels from the hot rail, he made a soft nest on the marble floor and settled her down in it.

'Now I know exactly how to please you, I can delay my own pleasure for as long as I like.' Testosterone lowered his voice and made his smile wolflike.

Kira moaned with anticipation as his mouth dipped to nibble one nipple while the pads of his thumb and index finger rolled the other into a hard peak of anticipation. She lost count of the number of times he sent her sweeping over the edge. When she was sure her body could take no more she opened her mouth to beg him to stop, but he anticipated her cry.

'Now it's my turn,' he growled.

Stefano woke her with a kiss. Kira opened her eyes and realised that at some stage they had left the bathroom and moved on, in more ways than one. Stefano was standing beside the bed. He was fully dressed and ready for work. Kira smelled hot coffee and warm pastry, and saw he was holding a tray. She struggled to sit up, the sheet slipping away from her nakedness again. His business suit was beautifully cut, but could not conceal the sudden rise of his manhood as he looked down on her appreciatively.

She looked from him to the breakfast tray. It was set for one.

'Are you leaving, Stefano?'

He placed the tray on her lap. It was complete with fruit, cappuccino and brioche, fresh from his kitchens. Kira gazed at the beautiful display in wonder.

'I'm afraid I must.'

'Two weeks ago, I stopped you coming upstairs in my own home. Now I'm in your bed,' she said faintly. Kira couldn't believe her luck, but wasn't sure whether it would turn out to be the bad kind of fortune, or the good. A long shadow was lowering over the best, most exciting job prospect she had ever been offered. Any woman would be a fool to trust such a dedicated ladies' man. She would be doubly stupid: mixing work and a man had derailed her life once already. It would take a special sort of idiot to fall into that trap a second time. Kira was determined to stay independent. And yet, to resist such an opportunity…

There wasn't much time to decide. Stefano was already heading towards the door.

'I must go. Multi-billion-dollar enterprises don't run themselves, you know.' He smiled at her. 'Take your time to consider my contract, and let me know what you decide. If you make the sensible choice, I'll send a car to collect you later today—I want to take you to Silver Island.'

Kira made a snap decision. 'There's no need. I've made up my mind—I'll sign it.'

Stefano paused, one hand on the door frame. Genuine pleasure, but no real surprise, lit his eyes for a moment. 'I am glad. We have a lot in common, Kira.'

At his reminder of what they had so spectacularly shared, nervous defiance flared in Kira again. 'I can't always be relied on to do exactly as anyone says, Stefano, and once I'm working for you we can't carry on…'

He nodded, and his bright blue eyes became serious. 'Of course. You are your own woman…apart from those moments when I make you mine. So, until later…'

He reached over and kissed her hard, driving all thoughts of rebellion from her mind and leaving her gasping. When he drew back she only just stopped herself reaching for him again. Stefano gave her a look that made her blush. It said he knew exactly what she was feeling. A moment later, he was gone.

CHAPTER EIGHT

KIRA gazed after him, hardly able to believe what had happened. It was madness, she told herself over and over again. It didn't make a shred of difference. All she could think about was the look in Stefano's eyes as he left. His eyes had been dark and full of longing. The memory worked away at her, slowly chipping out a special place for him in her stony heart. Her ill-fated liaison with the lecturer who seduced her had never been anything like this. Hugh Taylor had lied and schemed to get her—and other women—into bed.

Stefano isn't like that, she thought, and then told herself the only difference was his honesty. She had thought of him as Stefano the Seducer before she met him, and that may be true, but at least he was truthful about it. He was quite happy to be the man of her dreams, as long as she woke up afterwards. He never made any pretence at being in this for the long haul. He was out for what he could get, but on their first night together, so was she. Once he sated her desires, Kira delighted in what she could give him.

It had never been like that with Hugh. She had been so upset by the whole business she had abandoned her university course and turned away from academic life altogether. Making love with Stefano made her think and feel in totally new ways. This wasn't some hole-in-the-corner affair. It was an awakening, and one she could dream of experiencing with him again.

She had total recall of every single second she spent with Stefano. It was all so special. She couldn't stop smiling. It had felt so perfect....

Suddenly a shiver ran over her skin. Her smile vanished. The spectre of her past reached out a cold bony finger and tapped her on the shoulder. She had known Stefano for only a few hours, yet her feelings had a cast-iron certainty about them. It made her look deep into her heart. She had never felt this way about Hugh. Never. The firework of that brief infatuation with her tutor had been hot and dangerous, but it had never reached this pitch of perfection. She ached for Stefano with a longing that scared her. He was bound to be as faithless as Hugh. How could she risk her heart and peace of mind again?

The answer was simple.

Because it is Stefano, she told herself, and this time I'm the one in control of the relationship. I won't sacrifice the most exciting job I've ever been offered because I'm afraid of pain. I'll throw my heart and soul into my projects for him. That will satisfy us both, she thought.

When the maid arrived, she found Kira still sitting where Stefano had left her. She was gazing over the rooftops of Florence, lost in thought. Her conscience might be clear, but her eyes were clouded.

Stefano leaned back in his chauffeur-driven Mercedes and breathed a long sigh of contentment. He was still relishing the details of his night of pleasure with Kira.

Soon he would be relaxing on Silver Island with the world's most passionate woman. When they eventually returned to Italy, the Bella Terra villa would be ready for him to move in. Life did not get any better than this.

He felt his brow pleat at the thought of going back to the office. The contrast between these past carefree hours and the urban jungle could not have been more marked. A scowl was as necessary a part of his office uniform as a designer suit and a Rolex. All his working life Stefano had been perfecting that image. Now he had the kingdom to go with it. Everything should have been worthwhile, at last. Today, he had it all—or so everyone kept telling him.

The creases accentuated his dark, beautifully arched brows. Deep in thought, he braced himself for re-entry into the business world of concrete and cut-throats. That was his domain during the working day. Nothing was ever allowed to distract him from it.

Then a faint, feminine perfume drifted through his limousine. He looked around. He had no idea where the scent could be coming from, until inspiration struck. Turning up the lapel of his jacket, he sniffed it appreciatively. He had leaned so close to Kira when he kissed her awake, some of her delicious fragrance had attached itself to his clothes. It brought back all those soft, sweet memories of the night he had spent with his lady of the flowers.

For a split second his frown disappeared again, and he smiled.

Kira's new project was the only thing that could stop her thinking about Stefano. Even that did not work for long. She was continually drawn back by the memory of his whispers through their one unforgettable night together. As she walked along the corridors of his big old town house, she let her thoughts dawdle deliciously over him and his body.

But the moment she crossed any threshold, work took first place again. Daydreams were put on hold until she had noted down a room's aspects and angles of light. It was only as she left that she took a moment to look back and appreciate it. The whole building, every nook and cranny, was filled with faded splendour. All the modern art and electronic offices could not hide its beauty. Every passage was full of interest. The rooms were absorbing. She really relished the chance to choose plants to soften and beautify the balconies and public areas. Most of all she wanted to see Stefano's pleasure—in her work, and in her.

As she was dreaming along an upper corridor, her mobile began to dance.

'Stefano!' To her shame, she almost dropped the phone.

'I never thought one single word could be charged with so much guilt,' he lilted. 'Don't say I caught you with your hand in a cookie jar?'

'No...no, I was busy thinking about something, that's all,' she muttered, her voice indistinct with embarrassment. She had been thinking about him, naked, and spreadeagled across her bed. 'You disturbed me when I was working,' she countered more sharply, as she managed to bring herself back to reality. There was much more truth in her words than he could ever imagine!

'I'm glad to hear you're taking things so seriously. Clearly, this will be a really good relationship—a really good *working* relationship,' he corrected himself carefully.

In spite of her misgivings, Kira blossomed under the warmth of his voice and his small slip-up. It felt as though she grew several inches. Not for the first time, she found that smiling was compulsory whenever Stefano was involved. She couldn't help herself, especially when she heard what he said next.

'Go home and throw a few things into a suitcase. A car will be round to collect you in a couple of hours' time, and take you to the airport,' he announced in a voice that made her tingle with anticipation. 'I'm taking you to see phase two of your commission to landscape my properties.'

The next few hours passed by in a blur. Kira was whisked to the airport and straight onto Stefano's private plane. He met her at the top of the steps and kissed her hand in greeting. She hesitated, not knowing how he wanted to play this reunion. His lips still pressing against her fingers, he gazed at her. The look in his blue eyes was watchful rather than seductive.

'Kira…' He made her name sound so beautiful she blushed. 'Welcome. In a few hours you'll see an entirely new kind of paradise.'

He seemed to be waiting for her reaction, so he could fine-tune his own. Kira decided to play it cool, although the mere sight of him threatened to send her temperature off the scale. She looked around appreciatively. The jet was new and smelled of luxury. Inside, the spacious cabin was an extension of his elegant furnished suite in Florence. It was thickly carpeted, and softly upholstered with linens and silks.

'Paradise? I think I've already arrived,' she breathed, wide-eyed.

* * *

Their trip to Silver Island was smooth and fast. Anything Kira could possibly want was to hand. There was a selection of magazines, several shelves of contemporary and classic novels, but she took her lead from Stefano. After his watchful greeting, he turned to his work. Surrounded by papers, he was riveted to his computer screen. Kira was almost relieved. She had packed her laptop case with plenty of work, and cautiously picked a workstation on the other side of the aeroplane. It kept her within reach, while maintaining the privacy she usually guarded so fiercely.

Unfortunately, it no longer felt quite so natural to keep her distance from him. Many times during the flight she felt her eyes drawn across the cabin to where he sat. To glance at him openly was to run the risk he might start a conversation. Kira had no idea what she could to say to him, outside the subjects of bed and the plans for his properties. She wasn't sure words would come easily on those subjects, either. With relief, she fell back on her plans for the Florence town house and its roof garden. Soon she was lost in her imagination, but it was still impossible to forget Stefano's presence. Every few moments a strange feeling crept over her, as though she was being bathed in a warm glow. The first few times it happened, she glanced up at him. He was always hard at work. With a shrug, she would turn back to her work, puzzled. It was odd. She could practically feel his eyes on her, but each time she checked he was gazing impassively at his paperwork.

Finally, the pilot announced that Silver Island was coming into view over the starboard wing. Kira instantly looked out of the window. A scatter of green islands rose softly from a sea that was almost as tranquil as Stefano's eyes.

'Oh, I've never seen anything so lovely!' she gasped.

'I have,' Stefano said quietly.

Kira looked over her shoulder, ready to make room for him if he joined her for a view from the window. He never moved. Instead, he sat back in his seat, watching her with a steady gaze.

'And if you think that is beautiful,' he murmured, 'wait until you are framed by orchids, set against a tropical moon and a sky scattered with stars.'

They flew in to a private airstrip. Unlike the sun trap of the Bella Terra estate, this land was cooled by sea breezes. The atmosphere was as clear as crystal. As she stepped down from the plane Kira stretched her arms up to the sun and revelled in the sharp salty tang in the air.

'This is wonderful,' she breathed, but the dream was just beginning. A car swept up to take them to a nearby quay. There, brightly painted fishing boats bobbed alongside the sun-warmed boardwalk, but Stefano led her towards a very different craft. Handing her down into a sleek black-and-gold speedboat, he took the controls and headed out towards a blue-green cloud low on the horizon.

'This is where I thought to make my base, until I discovered the Bella Terra estate,' he told her as the speedboat skipped across the clear blue sea like a flying fish. Kira watched indistinct shapes in the distance become a necklace of islands set in the warm, shallow sea. High, forested mountains rose up from shallow shelving beaches of flawless white sand. As they ran into the shallows, she saw the tension ease from Stefano's face once more. Boys playing football on the beach raced to greet them. As Stefano handed over the mooring rope, Kira was seized by a mad impulse. By the time he moved to help her from the boat she had slipped off her sandals and jumped barefoot into the water.

'Careful, the surf runs fast here!' Stefano called, but his warning was too late.

Dizzy with travel and excitement, Kira was pulled in two directions at once. Her feet went from under her and she promptly sat down in two feet of surging water. Stefano reached down and hauled her up. She surfaced, spluttering, to roars of laughter from the beach footballers.

'Are you all right?' Stefano's concern was obvious, but Kira was laughing as hard as anyone.

'It's wonderful!' She giggled, pushing her drenched hair back from her face. Her skirt was sodden, and wrapped itself in clinging folds around her slender legs.

'Take a seat and catch your breath.' He took her towards the treeline, where coconut palms draped cool shadows out over the sand. Kira sat down thankfully on a perfectly placed trunk. Instantly, a waiter appeared at her side. He was holding a tray with two tall glasses of passion-fruit cocktail, clinking with ice.

'This is heaven!' she gasped. Stefano laughed.

'Not yet, but it will be. I've gathered a world-class team to create an island paradise, and you're here to see how it can be made still more stunning.'

Kira took a long, slow sip of her drink. 'It'll be a challenge—' she smiled mischievously '—but I'm sure I'll think of something.'

'There's no hurry,' he said softly. 'No hurry at all. It's been a long flight. Shall I show you where you can freshen up?'

Kira bit her lip. She had spent the night with Stefano. There could be no secrets between them now, but that was what made her afraid. He was about to lead her to his suite. She wasn't ready for that and knew she should refuse, yet at the same it was everything she wanted. Stefano barely seemed to notice.

'I've had one of the guest suites made ready for you,' he said, taking her hand and leading her across the white, warm sand. Her sigh was a strange mixture of relief and disappointment, and he looked back with a laugh.

'Did you think I'd forget what you told me? You said there would be no repeat of our passionate night once you had signed my contract. I don't intend to blur the line between employer and employee.'

'Thank goodness for that,' Kira said determinedly, but with a heart that had suddenly plummeted. *Fool!* she berated herself. *Don't mistake his flirtation for serious intentions. It's good that he wants to keep this businesslike.* Tell herself what she would, however, the idea that she might never go to bed with Stefano again made her feel as though she'd lost something utterly precious. Caught up in her thoughts, she nearly missed his next words.

'Although I like to keep my staff happy,' he went on, and suddenly his eyes lit up with a dangerous spark. 'So I always make a special effort for new arrivals. That's why I'm inviting you to dinner at my apartment this evening.'

He moved closer. Kira felt it with every heartbeat. If

he was trying to test her, she was equal to it. 'Like you, I always mean what I say, Stefano.'

His eyes twinkled in the dancing sunlight. 'Fine. I wanted to see if you had changed your mind, that's all.'

With a wolfish smile he lifted her chin with his hand. She had been remembering his touch all day, but her memory was nowhere near as powerful as the real thing. His skin glided over hers like a kiss of fire, drawing a gasp from her lips.

'Second chances make life worth living, don't you think?'

His voice ended in a whisper of longing. Enfolding her in the curve of his arm, he drew her the last few inches towards his body. His kiss was a long, slow promise of all the things Kira knew he was so brilliant at. She could not help but respond. She was aware of all the dangers, but they were nothing when matched against his powers of seduction. Knowing she should pull back, she forced herself to do it.

At her first hesitation he let her go. His hands drifted regretfully from her body. She took a step back from him, struggling to catch her breath. Her common sense was marginally easier to manage.

'Last night was a mistake. One of those should be enough for both of us.'

His touch slid down her back, lingered around her ribs and then fell away. Pushing his hands deep into his pockets, he shrugged.

'I know—' he gave her an irrepressible smile '—but you surely can't blame me for trying?'

'I've told you. Now I'm officially on your payroll,

there can be nothing between us. I'm only interested in doing the best I can for you.'

He cocked his head on one side and regarded her with the keen look of a bush robin. 'Ah, but in what way?'

'You're my employer, nothing more,' Kira said firmly, desperately in need of the reminder. She had managed to keep her emotions out of it—until now. She could feel herself sliding out of control. Equally determined to call her bluff, Stefano wasn't about to give her a second chance to back down.

'Okay. If that's how you feel, follow me, and I shall show you to your room.'

He was already walking away. Kira was drawn along in his wake, trying to catch up.

'Isn't it lovely? Silver Island is the ideal refuge for me—and anyone I choose to invite here.'

Those last words were thrown casually over his shoulder as he walked into the treeline. Kira followed him. She caught him up as he breasted a little rise where palms gave way to lush, leafy shrubs. This oasis of cool shade was the perfect place for a collection of freshly whitewashed buildings. Each was roofed with yellow ochre tiles, patterned with age.

'That's my headquarters.' Stefano pointed out the largest building as they crossed a clearing. 'Like all my properties, the first thing I do is bring in office staff, so I can keep my finger on the pulse of business, day and night.'

Kira laughed at the picture he painted.

'It's no wonder you never feel at home! You make everywhere into an extension of your office.'

Stefano frowned and did not reply. They drew closer to the buildings. As they crossed the pine- and balsam-scented clearing, a cloud of brightly coloured parakeets exploded into the air from the eaves of an apartment building. It was twice the size of La Ritirata. Unlike Kira's ancient little home, its roof was supported by all the walls in all the right places. She was instantly impressed. As Stefano showed her up the steps of her temporary home, she was already wondering what design ideas she could take back with her.

'Well? What do you think?'

Kira had been too wrapped up in her own thoughts to realise Stefano was interested in her opinion. When she jumped at his light touch on her waist, he dropped his hand and stepped back. Hurriedly, she went in to discover her apartment's air-conditioned luxury—and stopped dead.

'It's amazing!' she breathed, and it was true. Her luggage stood in the centre of a large, cool room. There were big, squashy chairs and a matching settee for loafing. The floor covering was thick and plush. Beautiful art stood on every shelf, while woven hangings added splashes of colour against the sparkling white walls. Everything was brand new—and it was all oddly soulless, as though the wraps had been taken off this apartment especially for her.

'Am I your only guest, Stefano?'

'At the moment, yes.' He strolled over to where a reclining nude sculpted from rich red wood stood on a side table. Drawing his fingers over its glowing flanks, he gazed at her thoughtfully. 'At least, you're the first to stay in this particular building.'

Kira didn't say anything. Instead, she let him show her around the bland and beautiful apartment. Everything was absolutely right, from the wall hangings to the ethnic rugs and the huge gold-and-marble bathroom.

'I think it's wonderful,' Kira said as she strolled into her new bedroom. A genuine Victorian bed stood at its heart. The pillows and thick, soft mattress looked so inviting—but to her embarrassment her first thoughts at the sight of such a bed were certainly not of sleep.

'I'm impressed you haven't followed me in here,' she said airily.

Her words provoked a reaction in him, but too late she discovered it wasn't the one she wanted.

'You said you wanted me to stop all that,' he drawled, leaning against the door frame.

With a pang, she turned to face him. Her first rebuke had worked better than she expected. One look at his beautiful face and she knew he could see through her flinty manner to the real, pulsating woman within. She flushed with shame as he continued to watch her, his gaze feeling heavy as a caress on her skin.

'From now on,' he said softly, 'you're the one who makes the decisions. For example, whether you want to have dinner with me this evening at eight o'clock is entirely up to you.'

It was a statement, not a question. Before he finished speaking he pushed himself upright and strolled away through her apartment.

Stefano caught himself smiling as he headed for his own bungalow. That was a surprise. He had known Kira was a passionate woman beneath her reserve, but he hadn't expected such untapped depths of sensuality. She had been so determined not to fall for his charm that usually he would have looked elsewhere without a second thought, but she was different. Her hands put a stop to their kiss on the beach, but her lips told a different story. Stefano knew women and Kira Banks was definitely a girl worth waiting for. She would make such a change from the extrovert capers of his usual women. She needed much more careful handling, and Stefano knew he was the ideal man to conquer her fears. A few days of his company, together with the allure of this tropical island, would slowly melt her English reserve.

Like a stalking leopard, Stefano settled down for a long wait.

Kira watched him walk away. He never once looked back, although something told her he knew very well that her eyes were on him. She stayed motionless, until he disappeared inside his bungalow and closed the door. It was only then she took refuge inside her own rooms.

Leaning back against the closed door, she looked around. This place was paradise. A wand of fragrant orchids peeped over the nearest windowsill. Outside, the parakeets returned, tumbling over the eaves and squawking with delight. Silver Island had everything—including the only man she could ever want. This should be the project from heaven, and more holiday than work. Yet Kira already felt stressed. She might as well have been back in England, trying to sort out her stepparents' chaotic finances.

She knew she should ignore Stefano's invitation to dinner. Her willpower would be under pressure from the moment she crossed his threshold.

Somehow, that didn't feel like such a terrible threat any more. A small smile flitted across her face. When

Stefano wasn't with her, she missed him. That was a totally alien experience for Kira. It made her feel unsure of herself. She didn't like it, but she did like Stefano—in a way that encouraged all sorts of outrageous thoughts.

She was having a particularly wild idea right now. Any truly independent, intelligent person ought to be able to accept his invitation to dinner. She had come a long way over the past couple of years. She was a successful businesswoman. A perfectly respectable dinner with a man she fancied was exactly the treat she deserved for landing such a lucrative contract. It would also be an opportunity to put herself to the test. If she succeeded in resisting Stefano this evening, she would be unstoppable. There would be no limit to what she could achieve, if only she could show her new boss that not every woman would roll over and beg for his body straight away.

If she failed, the worst that could happen was that he would ravish her senseless. Her heart and mind would never be in danger. They were safely locked away, somewhere Stefano would never be allowed to find them.

Kira felt she couldn't lose.

CHAPTER NINE

ONE long, luxurious bath later, Kira slipped into the single evening dress she had packed. It was a silky little emerald number she had worn for the most recent Chelsea gala night.

I'll show Stefano that when it comes to his charms, I can be chilled steel. I can resist him, she told herself a hundred times.

The mirror told a different story. Her eyes were dark with arousal. The tip of her tongue rested against the glossy cushion of her lower lip as she pinned her mane of auburn hair up into a sophisticated coil. The sight made her smile. She looked good, and knew it. Loose tendrils danced over the creamy curves of her neck and shoulders. Her dress was a sumptuous slither of sequinned silk. Its opulent shade of green complemented the rich tawny of her hair. With every movement it shimmered like the sea.

As she twirled and swirled in front of the full-length mirror, Kira went on deceiving herself. Instead of trying to put Stefano off by dressing like a drudge, she would make this evening still more of a challenge by making herself irresistible. Then, when he tried to seduce her and failed, her triumph would be complete. After all, when we met I was only dressed in dusty jeans and look what happened then! It's not the clothes he should be interested in, but what is inside them, she told herself, managing to limit her self-delusion right at the end. There was absolutely no point in imagining he was only interested in her brain. To her horror, the reflection looking back from the glass smiled instead of frowned. Stefano Albani was all man. He had proved it to her any number of times during their fantastic night together.

She checked her appearance again. Her smile faltered, and then returned with added self-assurance. She loved this dress, and for once the torture of a social occasion was going to be sweet, sweet, sweet.

She added one last finishing touch. It was truly spectacular. With her first impressive pay cheque, Kira had spoiled herself with a real diamond necklace. It contained the smallest stones in captivity, brilliantly cut and cleverly set to make them look larger. Tiny they might be, but she was really proud of her necklace. It didn't matter to her that she never went anywhere she could wear it. That wasn't the point. It was beautiful, and it was hers.

She laid the galaxy of tiny stars against her skin and fastened the catch. Then she took the matching earrings from their royal-blue velvet bed. It had taken her a further two years of careful saving to add them to her collection, and this was the first time they had been out of the box. Finally, glittering like moonlight on the sea, she set off on the nerve-racking walk to Stefano's bungalow.

Her nerves were tuned to a high C of tension by the time she reached his apartment. They weren't helped by movement sensors switching on a battery of security lights. Startled by the sudden blaze, a deer shot away through the undergrowth. It leapt like her heart as it dived into cover. That close shave did nothing for Kira's nerves. Feeling like a prisoner on the run under all the lights, she started up the front steps. Raising her hand, she knocked hesitantly. Five…ten…fifteen seconds passed with no reply. Then she noticed the bell. The bungalow was so large, the chances were that Stefano hadn't heard her nervous tapping. She leaned on the bell, and heard it echoing through the building beyond. He must have heard it, but it still felt an awfully long time passed between pressing the button and seeing the bungalow door open.

'Kira.'

Stefano loomed in the doorway, dressed in an immaculate white shirt and dark trousers. He looked magnificent, but it was his expression that snatched her breath away. He was looking at her with the same illicit pleasure she had seen in her reflection only a few moments before. 'You look incredible.'

'Thank you!' she said breathlessly, relying on the glittering diamonds, sequins, lipgloss and nail polish to speak for her. It was a risky venture. There was a fine line between untouchable beauty and come-hither.

He stepped back from the door with an inviting gesture. 'Come in and make yourself comfortable.'

Kira followed him into the bungalow. The building smelled of new money and even newer paint. It was as tasteful as her own apartment, and just as soulless.

'I've given most of my staff the evening off.'

Kira stared at him. He returned her look with one that danced with silent amusement.

Escape was still not impossible. She could have reached out and touched the door from where she was standing. All it needed was a quick goodnight. She could make some excuse and slip out into the safety of darkness, beyond the security lighting.

She didn't do any of those things. Instead, she looked around. Rather than cowering by the door, she began to unfold like a flower. After all, she told herself, there's no triumph in running away. She had accepted Stefano's invitation. If she took up the challenge of treating him like a trustworthy employer rather than a casual lover, that was even better.

Stefano began moving around the room with careful deliberation. Under Kira's gaze, he shook sofa cushions and dragged scattered magazines into a pile.

'Now you've had time to settle into your own apartment, why don't you have a look around here, and tell me what you think?' he asked her as he prowled around.

'I think you have a beautiful house, on a lovely island. The peace and quiet here make it almost as perfect as the Bella Terra valley,' she said simply.

'Almost?' Stefano asked.

Kira didn't answer him. The large main room of his apartment had been painted pale ochre, with the woodwork a slightly lighter shade. It was sparsely furnished, with polished boards rather than carpet on the floor. They gave it a rather hollow feeling. The whole atmosphere was light and bright rather than warm and welcoming. It echoed the impersonal touch that seemed to follow Stefano around, but she didn't know how to explain it to him. Instead, she went to investigate two long leather couches and a beautiful large glass coffee table while he headed for the sound system.

'Make yourself comfortable while I set things in motion. We're dining on the mainland, so I'll alert the launch.' He walked towards the nearest telephone.

'Oh…I thought we'd be eating here?' Kira could not keep the disappointment from her voice. 'Leaving this paradise and plunging back into the chaos of city life doesn't appeal in the slightest.'

Stefano had been studying one of his works of art with a critical eye. When she said that, he stopped and looked straight at her instead. A slow smile spread across his face 'Squisita! You are an unusual woman, Kira. Not everyone would choose a simple dinner rather than air-conditioned luxury.'

'Well, I would,' said Kira firmly. 'You are so lucky, being able to escape from everyone and everything whenever you like.'

His art collection forgotten, Stefano's attention was now firmly riveted on Kira. One hand in his pocket he strolled towards her, his eyes intent on her face.

'Is that what you think?'

Kira looked askance. 'Why would I say something I didn't mean?'

'You'd be surprised how many people do. All of the women I speak to, as a matter of fact. With one notable exception.' He inclined his head to her, interest very obvious in his beautiful eyes.

'That's what living does for you.' Kira was hardly aware of what she was saying. Only one thing mattered, and that was the lovely warm feeling that came from basking in his appreciation. 'It's easy to forget what life is actually about.'

'And what do you think that is?' He was looking at

her with intensity and his expression demanded nothing less than the absolute truth.

'I'd love to be able to say home and family, but I've only got experience of half that equation. I've got the home. It's better than I ever dreamed it would be, but I've never known what a happy family feels like. My idea of what it must be like is hopelessly romantic. Please shoot all my delusions down in flames by telling me your Italian family background is full of fights and bad feeling, and not a bit like the cheerful stereotype!' Kira tried to joke past the pain, but she wasn't the only one with issues. For the first time in heart-stopping minutes, Stefano avoided her eyes. It was a painful reminder that she might not be the only person in the world hiding inner turmoil.

Walking over to the fully stocked bar that stood in a far corner of the room, he spooned ice cubes into two tall glasses. 'What would you like?'

To take back the last thing I said, Kira thought, wishing she hadn't rattled on so cheerfully. 'I'll have a St Clement's, please,' she muttered.

As a distraction, it worked perfectly. Stefano left the bar and stepped through a pair of French doors. Kira watched him reach out and select the ripest fruit from big old citrus trees shading the veranda. When he returned, so did his smile. In one hand he held a spray of polished, dark green leaves. Nestling at their heart was a cluster of waxy white blossoms and purple-stained buds. He held it out to her gallantly.

'This is for you, to make up for the bouquet that would have been waiting for you at the restaurant in town.'

'Thank you!' she whispered, glowing with pleasure.

The heavy, sweet fragrance stole through the warm evening air between them. 'It's lovely!'

'Then it is exactly the right gift for you,' he said quietly, moving in still closer. 'Let me see how it can be fixed...'

'No!' Kira leapt back in alarm. It was already hard enough keeping him at arm's length. When he lavished her with flowers and soft words, it was impossible. 'I mean, no, thank you. The perfume is so powerful I'd rather have them in a vase on the table.' *And I can pretend to be looking at them, when I'm really looking at you!* The words raced desperately through her mind as she watched him walk back to the bar. He halved all the fruit and extracted the juice with powerful but deft movements. Then he presented her with a perfect cocktail.

'That's really impressive. You handled that knife like a professional.'

'Call it the legacy of a wasted youth,' he said, mixing himself the driest of dry martinis.

'I know all about that,' she said with a shiver as the ice rattled enticingly in her glass.

Stefano's shoulders visibly relaxed, as though he had ordered them to. Until that moment Kira had assumed he was always perfectly at ease. Now she knew better. The change in him was noticeable. The mask was back in place.

'I doubt that very much, but we can discuss it over dinner. What would you like? Name it, and my chef will make it for you.'

He must have been through this routine with a thousand women. Kira heard the ring of fine crystal echoing again across the glade from his kitchens. No doubt they were getting ready to serve a meal fit for the latest princess of Silver Island. She had no intention of being a temporary attraction. The reason she was here was to stake her claim to something much more important than that. Caviar and champagne counted for nothing if it lacked one simple ingredient. She wanted Stefano's respect. That was more important than any amount of cordon bleu cookery, and she intended to get it. Leaving her drink on the bar she strolled away to admire a piece of glass sculpture so that he would not see her smile.

'Do you know what I'd really like, if it's not too much trouble?'

'Dressed in silk and diamonds? Do you want me to offend your sense of decency?'

Regarding him with a cool, steady gaze she said slowly, 'I'll tell you what would make my evening complete. Something utterly simple. No distractions.'

'No oysters or asparagus?'

'Aphrodisiacs? I don't need them,' she said simply.

He laughed, but for the first time the amusement never reached his eyes. As he phoned through to the kitchen, Kira watched him with intense interest. Moving restlessly beneath her gaze, he showed her into the dining room.

'I'll bet you can't remember the last time you shared such a simple meal with a girl,' she said idly.

There was nothing half-hearted about Stefano's reaction.

"On the contrary, I'll never forget it.'

His tone was so strange Kira shot a quick look at him. In profile he had a gaunt, distracted look she had never noticed before. As she watched, he collected himself and added, 'She was a girl who knew her own mind, too. That's the reason she's not here to share all this, tonight.' He pushed a hand out to indicate the luxury surrounding them. Kira could not help thinking of the svelte, glamorous Chantal.

'Someone else who wouldn't stand for your womanising ways?' she said slyly. 'So that makes two of us.'

'No, only one.'

That must mean she won't put up with it, but he thinks I will! Kira thought indignantly.

She was about to spring to her own defence, but the words died on her lips. Something about the way Stefano abruptly turned his back on her warned her to keep quiet. He walked over to the long, highly polished dining table. Closing his long sensitive fingers around one of the chairs, he pulled it out for her to sit down.

'And now, no more questions. You accepted my invitation to dine, so it's up to me to play the part of charming host.' The tension drained from his voice as he watched her shimmer into her seat. Candles set in silver candelabra stood in the centre of the table. Stefano lit them. Instantly, a million sparkles danced over the diamonds at Kira's throat. The same cold fire ran over her silken dress. It melted the frown creasing Stefano's brow. She actually saw him catch his breath, and it was wonderful.

'Kira…you have never looked lovelier,' he murmured.

She couldn't answer. Deep in her heart she hoped it was true, and wished she could believe him. While she was preening in front of her mirror, the thought of him had transformed her. Now he was working his magic on her in living, breathing reality. She felt fantastic, and he was telling her she looked it, too.

I have to put a stop to this. Right now, Kira told herself desperately. She was only here to prove to herself that she could resist him, that this was an adult, business relationship only....

But when Stefano looked at her in that way, only the first part of her brave statement was true. Business was the very last thing on her mind. The idea of a hot, very adult relationship with Stefano pushed everything else out into the cold.

Only a discreet knock at the door saved her. Swift, sure staff presented dinner on silver dishes and the finest china plates. Kira barely noticed the food. She could think of nothing but the tussle between her body's needs and her common sense. Stefano was trouble; she knew it.

'This is spectacular!' she laughed as the waiters poured her a chilled glass of pinot grigio.

'My guests always enjoy the best.'

'Is this how you entertain all your women?'

'No.'

Kira paused and looked along the table to where he was sitting. He looked up and met her eyes.

'What's the matter?'

'Then what do you do?'

His puzzled frown was exactly that—puzzled. However hard Kira tried to be suspicious, she couldn't spot anything shifty in his expression.

'Why this sudden obsession with other women?' His gaze was equally searching.

'You said I was only the second woman to stand up to you.'

He laughed. 'Yes...' He paused, clearly turning something over in his mind. 'If you must know, each time you answer back you remind me of my little sister, Maria.'

'Oh…I thought you were comparing me to…'

Kira's voice sounded very small suddenly, as she became aware of how little she really knew this man. His eyes burned with cold fire.

'No. Never.'

Kira's mind worked with the speed of light. She pieced together enough hints to know this was a delicate area.

'Were you very close to your sister?' she risked, pretending to be busy with her meal.

'We were inseparable. We had to be, on the streets. She had no one else to protect her.'

He dropped his fork with a clatter. Kira looked up sharply. Elbows on the table, his fingers were netted in front of his mouth as though to stop any more words escaping.

'Maria was very lucky to have a brother like you looking after her,' she said, hoping to sidestep the awkward subject. Stefano was not so tactful.

'It was people like me who made the streets dangerous in the first place,' he muttered.

'I don't think so.' Kira tried to pacify him, but she was desperate to hear more. 'You must have been different, even then. You told me how you started your own business.'

'Maria's death was the only reason I changed.'

He stopped talking, and looked up to meet her eyes. He saw only sympathy and willingness to listen. Taking a deep breath, he continued, his voice hoarse and seeming to force the words out. It was the first time he'd told anyone the truth for more than twenty years. 'She was killed when a raid on a shop went wrong. She hadn't wanted to go—I convinced her, saying it was "for the good of the family." It was my fault. From that moment on I vowed to turn my life around, and I did.'

'Maria would be really proud of you now.'

Stefano exhaled so heavily all the candle flames fluttered.

'I'm not so sure. When I decided to go straight, I made a clean break. Since her funeral, I haven't spoken to any members of my family. I turned my back on them all when I abandoned that way of life. It was the only way to get out. The last time I saw any of them was when I was acting as a witness for the prosecution.'

Oh, why did I have to open my big mouth? Kira thought desperately. She wanted to reach out and comfort him, but didn't dare. Where would that lead for either of them? Placing her knife and fork carefully on her plate she hoped for inspiration. None came. Instead, Stefano sprang to his feet when he saw she had finished. Collecting the remains of their meal, he carried it out to the kitchen. Kira fought the impulse to follow him. She desperately wanted to apologise for raising the subject, hold him, share his pain and tell him everything would be okay. It was impossible. Stefano wasn't that sort of man. Expecting an agonising wait, she was relieved when he came back almost immediately with a confection of tropical fruit sorbets. They glittered like jewels set in crystal dishes.

'There are sponge cakes and wafers, too, in case you share Maria's appetite as well as her temper,' he told her, sounding perfectly normal. There was no trace of the anguish she expected. All the self-control was back in place. Astonished, Kira looked up into his gaze. He was expressionless again, but something in her questioning face seemed to relax him.

'You're right, Kira. There are plenty of things about my life of which Maria would be proud. I'd never thought of that until you said it.'

'Wasn't it obvious?' she said as he placed the delicious dessert in front of her.

'No. I'd genuinely never considered it. All I focused on was losing her, and then the rest of my family. I knew there had to be more to life than crime and handouts. I made myself master of my own destiny. Working gave me an outlet, and an escape. I channelled all my frustrations into learning as much as I could about my own city, and then other places, as I climbed the ladder to success. That single-minded toil dulled the pain, but it left an awful void. Maybe that's why I'm never satisfied.'

He drew back from her suddenly. 'I've never told anyone that before,' he added, with such an air of surprise Kira couldn't help smiling.

'Then thank you,' she said softly.

On impulse, she stood. Before either of them knew what was happening, she kissed him on the cheek.

Coming to her senses like a sleepwalker waking from a dream, she dropped straight back into her seat. Until a moment before, she had been ready to resist him. Now she didn't know how she felt. In that same instant, Stefano made her confusion worse. He reached out and squeezed her hand.

'Let's live in the present and future, not the past, Kira.'

With a final pat he left her side and went back to his seat at the far end of the table.

* * *

Much later, Kira lay back on one of the long, cream leather couches and felt a huge smile creep across her face. A threatened disaster was turning into the best evening she had ever spent. The rest of the night had passed in a glorious blur of conversation—the best kind. Sharing true thoughts and ambitions and dreams. She felt filled with utter happiness.

A sound from the doorway made her sit up quickly. Stefano stood there, coffee in hand, looking at her.

'I didn't mean to wake you,' he said softly. Suddenly the sensual tension which had been disguised with words drew taut again. His gaze was serious, clouded and full of desire.

'It's okay. I wasn't asleep.'

She stretched into a sitting position as he came towards her.

'You don't have far to go,' he said simply.

Kira watched him placing things on the glass surface beside her. He wasn't looking at her any longer, but her body jangled from his nearness. He turned his head suddenly and she was caught in his gaze, almost trembling.

'Kira, tonight has been fantastic. In fact, I can't remember a night like it.'

'Nor me.' She sighed. 'Before I met you, I was uptight all the time. You're quite a role model.' Taking the cup and saucer from his hands, she looked reflective. 'I really wish I could be like you all the time, Stefano.'

He chuckled and sat down a little distance away from her, cradling his coffee. 'What—cold, calculating and immune to human feeling?'

'You need a little of those qualities to really succeed

in business. Loss, and an unhappy childhood, forces that tough shell onto people. I know all about that.'

'I do, too—although your background is still a mystery to me.' He watched her sip her drink. 'I've got every qualification the school of hard knocks can deliver, but what can have been wrong with your childhood? You told me it was full of Cotswold Christmases.'

'I was the big problem in my childhood,' she told him glumly. 'My adoptive parents wanted a porcelain doll, but they ended up with me instead. I've always liked doing things. They simply wanted me to *be*. I've never been happy, acting the part of a dim ornament.'

'I can imagine.' He smiled with a warmth that encouraged Kira to open up a little more.

'But that's all in the past. Now I'm earning a decent living, my stepparents can forgive me anything—as long as I keep sending the cheques home.'

He grimaced. 'Maybe you're lucky to have a family to spoil?'

She wriggled around to face him as they sat together on the settee. 'I wish that was all they wanted.'

He leaned forward and lifted the plate of sweet treats up from the coffee table. As he offered it to Kira, she got a tantalising hint of his evocative aftershave. She breathed deeply, but despite the distraction could not resist a piece of crystallised pineapple. Stefano selected a strawberry dipped in dark chocolate before putting the plate back on the table.

'The problem is, settling debts comes right at the bottom of my stepparents' list of priorities. I can't bear to think of them being without heat, light or transport so I bail them out—at least in theory. In reality, they use most of my money to send more invitations around the country club.'

Stefano made lazy circles in his coffee with a silver teaspoon. 'Why don't you offer to settle their debts direct?'

Kira was aghast. 'What—go behind their backs? I couldn't do that!'

'Then you'll have to be tough with them, Kira, and say "no more,"' Stefano said sharply. 'It will hurt in the short term, but will end up saving you a lot of grief. I should know,' he finished darkly.

Kira rolled her lip, wishing she could take his advice. 'It's all right for you. You're always so self-assured.'

He looked at her long and hard before replying. 'You don't do so badly. In fact, I would say you are an unusually forthright woman. You were certainly very decided about our plans tonight.'

Kira laughed. 'I've told you before. I like simple pleasures. You can have too much of a good thing!'

'I know, but I never expected to find anyone who agreed with me.' He sipped his coffee in silence, and then slowly and deliberately put it down on the table. 'Am I one of your simple pleasures, Kira? Or too much of a good thing?'

Her eyes remained on his hand. He drew it back from his cup, and rested it lightly on his thigh.

She bit her lip. 'I don't know. I can't decide.'

He hitched his shoulders in a casual gesture. 'You accepted my invitation and came for dinner.'

'Maybe I shouldn't have done.'

'Yes, you should, and I know you enjoyed the evening. I did, too,' he said, so quickly that she couldn't possibly doubt it. But worrying was a tough habit to break.

'Are you sure, Stefano?' she asked uncertainly.

'I'm positive.'

Her willpower started to wobble. Nothing had happened...so far. When Stefano seduced her the first time, it had simply been physical, if spectacular. Now, having spent the evening with such a sweet, funny, charming man, she was terribly worried. If he loved and left her after this, she would never be able to bear it.

'I'm not sure at all. I can't trust my own judgement any more, Stefano,' she confessed. Surely it was best to tell him the bad news straight out. 'I give money to lost causes. I made a fool of myself over a man and got my name all over the papers as a result. It was hell, and I'm so afraid of it happening again.'

The words escaped from her in a rush. She looked down at her lap, stunned to hear herself speak the words she had held back for so long. Beside her, she sensed Stefano tense. Her fingers twisted painfully as she waited for the questions to start.

'It's no wonder you send out mixed messages,' he said quietly. 'I wanted you from the moment I spotted you from the helicopter. When you put up barriers, I held back. Normally, I'd simply walk away, but something about you keeps me coming back. What happened? Tell me.'

His concern was so genuine. Kira was touched. Still staring at her hands, she spoke in the hope that sharing her pain might soften it somehow. 'I made an idiot of myself while I was at university. If I'm honest I knew there was something wrong about Hugh Taylor from the start. He only gave me his mobile number, saying he didn't have a landline at home. We never went back to his place, which should have been the decider. When I discovered he was married, I was too weak and stupid to drop him like the rat he was. To my shame I let the affair limp on, but I didn't know the half of it. It was left to his poor wife—or rather, one of them—to expose his double life. He was already a bigamist when he moved to Oxford, and started on me. The story was horrible enough to make the papers, and ruin me.'

There. She had said it. All the shame and embarrassment rushed over her again. She covered her face with her hands, unable to bear Stefano's gaze and sure she would never be able to look him in the eyes again after this.

'I was such a fool...' she went on through her fingers. 'I'd led such a sheltered life. I didn't know any better and took his bait. To know everyone was talking about me behind my back was awful. And my stepparents won't let it rest, even now.... There was no way on earth I could have carried on with my course after that. The shame was unendurable.'

Oblivious to everything but her pain, she had been rocking backwards and forwards. It was only when a light touch fell on her shoulder that she came to her senses. When Stefano spoke, she almost lost them again.

'How could anyone treat you like that?' he whispered.

'It's what people do. They use you, and then walk away,' she muttered, overwhelmed by the grubby scandal of it all.

'Yes. Life is hard for the weak.' Stefano's voice cut through the silence like a knife.

Kira dropped her hands and turned a simmering stare directly on him. If there was one thing she found more painful than self-hatred, it was someone else's pity.

'I am *not* weak,' she said, with absolute conviction.

'I know.' His reaction was equally unexpected. 'I was blaming myself for things I did, long ago. Seeing you like this has made me put my own past under the microscope. It isn't pretty,' he said grimly.

'You aren't a bit like Hugh!' She frowned.

'I was. I am,' he persisted. 'I may not have deceived my lovers—we had fun, but that was the extent of it. Sometimes I know I have left broken hearts behind me through not resisting temptation. You knew that when we slept together, didn't you?' he looked for her agreement.

'Yes. I'm under absolutely no illusions about you, Stefano,' she agreed. An odd expression flashed in his eyes for a moment, but then he continued.

'That's just as well. While I was on the streets I saw too many relationships driven apart by abuse and desperation. I was determined not to be like that, so I've never made any promises I can't keep. Giving a woman overwhelming pleasure is one thing. Promising to bind myself exclusively to her—never.'

'I understand.' Kira nodded. 'For me, you've always been Stefano the Seducer. Nothing more—and most definitely nothing less.'

The crease between his brows deepened a fraction.

'It almost sounds as though you approve of what happened between us, Kira.'

Unable to stop her memories warming her voice, she smiled. 'I can't help it. I do.'

Stefano's frown eased, and she corrected herself quickly.

'That is...I mean...I did.'

'You don't sound very sure?'

Slowly, almost hesitantly, his hand moved towards a curl of her hair that had strayed out of place. Coiling it over her shoulder, he smiled.

It was her turn to frown. 'I'm not.'

'Then let me help you to make up your mind. What you mean is, that as long as we are both completely honest with each other, no one will get hurt. Is that right?'

She nodded.

'I'm not sure I agree,' he said softly, shaking his head. Then his voice dropped to a whisper. 'For example, if I told you now that my deepest desire was to take you to bed, and you said that was the last thing you wanted to do, I would be crushed. Absolutely.'

His hand was still hovering near her hair. His eyes were very blue and clear.

Kira could barely breathe. She tried to speak. 'B-but then, if I said that, I would be lying...' she began, but could not finish.

Stefano anticipated what she was going to say. With the urgency she craved so much, he reached out and brought her within the circle of his arms. She could offer no resistance, and didn't want to. Stefano drew her towards him until their lips met in a kiss that swept away all her worries. She relaxed into the delicious warmth of his embrace. While his kiss held her captive, he drew his hand slowly up over her ribcage. As his fingers brushed the curve of her breast she shivered with anticipation.

'That is exactly the type of persuasion that can lead a girl astray,' she murmured.

'I know. Now, where would you like me to lead you—to your place, or mine?' he whispered, lifting her into his arms.

CHAPTER TEN

STEFANO undressed her right down to the diamonds. With a huge moon riding the velvet night outside, he worshipped his goddess of the flowers. 'I said you would be perfection, framed in honey orchids and silhouetted against the tropical sky,' he breathed, and it was true. He could not get enough of her, his lips sipping kisses from the yielding softness of her skin.

He made love to her the whole night long. No sensation was too divine. She fuelled feelings within him he had never experienced before. Each time she moved beneath his hands, a possessive need made him hold her ever more tightly to his body. He could not let her go. As their bodies entwined in a vibrant search for satisfaction, a truth began to slip in and out of the shadows shielding his mind. He had never before found such a perfect fit for his body, his mind and his senses. Kira had to be his for evermore. He wanted her—but his feelings ran far deeper than mere sex. He had wanted plenty of women in the past, and taken them all. But Kira was different. She was an experience he could not afford to lose.

Much, much later, Stefano swam back to consciousness through warm waves of satisfaction. Then the gravity of his feelings pulled him back to real life. Something incredible had happened last night. His seduction hadn't gone as planned; it had been spontaneous and reckless in a way he had never experienced before. The realisation opened his eyes wide. Then two words hurtled back at him and he shut them again, fast.

Love me.

Had he really said that? No, it wasn't possible. He wouldn't have—couldn't have—said it. He'd never done such a dangerous thing in his entire life. Although…he definitely remembered those words pulsating through the heat of his passion. Twice, in quick succession.

He must have imagined it. Yes, that was it.

With an exhalation of relief, he opened his eyes again. The room was still close and shadowy in the purple light before dawn. The sun outside had not risen high enough to penetrate the trees sheltering their refuge. He moved to check his wrist, but it was bare. He had tossed his watch aside in case it rubbed harshly against Kira's delicate skin. It was the first time he had ever done something like that, too. He wondered idly what time it was, but found he didn't care. Kira wouldn't mind, either. She liked it here on Silver Island as much as he did. They had lain awake for hours, listening to the mournful night birds outside, and wondering about the bright star that flickered down at them through the jalousie slats.

He tried to move, but couldn't. He had fallen asleep with Kira wrapped protectively in his arms. Until she wanted to escape, he was trapped.

Escape… The word rang through his head like an alarm.

Suddenly he stopped wanting Kira to wake. More

memories were racing back to taunt him. Before the wonderful abandon of bed, they had talked about her past last night—and his. That would mean she could never look at him in the same light again. Her image of him would be tainted by what she knew about his past. When she woke and gave him that lovely smile, what would be going on behind those beautiful eyes? His heart began to race. What exactly had they talked about last night, before words became unnecessary? He dimly remembered saying something about life being hard for the weak. Him? Weak? A hot wave of resentment washed over him, throwing more conversational flotsam back in his face. He had admitted turning his back on all his relatives. This, after Kira had been desperate to believe in some idealised dream of Italian family life. Well, he had shattered that illusion beyond repair!

Talking after sex, stargazing… Stefano was losing count of the number of firsts he had shared with Kira last night. There was no knowing where all this might lead, but he had his suspicions. Mercifully, another memory came back to him. He had stressed his independence again to her, hadn't he? She must understand that by now. Surely a man who could abandon his family couldn't be expected to be faithful to anyone else. In any case, where women were involved, Stefano considered himself a hunter, not a pet. Kira knew he was a lone wolf. Animals like that walked alone.

Beside him, she moved in her sleep. It was a luxurious movement, stretching out across the bed and freeing him.

A wolf walks alone, Stefano told himself. He hadn't been backed into a corner by anyone since he was a child.

Taking his chance, he began inching his way towards the edge of the bed. He had to escape. Last night, Kira had seen past his act of emotionally detached, successful businessman. She had captured some of his spirit. If he stayed by her side any longer, she would surely consume the rest.

He had to go. Now.

Peeling his body away from the last temptations of her touch, he eased his legs over the edge of the bed and inched into a sitting position. His clothes were scattered all over the place. As he reached for them, he tried not to think of the spectacular passion he had shared with Kira only hours earlier. Pulling his still-buttoned shirt on over his head, he stood, stifling a sigh of relief—but not well enough.

The rhythm of Kira's breathing changed. Stefano froze. So did she—and then she rolled over to greet him with that smile….

He swung away, unable to look her in the face.

'Stefano? What are you doing? It's too early to get up.'

Her voice was as velvet smooth as the touch he could never risk experiencing again. He shook his head.

'I'm sorry, Kira. I—I have to go. It's business. An urgent call. You know…' His voice disappeared. When Kira sat up and the silken sheet slipped away from her stunning nakedness, his willpower almost followed his voice.

'I never heard anything?'

'My phone was on vibrate. I really didn't want to wake you,' he added, with a sudden attack of the truth.

'So tell me—what is so important that it can pull you out of my arms?'

'You don't want to know.' Stefano went on dragging on his clothes.

'Yes, I do. Everything you do interests me, and I don't know the first thing about your work. All you've told me about so far is your past.'

He stopped and stared at her.

'Dio! Forget that. I shouldn't have said anything,' he muttered hurriedly. 'I—wanted to see how you'd react if I shot your dream of Italian family life down in flames. It was nothing. Forget everything I've told you.'

'No!' With a giggle she reached out to him, ready to tug him back into bed with her. 'First you try and sneak off without waking me, now you're backtracking on everything else as well. What's the matter, Stefano?'

He leapt back as though her touch was a threat. 'I've told you. It's nothing.' Making his face as bland as possible, he stared at her, daring her to contradict him. 'I must go.'

Kira had stopped laughing. The silence that fell between them now was deadly. There could be only one reason for his sudden coldness. He was leaving her. She gazed at him, unable to quite believe it.

'Why are you going? Tell me. I want to know.' Her voice crackled with emotion.

Stefano reached for his jacket and pulled it on. With short, sharp movements he checked that it contained his keys and wallet. 'All right—if you insist. I'm not going to lie to you, Kira. Have you thought you might not be the only one who could have second thoughts about all this?'

There was frostbite in his voice.

'It sounds like you're getting ready to abandon me.' Her voice barely trembled, but the tension was there.

'Of course that's what you must think.' Stefano's reply ricocheted back like a bullet. 'After what you've been through, it's only natural.'

Kira watched him brace himself, and take a step towards the bed. If kissing her goodbye took such a visible effort, she didn't want it. She sat back on her heels, distancing herself from him.

'Can you blame me, Stefano, when all men are so alike? I thought last night was something exceptional, but now it turns out every move you made, every word you spoke, was fiction,' she snapped.

Stefano drew back. The rising sun outside lit a shimmering aura around him. Despite the growing dawn, no bird or insect dared disturb the horrible silence as he formed his next argument. 'That's not true. But don't say you've never felt the need to nip a situation in the bud, before things get out of hand?'

She could hardly believe what she was hearing. Clutching the sheet against her body like a shield, she tried to make sense of this sudden change in him.

She was losing him. Unable to think of anything she had done or said to make him cool so abruptly, she began to panic.

'What is it? What can possibly have changed between us since last night, Stefano?' she implored.

'Nothing…and everything.'

His face was hard with an alien emotion. Kira gazed at him. The man who had seduced her with soft words and intoxicating caresses stared back at her in bitter disillusion.

'My US agent rang with details of an ideal investment property in upstate New York. That's where I'm going,' he said at last, each word drawn out and hesitant.

Kira's heart leapt. For a moment things didn't seem so bad. Looking around Sir Ivan's old house with Stefano had been wonderful. Maybe she could persuade him to include her in this next invitation? Her excitement was quashed by his next words.

'I'm leaving right away to go and view it. You can stay on here for as long as you like. Just tell one of my pilots when you want to go home.'

'So…you're flying to America alone?' Kira said slowly. With heart-rending effort, she managed to stop her smile sliding straight into despair.

He nodded. Grabbing his phone from the bedside table he dropped it into a pocket. Motionless with shock, Kira could not do or say a thing. It didn't matter. Stefano was perfectly prepared to do the talking for both of them.

'When I want to get away from people, I get right away from them. Once you've finished checking out Silver Island, you can go back to living in the grounds of Bella Terra, and working at my town house in Florence. While you're doing all that and flitting from one place to another, I'll keep well out of your way, until you've finished.'

'Why? There's nothing to stop you coming and going wherever you please. I'm won't be in your way,' Kira said, confused.

'I need space. I can't let you interfere with that.' Stefano's voice soared through the silence that fell between them.

It wasn't just a statement, it was a warning. Kira didn't need to be told twice. Gathering up her last reserves of courage, she stared him out.

'Don't worry on my account, Stefano. You know I'm

happier alone,' she said brusquely. 'I'll be fine. Once I leave here, I'll be totally absorbed by the Florence project. Go and find yourself another new house. Maybe you'll have better luck turning that one into a home, although I very much doubt it.'

'I can hope,' he said coolly.

'It won't take me more than a few hours to do my preliminary checks here. I'd be grateful if you'd arrange for me to be flown home this afternoon,' Kira countered, turning to hide her rage and shame as she got out of bed. Wrapping the sheet tightly around her body she stalked towards the bathroom. Ice-cold reserve was the only way she could deal with this situation. She expected Stefano to agree to her demand without question. His reaction came as a shock. As she strode past him, he grabbed her by the elbow.

'No. Stay here, on the island.'

'What?'

'That way I'll know where you are.'

'Now, wait a minute!' Kira flared. 'I may be on your payroll, but that doesn't mean you're in charge of my schedule. When it comes to my work, everything has to be done in the right order.'

And first on the list is getting you right out of my system, she thought painfully.

'I've got so much admin work to do back at home, I'll need to get started on it as soon as possible,' she went on, pulling her arm roughly from his grasp. 'Then there's the prince's project to sign off, and that's before I've even thought of starting work on your town house....'

Hugging the sheet tightly to her body, she started for the shower again. Hearing Stefano take some quick steps in pursuit and knowing that if he laid another hand on her she would be lost, she turned to confront him. She didn't want his touch clouding her judgement.

His expression gave her another jolt. He looked white-faced, almost lost, and as far from the smooth, composed Stefano as she had ever seen him. A moment later, and he was impenetrable once more.

'I'm glad you'll be keeping yourself busy,' he said, with all the passion of a diplomat.

Kira met his chilly good manners with a hard frost of her own. 'Don't talk about my work as though it is a hobby, Stefano. I signed that contract for you, don't forget.'

Her glare drew down shades over his expression. Any softening of his manner was instantly hidden from her, and from the world.

'How could I?' he said bitterly.

Stefano stormed away from Silver Island. He didn't need his newest employee lecturing him, even if her name was Kira Banks. Her anger worked away at his pride like a mountain stream running over rocks. An endless loop of her words went around and around in his head, and worse still, for the first time ever, Stefano could not settle to work on the plane journey. He hardly heard a word his agent said as they drove towards his latest dream property. His mind was a complete mess of regret and confusion. What did he want with another soulless palace? None of the others had brought him a moment's happiness or satisfaction. He had found both in Kira's arms, and then turned his back on her. Where was the sense in that? All he needed in his life was Kira, and her homely touch. Why had he ruined his only chance of happiness by letting slip his murky past, and the way he had abandoned his family? It would only reinforce her picture of him as a shallow pleasure seeker, flitting from one set of values to another. Kira deserved better than that, and she knew it.

She wouldn't want him now.

He barely noticed the colonial mansion he had travelled thousands of miles to inspect. Unable to make a decision on it, he retreated to Manhattan. His apartment on Fifth Avenue was as cheerless as any of his other homes. He roamed about, trying to put Kira out of his mind. It was hopeless. From the contrast between her cosy little home and his soulless apartment to the sight of lovers strolling hand in hand through Central Park, everything reminded him of her.

Finally, he went out, throwing himself into the surf of crowds and noise swirling through the city streets. It was supposed to block thoughts of Kira with the white noise of chaos. It didn't work. Each woman he saw was automatically matched against her memory, and found wanting.

Eventually, he washed up at an all-night club. The atmosphere was intended to stifle Kira's memory. Instead, her voice echoed in his brain. It cut straight through the racket, as he remembered how she had chosen to spend the evening with him on Silver Island—no distractions—rather than be wined and dined in the city. They wanted the same things out of life. Why didn't he trust himself to share them with her? The answer to that circled him like a shark but he didn't want to face it. Instead, he told himself that he'd done the right thing. She had been hurt before, and he'd only hurt her again—he had left her to protect her.

After a sleepless night, he went into the Manhattan

offices of Albani International. That was another disaster. He lasted twenty minutes. Unable to work, he spent the whole time resisting the urge to pick up the phone and ring Kira. In the end, he had to walk out and ask a secretary to order a car for him. He couldn't trust himself to make one simple, innocent business call. Once he lifted that receiver, he knew he would end up ringing Kira instead.

Kira tried to make a full and detailed assessment of Stefano's tropical paradise. It was impossible. She made some silly mistakes, and couldn't complete the simplest calculations. Her emotions were too raw. He had swept her up to heaven, and then dropped her the morning after. It was history repeating itself, and she felt empty, completely crushed. As soon as she had filled a few pages of her notebook, she made arrangements to board one of his private jets and leave the island chain.

The flight home was agonising. She did her best to make it look as though she was enjoying every second. She had a lifetime's experience of putting on a good show. She watched a romantic comedy, and took care to laugh in all the right places. She smiled and chatted to the cabin crew, and ate every meal and titbit they offered her. In contrast, she took only a solitary glass of white wine with her dinner, and most of that went back to the galley untouched. No way was she going to let anyone think Stefano Albani had driven her to drink!

One of his fleet of cars was waiting for her at the airport. The chauffeur said he had instructions to whisk her straight back home to La Ritirata. Kira had other ideas. She asked to be taken directly to Stefano's town house in Florence. That would put some distance between her and the valley she had left with such high hopes, only a couple of days before. Stefano had already infused the entire Bella Terra estate with so many memories for her. They had talked and laughed there. His new town house did not mean quite so much to her. As long as she kept well away from the place where he had seduced her, it had no hold over her. Stefano's offer to let her stay there while she worked on the project had seemed wildly overgenerous. Now she was glad of the opportunity. A break from La Ritirata was exactly what she needed. It would give her some time away from his memory.

Stefano suffered through another sleepless night, and that morning he knew he had to come to his senses. He couldn't think of anything but Kira and there could be only one outcome. He wanted her, and he would never get any rest until she was safely in his arms again. He didn't need to think any further than that. Summoning a car, he headed straight for the airport. Then he blazed a trail across the world. He hadn't thought beyond the fact that Kira had bewitched his mind and his body, and he could not live without her for a moment longer. All he wanted to do was reach her side. This was such a new sensation he had no idea what he was going to say, but right now, he didn't care. He needed her. The moment he saw her, the words would come. He knew it.

Driving towards the Bella Terra villa felt like coming home. It reinforced all his deepest feelings. This was where he wanted to spend the rest of his life. Now he was going to claim the woman he wanted by his side for all eternity. Leaping out of the car before his chauffeur had brought it to a standstill, he strode straight across the valley towards La Ritirata. He still hadn't worked out his argument, but words could wait. His first kiss would tell Kira all she needed to know.

He was so consumed by what he would do, it took him a while to realise something was wrong. The day was hot and the sky stormy, but all the windows of Kira's little home were tightly closed. As he registered that fact, he smelled smoke. The countryside was dry as dust. Fire was a constant threat, but now he saw it was a reality. Smoke was curling up from the back of La Ritirata. He started to run.

'Kira!'

Pulling out his phone as he ran, he summoned help from the villa but didn't wait for it to arrive. The woman he loved was in danger. Kicking down the front door, he burst into the living room. It was a furnace, centred on the burning kitchen door. A thick haze of smoke rose to fill the house, but Stefano never hesitated. Dropping to the floor where the atmosphere was clearest, he made straight for the burning room.

'Kira!'

There was no reply. He held his breath. The kitchen was well alight, but empty. His heart started to beat again. There was still hope. Calling her name, he quartered the living room, searching through the smoke and straining to hear the smallest noise. The crumble and crackle of feasting flames threatened to silence everything in its path.

Time was slipping away, dragging a suffocating chain ever tighter around his chest. He cast a desperate look at the fresh air outside, but could not waste a precious second. Reaching the staircase he went up on all fours. Keeping his head below the level of the smoke was good in theory, but the fire was sucking all the available oxygen from the air. If Kira was here, he had to get her out within the next couple of minutes. He ran into her bedroom, his movements now desperate Walking away from her was the worst mistake he had ever made, and if he had now lost her for ever…

The town house in Florence was every bit as tempting as Kira remembered from her first visit but the unfinished business with Stefano hung over her like a thundercloud. Nothing could distract her. Flipping on the TV, she tried to get interested in the news. Gazing out of the window, she was only half listening to the babbled headlines. The sky outside was crying. She stared out over the sodden rooftops of Florence. If only Stefano had not tried to shut her out of his life so abruptly. She might still be lying in his arms. The silver sand would be soft and warm beneath their skin, while sunlight danced in patterns overhead, sparkling through palm leaves.

Here in Italy, it was wet and Kira was miserable. She closed her eyes and inhaled, imagining the warm, fertile perfume of her garden back at La Ritirata after a shower. All it needed to make her fantasy complete was Stefano. He had broken her heart, but she could not stop yearning for him. Angry with herself for being so weak she reached over to switch off the useless distraction of the television when her hand froze in midair. Half a dozen words snatched her attention and held it, breathless.

'Mystery fire rages at billionaire's hideaway…'

The plasma screen was alive with flames and thick funnels of smoke. As the presenter droned on, the scene changed. A bird's-eye view showed again the frighteningly familiar landscape. The pictures were so huge and horrific she could practically feel the heat. The news report said only that a house on the estate of a reclusive billionaire had been destroyed, but Kira didn't need any more details. Despite the flickering flames and jagged camera work, she recognised La Ritirata.

Her home had been destroyed.

Alight with fear, she called a hire car and drove straight to the Bella Terra estate. The smell of smoke was almost overpowering as she drove up the track towards the villa. She had to close all the ventilators. It was impossible to miss the turning for La Ritirata. The TV item had been recorded earlier in the day, so the news crews and fire services had vanished. Only the mess remained, where all their vehicles had been stationed. Grass and bushes were flattened, and the recent rain had surrounded the blackened stinking ruins of her little house with mud.

Kira put a hand up to open her car door, but stopped before she made contact. She couldn't do it. She couldn't step out into this disaster. Unable to bear the horrible sight any longer, she turned the car around and headed for Stefano's villa. The sick feeling inside her was made a hundred times worse by the reek of smoke that crept into the vehicle. There could be no escape from the after-effects of the blaze. They would linger for a long time, and in her memory for ever.

She brought her car to a halt on the grand terrace where Stefano had once parked his helicopter. She got out of the car, and plodded up the steps to the great front doors. There she pulled on the bell, which echoed like an alarm through the rambling old house. She purposely kept her back to the wreckage of La Ritirata, unable to look at the damage.

When the villa door opened, the interior came as

a complete surprise to her. It had been transformed. Although Stefano had owned La Bella Terra for only a few days, an impressive desk and banks of telecommunications equipment had already been installed in the reception area. As Kira stepped inside, a woman rushed forward and grabbed her hands. Her face was tight with panic and stress and it took a few moments for Kira to recognise Stefano's senior PA beneath the smudges of mascara. That was a shock. Kira had last seen her arriving on Silver Island, and assumed she would have followed her boss to the USA.

'Is there any news, Miss Banks?'

'What about? And why are you here?' Kira stared at her, puzzled, the chaos surrounding her house momentarily pushed to one side. 'I thought you stuck to Stefano like a Post-it note?'

At the mention of her boss the woman went even whiter.

'Oh, I am so sorry, Miss Banks…'

Feeling panic rise, Kira prised herself out of the PA's grasp. To be clutched at by a stranger was almost as bad as seeing her house in ruins.

'It's only sticks and stones,' she muttered, embarrassed by such a show of emotion from someone she hardly knew. Stefano mustn't be allowed to see her fail. If she could walk away from him on Silver Island, she could carry on holding everything together now. She avoided thinking in too much detail about how much she had lost. All of her hard work over the years…

'It isn't as though there were lives at stake,' she went on, keeping a skin of ice over the turbulent depths of her true feelings. 'Could you send a message to Signor Albani, please?' she asked briskly. 'I was only going to be staying in Florence while I worked on his town house, but now I've lost my home, I've got nowhere to live. I'll need to stay in town on a permanent basis, until I can sort things out....'

The girl was looking at her in confusion.

'Miss Banks! You mean to say you don't know what happened? Signor Albani has been rushed to hospital!'

Kira's mind went completely blank. She fell back, aghast.

'He tried to save your house. He put his life on the line, looking for you, and for what? You hardly seem to care about him, or your home!' The PA was clearly fighting tears.

Kira was suddenly aware of the villa's entrance hall filling with faces. Builders, architects and members of staff poked their heads from doorways or looked over the banisters from the upper floors. Covered in shame, she wanted to run away and hide, but she was too thunderstruck to do anything but gawp at the collection of furious, accusing faces.

'Me? What have I done?' she said faintly. 'It's not my fault!' No answer came. The PA had turned away and Kira was left to her own thoughts. If Stefano had not gone looking for me—*why was he looking for me?*

'I had no idea he was in the country. I thought he was still in America,' she whispered to herself.

Kira's heart solidified inside her chest. Stefano had left her, that last fateful day on Silver Island. He had betrayed her, forcing mental and physical distance between them. Now she was expected to believe he had taken a pointless risk by searching for her in an empty house! It was too much to take on board.

Ignoring her audience, she marched straight back out to her car. On the way, she steeled herself to take another glance at the smoking ruin that had once been her home. It was terrifying. Stefano had been in there. She had to find out why.

CHAPTER ELEVEN

ONCE at the hospital, rules and regulations held her up for ages. Getting into Stefano's private suite took longer than the drive from La Bella Terra had done. When she was finally allowed to enter, her nerves were put to their stiffest test. Stefano lay motionless in the bed. His eyes were closed, and the only colour in his face came from a network of cuts, scratches and bruises. His natural colour had drained away to a deathly grey. Once the orderly had shown her into the room, he left. When she was completely alone with the patient, Kira could not contain herself any longer. She rushed forward and grabbed his hand, which was swathed in bandages.

'Stefano!' she gasped.

He flinched, scowled and opened his eyes, in that order. Kira instantly dropped his hand and stepped back, his cold eyes reminding her of the distance between them.

'What are you doing here? I gave express instructions that you, above all people, weren't to be allowed in.'

Digging both elbows into his bed, he struggled up into a sitting position. Once there, he reached for the alarm button on his side table.

'Stop! Don't blame the staff. It's nobody's fault but

mine,' Kira said. 'I waited until the shift changed on reception and then said I was one of your PAs, coming to consult you about some paperwork.'

Stefano let his hand fall back to the bed, winced and then managed a half-smile at her ingenuity.

'Why do you think I issued that order? I didn't want you to see me like this.' He wouldn't meet her eyes.

There was a silence. Scrabbling for words, Kira said with an awkward laugh, 'I did all that work making my house beautiful and comfortable, but never got around to fitting a sprinkler system!'

'Dio! It was a country cottage, not the Uffizi Gallery.' They both paused again.

'Are your burns very painful?'

He looked at her finally, but only for a moment. 'They're not too bad. I'm only in for observation.'

Kira poured him a glass of water, but he shook his head.

'Why did you risk going into a burning building?' she burst out, unable to wait any longer.

For a moment she thought he wasn't going to answer her, but then he sighed and spoke.

'I thought you were inside. I assumed you would shut yourself away in La Ritirata after getting back from Silver Island.'

Kira watched him intently. He brushed folds from his coverlet, picked up his watch from the bedside cabinet and put it on, but he did not look directly at her.

'So…you actually went looking for me?' she said at last.

'It was the least I could do,' he said, still avoiding her eyes. 'I realised that, however much you claimed to understand I wasn't offering you anything more than a good time, I had hurt you. I was determined to make up for that. I saw smoke, thought the worst and broke in. I thought maybe you were asleep, or unconscious, or...'

'You risked your life for me,' Kira said slowly. 'I never imagined anyone would do that.'

'I couldn't help myself.' Stefano evaded her eyes. 'The flames took hold very quickly. When I realised you weren't there I concentrated on getting as many of your belongings out as possible.'

'You saved some of my things!' Kira's heart leapt for a moment, before shock distracted her. 'You stayed and did all that when I wasn't even in the house, Stefano?'

'They were your things. You made a perfect home. You weren't going to lose anything, if I could help it,' he said simply. 'Things matter to you.'

And so do you, she thought painfully.

Shutting her eyes, she sank down in the nearest chair. When Stefano first abandoned her, she had been filled with anger. That evaporated the second she heard he had been injured. Now she felt weak, confused and resentful that he should force her through such an obstacle course of emotions.

'You might claim to know my mind, but you're a total mystery to me, Stefano Albani. I thought you didn't ever want to see me again. And then you go and do something like this,' she said quietly.

'I've told you. I couldn't help myself.' Stefano sounded as though he could hardly believe it himself.

Kira did not need to search his face to see that he was telling the simple truth.

'Did you buy that house in America?'

He shook his head. 'It didn't seem important any more. Once upon a time I had nothing, but now I can have what I like, and make a home anywhere I want. It's enough to know that. I don't need to follow through.'

'But you can't make yourself any kind of home, can you? That's what all this is about!' Her eyes flew open. 'On the day we first met, you spoke as though the Bella Terra estate was the answer to all your prayers. You were going to make your home there, and settle. But it wasn't good enough, was it? I should have seen the warning signs when you showed me around the town house in Florence—that must have been your previous "ideal home." It would have been the solution to all your problems—until you lit upon my valley. Before that, it must have been Silver Island. All these places have one thing in common, Stefano. You haven't been able to make a home out of any of them!'

Breathless, she ran out of words. Stefano had watched her in silence. Now he laced his fingers together, winced and straightened them carefully again before speaking.

'We're alike, you and I. Neither of us likes to be out of control. Neither of us appreciates surprises.' He paused before adding, 'But my existence has been anything but predictable since I met you.'

His calculated tone was in such contrast to her outburst, Kira sat back in surprise. He seemed to have somehow retreated from her, in spite of not having moved from his bed.

'I'm a free agent, Kira.' He spread his hands in a bleak gesture. 'I need to be able to come and go, in the same way you do. Work defines both our lives, doesn't it? We can't devote ourselves to our careers if we're always looking out for the other, can we?' he finished, with a hint of defiance.

Over the past few days Kira had begun to reassess her life. She was beginning to think work was playing too big a part in it. Her heart sank as she realised that Stefano had clearly done no such thing.

He grazed his teeth over his lower lip. 'What are you going to do about La Ritirata now? I doubt if it's habitable.'

'There isn't much left standing.'

Always restless, Stefano reached for the water Kira had poured him. After taking a sip, he slid the glass across his bedside table. He did not look at her as he spoke.

'Look—don't take this the wrong way, Kira, but why not consider selling what is left of your house to me? I can take it off your hands, give you a good price and you can start again. I can make everything all right for you again. You were never keen on a stranger moving into Bella Terra. This way, it won't matter to you.'

Kira stared at him, looking for any trace of the man she thought she loved. All she could see was the cold, hard exterior. She forced herself to ask, 'You—you'd like me to go back to England?'

'Well, it's obviously up to you,' he responded mildly. 'I'm simply offering to help you. That heap of rubble is nothing but a liability to you now.'

The truth hurt. Kira was so used to it, she only knew one defence. She squared up to him again.

'A liability? You know all about those, of course. Apparently, that's how you saw me on the morning you abandoned me on Silver Island.'

She rose from her seat, all the hurt rushing back as fresh and raw as that first moment when she saw him getting ready to leave her.

'I served your purpose, and then you left.'

'Oh, Kira…' For a moment she thought she saw a flash of something deeper in his eyes, but then it was gone, and when he spoke again, his voice was carefully controlled.

'That night on Silver Island, you seemed to understand me better than I knew myself. You know what I'm like now, which is more than anyone else in the world does. I didn't want you to get too fond of me, so I went to look at a property. That's all.'

Kira looked at him, really looked at him. His white face and guarded eyes. He was lying. She knew it. Somewhere deep inside, he must know it, too. Her sadness was suddenly gone, eclipsed by anger at his stubborn blindness. Her hands flexed in impotent rage. 'You are a coward, Stefano. We had something incredible between us—I know you felt it, too. Deny it all you want, but I hope one day you'll understand what you have thrown away. Property? You've already got more of that than you know what to do with! Why don't you start looking closer to home, Stefano? Oh, I'm sorry, you don't have one of those!' Grabbing her bag, she threw herself towards the door.

'Wait, Kira! Where are you going?'

'I'm going to show you how to make a home from absolutely nothing, Stefano. I'm going to rebuild La Ritirata stone by stone, if it takes me the rest of my life,' she finished, with steely resolve.

Swinging out of his room, she let the door slam shut behind her.

Shell-shocked, Stefano dragged himself out of bed. He didn't want things to end like this. They needed to finish on his terms—he needed the last word. He flung open the door of his private room. She was already gone, straight out of his life. It was too late.

It was almost dark by the time Kira reached her car. With a heavy heart she decided there was no point in going back to La Ritirata until the morning. Nothing could be done by night. Instead, she headed back to her guest suite in Stefano's Florentine town house.

Hours later, she wished she had returned to the Bella Terra valley anyway. Sleep was impossible. Inspecting the ruins of her home by torchlight would have been a better use of her time than tossing and turning in bed. She got up while it was still barely light, and went out for a short walk around town. It was supposed to clear her head, but her mind was too full for that. She thought about the home she had lost, and how much more terrible it could so easily have been. Stefano might have been killed. When it came to matters of life and death, possessions didn't matter. They could be replaced. People couldn't. When he left her on Silver Island, Stefano had torn a hole in her heart. While he was still alive, there was a chance it might be repaired. If he had died in the fire, he would have been lost to her forever.

At least today she still had hope, where there might have only been tragedy.

Kira was a perfectionist, but when it came to Stefano's town house her standards reached new heights. She went into overdrive. When she wasn't busy with her contract to beautify the house, its roof and courtyard, she sat in her borrowed suite and co-ordinated the rebuilding of her own home. It was so painful to be confronted by the ashes of her happy life, but she refused to be beaten. Her vow to recreate her home was written in smoke-blackened stones. She poured all her anger and disappointment into her project to rebuild it. Each day she concentrated on her work at Stefano's town house, determined to fulfil her contract impeccably. Each evening, she drove to La Ritirata and worked on until it was too dark to see. She did all the odd jobs that might otherwise eat into the builders' time: making phone calls, sweeping up and washing down. Everything had to run according to her plan. Nothing must go wrong. She wanted her house to stand as a monument to her iron will.

Her commitment to both jobs never wavered. Her self-control often did. She was so glad that this was something she could do alone. For anyone else to see her anguish would have been unbearable. Each time she walked out onto Stefano's new roof garden, she kept expecting him to appear. He never did. As she walked through the cool, beautifully designed rooms of his suite, she knew that other women would have the benefit of the emperor-size bed and the shower that was big enough for two. She had lost him. Her bridges were burned, along with her house.

She had turned out to be the architect of her own unhappiness, and that was the most painful thing of all.

Kira's punishing schedule began to take its toll. There were times when she could barely drag herself from one project to the other. Her body was numb with exhaustion. She kept her mind blank with the anaesthetic of work. If she let it wander for a moment, it homed straight in on Stefano.

Rebuilding La Ritirata would take a long time, and more money than she could bear to think about. Her beloved garden was wrecked. It sagged beneath the weight of disaster. Nothing had escaped. Plants had been scorched, crushed beneath falling masonry or trampled and drowned by the emergency services or the builders.

Her house could be replaced, but its heart and soul would take a lot longer to repair. Wandering around the site, Kira couldn't help wondering if it would feel as soulless as all Stefano's properties did. There would be no love in it. She had none left to give. The rebuilt La Ritirata would rattle with emptiness, and smell of nothing but new paint and plaster. They were nice smells, but as impersonal as a hospital. The place would be eerily silent, too. Kira had grown to love the little creaks and moans her old house made. All its imperfections would vanish, like the original building. None of the new windows would jam, and the front door would open first time, every time. The usual pantomime of wiggling the key and bumping her shoulder against one particular spot would be a thing of the past. This new house should be ideal in every way, but somehow she knew it never would be. Something would always be missing.

All she had ever craved was a quiet life, far away from strangers, in her old house with its funny little ways. Now she had lost everything. Looking out across the valley at the Bella Terra villa, all Kira saw now was the wrong sort of isolation. She wanted to carry on being alone—alone, together with Stefano.

It was the end of her wonderful dream. She had lost her home, and the only man she would ever love or need or want. Stefano had been on to something. She should have accepted his offer to buy the ruins of La Ritirata. Her contracted jobs were well on the way to being finished—they didn't need her any longer. There was nothing in the Bella Terra valley for her now. Sadly, regretfully, she pulled out her mobile phone.

He had been right all along. All she had to do was tell him.

It was ironic. Stefano's problem was that he could never be satisfied with what he had. Kira's problem was the exact opposite. She loved what she knew, and never wanted it to change.

Her message to him was a simple one: You've won. I don't want to replace my home here after all. You can have it.

It had been hard enough to begin. Finishing it took forever. Every ending she added felt desperate, so finally she put the single word Kira and pressed Send.

She had a long wait. Her time in Florence, which should have been spent packing, kept being interrupted by checking her email in-box. Each time she opened it and there was no reply from Stefano, it felt like another rejection. She usually spent her time avoiding office work and the computer. Today was different. Finally, eyes dry and gritty from staring at a screen that refused to come up with the only name she wanted to see, she flung herself away from the desk with a cry of desperation. Blindly, she dashed up onto the brand new roof garden she had designed and built for him.

For as long as she could remember, gardens had been Kira's sanctuary. That magic did not work today. Solitude could not help her. She drifted around, unseeing. Moving from the flower boxes of pelargoniums to the terracotta pots of lemon trees and back again, she was locked inside her own thoughts. It was not a happy place to be. The only thing that could distract her was the idea Stefano might have replied to her email, and she had missed it. Within minutes of escaping from the screen, her nerve broke and she fled back inside.

Inevitably, she discovered her message had been answered almost as soon as she abandoned her laptop. Excitement plummeted to despair as she opened Stefano's message to find only an automatic response. He was going off-message until further notice.

Kira put both hands on the edge of the table and pushed herself back from her computer. That made his feelings pretty clear.

The rest of her day went to waste. She could not eat, or settle to anything for more than a few moments. As evening approached she gave up and drove to the Bella Terra valley. The place had always healed her in the past. It didn't happen today. Gazing at the foundations of the new house, she wondered if the next person to live in it would be truly happy there.

A chill breeze ruffled her hair. High in a nearby pine, an owl quavered its mournful cry. Cold weather would soon be on its way. One of Kira's great pleasures had been to feed the creatures driven close to her old home in winter. When she left, she would lose that. It would be a terrible wrench. She might hate this new house, but she still loved the Bella Terra valley.

On impulse, she decided to recreate some of the best things about her life at La Ritirata. She shook out some biscuit crumbs onto an upturned oil drum. Within seconds a robin returned to investigate. Gathering up small branches from beneath the trees, she began rebuilding the wood pile. It would be ready for burning by next winter. The memories of the sound and fragrance of crackling wood might make this soulless new house feel a little bit more homely. The new owners would enjoy that.

She was kneeling on the ground, picking up pine cones, when a sound made her whirl around in alarm. What she saw almost stopped her heart.

'Stefano!'

Without waiting for her to say any more, he walked across what had once been her garden. She froze. As imposing as ever, his long shadow fell across her. Sitting back on her heels, Kira tried to push her tumble of coppery gold hair behind her ears.

'Yes,' he said mildly. Reaching down, he brushed a fragment of dried grass from the crown of her head. She held her breath. He leaned back, carefully under control, and she breathed again,

'You've lost weight,' she said faintly. He laughed.

'I've been too busy to eat. I've found a new purpose in life.'

'That American property tempted you after all?' She smiled, dying inside. He shook his head, but that gave her no cause to hope. Instead, she became defensive.

'I've gone beyond the point of playing games, Stefano. Did you get my email?'

'Yes. That's why I'm here.' He was equally forthright.

She watched him speculatively. 'Why hasn't your office answered any of my messages?'

He flipped his keys into his pocket. 'They had nothing to tell you. They couldn't contact me. I was on my way here.'

'Why? Of all the places in your empire, why visit here?' Kira asked, hearing her voice trembling slightly.

He paused for a long time before he answered. The only sound was the idle clink of coins in his pocket. It cranked up the tension to a point where Kira jumped when the lonely owl called again.

'I'm not visiting, Kira,' he said at last. 'I'm back in the valley for good.'

She stared at him, wondering what to ask and where to start. 'Until five minutes ago I knew exactly what I was going to do. I had everything planned. Now you've parachuted back into my life, and I don't know what to think.'

'So don't think anything.' He came towards her again with a huge, beautiful smile and she stood, legs wobbly, to meet him. 'Just feel. All you need to know is that your problems are over, tesoro.' He reached out for her and Kira took a hasty step back. Her body was already reacting to his presence, and she knew that if she let him take her in his arms all would be lost.

Anger bubbled up inside her. How dare he just return so casually? 'I don't think so, Stefano. I have a feeling they may only just be beginning. Do you think you can flit in and out of my life on a whim? You abandoned me once, remember? How do you expect me to trust that you won't suddenly change your mind again?'

Stefano's smile faded.

'I want to explain.'

'What is there to say? You deceived me!'

A lightning bolt of anger galvanised his body. 'That's not true, Kira, and you know it! We both said we wanted to resist mixing business and pleasure. When it happened and I made a move, you could have said no. I would have respected that. We are so alike, both wary of entanglement. We knew the dangers. That meant you were never under any pressure to respond, and neither was I.' He had started angrily, but the bitterness in his voice melted away as he added, 'But we did, and there can never be any doubt that you are a woman who knows exactly what she wants. I wanted the same thing,' he finished quietly. 'And I still want it.'

Kira bit her lip as her eyes threatened to fill with tears. His words had some truth to them. He had been cruel to her, but she had been naive. 'I always said I would never let myself be so vulnerable again,' she said eventually.

'I know, and that was why I had to leave!'

His words escaped in such an explosion, Kira's head jerked up.

'I told you too much about myself on our last night together, Kira. That's why you must have realised I'm not to be trusted.'

In the days they had been apart Kira had combed every magazine and newspaper, steeling herself to read about Stefano and a string of other women. There had been nothing.

'I don't know what you're talking about, Stefano,' she challenged him at last. 'And you can't possibly say something like that without following it up!'

'I don't know if I can,' he said, with difficulty. 'You learned more about me in those final hours than I have ever revealed to anyone else. Telling you about Maria and my family lifted a weight off my mind. At first it felt good. But next morning...' He shook his head wordlessly.

'I realised I had gone too far. I had to get away.'

Kira waited, hardly daring to breathe. It was a long time before he spoke again.

'I told you the darkest secret of my life—that in order to make myself a success, I turned my back on my birth family.'

'You also told me you chose honesty when you decided to leave them,' Kira said quietly.

He nodded, pushing a hand through his hair in a sharp, agitated gesture. 'But at the time…the thought of you discovering I couldn't be any more loyal than your faithless Hugh…it was too much to bear.' He exhaled in a rush. 'And knowing you knew my secrets, what my childhood was really like… I've never told anyone that since I escaped it. I kept imagining you looking at me with disgust or—far worse—pity.' He lowered his head for a moment, the sharp planes of his face tense and pale.

'Stefano,' Kira said softly. 'You must know your past could never make any difference to me. It made you the man you are now, the man I—' she stopped herself and swallowed hard before continuing '—I know. I understand exactly how you feel. I panicked after the first time we spent the night together. I couldn't believe how perfect it felt—there was no way I could trust it to last. I knew it would crush me when it fell, when you decided I wasn't good enough—or met someone else…'

'What changed your mind?'

Kira sighed. 'To be honest, I couldn't stay away from you! I wanted to keep my distance—but I didn't want to lose touch with you either. I think I was lost from the beginning, really. Ever since you gave me your business card, I've been treating it like a holy relic,' she finished ruefully.

'You wouldn't be the first,' he assured her.

They stood and looked at each other—and then they laughed.

Stefano reached out to her again, his touch gliding over her cheek. In that moment, Kira forgot all her fears. All she wanted to do was check that her body was still a perfect fit for his arms. Closing the gap between them, she looked up into his eyes. They were intense and totally focused on her face. His smile enclosed her in warm, honeyed security as his touch brushed like silk against her skin.

'I—I don't know what came over me when we made love on Silver Island, Kira. It was every bit as good—no, it was better than when we were in Florence. That was the problem. First I couldn't get you out of my mind, and then I didn't want to let you out of my bed. I'd never felt like that about any woman before. It was such an overwhelming experience, I had to get away. I thought I was lost. In fact, the exact opposite was true. Once we were apart I discovered you are my anchor in life, Kira. That's why I could never resist coming back to you. You're strong, and centred, and keep me grounded in real life. When I abandoned you on Silver Island, it was like leaving behind part of myself. It was the best part, but I knew it was safe with you because after we made love that night, something changed. I became one half of a couple. Do you realise what that means? Since then I've been lost without you, adrift. We are meant to be together, Kira. You make me whole. There can be no going back now—for either of us.'

She shook her head in disbelief. She had never dared

to hope that his feelings might run so close to hers. 'That's exactly the way I felt, after Florence,' she told him quietly. 'For the first time in my life, I didn't want to be alone any more. That scared me, because it felt so different.'

He nodded.

'The moment I left you on Silver Island, I discovered you were inescapable. I was carrying you everywhere. You were inside me—in my thoughts, and deep within my heart. I went back to find you in La Ritirata, but the fire got in the way. When you found me in the hospital, I couldn't find the words to tell you the truth—I was still scared. I drove you away again, stubborn fool that I am. When you left, I tried to convince myself it was what you wanted. That it was the right decision, and I tried again to let you go. But I was lying to myself. Kira, we need each other. Together, we can show the world what family really means. Together, we'll be unbeatable. That's why I came to find you. Kira, my only love, am I too late?'

He was gazing into her eyes, trying to read her thoughts. Kira feasted her eyes on him for a long time before replying, but there wasn't a doubt in her mind. 'Too late?' she said finally in a soft, slow voice. 'You can't be, for here I am.' Stefano's face lit up with blazing joy as he pulled Kira against him.

'And here you stay.' He cupped her face in his hands and passionately kissed her as she melted against him. 'With me, for ever.'

JOIN US ON SOCIAL MEDIA!

Stay up to date with our latest releases, author news and gossip, special offers and discounts, and all the behind-the-scenes action from Mills & Boon...

 millsandboon

 millsandboonuk

 millsandboon

It might just be true love...